I'm Not the Hero

Book 3 • An Education in Magical Affairs

SourpatchHero

Podium

For Sarah:
My best friend, confidante, mashed potato taste tester, and partner in crime. The best part of my life began when we met.

And for Oliver and Milo. Every single day is better when I get to play, read, and talk with you two. Love you, buddies.

Cover design by Francell Garrote

ISBN: 978-1-0394-5431-6

Published in 2025 by Podium Publishing
www.podiumentertainment.com

AN EDUCATION IN MAGICAL AFFAIRS

Chapter 1

Orrin's body hit the cobblestone floor of the cell. He was one door down from the small room Brandt had occupied hours earlier, the broken barred door still on the ground outside. He rolled until he hit the far wall hard. Without [Mind Bastion], he would have passed out from the pain long ago.

Caught and imprisoned.

When Madi had approached them with the information that their party member Brandt had been captured, Orrin and his friend Daniel had raced to the rescue. From the moment the two of them had been forced into this world, Orrin and Daniel had stayed by each other's side. Friends for years before a runaway truck had killed them on Earth, the two high school boys had woken up naked in a new world with magic, levels, and a system. Just like the stories that Orrin used to read.

Daniel was a [Hero], the legendary class that was destined to save the world. Orrin could admit to himself in this low moment that the class fit his friend perfectly. Daniel had always been the popular one in school. He succeeded at whatever he put his mind to, treated everyone like a friend, and had just a tiny bit of an ego to go along with his good looks.

Orrin's class had seemed lackluster at first. [Utility Warder] was a back-line support class, something the world didn't value as much as the ability to lay the smack down on the monsters that existed here. In a world where the growth of your class depended on how many monsters you could defeat, healing and support were rarely a first option. He'd slowly, over time, shown those close to him the value in a healer, shield maker, and stat-increase spell bot. What nobody could have expected were Orrin's other powers. Administrator powers. Orrin's rebirth had caused some sort of problem in the system that governed skills, spells, and classes. He'd unlocked a power that nobody alive knew much about. He had only started to find out more about it himself when he, Madi, and Daniel had left the protection of Dey and stormed the enemy country of Odrana on a suicidal rescue mission. Their friend Brandt had been captured and slated to die. They'd planned the best they could, but the one thing working for them was that nobody knew they were coming. With any luck, they'd be able to get in and free Brandt without anyone knowing.

Of course, Orrin should have known better. They were never lucky.

Orrin remembered bits and pieces before the beating Lord Sanerris had put on him. He'd hinted that Brandt's imprisonment had been a trap to draw them in. Orrin had convinced Daniel to use his party escape spell to save Brandt and Madi. He would have escaped, too, if one of the Odranan thugs hadn't snapped a collar around his neck, which had severed his party connection and access to most of his spells.

Orrin's right hand reached up and touched the smooth metal around his neck. It was slick with his blood, and he couldn't find a clasp or edge.

He groaned as Lord Sanerris, the ruler of Odrana, sneered down at him. Two guards had dragged him back along the long path before dumping him on the ground. They proceeded to strip him down to his pants and threw his cloak, armor, and potion vials into the hall.

Orrin tried to find a more comfortable position on the ground. At least one arm was broken, and if the dull burning in his sides was any indication, Sanerris had shattered a few ribs. His leg hurt as well, and he was scared to put weight on it to see how bad it was. It took most of his remaining energy to prop himself up and spat at Sanerris.

"You might as well let me go right now," Orrin said, his voice gravelly. He must have taken a few hits to the neck. "You don't want an angry [Hero] coming back for me."

Sanerris lifted an eyebrow. "I'm amazed you can still speak. I am not used to being denied what I want, and twice now you and the [Hero] have surprised me. I will see to it that it doesn't happen again."

"Seriously, take the collar off me and I'll try to convince Daniel not to level your country. He has a bit of a temper sometimes."

One of the guards moved to hit him, but Sanerris grabbed the man's arm. "Don't kill him yet. The slave collar will keep him from attacking anyone." To Orrin, he only smiled. "I'll be back tomorrow. I have so much to plan and so little time to inform your friends of your upcoming execution."

"Huh? I thought you wanted to learn about my skills?" Orrin backpedaled quickly. The flickering light of the guard's torch lent a crazy glint to Sanerris's eyes.

"I'll get what I want," he said with a sinister smile. The man swept from the room. One of the guards closed the cell door, and the lights retreated until Orrin was sitting in darkness.

Orrin's mind worked through the inconsistencies of what Sanerris had said. He was going to execute him but still learn how his class worked? That made no sense. Why would he need to tell his friends that he was going to be killed . . . unless . . .

He's trying to do it again. He wants to draw Daniel back to Odrana in another rescue mission. Orrin sighed in relief. Sanerris was playing mind games. He wasn't going to kill him. He'd beaten him to a pulp but kept him alive.

I can't let him know about my Administrator powers. Orrin pulled up his list of skills and spells. *I need to figure out how much I can safely give away.*

Orrin was under no delusion that Sanerris wouldn't torture him. He was honestly surprised that it hadn't started right away. He was weak and vulnerable after his friends had been forced to leave him behind.

Lord Sanerris had the ability to freeze a person in place. Orrin's theory was that it was time magic. *He can only focus the spell or skill on one person at a time, though.* That was how Orrin had figured out a way to get everyone else to safety. He'd hoped that once the rest of his party was safe, he could escape himself.

After Orrin had been frozen in time, Sanerris had snapped the collar around his neck. Orrin knew slaves existed in Asmea but had avoided that seedier part of town. Now he wished he had learned a bit more. Once he'd been collared, he hadn't been able to use any of his spells or skills except [Mind Bastion], one of the first skills he'd ever received, which had become a blessing and a curse in Orrin's mind. While it allowed him complete control of his thoughts, turning him into a logic-driven machine, it also could be used to negate or at least slow down the effects of overusing man—or, in his current situation, ignoring the pain receptors his body was firing in an attempt to let him know just how badly he was hurt.

If [Mind Bastion] is still working, this collar doesn't block the system completely.

The first ray of hope sparked in his eyes. It was time to figure out the limits of what he could do.

Orrin breathed heavily, trying to calm down. He'd almost killed himself.

That's what I get for not taking it slow, he berated himself.

Obviously, the first thing he'd tried to do was heal himself. The slave collar took the mana that was swirling inside, ready to be used . . . and fired it at him in a painful backlash that left him crying on the floor, even with [Mind Bastion] running. It took him five minutes of deep breaths before he gathered the courage to even move.

"No healing spells with this thing on, then," Orrin said aloud to the darkness. He reached up and flicked the collar. "Probably should stay away from casting spells at all."

The way the collar had collected his mana hinted that he wasn't going to be using magic to get out. He was relieved that he hadn't tried to [Teleport].

[Mind Bastion] was working, and Orrin could still use [Map] to see his surroundings. Being underground, he could only make out the system of caves that he'd led the group through just hours ago. One guard was stationed by the stairs.

He only left one guard?

Orrin reached into a pocket and almost let out a whoop of excitement when [Dimension Hole] worked. He pulled an extra health potion out and had it on his lips before he stopped.

They'll know I was healed. He wasn't sure there was a way to block his skill from working, but it was better to keep it a secret for now. Orrin looked quickly at his broken arm and sighed. He'd have to deal with it for the time being.

Luckily, this room had a mattress on the floor and a small latrine. *Lucky* wasn't really the word for it, however. The toilet was nothing more than a wooden box over a hole in the ground. A small bit of water from the ocean somehow made it all the way to the small carved-out hole to flush away whatever filth was thrown down it.

The mattress was . . . *The less said about the mattress, the better,* Orrin thought with a shiver.

He pried the top piece of wood off the toilet, letting the fresh smell of salt water waft up. His first true piece of luck was that nobody seemed to have used it in a long time. The wood was near rotting but stiff enough for his purposes. He pulled a knife from his pocket and paused again. He sighed and put it back. *I have to avoid doing anything that might hint that I have a storage skill.*

Using one arm, he positioned the wood lengthwise along the metal base of the gate. He hobbled up to his one good leg and jumped. It took three tries before he landed on the wood and snapped it into two long pieces of unequal size.

Using the sheet that was crumpled up near the mattress, Orrin fashioned a splint for his arm and his leg. Thanking his mom for making him take that first aid class years ago, he clenched his teeth as he tightened the bands he'd made. He had a lower left arm break that was more annoying than painful, in that it left him only able to use his right arm. The right leg break was worse. It took longer to set it before applying the splint, and he'd passed out twice despite [Mind Bastion] blocking most of the pain.

Covered in sweat, Orrin started breathing heavily again. It was a few minutes before he realized he was using [Meditate] unconsciously. That last piece of information clicked in his mind, and he realized what the slave collar did.

It blocked external mana use.

Orrin could still use skills that didn't depend on using his internal mana reservoir. [Meditate] wasn't using his internal mana but adding to it. *To-do list: Figure out how [Meditate] uses mana around the slave collar.*

He could use [Obscure], [Analyze], [Identify], [Map], [Mind Bastion], [Dimension Hole], [Meditate], and [Merge], although he didn't try to actually merge any spells. He hesitantly pulled up [Way of the Water] and got the prompt to reenter the training room with Styx.

Worst case, I can try and fight my way out—as long as Sanerris isn't around. Orrin moved to train with Styx. The time dilation of the training room might give him a few extra hours to come up with a plan. Before he selected the skill's acceptance option, he had another thought.

With a deep breath, Orrin tried to select his ace in the hole.

The Administrator options appeared. Orrin smiled in the darkness. He had options. He'd find a way out of this, and if he couldn't, Daniel would be back soon. Orrin had kept to Rule One: he'd survived. Daniel had only left him because he had to save Brandt and Madi. Rule Two was to stick together. *We're a team. He'll come for me. They all will.*

Chapter 2

Cold water splashed down on Orrin, waking him from his sleep. He'd been exhausted from the multiday run to rescue Brandt and drifted off while going over his escape options.

"Get up," the voice belonging to a new guard ordered. He dropped the bucket he carried and let it roll away. Orrin caught a glimpse of the clothes that had been stripped off him the day before. His small pile of possessions was crumpled against the wall opposite his cell door.

He tried to push himself to a standing position but took too long. The butt end of a spear cracked on his shoulder, sending fresh waves of pain into the broken arm.

"Faster!"

"Donte, the order is to bring him upstairs, not kill him." Orrin could barely make out the second guard's form as she opened the door to his cell and knelt over him.

"He's got weapons on him."

The female poked a finger under his makeshift splint and huffed in annoyance. "He set a break on his arm . . . and his leg, too? Strong little shit. Donte, I know your family had the coin to heal every little boo-boo you had growing up, but even you should know the difference between a field splint and a shank. Get in here and help me pick him up . . . Why is he wet?"

Orrin got his breathing settled in time to see Donte's satisfied smirk. "He needed a shower."

While Orrin had a faint hope that the nicer guard would help, he was quickly disabused of any dream of escape. The female guard kicked his good leg when he didn't move fast enough. Donte cheered her on and Orrin caught her name. Imani.

Orrin filed the names away for later.

The two guards dragged him from his prison and up the stairs to Lord Sanerris's house. His cries of pain were ignored and he was tied to a chair in a small room he hadn't seen before. It wasn't as richly appointed as the rest of the castle. The one door, stains on the ground, and sheet-laden table with menacing shapes underneath let him know where he was.

Donte spat on him as he pulled the ropes tight on his broken leg. Orrin gritted his teeth and let [Mind Bastion] wash the pain into a numb background noise.

"You're not so strong alone, are you?"

Orrin processed his words and noticed the quiver in the man's voice. "You knew someone who died? One of Sanerris's mages?"

His guess landed solidly. Orrin didn't see the fist that hit his face. The room spun, and the next thing he saw was Imani pulling Donte back.

"Leave." The commanding voice of Lord Sanerris broke over Donte's curses.

The leader of Odrana entered the room, accompanied by an old woman. Orrin could barely make out her face under the heavy hood she wore. The guards quieted and left without complaint. Orrin rolled his jaw.

Sanerris started talking. "I'm sure you're wondering why I haven't killed you." He snapped his fingers, and a servant carried a plush chair into the room. He waved a hand in dismissal before sitting down across from Orrin. The door clicked shut. Orrin was alone with Sanerris and someone he hoped was not a torturer.

Orrin had a plan. He was going to be cool and collected. Sanerris was the kind of person who kidnapped people he wanted and killed those he didn't care for. Torture was a given. Orrin was going to do what Daniel would and not say a word to him. His smile would be the only response Sanerris would get today.

"This will go much easier if you answer me. You were unfortunate to see my . . . less controlled state earlier, and I apologize for that. Do you require healing?"

Sanerris waved the old woman forward. Orrin clenched his teeth and sat straighter in his chair. Her hand touched his head and she let out a gasp.

"What is it?" Sanerris sat forward in his chair.

"How are you . . . My lord, he's . . . I don't know how he's conscious right now."

Sanerris turned away, his expression what Orrin would have called a guilty look on anyone else. "Heal what you can."

"This is beyond what I can do alone. I'm going to need two, maybe three days to set his injuries."

"That long?" Orrin let the words slip out and closed his eyes at his stupidity. His curiosity had gotten the best of him. *Keep your mouth shut.*

"Do what you can for today," Sanerris ordered. "If you are well enough to speak, we have some things to discuss. If you will not answer my questions, it changes nothing. You will be executed for assaulting the lord of Odrana on the day after next. I afford you this bit of respite from the injuries I gave you for my own conscience. I despise beating a child such as yourself, but I am . . . not used to losing. Twice now, your friend Daniel has evaded me."

Orrin focused on the way the healing magic entered his body. It felt different than his own. When he used [Heal Small Wounds], he focused on the specific area and imagined the wound closing. He could see his mom's medical books and pictures in his mind as the flesh closed or the bones reset. This lady's magic permeated his entire body without focus. He tried to reach out and direct the mana to his leg and arm but felt the collar restrict control. He listened to what his capturer was saying but continued to try and give a gentle nudge to the woman's magic.

Orrin noticed she was paying more attention to what Sanerris was saying than he was. Focusing down more, he turned to his own body. [Mind Bastion] was still running.

Maybe . . .

[Mind Bastion] was one of his first skills and still something he didn't fully understand. The description was something about controlling his own mind and part of his body.

If I can't use the mana, maybe I can block her magic off from everywhere but the broken bones. He visualized the bones, muscles, and nervous system and squeezed the muscles of his good arm. He imagined the mana being blocked by [Mind Bastion], forcing it to consolidate elsewhere in his body. The steady stream to his fingers slowed, and a minute later, Orrin had to repress a smile.

He'd done it. He wasn't controlling her healing but redirecting it by setting up roadblocks. He clenched different parts of his body and felt the healing to his shattered bones triple. He left a little flowing through his chest. Sanerris had done a number on his ribs.

"I was informed you could [Teleport] but don't know how you were able to get to my city so quickly. I had multiple groups watching the roads for the three of you, but nobody saw you. You didn't hire another [Locationist]. Tell me how."

Orrin's lip twitched. The bandits they'd evaded were likely one of those groups. Smart of them not to report their failure to this kind of guy. He wasn't one to reward incompetence.

"A smile? So, someone did find you. Did you pay them off or kill them? I've finished a dossier on Daniel and Lady Catanzano, but you are a mystery. A [Healer] but you can [Teleport]. The spells you hit me with in the elven forest were unique. I've been unable to find a targeted debuff like that in any book. Before you die, would you like me to record your class? It would be a shame to lose that kind of knowledge."

"My lord, I am almost out of mana," the lady interrupted. Her hand was shaking. "I was made to leave my supplies at the front door. I'll need a mana potion to continue."

Sanerris smiled politely at the woman. "Of course, Margery. I'll have one brought. One moment."

He stood and knocked on the door. It opened, and he began to have a hushed conversation with someone outside.

The healer, Margery, leaned in close and spoke so quietly in Orrin's ear that he felt her breath raise the hairs on his neck. "The lord of Dey is coming to rescue you. Hold out for one more day."

Without [Mind Bastion], Orrin would not have been able to control the smile he felt rising up in him. *Of course, Daniel wouldn't let them kill me. He probably had Silas [Teleport] them all right back to Mistlight. Sanerris wouldn't risk a political debacle.*

His heart alight with the thought of rescue, Orrin refocused his energy on better blocking her mana to unnecessary parts of his body. He wanted to talk with her, but Sanerris was already on his way back, holding a vial not unlike Orrin's own.

"One of my own; It should restore your entire mana pool."

If Orrin didn't know any better, he'd swear the man was nice. He treated Margery with respect. A far different attitude than how he'd treated Daniel . . . or Brandt.

Orrin couldn't take it. "If you're going to kill me, why have me healed? You kept Brandt in that cell near death for however long and didn't care. What's your game here?"

Sanerris settled back on his chair and watched Margery work for a bit more. In five minutes, she'd pushed what Orrin approximated as six hundred points of healing magic through him. Something he'd noticed over the last few months of healing was the health points of a person didn't directly correlate with an injury. Someone could have full HP and be hurt. Silas was the perfect example. Orrin knew that something must be wrong in the man's spine to make him use a wheelchair, but he could only guess at how much mana it would take to fix that. A broken bone that was set healed easier than a protruding bone. Now he was wondering if his knowledge of the human body, however rudimentary, was helping his own healing. His friend Amir had commented on it once, but Orrin had brushed it aside.

"That will be all, Margery. Thank you for your service. I'll send the usual donation to the Hospital later today. You can return in the morning for another round if you are up for it."

The old woman was hesitant to leave. Even Orrin could see that, and he didn't want Sanerris to get suspicious.

"Thank you for the healing," Orrin said, nodding at her. *I'll be fine.*

"I'll take my leave then, my lord."

She paused at the door but thought better and left.

"I'll make you a deal," Sanerris said, turning back from watching the door close. "You answer a question of mine and I'll answer one of yours."

"Why do you keep trying to kidnap Daniel?"

Sanerris laughed. "Your first question isn't about your own life? What does this [Hero] have that inspires such loyalty?"

Orrin wiggled his arm. The pain of the fracture was gone, but he knew from experience that a recently healed break was fragile. Margery had fixed his arm and his leg was about halfway to healed, but he had a long way to go still. If he focused again tomorrow while she healed him, he could probably be in decent enough shape to fight when they came for him.

"You'll answer my question first. What is your class?"

Orrin reasoned there was no harm in giving out the name of his class. He'd created it with the system, so it wasn't something that Sanerris could learn more about. Plus, he was pretty sure he'd told a lot of people the name by now. "[Utility Warder]."

"Interesting. I've not heard of that class before. As for your question, I need a [Hero] to save the world. None of the other leaders on this side of the Pass seem to care about what is happening. I have a plan and it involves your friend. What are the names of your spells?"

"I'm not telling you the names of all my spells," Orrin said and rolled his eyes. "I might as well ask you how do I get out of being killed."

"You aren't being killed."

Orrin stopped trying to fiddle the rope undone. "What?"

"You are not going to be executed. I know that Margery is a spy for Dey. I know that Lord Catanzano is in my city. Tomorrow, a criminal wearing a [Glamour] of your face will be executed in the town square and his body thrown out to sea, as is custom for criminals in Mistlight. I will keep you here and chat with you from time to time. My question about the names of your spells doesn't need to be answered today. We will have months, maybe years, to get to know each other."

Orrin's heart dropped.

Chapter 3

Orrin hit the cell bars in frustration.

Sanerris had had him escorted back after dropping that little bomb on him. He'd straightened his shirtsleeves and talked more at Orrin, but the words were nothing more than a faint buzz to him. Orrin had been thrown back into his prison cell, and nobody had returned for two days.

That was two days of no food or water . . . or so his captors would think. Orrin had enough food and drink in [Dimension Hole] to stay alive for months.

Not that he planned on waiting that long. Orrin didn't think Sanerris was lying about the execution, but Daniel and Madi were smart. They'd figure out it wasn't him. He just had to be patient and ready for when they came for him.

In preparation for his rescue, Orrin trained the few internal skills he could. He used [Analyze] on every item he could find. The information he gathered wasn't useful, but it kept him from going crazy. [Map] worked well but only on the floor he was on. Nobody came down the stairs while he was watching. He meditated a lot, using the skill to calm his mind more than for any need of a mana regeneration increase.

He thought about using [Obscure] on all his spells and skills. His friend Tony the mind mage had instructed him to purchase the skill ages ago. Orrin had originally used it to hide [Blood Mana] and [Mind Bastion] on his status screen. If anyone tried to use [Identify] or [Analyze] on him, they wouldn't find those two skills. He didn't hide everything for one reason: a lack of powers would be suspicious.

Orrin spent the first three hours of his imprisonment pushing his mind to the limit, picking what skills he could afford to eventually give up. He didn't know if Sanerris would torture him. He picked bright lines of things he would not reveal and selected a few more of his abilities that he figured he could hide. [Dimension Hole] was quickly grayed out on his status. The ability to keep food or weapons hidden was a perfect card to keep up his sleeve. [Merge] was his second pick. Madi had warned him about the skill's history, and he did not want to become a spell farm for Odrana.

He also hid [Through the Ages], the [Hero] skill that Daniel's predecessors used to send notes to future [Heroes]. He left most of his spells discoverable, as he was sure Sanerris had paid attention during the two fights they'd had. The only exception he made was [Way of the Water]. He felt strangely protective of Styx and his fighting style.

He didn't try leveling [Way of the Water] for now. He had no clue what schedule they would keep him on. The last thing he wanted was to be catatonic in his training when they came for him.

[Merge] would still work on the spells he couldn't access with the slave collar around his neck, but making more spells that he couldn't use didn't appeal to him. Instead, Orrin played with the skills he could use. Nothing matched up into anything useful. [Way of the Water] was still not complete. He thought [Analyze] or [Identify] would mix well with [Map], but he was given the extra [Map] options that he'd already purchased. Nothing new appeared.

[Analyze] did give him a new piece of information.

[Slave Collar]—[In Use]

Orrin pushed through until a full description appeared.

[Slave Collar]—Blocks access to the system and mana use. Made in Odrana. [In Use]

Orrin frowned when he read it. The collar wasn't blocking his access to the system completely. He'd felt the mana that the [Healer] had used to heal his broken bones, so it also didn't block access to mana. He didn't know if his skill was acting up or if something else was at play.

Orrin pulled snacks out of [Dimension Hole] and scarfed them down while watching [Map]. He was sitting on the edge of his mattress. Two days had passed. He bounced his leg and counted the holes between the bars again.

He wore nothing but his pants, and the small blanket they'd left him did nothing against the cold wind that blew in from the outside at times. He'd taken to walking in circles after waking with pain in his joints after his first fitful sleep. He had to keep warm. He could see his clothes right out of reach but hadn't tried to retrieve them. He was worried they might punish him, and the thought of being left down here wet or beaten was enough to keep him from trying.

At least it had been before now. Orrin checked [Map] before pulling a spare spear he kept for Madi out of [Dimension Hole]. Reaching his arm out, he snagged his cloak and shirt with the metal end and pulled them back. He took the risk of grabbing his potion belt and hiding it away in his [Dimension Hole]. He hadn't seen anyone take an inventory of what was in the pile.

The armor he left for now. They might let him get away with some extra clothing but if he put his armor on or it disappeared . . . He didn't want to get beaten again. A few potions they might overlook. The intricate armor that he'd been wearing was harder to ignore.

A glint of metal under his shirt caught his eye. It was his guild ring. Orrin had long ago forgotten he even wore the tiny copper band on his pinkie. He spent another few minutes pinning it to the far wall with the spear and walking the haft backward at an angle to get it. He slipped the beaten metal into his pocket, letting his storage skill take the jewelry.

With his shirt on, he sat down with his cloak around his shoulders. He closed his eyes and tried to [Meditate] again. He'd found that he could pass a few hours with the skill if he let his mind go. It beat pacing around the small cell.

When he came out of his meditation, Orrin stood to stretch his back. He groaned as multiple body parts cracked. He moved again and felt his body fall into Formless, the base stance of his fighting style.

Orrin instinctively moved through a few katas, letting the warmth of the movement spread into his joints. He moved around the room for another twenty minutes before pushing two hands together in one of the final moves he'd learned.

A bead of water gathered and splashed to the floor when he lost his concentration.

"What the . . . how?"

Orrin sat in the corner, letting the drop of water move between his hands. When Styx, the shadowy figure that taught him how to fight, had shown him how to do this during the last training session, he'd assumed it was some sort of mana-using spell that would be incorporated into his fighting. With the collar on his neck and after a lot of practicing, he knew for sure: there was no mana use in moving the water around. It was magic . . . but unlike anything else he could do.

It makes no sense. I'm not using any mana. I can't track my stamina, but I'm not tired after doing this for half an hour. Orrin let the water drop again. *It has to be using stamina, right? But a slave collar would block the skills of a nonmage, too, or only magic users would be able to be controlled. What is going on?*

Orrin's thoughts were interrupted by the distant sound of a key rattling in a lock. He smiled. His friends had finally come to rescue him. He pulled up [Map] and felt his heart drop.

The guards who arrived a few minutes later were different than the ones he'd seen before. They wore different colors than Sanerris's other guards had, with a subdued blue and dark gray mottled in. It reminded Orrin more of army camo from his world than the showy outfits the lords had their retinue wear.

"Put this on your head," the shorter one said, throwing a bag at Orrin. He caught it on reflex.

"If I don't?"

The taller man pulled a cudgel from his side and slapped it on his hand menacingly.

Orrin gave one last glance at his armor in the corner. It had served him well. He should have tried to hide it as well, but it was too late now. He pulled the bag over his head.

The cell doors swung open and Orrin was frog-marched out and up the stairs. The next few hours were spent in a carriage. His two new "friends" made him get out and walk at one point before they got into a second carriage. The hood was likely to prevent him from finding his way back or knowing where he was going.

[Map] kept track of everything. Every person within range appeared as a gray mark unless they were part of his party. There were no blue spots marking his friends nearby.

Orrin watched the thousands of dots of Mistlight disappear as he was moved farther east. His nose told him he was being transported mostly along the coast. The sea air was crisp the entire time, with one of the guards keeping him company in the carriage while the other drove.

The destination held three additional people, but Orrin's hood was not removed until he'd been taken inside whatever house or castle he was in now. He blinked hard as the light stung his eyes.

He stood with the short guard in a decently sized room. A bed with a few sheets was in the corner. A long chest of drawers sat beneath a window that looked out over the ocean. Orrin didn't know how large this house was, but it was high up on a cliff. If he tried to go out that window, he would fall a long time before hitting the water.

"Where am I?"

The shorter guard that had been with him in the carriage answered by slugging him in the gut. Orrin let the hit connect. He could have dodged it with [Way of the Water], but the more surprises he could store for later, the better.

"You are a prisoner of the Sanerris house and will not talk unless directed to speak. If you speak without leave to do so, you will be punished. You will keep this room clean and do as the mistress of the house demands or you will be punished. You will wake at first light every day and be ready to work or—"

"I'll be punished. Yeah, I get it."

Orrin dry heaved on his knees and spat blood after the guard stopped hitting him.

"You are not in Mistlight. This is not Dey. Nobody who cares for you knows you are here and you will likely be dead in a month." The man squatted as he whispered to Orrin. "I know you were part of the kill squad that took out my brother. Give me an excuse and I will gladly end you."

Orrin was spared having to ask what a kill squad was or why this guy thought he'd taken out his brother by the door opening. An woman, older but still regal in her posture and clothing, entered so quickly that if Orrin hadn't been facing the door, he would have assumed she'd teleported in.

"Jann, you can return to the city. Your services are no longer required."

"My lady, I apologize if I overstepped. I was given clear instructions by yo—"

"Leave at once or in pieces. These are your new instructions. Choose."

Orrin kept his eyes on the ground. The coldness that seeped into the room from that open door chilled him more than the sea air had in his cell. Jann, the short guard, didn't say another word as he scrambled from the room.

The cold wafted out with him, and warmth replaced the chill air. Orrin kept his eyes on the floor.

"You are made of sterner stuff than that. Get off the floor." Her voice didn't demand; she simply spoke what would be. Orrin raised his head and caught her eyes.

Emerald eyes that glittered with silver specks caught him back. The lady of the house raised an eyebrow as her golden hair bounced over her shoulders in long curls. She wore a dress that Orrin was sure by just looking at it must have cost dozens of gold pieces. Her fingers rested lightly on a small wand holstered on her side, letting him know she was a magic user. From the righteous expression on her face and the haughty way she carried herself, he saw one more thing about her. A clear family resemblance.

"Lady Sanerris, I'm guessing?" Orrin said as he stood.

"You are the one who came with the [Hero] and bested my son?"

Orrin put a finger under his collar and flicked it. "Didn't really win that fight, did I?"

The mother of the leader of Odrana laughed. "You had your party make a tactical retreat after brazenly walking into a trap. A trap that cost hundreds of gold and two now-useless spies. You intrigued and upset my son so much that he has sent you to me. Do you know what that means?"

"I didn't know he was such a sore loser." Orrin didn't know where his mouth was coming from, but something deep inside him told him that showing weakness to this woman would be a mistake.

Her broad smile showed too many teeth. "I think we are going to have a lot of fun together."

Chapter 4

"My name is Anabella Sanerris. My son is Arvin Sanerris, the lord of Mistlight and ruler of Odrana. You've been sent here to be tortured. You may have some information crucial to defeating the [Hero] and saving our world from total annihilation at the hands of the demon armies that will soon invade our lands." She paused dramatically and smiled. "Do you know how to play Kala?"

Lady Sanerris was giving Orrin a tour of her little villa. The other people in the house were kept out of sight, so he wasn't able to place the dots on his [Map] to faces. Anabella moved Orrin throughout the house without a care, pointing out the different rooms. Orrin was amazed at how easily she gave out information.

This room was where the help prepared the food. This room was where the two guards who stayed on-site slept in shifts. The front door opened to a path that ran down a long stairway carved into the cliff base. Nobody could go up or down without using those stairs. More guards were stationed at the bottom and would only allow those on Lord Sanerris's list to go through.

"Aren't you worried I'll try to escape?" Orrin couldn't help asking after she showed him the back patio that captured a picturesque view, which he couldn't appreciate at the moment. The sunlight dancing along the waves of the ocean below their feet and the expanse of blue that spread out as far as he could see were ignored.

"My son sent you here to vex me." Anabella held open the door and ushered Orrin back inside. "Since he usurped my position, he has tried many times to force me to accept his rule and give him aid. If you were to escape, I would return to my studies or perhaps try writing a book. Nothing of worth, mind you. I won't give Arvin one more hint about magic. However, I have been toying with the idea of a romance novel . . . I see that you don't care. If you try to escape, you will most likely die. Your collar is set to restrict all your skills and spells. It also will glow with a dull light if you move too far away. I would recommend finding me quickly if that happens. Here we are."

She opened a door on the opposite side of Orrin's room. The small chamber was similar to his own, except a set of doors opened onto a veranda that could comfortably seat two. A small table for tea or coffee was pushed up against the rail, and two weathered but comfortable-looking chairs were set to either side.

Anabella opened a wardrobe and pulled out a board for Kala. She set it on the small table and pressed a lever on the bottom of the board. A spring-loaded insert popped out, containing the needed cards and marbles.

"Shall we?"

Orrin sighed. Why did he meet weirdos wherever he ended up?

"I don't have a choice, do I?"

Anabella had already begun to put the marbles into a velvet bag for the pregame selection. "You always have a choice. The consequences of your actions are your own to bear."

Orrin slumped into the proffered chair. "If I don't play, I get tortured. If I do play, I still get tortured. Yay for torture."

He noticed a slight pull at her lips as she shuffled the cards. *She likes a bit of impertinence and bravery in the face of danger.* He needed every edge he could get until he figured out a way to escape. "How many prisoners have you played Kala with?"

Anabella raised her eyebrows in feigned surprise. "Prisoners? None. I haven't played Kala in two or three years at this point."

Orrin reached into the bag and pulled out his eight marbles: four white, two black, and two green. Like a game of checkers, the objective was to either take all the opponent's marbles off the board or reach the back line for an automatic victory. He could set his eight marbles anywhere on the three lines closest to him on the eight-by-eight grid board.

The white stones were the workhorse of a basic game. They could move forward or back, one space at a time; however, they could only attack diagonally one space as well. Orrin had drawn half of his pieces as the easiest-to-lose forces.

He rolled his two green marbles in one hand. By far his luckiest pull, a green marble created an imaginary forest line that the attacker could not pass until the marble itself was attacked. Good placement during setup could ensure victory unless he screwed up bad.

The last two black marbles were the other common piece. They could be moved diagonally one square at a time but could only attack vertically.

Orrin hadn't pulled any red marbles. Those could be placed on the person's own half of the grid at any time during the game. Any piece that surrounded it was destroyed. Orrin had once called it a bomb before Madi had corrected him—it represented any magical attack that could take out a force in number, but most referred to it as a fireball.

After ten turns, each person could draw an extra two marbles. This continued until someone won or they ran out of pieces and capitulated to a draw.

Orrin ran the rules of the game through his head once more. He had played with Silas and Madi a few times. He had tried to get Daniel into it, but he'd insisted on playing checkers instead. Not surprisingly, Madi had humored him and learned to play.

"One- or two-card draw?" Anabella laid the shuffled deck down. Orrin grimaced. He hated the cards. They added another element of randomness to the game, and he'd avoided playing with them for the most part.

Only ten cards, and yet they could make an entire winning strategy irrelevant. The two lightning cards could destroy a green forest line, effectively taking a marble from the opponent from the very beginning. The two rain cards were perfect against the red marble, played immediately after your opponent used the fireball stone. The red stone would be discarded, rendered inept.

Four of the remaining six cards were color-change cards, used to change one of your white marbles into a red or green depending on which color card you had.

"One card," Orrin answered. He always tried to minimize the randomness. It was harder to figure out the odds and make the best moves with more cards in play.

"Live a little." Anabella smiled and drew the top two cards. "Let's use two."

Orrin cursed under his breath but selected the next two cards. The rules stated the players had to agree on how many to use, but he didn't see disagreeing with Lady Sanerris going well. He had to bite his tongue to keep him from cursing louder. He'd pulled one of the last two special cards.

The art on the card was exquisite, showing a shadowy being lounging on a throne of gold. Orrin had drawn the Demon Lord, the sister card to the Hero. He could use it to summon two black marbles to his back line for three turns. It was a last-ditch defense card and was used mostly if a person was losing badly.

If I had to get one of the special cards, the Hero would have been better. I could use the extra white marble to press the attack. Orrin checked the red color-change card he'd also drawn and put them both to the side. *I'll just ignore them both and go for it.*

Orrin placed a green marble on the leftmost spot of the third line and on the rightmost spot of the second line. He spaced the two black marbles on the second line as defense, having them cover as much of the middle of the board as he could with their ability to move diagonally for a quick attack. The four white marbles he placed along the front. He'd need to play aggressively and move into the middle of the board quickly to keep Anabella on her toes.

Even under the encompassing calm of [Mind Bastion], Orrin's nerves snuck through and his stomach clenched. However, he felt a little excited, too. He wasn't half bad at this game. He'd impressed Silas with a few moves, even if he'd never beat the lord of Dey.

"Ready."

"Hmm." Anabella raised an eyebrow at his setup. The advantage of putting your marbles down first was you moved first. However, Anabella would be able to set down her marbles with an eye on defending against whatever was on the board. "You play like a child."

"Excuse me?" Orrin double-checked to make sure [Mind Bastion] was running. He felt a little heated.

"You scream to the world, *here is my plan.*" She placed a green marble in the middle of her second line and three white marbles and three black ones at confusing points around the same. She held one back in her hand, so Orrin knew she had one red marble as well. "Make your move."

Orrin had to admit, Anabella had his number from the beginning. While he rushed his marbles in, she maneuvered her pieces so he couldn't attack but found himself getting taken piece by piece before he reached her forest line. She played a lightning card to destroy his first forest line and sacrificed a black marble to take out his other before he finally took hers down. She retaliated with a fireball that took two of his pieces at once. He'd tried the same, sacrificing one of his last two white marbles to make a red, but her other card was a rain card. They'd danced back and forth on the sides and drawn two more marbles each, but Orrin was losing and he knew it. He had one white marble left, running it from two of her black marbles, while she had two moving in to take his back line.

He played his Demon Lord card, trying to buy the next three rounds for another marble draw.

Anabella smiled. "I wondered if you were saving that. You fight with all that you have. I respect that. I sacrifice one of my whites for another card."

Orrin barely remembered that as a rule. Neither Madi nor Silas had ever played that way, but he could remember reading or hearing it a few times. He watched as she took one of her two attacking pieces and moved it off the board. She picked up her new card and smiled. Orrin knew he'd lost.

"I play the Hero. All your Demon Lord pieces are gone, as well as half the pieces we have left. We both have odd numbers left. If we round up, you have no pieces left. If we round down, I still block you with this one and have my marble here to move in the next round. Do you yield?"

Orrin nodded. "That was a brilliant game. If you hadn't pulled the Hero card, I might have won."

Anabella scoffed and shuffled the cards. "You win or you lose. Again?"

After the third game, Anabella packed up the board and stretched. She was smiling, and Orrin thought it was due in no small part to how poorly he had played in the last game. He'd thought he had her again, but each time she'd managed to move her pieces in a way that messed up what he planned to do.

"Don't pout, it's unbecoming. What was it you said earlier? That was a brilliant game. I'm sure you'll manage a win in a month or two."

Orrin clenched his fist and moved to the railing with her. "I don't plan on being here that long, but at least I have good company."

The mother of his captor leaned back on the rail and studied him. "Why does my son fear your friend? Did your [Hero] not understand what is at stake or does he not care that we will be destroyed?"

"Your son tried to kidnap him. Twice, actually. He blackmailed our friend using his family and caused his death. He has never tried to have an actual conversation with us, not that it would matter. Daniel was already aware a Demon Lord was on the way to Dey. We were training and ready to stop anything from happening when we found out he was going to kill another one of our friends."

"The man who snuck into Mistlight and tried to assassinate him?"

Orrin scratched his elbow. "I mean, yeah. It's weird talking to you about this. I feel like I'm telling on someone to his mom."

"You are." Anabella smirked. She clenched one hand tightly before turning toward the sea. "So, he didn't tell you. What are you hiding, Arvin?"

"Tell us what?"

The elegant woman standing in front of him sighed again. "This is what comes of keeping me secluded and not informed. He wants answers but gives nothing to those by his side. It's why I'll be back in charge within a decade. Oh Arvin, you impatient little shit."

Orrin tried to keep up with her jumping thoughts but felt like he was missing something. "He didn't need to tell us the Demon Lord was coming. Daniel has a Quest to stop it from happening. Even without me, he'll be—"

"The Demon Lord is a black marble moving on the board. My son is playing Kala on a level you aren't ready for. We've known about his forces amassing for years but knew a [Hero] would come along to fight him. History repeats itself, no matter how long it takes," Anabella said and unclenched her fist. Orrin saw the dark marble in her hand but couldn't see what color it was from the angle she held it. "He isn't worried about the Demon Lord or a silly little Quest. He is preparing to fight the man who made the Demon Lord. The man who wants to end humanity and make all races into demons."

Anabella flung the marble. It was tiny against the crashing ocean below, and Orrin missed its splash against the foamy white waves. "My son is trying to stop the end of Asmea."

Chapter 5

Anabella hadn't spoken for ten minutes, just staring off into the distance. After dropping such important information on him, Orrin had assumed she'd want to share more. Instead, she'd dismissed him back to his room.

The next three days passed slowly. He spent time playing Kala, eating with Anabella, and learning the staff's routines. He ran into one of the two guards stationed here. She'd introduced herself as Jinx before giving some unsolicited advice.

"Stay away from Lady Sanerris and don't offend her. She's too smart. It's best to avoid conversations with her altogether," Jinx said, tapping her fingers on the mage's wand she kept on her hip. "Wait it out and Lord Sanerris will send for you. I don't want to have to get rid of another body."

Lady Sanerris hadn't asked more questions or spoken to Orrin at all. During their games, she'd point out flaws in his strategy or compliment him on a well-thought-out move, but she didn't broach the topic of demons or heroes again. She didn't let him win a single game. The one time that he had come close with a last-minute red marble, she had played a rain card and thrown the offending marble into the ocean.

Well . . . Orrin knew it would hit the ocean eventually. Her casual throw had rocketed the tiny stone away so quickly that Orrin couldn't see how far it had gone.

Orrin's only solace was [Way of the Water]. He trained every night, moving a drop of water faster and faster between his hands.

On the second night, he checked [Map] to confirm everyone was in their room except one of the guards stationed in a small guard blind built into the roof. Orrin decided to chance it. He was going to need everything he could to get out of here.

> **[Way of the Water] 30% 6/20 completed.**
> **Continue?**

Orrin snapped his fingers and went to it.

"Hey, Styx, you won't believe what's happened to me," Orrin said with a wave at his sensei. The watery figure bowed his head in welcome but didn't speak.

Orrin ignored the actual trial he was supposed to be doing and told Styx everything that had been going on. Styx didn't respond when Orrin told him how Silas, the lord of Dey and Madi's father, had been considering murdering their friend Brandt. He described the mad rush to Mistlight with his friends and the fights they'd gotten into. He confided his fears that Daniel might think he was dead and his dread at the possibility he wouldn't be able to escape. He talked for a solid twenty minutes before he ran out of steam and plopped on the floor.

"That's been my life recently. How about you?"

Styx didn't respond. Instead, he gestured for Orrin to stand. Orrin groaned as he crawled back to his feet. Even though his body wasn't really in this . . . simulation . . . he could still feel it. He'd taken a look at himself with his skills that morning before his daily game of Kala with Anabella and found that his fractures were mostly healed. His body was still covered in bruises of violent shades of green and yellow, but he was on his way to his old self.

"Take it easy on me today?" Orrin asked as he wobbled to his feet. "I'm still on the mend."

Styx fell into Formless, the base stance of his fighting style, and held his hands a little less than a foot apart. A drop of water condensed and floated in the middle.

"That's what we did last time," Orrin complained as he also took the starting form of [Way of the Water]. He felt confident in keeping his own drop of water levitating between his hands. He'd been practicing it. There was a calm to doing it, even if he didn't know what he was actually doing yet.

"PROTECT." Styx spoke his one-word command.

"Protect wha—" Orrin couldn't finish his sentence as Styx threw a kick at him. Dropping his left hand, he blocked the foot and spun into Styx's guard, ready to attack. He threw a punch and . . . Styx was gone.

Orrin checked behind him to see a puddle of water moving along the floor. It rippled once before Styx re-formed up into his humanoid form.

"What was that? Am I going to learn to turn into a puddle of water?" Orrin was excited. If he could completely avoid hits like that, maybe he could flush himself into the ocean. On second thought, that sounded terrible. He'd rather stay a prisoner.

Orrin could have sworn Styx shook his head but when he looked closer, the man wasn't moving. Instead, he took up Formless again and held the bead of water in his hands.

"PROTECT."

He didn't attack again. Orrin moved toward him and swung, but Styx's defense was leagues ahead of him still. This time, Styx didn't attack but retreated. Orrin felt like a kid running after an adult trying to play tag. After five minutes of keep-away, he shook his head and quit.

"Styx, I'm never going to hit you. What am I supposed to do here?"

"PROTECT." Styx held his hands up, gesturing with his head at the bead of water he held with the force of his will.

"You're doing great at protecting your water . . . Protect my own?"

Styx's body rippled in excitement. He nodded.

Orrin sighed as he took the Formless stance again and summoned a drop of water between his hands. "You need to learn to speak better. These half-assed instructions are terrible. We'll find a way."

"LEVEL."

Orrin dropped his water. "Did you just sass me with a straight answer?"

Styx didn't respond. Orrin got ready and nodded at the man. "Protect."

An hour later, he collapsed on the floor of his room. He'd spent so long in the time dilation trying to keep away from Styx's attacks he could feel the crick in his neck. *Next time, lie down on the bed, not sitting up,* he told himself. He checked his status. [Way of the Water] was at 35 percent. All it took was keeping the drop of water from falling for a single minute . . . while his teacher attacked him with everything he had.

Orrin pulled a piece of spiced bread with nuts out of his [Dimension Hole] and ate it. They fed him pretty well, but he was starving after the exercise.

"All so I can move a bead of water around while dodging. I should have researched [Way of the Water] more in Dey. Somebody has to know what this fighting style is."

Orrin grumbled some more before turning in for the night. "Daniel, you better come rescue me soon. I'm talking to myself already. I'll be completely crazy in another two days."

On his third day of captivity with Lord Sanerris's mother, Anabella surprised him.

"My son told me that you can heal and you have spells that can increase stats. I would like to see them in action. Come here so I can reprogram your collar to allow use of those spells."

Orrin considered his options. He hadn't known the slave collar could be programmed to allow spells to be cast, but it made sense. What was the point of having a slave with great and powerful powers if you restricted them from using them all the time? If he let her open up his abilities, he'd have an easier time escaping, but there was no way he could make an attempt right now. He couldn't use [Identify] on her, but from the casual movement and the one display of strength she had displayed, he would guess she had to be at least thirty or forty levels past him, if not more. If he declined, he could keep his powers a secret, but she'd probably start the actual torture.

"This is not your moment," Anabella said quietly as she placed her cup on the table. She was drinking a clear fruit juice of some sort that sparkled in the sunlight. "Move here, now."

Orrin frowned as he approached her. "What do you mean, it's not my moment?"

Anabella turned him bodily and fiddled with the collar. "You know what I mean. I will not let you escape while I am in front of you. Don't make me hurt you . . . or worse. I am enjoying our games. Do you know that most of my old peers would give up after only a loss or two? Or worse, they would let me win to try and curry favor. You play with passion and intelligence. You learn from your mistakes and rarely repeat the same ones. I was playing Kala when I was eight. I've played for decades. You've only been playing for, what . . . a handful of years?"

"Less than one. We didn't have Kala where I grew up." Orrin focused on the feeling of magic that was coming from the collar. He felt the tiniest movement of . . . something. Before he could get a hand on what it was, Anabella twirled him back around.

"Truly? A year?"

"Silas, um, Lord Catanzano taught me. He said I was decent, but I couldn't win against him, either," Orrin said, choosing to not push the issue of escaping. "Is it done?"

She nodded, and Orrin pulled up his status. He had to focus hard to keep from smiling. She'd opened up more than she'd wanted to.

"You should have access to internal modification spells. I have a list of your suspected spells, so I'll warn you now. Jinx can see through most forms of concealment. If you try and slip away, she will find you and you will be killed."

Orrin's joy turned to ash. [Camouflage] was the spell that was now free to use. Jinx wouldn't be able to watch him all the time, though.

"I'll also be reprogramming the collar before you leave the room."

Damn it.

Anabella smiled. "I'm sure you have other spells you could try, but if you do, my son learns of those spells. The only reason I've agreed to do this is the rarity of buff spells. Can you truly use them on others?"

Orrin resigned himself to giving up some information and nodded his head. "I could show you if you want."

Anabella's smile gentled. "No, you could not. If you try and cast a spell that affects anything or anyone other than yourself, the collar will cause you unbearable pain and revert to the original programming. You'd lose access to everything again. I'll be observing as you heal yourself. I know you are still hurt; I see you wince when you sit. Perhaps if we have time today, you can show me the strength increase. That should be the easiest to demonstrate and measure."

"Measure? What would you measure?" The investigator part of Orrin's mind churned.

"First, we should find your base strength score. Not what the system says is your strength but how much you can actually lift or carry. I have some potions that will allow you to use the full strength of your system score and then we can play with the increased stat of your spells as well. It's fascinating, isn't it? I once had a [Berserker] let me do this with him, but we couldn't get good data because . . . well, he kept trying to kill everyone. But with you, I can pick apart another part of the puzzle of stats and the system."

Orrin now knew what Daniel felt like when he went off on his own system knowledge tangents. "So, I'm a test subject?"

Anabella's eyes gleamed with a dangerous fire. "That sounds like I'm going to dissect you when we're done. I like the phrase *experiment colleague.*"

Orrin closed his eyes and took a deep breath. "Can I heal myself first, at least?"

Anabella picked up a pad of paper and a pencil. "Of course. But first, I have a few questions. What type of healing spell are you using?

What is the baseline health that you recover? Do you give weight to the idea that healing spells increase a body's own regenerative power or that you are using mana to rebuild something from nothing?"

She continued with her questions and Orrin realized he was already being tortured.

Chapter 6

Orrin sighed in defeat and fell back on the bed. The last few hours had been terrible. Anabella hadn't needed him to give her his stats. She already knew them. She had a version of the upgraded [Identify] like he did. Of course, she hadn't told him that until after he'd been humiliated.

Orrin groaned again and rubbed his eyes in frustration, remembering their conversations.

"Don't lie to me." Her voice took the cold tone of teachers from his past when he'd forgotten homework. Orrin's neck hairs tingled.

"My will is twenty," Orrin tried to lie. "I'm telling the truth."

He found himself floating upside down in the middle of the room. Anabella held a knife in her hand and advanced on him.

"If you won't be honest, I'll study the effects of your healing with actions." She pressed the cold blade against his abdomen. "It is your choice."

After he'd told her his will, intelligence, strength, dexterity, and constitution, she'd tilted her head. "Why [Mana Pool]?"

"I needed the extra MP to heal . . . how do you know I have [Mana Pool]?"

The vulpine smile that spread on her face reminded Orrin that this was the mother of Lord Sanerris and the former ruler of Odrana. "Now that we have an understanding, I'll ask again. What are your theories on the different branches of healing and how they relate to . . ."

Orrin took a deep breath and steadied his mind with [Meditation]. He'd been able to glean some interesting facts regarding his own magic from her inquiries. [Mind Bastion] had played against him for the first ten minutes before he realized his need for a logical solution was making him argue with her on the finer points of [Heal Small Wounds].

He'd also let slip the equation he'd worked out for his first-level increase-stat spells, the will-to-stat-increase math that he'd worked so hard to figure out, but Anabella had waved her hand in annoyance.

"Everybody knows that," Orrin mocked in a poor imitation of her voice.

He turned over the few bits he'd been able to steal back from her. He'd had to turn [Mind Bastion] on and off, which felt like jumping from a cold pool into a sauna every few minutes. However, he'd begun to piece together a few interesting ideas.

First was something that Arandir had already hinted at: even if Orrin increased a person's strength to the maximum value of one hundred, they couldn't use that newly attained strength to its full extent. Anabella had mentioned constitution playing a part in how quickly a person could acclimate to their increased skill, using the example of a [Berserker] again. She must have talked with one extensively in the past.

Orrin could see how that made sense. He'd already had a theory that Daniel's skill [Summoned Hero], which gave him double the stat power for his strength, dexterity, and constitution, had something to do with why he didn't suffer from stat overuse. It conflicted with his own case, as Orrin also had some sort of immunity to overincreasing his stats. The Dragoon team's ability to not pass out after being buffed also supported the argument that a higher level and constitution could negate the aftereffects.

Second, Anabella knew her healing. This was where Orrin was scared that he might have screwed up. He'd slipped back into [Mind Bastion] for the calming effect and better recall it gave while arguing with her about the way [Heal Small Wounds] worked. Orrin hadn't worked with other healers to a great extent, but what Anabella was telling him was wrong.

"You can't focus the healing on a specific part of the body. You must let it spread so the person's own magic can direct it where it is most needed." Anabella had pulled out books on healing and was able to find direct quotes without using a reference guide. "This study proved that generalized healing worked better than trying to apply personal knowledge of a wound's nature."

"That looks flawed to me. There's no mention of anatomy education or knowledge from these healers. This passage says one of them tried rubbing mud on every wound before to help his nature magic work better. Wounds should be clean, and knowing how the layers of skin would react to something like that would be—"

"Layers of skin?"

Orrin had tried to backpedal, but once Anabella had her sights set on something, she eventually got what she wanted. He'd explained the various layers of the human body in the broadest terms he could. Three layers. The first that kept things from entering your body, unless it was cut. A second layer under that contained fine-sensation nerve endings and small blood vessels. The third held the fat layers, more nerves, and the bigger blood vessels.

"How do you know these things? Have you cut the skin to see yourself?"

"My mother taught me," Orrin had repeated. It was the easiest way to get out of further questioning.

They'd talked more, and Orrin learned a few more topics about healing that he hadn't been able to find in books. Some of the things she told him contradicted what he'd discussed with his healer friend Amir or Lyra, the elves' elder of healing.

"You're sure that [Diagnose] isn't required? I was told it is—"

"A requirement for multiple fields of healing. Yes, I've heard that before." Anabella had the annoying habit of finishing Orrin's sentences for him. It was like she was impatient to continue the conversation. "One of the things that I was trying to reform was our Hospital and general healing knowledge. I upset a great number of old men. One reason on a list as long as my arm of reasons my son was able to snatch my power away."

"You seem pretty strong still," Orrin had said, rubbing his stomach.

A rare warm smile flashed across her lips. "My powers remain mine. I meant my rule. I tried to be too involved in projects I was interested in and lost sight of the greater scheme."

Orrin had kept quiet, and her small smile turned predatory again. "Of course, now I have the time to delve deeper into what interests me. Back to what you said about nerve structure . . ."

The third and final thing he'd learned from Anabella was how little he knew about magic. She'd been asking him what spells he had to use against enemies. He'd tried to be cagey until she shook her head in disappointment. She spent a long minute staring at him, which made him distinctly uncomfortable.

"You have too many spells in different areas. Why did you buy [Tilth]? I'm not sure anybody has used that in centuries."

Orrin had pulled back in shock. "How do you—"

"I used [Identify]. Anyone of sufficient power gets it eventually, and I see you already have it. I'd recommend you not use it on me if I open your collar up more in the future. What is the reason you have such a wide array of magic? These wards you have seem to . . . I see. Do you have a growing class?"

Orrin had to slip back into [Mind Bastion] to keep up with her thoughts. "When I get a new spell type, I sometimes get a new ward option . . . if that is what you're asking. What's a growing class?"

"A growing class versus a static class. Some classes give access to every skill or spell from the first level. It makes the class common, easy to record, and safe. A [Farmer] will know every ability he can use and it is only a matter of time before he charts his path to the most profitable outcome. A [Fire Mage] is a growing class. It has a set of base spells but can add more depending on what is chosen or if other actions are taken."

"I guess I'm that kind, then."

"Wonderful. If you have a spell of each type of magic, along with a ward for each type as well, you'll eventually be able to see the changes of magic for each one. I'd recommend you not purchase any other types of useless spells. You don't have a metal spell or any wood magic. I'm going to open up your [Tilth] spell. I'll have them send some dirt to your room. Try using the spell and see if you can watch the magic leave your body."

"Huh?"

Anabella took a pitcher of water off the counter and poured some into a glass. "Watch."

Orrin watched as she moved the water with a spell. It lifted out of the glass and spun in the air, creating a circle. She twitched her fingers and the water froze. It fell to the ground and shattered, sending small chips of ice against his legs.

"Did you see?"

"You froze the water? I don't have a spell to do that."

Anabella had dismissed him after that, telling him she wouldn't teach imbeciles.

Someone had brought a bucket of shitty soil into his room. Actual soil with what smelled like horse manure mixed into it. Orrin tried to use [Tilth]. He felt the mana draining, but to his untrained eye, he had no idea what to look for.

Orrin's dad had taken care of the garden in their backyard. He'd had green plants around the house that he watered and sang to. Once he'd gone, Orrin's mom tried to keep them alive, but she was busy trying to get the police to look for him or working to keep the house. As such, the plants had fallen to the wayside. Orrin had tried to pick up the slack and keep them watered at least. He'd even brought the hose around the back of the house to spray the small vegetable garden his dad was so proud of. It only grew carrots and small tomatoes.

Everything had died within a week of Orrin taking over.

He kept at it, mostly because he had nothing else to do. He could only spend so long pacing or running different spells through [Merge]. He was hesitant to create anything new now that Anabella had seen his spells. If she looked again and something new popped up, he'd have to explain why he bought it.

Orrin still had ability points and administrator points as well, but what could he possibly use them on in his current predicament? He'd need to find something in the store that was internal magic only and would help him escape.

Every cast of [Tilth] made the soil blend, for lack of a better word. He mixed the soil over and over, feeling the mana move away from his body. Anabella had also left [Heal Small Wounds] unlocked, and he had quickly brought himself back to full strength. He was slightly angry to find himself counting the casts and mana used versus how much better he felt after each cast. It wasn't something he was going to tell her. He did it for his own knowledge . . . right?

He didn't go back in to train with Styx. Anabella had sent him back to his prison early, but he knew dinner was right around the corner. Maybe after he ate and everyone was asleep, he'd try to increase [Way of the Water] to the—

What was that?

Orrin cast [Tilth] again.

It must have been my imagination.

He cast three more times before it happened again.

As Orrin cast the spell, he focused on his hand. He'd long gotten used to shooting his spells with finger guns, but it wasn't necessary. He knew that in theory, he could cast from any part of his body but most casters used their fingers or palms.

As [Tilth] ate his mana, Orrin felt the magic. It was similar to when he'd redirected the healer's magic to his broken bones, but instead of touching the magic, he just observed.

The mana within him was a calm sea of power. As he activated the spell, it was pulled to where he had visualized. A small drop of his mana raced down his arm and to his fingers. It spread and drifted out of his skin, laying itself over the soil.

Except as it left his hand, his mana sparked . . . or maybe *grew* was more accurate. It changed from potential into something hearty and musky. The flowing blue power within him morphed into a sludgy brown energy that spread into the dirt below.

Orrin cast again. He watched. He tried it with [Mind Bastion] and without. After twenty minutes, his mana was getting low, but he succeeded nine times out of ten now in watching the magic move and change. He wasn't sure what good it would do, but he smirked.

"Who's the imbecile now?"

Chapter 7

Orrin smirked as he described the change of his mana while casting his [Tilth] spell the next day. Anabella nodded her head slightly to him. It was the same as enthusiastic applause from anyone else. They were halfway through another game of Kala.

"Watch again," she commanded and repeated her water trick. The coil of liquid lifted into the air and spun before turning to ice. It fell to the ground and broke into pieces again. "Did you see?"

Orrin had her repeat the spell twice before he saw it.

"You changed the magic somehow when it reached here." He pointed to the space in the air. "How?"

Anabella kept her lips pursed and stared at Orrin. He had the impression that she was judging him in some way, but everything about his interactions with her so far was confusing. He was just trying to keep her from torturing him before Daniel arrived to rescue him.

"Before I discuss secrets with you that many at my school haven't grasped, tell me why the [Hero] is so upset with your death that he threatens my entire country."

Orrin felt his feet fall out from underneath him. He'd assumed Anabella had a way of getting news from the outside world, but he'd been living in isolation. If Daniel was making threats against Odrana, he must have bought the ruse of Orrin's execution.

That means I'm alone. I have to escape on my own.

"You have no chance of escaping without my help." Anabella's voice cut into his thoughts. "Is he a lover, perhaps?"

Orrin felt his face turn tomato red. "He's my best friend."

"Daniel told my son that Odrana will fall after he is done defeating the Demon Lord. How strong is this [Hero]? Does he have a moniker yet?"

Orrin remembered the time two of Daniel's soccer teammates had dropped him in a half-full garbage can during lunch freshman year. They'd received detention when a teacher caught them. Orrin had heard the coach had threatened to bench them for a game. The one who had started it, Jordan, had bragged the next day that it was all a bluff. He was a star on the team and the coach wouldn't do it.

Orrin could remember the way Daniel's hands had clenched on the book he was holding.

Orrin had gone to the game to cheer on his friend. When the coach subbed Jordan into the game after twenty minutes, Daniel walked off the field. His coach yelled at him and begged him to go back in. As crucial as Jordan thought he was to the team, the entire school knew Daniel was the true star player, even as a freshman.

Daniel never moved off the bench. The team lost by two goals.

When Orrin had confronted Daniel, his friend had shrugged. "Coach didn't keep his promise. Jordan's dad had scouts at the game, so he let him play. People's actions needed to have consequences."

"After Daniel kills the Demon Lord, I wouldn't want to be in Odrana."

"Good to know. He does have a moniker, then."

"I never—"

"You didn't ask what it was. Not many understand the full name of a [Hero]. There was recognition in your eyes."

Orrin kicked himself. He'd given her more information again.

"I would have Daniel not be an enemy of my people. If I released you, would that save Odrana?"

Orrin's head snapped up. "It couldn't hurt."

Anabella tilted her head. "No, it could. It could do much harm. However, there might be another way . . ."

Orrin waited for her to continue. "I'm all ears. I really don't want to be tortured."

Anabella waved her hand. "We're past that. Arvin pawned you off on me to bide his time. He underestimated how quickly the [Hero] would mobilize Dey against him. The elves as well. Either your friend is very persuasive or very powerful, or you have more friends than you know. My son directed me to get whatever information I could out of you and turn you back over to him once things cooled down. He's surrounded himself with sycophants and has forgotten his place. No . . . I think I will have to take over again."

A low sigh escaped her lips as she moved a white stone forward on the board. "I'll win in two moves. Concede?"

Orrin couldn't see how she thought she'd win, but he had no cards left. He'd learned to trust her when she said she would, though. He nodded.

Anabella picked up the pieces and put them back in the bag. Normally, this was when Orrin was dismissed, but she waved him back into his seat.

"The words you just heard are enough for a commoner to be tried and jailed for sedition, if not murdered. How much do you know about my family?"

Orrin shrugged. "You rule Odrana."

That rare smile peeked out again. "Yes. We do, but not in the way you think. Each of our five territories has a chancellor. Technically, my son is the chancellor of Mistlight. One chancellor is elected as the de facto leader of our country by the group. He is the tiebreaker in votes, but over the years, my family has amassed power and wealth. We rarely need to break a tie, as the other families stay in line."

"Ruler in all but name," Orrin commented.

"We know what is best for our country. At one time, we tried to work with the families and the people, but squabbles over breadcrumbs took opportunities away from all. We do what is necessary for the good of everyone."

Orrin kept his mouth shut, even though he wanted badly to argue with her.

"My son believes there is someone behind the Demon Lord. Someone with powers that we've thought lost to us forever. I know you've met with the elf Arandir. He has powers that are similar but pale in imitation to what we call Administrators."

Orrin felt sweat drip down his neck. He activated [Calm Mind] and [Mind Bastion]. *If I've ever been able to have a good poker face, now's the time for it to shine.*

Anabella continued, "We believe that someone with powers like Arandir is behind the new Demon Lord. They want to destroy all of humanity. A demon has the ability to kill another person for experience. They can live and breed with nearly any race. In a few generations, everyone would be a demon. Do you understand what that would do to society?"

When she stayed quiet, Orrin realized she wanted a response. "I can't imagine it would be good . . . but if they can kill each other for experience, how does the Demon Lord keep an army in check? Or how have they not all killed each other by now?"

"Nobody understands demons. All that matters is they are attacking and we must defend. Arvin thought we needed to create new spells and better magic. He's been trying to get Arandir to work with him, and when that failed, he thought he had enough power himself to force the elves to work for us." Anabella sighed and rubbed her eyes. "I love my son, but he's an idiot sometimes."

Orrin tried to piece together what he knew. Arandir's story about a [Hero] in the past came back in a rush: a [Hero] had been betrayed and broke the world. Demons had been left on one side of the mountain range, and the people of Dey, Veskar, and Odrana on the other. Arandir's ancestor was the last Administrator and had found a way to pass on some of his powers through his family line. Arandir had a small sample of the powers available to Orrin. The powers he still refused to learn.

If Lord Sanerris learned he was an Administrator, he wouldn't be squirreled away with his imprisoned mother. He would be a national treasure, kept under lock and key for the rest of his life.

"What would you have done differently?" Orrin tried to steer the conversation back to Anabella's favorite topic—her own brilliance.

"When our spies in the demon lands returned with news that a Demon Lord was gaining power, I began talks with Dey and Veskar to combine our forces. We could set up ambush points, choke the Pass, or even sue for peace. They have no reason to attack us. We've lived separately for thousands of years. My son urged me to consider a more permanent solution. If we attacked the demons, we could wipe them from existence. Their numbers must be low, as they've undoubtedly spent years killing each other."

Orrin could see Lord Sanerris wanting a fight. He had loved watching the fight between Orrin, Daniel, Madi, and the elven council. He'd only joined when Orrin had started using spells he wanted to know more about.

Luckily, Arandir had almost crushed him with a big tree.

"I want you to help me."

Orrin had to hold back a snort of derision. "Why would I help you?"

Anabella leaned forward in her chair and grabbed the back of Orrin's collar. "Consider this payment for hearing my proposal. Use your [Water Reservoir] and set a slow flow into this pitcher."

She cleared everything off the table and set the empty water container in the middle. Orrin complied, having learned not to waste her time. Her cutting rebukes hurt more than fists sometimes.

"Slow the mana more. It works best with a smaller amount. That's perfect," she guided him.

Orrin concentrated on the mana. Once again, his mana changed as soon as it left his body. Orrin could feel his cool blue mana drifting along through his body. Like a sleepy beast, he unleashed it from his palm. The mana moved differently as soon as it left his hand, moving in a more fluid way.

"Feel the mana outside your body. Can you picture it?"

Orrin nodded.

"Change it into a [Ice Sword]. Tell your mana to alter its form."

Water splashed over the top of the pitcher. Anabella stepped away with grace, barely getting her feet wet.

Orrin was soaked.

"What?" Orrin turned to the beautiful older woman. "What was that? You can't just tell me to change the magic midcast. What happened?"

A glimmer of something playful entered her eyes as she responded. "You tried to control the wild mana that you released. It remembered that it was yours and tried to heed your command."

Anabella stepped forward and turned the rest of the pitcher over. To Orrin's surprise, only a cup or two dribbled out. A large chunk of ice had formed in the middle.

"This is one of the most advanced courses that we teach at the Sanerris School for Spells. We teach our students how to cast one spell and alter it as many times as they can before the mana becomes set and unchangeable. You've grasped in a few days what many take years to do. I do not know if letting you go will appease the [Hero], but unless I kill you here and now, you're likely to become a powerful enemy in the future. Or a powerful ally."

Anabella opened a cabinet and pulled out a towel. She held it out to Orrin. "I'd prefer not to kill you. You're halfway decent at Kala."

Orrin took the towel and dried his face. "I would also like to not die. I don't know how strong I'll be in the future, but I'll at least turn Daniel away from Odrana and back toward the demons."

"No, you don't understand," Anabella said, waving her hand. "You're going to help me take over Odrana."

Orrin screamed into his pillow.

Anabella's plan was half-baked, relied on luck, and would likely result in his death anyway. The alternative, as she so aptly described, was having the guards throw him from the back of the house into the sea below. If the impact didn't kill him, the monsters in the water would. All her talk of working together and at the end of the day, he didn't have a real choice.

When Lord Sanerris had taken over from his mother, he had gathered support from three of the other four chancellors. Their votes and Sanerris's well-timed forced retirement of his mother had led to the current situation.

Lord Sanerris would visit in a month. Before that, Anabella was going to help Orrin escape. She was going to enroll him at the Sanerris School under a false name. She had a list of names. Three students. Each was the heir to the chancellor's position if something happened to their parent.

Orrin was to infiltrate the school, befriend these students, and help them take over power from their families.

"I'm dead," Orrin muttered and resumed screaming in frustration.

Chapter 8

Orrin sat across from Anabella as she sorted papers into three different piles.

"These are the chancellors' children at my school. You'll need to—"

"Why do you keep calling it *your* school?" Orrin interrupted. He'd barely slept, trying to figure a way out of this crazy plan. "Also, I've thought of a hundred ways this can go wrong. Nobody is going to be friends with a slave at some prestigious school. Your son had me executed in Mistlight. How is it going to look if I show up alive and well? Why are you smiling like that?"

"It is the school my ancestors founded, and even though I am deposed, I am responsible for it. As to your other concerns . . ." Anabella lifted a hand from her side. She held the wand she kept holstered high and tapped Orrin on the head.

The tingling started where she touched him but rapidly spread over his entire body. At first, it was only a slight tickle against his senses, but the flash of fire he felt made him let out a cry of pain.

"What was that?" Orrin ran his hands over his face and rubbed his hands together.

"A semipermanent [Glamour] I cooked up just for this," Anabella explained with a smile as she put her wand away. "You'll look like this until I remove it. Nobody will be able to see the collar, either. Take a look."

She waved her hand to a full-length mirror across the room. Orrin didn't need to move closer.

He looked hot.

His light hair had darkened slightly and hung in long ringlets just below his chin. He could see traces of himself in the illusion, but this him had a stronger jawline, better cheekbones, and dimples. His body was buff but without the oversize muscles of a bodybuilder. He had a leaner build with broad shoulders and arms that looked like they could throw heavy things around with ease. The collar appeared to be a necklace. Orrin ran his finger around it. It felt the same to him.

"You haven't changed. If anyone touches you, they'll be able to figure out that magic is making up about twenty percent of you currently."

"Only twenty percent? You made me into someone else entirely," Orrin whispered in awe.

"This is you. There are some embellishments, but with enough training and time, your stats will hone your body to this." Anabella waved her hand over Orrin. "I did have to tweak the hair and face. We can't have anyone recognizing you as the executed assassin."

Orrin continued to touch his face. He couldn't feel the longer hair, but it moved when his fake hands moved through the illusion. He'd known Anabella was strong, but this was not the kind of magic he'd thought she'd use. He expected lightning or great balls of fire. To be honest, from the way she sucked the warmth out of rooms when angry, he'd have bet she was an [Ice Mage].

"Stop doing that and come study these dossiers. I want your input on how you plan to approach each one and befriend them. We have twenty-eight days before my son will be here to take you away. It is not enough time, but I would prefer trying this over fighting him head-on."

"I'm not sure that would end well," Orrin muttered as he sat back in his chair and picked up the top paper on a girl named Maeve Wellan. "He can stop time. You can't fight against that without an army."

Anabella smirked. "Or with time-delayed attacks set up before he targets you, but I'm not going to discuss ways to defeat my son with you. Read."

Orrin grunted but acquiesced. The one fraction of a plan he'd been able to put together did hinge on being able to befriend these kids.

"She's twenty-one," Orrin groaned. "How am I supposed to make friends with girls older than me?"

Anabella rolled her eyes and gestured to Orrin's new physique. "Maeve is a smart girl, but she has never had friends. She's never been part of the female social groups, and although she is pretty enough, no suitor has pursued her for long. Be charming and ignore her bad habits. She'll latch on to you without a problem. I'm least worried about her. As it is, her father sided with Arvin out of a desperate concern that Maeve wasn't safe. Threatening the welfare of my enemies' children is beneath my family, or so I thought."

Orrin read more. Maeve was older than him but had been tutored mostly in her home estate. Her class wasn't recorded, but she could use wood and earth magic. Her father was the chancellor of Ceraun, and he . . .

"I've got a problem." Orrin winced as Anabella glared down at him again. "I never learned much about Odrana."

Anabella's frown deepened. "What do you need to know?"

"I'm not sure where Ceraun is or how it relates to the rest of Odrana. If I'm supposed to be friends with the children of the people in charge, it'll look weird if I don't know where their home is located."

"Have you never seen a map?"

Orrin shrugged. "I've had more important things going on in my life. Learning the names of countries I never thought I'd visit seemed like a waste of my time."

The temperature in the room definitely dropped a few degrees as Anabella swept out the door. She returned a few minutes later with a framed map of Odrana.

"Take notes. I won't repeat myself," Anabella demanded, pointing at the paper and pen she'd left out for him. She ran her hand over the map.

Orrin studied it. While he'd seen a few of Silas's maps, most of them just had Veskar and Odrana as two separate parcels of land to the east of Dey. This map was more detailed, showing the turned-boot shape of Odrana. The country was squat but long across the drawing, with an upturned peninsula jutting away on the northeastern side. Dotted lines separated the land into five uneven sections.

"The lands of Odrana that abut the lands of Dey and the elven forest is the territory of Idrisid. It's largely forested lands, with a few other small industries. The Palmer family has ruled for five generations and has done so admirably. They supply lumber, charcoal, and even some hunted game across Asmea. Lord Palmer is the only chancellor who stood against my son. He has no family to threaten and lives for the hunt," Anabella explained with a smile. "This section that takes up the majority of our lands is Ceraun. It exports more grains, livestock, and grown foods to the rest of the world than every country combined. Every person would starve without the Wellan family. They trace their line back to before the foundation of Odrana. As I explained, Lord Wellan would likely have voted with me if my son had not threatened his daughter. He is fiercely protective of her."

Orrin watched her long finger drag up to the smallest section of the map. A semicircle of land was carved in between the two prior territories. "You know Mistlight. The heart of Odrana and seat of power. Also the home to my school. We trade with the elves and Dey from this port. We can also move product east and down the coast to Veskar when the savages gather enough coin to pay for it."

Orrin pointed to the long stretch of land that ran along the southern border to the eastern sea. "Why is this one so long and skinny?"

"Ronden protects our borders from Veskar. The Madvarr family has ruled there for only two generations, but they've done so without a single lost battle against Veskar skirmishes. Their . . . son, Finley, is a little older than you. He is a battle mage, although of what sort I do not know." Anabella put her hand on her wand as if checking it was there. "There is a rumor that he turned back a group of raiders at age fifteen by himself. The Madvarrs have a flair for the dramatic, but they never lie about a fight. That leaves only Goldenhall."

The shoehorn located at the top right of the map. Orrin waited for Anabella to continue, but she was lost in thought. After a minute, he gave her a nudge by pointing. "What family?"

"Lady Tonsa. She is shrewd and intelligent. Her betrayal stung the worst. Goldenhall mines the mountains along the northeast sea. It's a dangerous job but necessary—one swing of a pickax in the wrong place can flood a mine with seawater. Her son, Rhys, is young like you. She's kept him away from Mistlight until recently. I've never met the boy."

Orrin flinched at being called young but kept his mouth shut. "What do they mine that's so important?"

"Precious metals, like gold, silver, and sometimes cold iron. There was a vein of Mythril years ago, but that dried up. The Tonsa family took over after the last family failed to keep up with demand. They pushed for the freeing of our orc slaves and then acted surprised when their quotas weren't met. Lady Tonsa turned it around."

"Did you kill them?" Orrin asked, horrified.

"What? No. They relinquished their claim to the chancellorship and started a school of magic or something. They're alive. Tonsa's son is the one I want you to befriend the most. I can most likely get Palmer and Wellan to side with me against Arvin, but I'll need the third vote to break the tie. Madvarr is an unknown either way."

Orrin felt the pit in his stomach growing. "You're asking me to become this guy's friend so you can kill his mother and have him vote you back into power? Why would he do that?"

Anabella's smile turned absolutely evil. "I'm not going to kill her. You do your task and I'll take care of the rest. If you can befriend all three, all the better. I'll have someone leave you instructions every few days. Go to class, learn something, and make friends. If you do what you're told, in a month's time you can be back with the [Hero]. You'll have a powerful ally in Odrana and my promise that we will leave you and the [Hero] alone."

Orrin studied the map for a bit longer, trying to think of any other questions. He asked a few more details on the five sections of

Odrana but could tell Anabella was bored with him again. The only extra information she deemed worth discussing was the internal processes of the Sanerris School. Orrin got tired of that information and picked up the dossiers on the people he was supposed to trick into being his friends.

Orrin began to read.

Maeve Wellan had been a student at the Sanerris School of Spells for two years. She was twenty-one and had no close friends at school. Despite stellar marks from her teachers, she'd yet to find an adviser for a thesis. Anabella explained that most students required three to five years of study before they picked a topic for a thesis. A teacher would walk them through a rigorous process of trial and error, research and experimentation, and, more often than not, healing and recuperation after deadly results. A thesis was not a requirement to graduate. In fact, the Sanerris School had no set graduation process. Students simply left when they felt they had learned what they could. Some went through the thesis process for no other reason than bragging rights.

She's a recluse but brilliant. Either she doesn't care about making friends or she's too busy studying to try. I'll need to get into a class with her and connect. Orrin couldn't make a better plan until he saw a class list, something Anabella promised was coming. Classes ended when the teacher was bored or jumped to another topic. Students could teach classes as long as they'd been given prior approval, but the classes changed month to month. Nobody could be bothered to help share information on a long-term basis.

Rhys Tonsa was sixteen. He'd only gotten his class recently, and no information beyond a vague description was in his file.

Finley Madvarr was nineteen. His file was mostly reports of fighting along the border of Veskar. From the few clues he could find, Orrin figured Finley was more of an up-close fighter with a little dash of magic. Nobody who threw spells would need to be "dunked repeatedly in the river to wash the stench of offal from his clothes" by his comrades.

Orrin rubbed his eyes. Maybe he should take his chances and let Anabella throw him into the ocean.

Chapter 9

Anabella sighed as she put the Kala board away. "I will miss our games. You've been a good opponent."

Orrin muttered under his breath.

The older woman smiled as she sat down across from him again. "Don't be angry. Give it a few years and you'll win a game or two."

The two of them sat in the same room they always did. The door to the terrace was open despite the pouring rain outside. Orrin noticed no water reached past the door frame. *Magical fuckery,* he thought as he turned a pen around in his hand. He steeled his nerve and put the pen on the table.

"I'm not sure this is a good idea," he started. Anabella raised an eyebrow. "I'm sure you've noticed I'm not the most social person in the world. You want to send me into a place with the richest and strongest magic users around and hope I survive. Do you think any of these people are going to want to be friends with me?"

Anabella steepled her fingers together and rested her chin on her thumbs.

Orrin continued, "You said I have twenty-eight days before your son comes back. That was yesterday. Assuming I do get to the school and assuming I do make friends with anyone, how am I going to do magic with this?" Orrin dragged a finger along the metal circle around his throat. "You aren't going to give me my magic back because you know I'll escape. The first time a teacher calls on me to perform some magic, I'll be screwed."

Anabella held up her hand, stopping Orrin's rehearsed speech. "I have someone coming today to bring you there. You'll start class tomorrow. I've picked your courses. You should have at least one class with each of your new friends."

She plucked her wand off her hip and pointed it at Orrin. "I will be giving you access to your magic, but with a few restrictions. You won't have access to [Teleport] or [Camouflage], but I'll leave your other spells free. Before you think about it, we found the collar you removed from your rescued friend. [Toxic Touch] shouldn't have done that to a collar. Even so, I'll be restricting that as well. You should also think about this before you escape."

A twist of dark-purple strands erupted from the end of her wand. Orrin tried to move but felt the collar tighten. The thin gossamer wrapped around his neck. He felt ice touch his skin before the heat burned him.

"Damn, that hurt. What was that?" Orrin rubbed his neck, the pain already fading.

"Insurance. The collar is keyed to me right now. You cannot be too far away from me. It will be reconfigured for the school grounds. I suggest you not wander beyond the walls. However, if you do manage to break out of a slave collar . . . a feat that is nearly impossible on your own . . . I will know. I will be able to find you, and I will not give you a second chance."

Anabella leaned forward and took Orrin's hand off his neck. She laced her fingers into his. "I am taking a chance on you, friend of the [Hero]. You may think what you want about me, but know that everything I do is for the good of us all. You do not need to become a trusted adviser to these children. Just friendly enough that they may come when you call. You'll receive more instructions when the time is right. Take this as an opportunity to learn. You have a keen mind and one of the most . . . diverse sets of spells I've come across in a long time. If this nonsense with my son wasn't happening, I might steal you away for a few years to train you myself."

Orrin blushed at the praise. Anabella didn't appear to be one to sugarcoat words. He was worried about what further instructions she would send, but knowing that he just had to be friendly with his targets made him breathe a little easier. He kicked himself over the lost opportunity of using [Toxic Touch], but there wasn't much he could do about it anyway.

"I thought I was going to have a say in what courses I took?" Orrin asked absentmindedly. He didn't particularly care which indoctrination class this terrible country was going to push on him, but knowing was half the battle. He'd also hoped to avoid any class that would make his knowledge of the world obvious.

"Maeve is taking only two classes at the moment, and you haven't taken the prerequisite for Rapid Acceleration Agriculture. Luckily, she appears to be trying to win over Professor Cade to back her thesis. Defensive Earth Magic is a first-year course. From what I've heard, Maeve has no need for the class but Cade won't advance any student who doesn't take the basics first."

"Defensive Earth Magic?"

"You'll be fine. If anything, I'm worried your ward magic might make Cade go into early retirement. I debated locking those spells as well but decided that letting you be unique might play well for you in befriending these three," Anabella explained. She also handed Orrin a small book entitled *Earth and You*. "That is Professor Cade's book. Study it before the class begins. He never asks questions that you cannot find the answer to in here." She tapped the cover.

"Thanks, I guess."

Anabella's eyes flashed. "This class costs several hundred gold for most. Do try to be more appreciative."

Orrin sat up a bit straighter. He was going to an Ivy League prep school for magic. *Even if everything goes like I want, I'll be there for a few weeks. Maybe I should take advantage of this.* "I'll read it tonight."

"The Tonsa boy is just starting as well. You'll be taking Magical History of Asmea and Surviving Spell Attacks with him. Both are obvious first-year classes that you should do well in. Be polite and don't argue with the history professor, whoever it ends up being. The staff rotates it out as a punishment for internal conflicts and they all have their own . . . prejudices they bring with them to the class. It won't be difficult and should give you the most time with Rhys."

"Surviving Spell Attacks sounds . . . daunting," Orrin said, trying to be diplomatic.

Anabella chuckled. "It is mostly theory and little actual practice. You'll be fine. Finley is our biggest setback. He hasn't signed up for any classes as of yesterday."

"How do you know?"

Anabella pointed at herself. "It's my school, remember? Even here, I keep my finger on the pulse of my school. Final sign-ups are due by tomorrow . . . when you'll show up. I've narrowed it down to a few that Finley is likely to take. He's already taken Magical Combat and might try an advanced version of that class, but you wouldn't have the prerequisites."

"Or any inclination to take a class called Magical Combat," Orrin muttered.

Her teeth flashed as lightning struck outside. "Yes, I'm sure the boy who fought off the leader of Odrana twice would be terrible at magical combat. You don't need that class. Instead, I've signed you up for Battle Class."

Orrin felt a pit form in his stomach. "What is Battle Class?"

"It is only a class in the loosest sense of the word. Students sign up to fight each other and then analyze how they could do better. There are teachers, but mostly it is student-led, hands-on practice."

"That sounds . . . dangerous."

"Finley won every match last semester and only lost two the semester before that."

Orrin distinctly did not appreciate the smile on Anabella's face. "Why did he take it twice?"

"Finley has taken Battle Class four times. Most students take it at least twice if they have a combat magic class. It's the best chance at connecting the two of you."

"I don't have a say in this, do I?"

Anabella didn't answer and instead spread out a few more papers. "The problem is what to take for the last class. He's taken a few classes on fire magic in the past, but his attacks use a sword. I'm not sure what kind of other class he would take at this point, but . . ."

Orrin tuned her out as he caught the name of another class on the list. "What about this one?"

Anabella went silent. "Dungeoneering is not a first-year class."

"So I can't take it?" Orrin glanced up and made sure to look Lord Sanerris's mom in the eyes. "I thought you said this would benefit me as well?"

"Why would you want to enter dungeons?"

Orrin shrugged. "Why wouldn't I? They're a blight on the world and need to be destroyed. It's not like you send these students into real dungeons, right?"

She didn't respond.

"Are you kidding me?"

"The final test is surviving at least two floors of a dungeon in a group."

"Okay, never mind. I'm sure we can find something safer."

Orrin and Anabella went over the list for another hour, weighing the pros and cons of Fire Magic Basics and Learning to Fly with Air Magic. It wasn't real flight, Anabella explained. Just falling from a high altitude without dying . . . most of the time.

He sighed and rubbed his fingers across his eyes. "This isn't going anywhere. When do you find out what other class Finley takes?"

"By the time I find out, you'll be in Mistlight." Anabella was stirring a cup of tea that one of the maids had brought in. Orrin had been offered nothing.

"I could wait to see what he picks and copy a class, I guess."

Anabella tapped her spoon on the porcelain and placed it on a napkin. "You could try, but it would be risky. If he caught you spying on his classes and then you showed up in that class, he'd be suspicious from the start."

Orrin was tempted to pull a coffee press and beans from his [Dimension Hole] just to see how she'd react but resisted. "I can be sneaky if I need to be."

"You want me to leave you a spell that allows you to bypass security systems and potentially escape for the chance to get one extra class with the younger Madvarr?"

Orrin shrugged and leaned back in his chair. "You already said I had no chance to escape. It might be helpful to be able to go places no one else can."

Anabella sipped her tea and peered at him over the rim. She placed the cup on its matching saucer and gestured to Orrin. "Come here."

When Orrin was close, she turned him and again fiddled with the collar around his neck. Orrin could feel his access to the system being restored. A quick check left him sure that his spells were available again.

Except [Teleport] and [Toxic Touch].

As he smiled, Anabella's hand gripped his chin and held him tight. The room's temperature dropped, and Orrin could swear he heard the rain hitting the balcony turn to hail. The pinging of ice on the tile backdropped her voice as she spoke.

"I am giving you a modicum of trust. Don't betray it."

"Lady, I just want to get out of your country. If helping you does that, I won't rattle the cage."

She stared into his eyes for a moment more before releasing him. "The [Locationist] I've hired will be here in a few hours. Take the four classes that we've discussed and whatever class you can find Finley is interested in."

Anabella reached into a pocket of her dress and took out two notebooks the size of her palm. She held one out to Orrin. "Do not lose this. Do not let others see it. Every night before you sleep, you are to write a succinct report of your daily activities in it. Every morning, check for a reply. I have the twin."

Orrin was fascinated as he watched her demonstrate. Each book had a stylus that clipped into the spine. As she wrote in one book, the words appeared with a slight delay in the other. She taught him how to clear a page by tapping the pen three times against it.

"They have been cleaned from their last use. It is imperative that you clear the pages after reading or sending a message. If anyone sees you using this, I need their name. You are not to speak of these books to anyone, including my son. Do you understand?"

Orrin agreed and put the book in his pocket. Anabella wished him good luck and dismissed him. It wasn't until he made it back to his room that he pulled the book out again. On a hunch, he tried using [Identify]. It took him two tries to get a response.

Twin Book of Sending. Relic.

Chapter 10

Orrin studied the small black book in his hand.

Twin Book of Sending. Relic.

Other than her insistence that he clear the book after using it, Anabella hadn't hinted that the item was a relic. Madi had once pushed him to take the Create Relic skill from his Administrator power list. The rare and permanent magic items cost enough that even her father, one of the leaders of Dey, would be bankrupted if he purchased one.

And Anabella gave one to me without a second thought. How rich is Odrana? Orrin thought as he turned the book over. Nothing was written on either cover. Orrin wouldn't be able to differentiate this one from a hundred versions available at stores throughout Dey.

For now, Orrin put the relic in his pocket but didn't store it in his dimensional storage. If Anabella asked to see it, he couldn't show off his trump card this early.

He pulled up the list about Maeve, Finley, and Rhys. Rubbing a thumb along the edge of Maeve's folder, Orrin considered what he was about to do.

Anabella was calculating. She was cold. She talked about how everything she did was for the greater good of the people of Odrana and also the rest of Asmea, but Orrin had watched enough documentaries and anime to know the leaders who spouted those things were after one thing only: power. If he was able to gain the trust of these three, Anabella would use them through him. He didn't know exactly how she would ask him to do it, but Orrin would be expected to betray their trust.

Orrin's one friend growing up was Daniel. Even when he'd become more popular and should have dropped Orrin as a friend, Daniel had carved time out for him. He'd defended him from bullies and pranks. He wasn't perfect, and they'd fought multiple times over stupid things like who would win in a fight between Superman and Batman, but Daniel would never betray Orrin. Orrin had never been put in that position of power over Daniel. He never had been tested like Daniel had, and facing this situation made him appreciate what his friend had gone through for the past decade.

Orrin flipped open the binder and began to read. *If I become friends with any of these people, I won't let Anabella use them. I'll figure out how to come out on top.*

A few hours before dinner, the storm outside was still raging. Orrin heard a noise at his door and looked up from the papers he'd been memorizing.

"Hello?"

A fist hammered on the door harder.

"Sorry, one second," Orrin stood and made his way around the small table he'd been given as a desk. "I didn't even realize these doors were locked. What do you nee—"

Orrin's hand was on the door handle when the entire door was shoved open, smashing into his nose. His hands went up to cover the pain as he landed hard on his butt. Blinking through the flashes of lightning through the window, he stared in confusion at the guard in his room.

"Jann? What are you doing here?" Orrin tried to ask, but the mumbled noises that he heard escape his mouth only further demonstrated that his nose was broken.

"Lord Sanerris sends his regards. You're too dangerous to be left alive any longer," Jann, the short guard who had brought him to Anabella's prison home, answered. Orrin didn't see the knife in his hand until it entered his side.

Damage taken!
HP 85/140

"What?" Orrin stared at the knife in his side. [Side Steps] hadn't triggered. He hadn't noticed the weapon, and [Way of the Water] hadn't helped him. The pain slapped the breath from his lungs a moment later. "What?" he repeated.

"That's for my brother." Jann ripped the dagger out of Orrin and raised it above his head. "This is for trying to kill Lord Sanerris."

As the knife moved through the air, Orrin reacted. He was on his back, bleeding into his lung from a stab wound, but his training with Styx kicked in. He swung his arm into the down strike of the dagger, taking a deep cut but deflecting the killing blow.

Damage taken!
HP 63/140

Orrin threw a wild punch, not backed by his fighting skill. For a few scrambling seconds, he forgot about [Way of the Water]. He forgot about magic. The adrenaline coursing through his body at being attacked kept him moving through the pain, and he flailed like a child against the trained guard. Jann was stronger and kept him pinned down.

"Don't fight it, boy." Jann slugged Orrin across the face and reached for the dagger that had been knocked from his grip. "Nobody is coming to help you."

Orrin finally let a thought into his mind and used several skills and spells in rapid succession. [Mind Bastion] closed off the pain to a dull roar as his body's adrenaline began to sag behind. [Heal Small Wounds] clotted his two stab wounds and stabilized the bleeding enough for the moment. He twisted his body with [Way of the

Water], using Rain to avoid Jann's last few attempts to hold him down. Orrin reached for his inversed-stat spells, but the cold logic of [Mind Bastion] reminded him of the newly created spells from [Merge].

[Decrease Strength]
[Decrease Strength]
[Decrease Strength]
[Decrease Strength]
[Decrease Strength]

Orrin hit Jann with five rapid casts of [Decrease Strength], watching the man's confusion as he slumped over top of the kid he'd been sent to kill.

Orrin pushed his way out from under Jann and ran into the hallway. He bounced into something hard and unyielding. For the second time in as many minutes, Orrin found himself clutching his nose while on his ass.

"What is going on?" Anabella's voice came from a long way away.

Orrin saw the cudgel of a second guard moving through the air. He'd been a fool to think Lord Sanerris would send only one person to murder him. He didn't care why the asshole had changed his mind. Orrin felt something rising up within him. [Mind Bastion] disengaged itself as a hatred and rage that he'd kept pushed down for too many days pushed at the cage bars like a hungry tiger.

The guard's eyes were shining behind his glasses, and his lips were blue as the weapon . . . *Huh? Those aren't glasses. Why is he not moving?*

"Orrin, are you alive? So much blood . . . no, bring me a health potion. Don't just stand there, run."

Orrin studied the ice sculpture. He'd thought it was a guard. When had Anabella put an ice statue outside his room and why was she yelling at him?

"He's in shock." Anabella's voice was far away. "Don't just leave him, bring him downstairs. No, put Orrin in my room. Send the [Locationist] to me as soon as he arrives. Go."

Orrin felt a hand run through his hair and delicate fingers wipe blood from his face. Anabella's eyes were wide with something between delight and frenzy as she moved Orrin's head to stare up at her. "Don't die on me yet."

[Mind Bastion] turned itself back on a few minutes later. Orrin wiped the blood from his broken nose and healed himself. He had to cycle an entire mana pool, but the stab wound in his side closed over, his nose popped back into place with a skin-crawling crack, and the general haze, which he was thinking was likely a concussion from being hit in the head by the door, cleared.

He almost wished the concussion hadn't gone away when he realized where he was. Anabella's personal chambers. He was in her bed.

While the rest of the house was functional but spartan, Anabella's room was covered with paintings, bookshelves, three desks with scattered papers, and a four-poster bed with an actual canopy draped over the top.

"Nice room," Orrin muttered. *Maybe the concussion isn't fully gone.* Orrin quickly cast another [Heal Small Wounds] on himself. "Did you kill the second guard or did I do that?"

Anabella was sitting at one of her desks, furiously scribbling on a piece of paper. "What? I froze him. You don't have a spell like that, do you?"

"It's all a blur," Orrin answered evasively. "Is Jann alive?"

"For the moment, he is." Anabella finished writing and folded the paper into an envelope. She took a block of red wax and held it over a candle for a few seconds. A drop of the wax sealed the letter, and she pressed her thumb into the hot dripping. "What was the spell you were gathering to cast on him? The one at the end before I arrived."

Orrin shook his head in confusion. He'd felt power growing in him in the same way that he'd felt when fighting Samara, the whip-wielding right hand of the deposed Lord Wendeln. At the time, he hadn't really known what was happening. He'd been given a prompt in his blue box and stolen Samara's constitution points . . . permanently. It had only cost Orrin a few of his own constitution points.

No words in a blue box had appeared this time, but Orrin had the feeling something similar would have happened if Anabella had been a few seconds slower with her spell.

"I can't remember," Orrin lied. "Everything happened so fast."

Walking to the door, Anabella whispered something, and Orrin heard footsteps running away. The letter was gone when Anabella turned back to Orrin. "Regardless, you survived. The first step of my plan proceeds unhindered."

Orrin pushed himself into a sitting position. "Survived? You knew I was going to be . . . that someone was going to try—"

"To kill you, yes. Your friend the [Hero] is threatening to lead a group from Dey into the elven lands and push our troops back to the border. The only thing stopping him is reports of movement from the Demon Lord's troops. My son sent me a letter to dispose of you quickly. He fears Daniel will learn you are alive and come to rescue you. He needs Daniel occupied with the Demon Lord for his plan to succeed."

"What plan? Wait, are you going to kill me?" Orrin tried to process the information, but he was still trying to get over the fact he'd nearly died . . . again.

"I told my son days ago that you were too interesting to kill." Anabella waved her hand and sat at the foot of the bed. "Our plan still holds. You'll be at the school tonight. Follow my instructions. Don't draw too much attention to yourself."

Orrin scratched his side. The new skin over his ribs itched fiercely. "What are you going to do when he shows up to kill me himself? You should just let me go. I can help Daniel fight the Demon Lord and you can take over after Daniel kicks your son's ass."

"I do not want the [Hero] murdering my son." Anabella's voice chilled the air. "I will deal with Arvin. You left Jann alive. That gives me a body to work with. I can do the same to him as I've done for you.

His appearance will look like you, and if Arvin comes to check, I'll make him scream like you would as well."

Orrin shivered at what might happen to Jann. Sure, the guy had tried to kill him but . . . actually . . . yeah, he was fine with whatever happened to him. People kept trying to kill him. This wasn't Earth. He needed to remember that and act a bit more ruthlessly. It was the only way that he would survive.

Noticing she was still watching him, Orrin gathered the courage to ask something he'd been curious about since the first day they'd met. "What kind of magic did you use to freeze that guy? Are you an [Ice Mage]?"

Anabella smiled. "That spell is a creation of mine. A long time ago, I was able to change the mana signature of a common spell to such an extreme that the system rewarded me with it. It's mana intensive, but in a one-on-one situation, I've yet to find a better option. I'm not an [Ice Mage], although it isn't a bad guess."

Orrin waited, but she didn't elaborate more. "What do you mean, you changed the mana signature of a spell?"

A knock on the door startled Orrin. Spells jumped to his mind and he readied for another fight.

"You'll learn more about that in class," Anabella said as she stood from the bed and smoothed out the wrinkles on her sleeves. "Your ride has arrived. Time to go to school."

Chapter 11

One of the staff passed a bag through the door. Anabella took it and crossed the room, handing the small satchel to Orrin.

"You'll find two sets of clothing inside, along with a small amount of gold. You'll need to buy supplies for school, clothes, and a weapon for Battle Class. I'd suggest a sword or a spear. They are the most common and will help you not stand out," Anabella explained. "You should keep your buffing magic a secret as long as you can. If rumors get back to my son, you will be too far away for me to help you."

Orrin opened the bag and peered inside. The "small amount of gold" was three long cylinders of coins with a hundred in each container. *She gave me three hundred gold as an afterthought.*

Orrin's mom worked hard. She'd had to after his dad left. She supported Orrin, and he'd never needed for anything. That didn't mean they were rich. He usually had the last-generation video game console, wore off-brand shoes until they fell apart, and brought his lunch to school. When greedy companies started the trend of releasing the newest games only on the most current console, Orrin had to pray his ancient PC would be able to handle the computer version or hope Daniel would get it. He'd tried mowing lawns in the neighborhood for extra money, but most of the dads didn't want someone taking away their favorite weekend chore. The one neighbor he'd convinced, old Ms. Fleebecker, had chased him off her grass when he accidentally rolled over her flowerbed.

Even with the gold that he'd been collecting since arriving in Asmea, Anabella's present was staggering. Her casual disregard for the value of money bothered Orrin. Not enough to say anything, but he filed away how little she cared for three hundred gold coins.

"Thank you for the supplies and the spending money." He pulled the strap over his shoulder.

"The money is for the final class you select. If it costs more than three hundred, send a note to me and I'll have the balance taken care of." Anabella waited for him to nod before continuing. "There's also a folder with your new name and family history. Memorize it quickly. Destroy it as soon as you can."

"Wait, what?"

Pulling her long blonde hair beyond her and tying it into a ponytail, Anabella reached into the bag and withdrew a folder not unlike the ones she'd given him regarding his targets. "Casimir Hale. Your family moved here from Veskar three generations before you. Your great-grandmother was recruited for her skills in array magic, but each new generation has worked mostly as clerks, grocers, and couriers. You are an only child, raised by your retired grandmother after a bandit attack on the road took your parents. That is the gist of it. Any questions?"

Orrin reached up to scratch the skin under his collar. "Casimir? Is he . . . was he a real person?"

Anabella pushed the papers back in his bag with a sigh. "It's all a fiction. The paperwork will hold up to moderate scrutiny, but try not to make waves. If anyone tries to find your dear grandmother, they'll find me waiting."

"Nobody would believe you're a grandma," Orrin muttered, dropping his hand.

"Flirt like that with Maeve." Anabella placed her hand on Orrin's shoulder, fixing his shirt under the satchel's strap. "You'll have her eating out of your hand in a week."

"I wasn't flir—"

"Come along. We have a narrow window of time to drop you off."

Orrin wondered about that. He'd thought Anabella a prisoner in her home but the more she revealed about her continuing power in Odrana, Orrin was beginning to think of her as a beautiful black widow pulling the threads around her country. All while the fly—her oblivious son—danced to her tune. *She isn't being kept here. She has retreated somewhere safe with plans to strike back when she's ready.*

A chill ran down his spine when she turned and smiled at him. "He's in the foyer. Be quiet and let me do the talking."

The man waiting was studying a painting of Anabella hanging on the wall as they rounded the corner. He held his glasses at the tip of his nose as he kept his face close to the portrait.

"Chaminda, welcome back," Anabella said, smiling and reaching for the man's hands. Orrin could see his eyes widen in glee as he touched her fingers for a brief moment.

"My lady, I came as soon as I received your call," Chaminda replied, his dark hair spilling over his face as he bowed his head. "I am always yours to command."

"You flatter me, Chaminda. No bowing is required in my home, and I've told you before to call me Ana."

Orrin watched the spider pull its prey into the web. [Locationist] was the premier class for teleportation. It wasn't uncommon for a noble house to have an agreement with one for quick travel, but outside of emergencies [Teleport] was expensive. Most people didn't have Orrin's ability to regenerate mana daily, having to wait until they got a full night of sleep to be able to move a group of people around.

Of course, Orrin could have used [Teleport] to bring himself to the Sanerris School for Spells, but Anabella would never trust him that far. Instead, she was playing this sucker along.

"I could never, my lady," Chaminda mumbled. His eyes took in Orrin standing behind Lady Sanerris. His dark eyes narrowed. "But where are my manners? Whoever could this handsome man be at your side? Have you taken a new husband since last we met?"

Anabella's laugh was a little too genuine for Orrin's liking. "He's a student, nothing more. You know better than any that my heart died with my dear husband. If I could still love . . ."

Orrin watched the two adults play out the bad soap opera and did his best to not yawn. Either Chaminda knew Anabella was using him but didn't care due to some nebulous advantage being in her good graces got him . . . or the man was a monumental idiot.

Not that Orrin could blame him. Anabella might be a lot older than him, but she was hot. Sure, Lord Sanerris's mother was a babe, but something about her usually cold and intelligent demeanor was attractive in itself as well.

Orrin had to remind himself that she was probably older than she appeared. Standing by her son, Orrin would have thought they were brother and sister. Lord Sanerris was probably in his thirties, which meant she was . . . closing in on fifty? Likely older?

She laughed at something Chaminda said, throwing her head back. Orrin had to give her credit. She'd positioned herself under a candelabra perfectly. Her hair reflected the light, and even Orrin's eyes followed the shiny dapple upon her skin down to her—

She's your enemy's mom and current jailer. Stop it.

Orrin glanced out the window into the rain. A bolt of lightning briefly illuminated the path down the mountain. Orrin bit his lip and hoped he was wrong.

"Lady Sanerris," he whispered and tapped her shoulder. Orrin missed the glare Chaminda threw his way. "Am I seeing things or . . ." He pointed out the window.

Anabella strode across the foyer and peered into the night. Orrin opened his mouth to explain what he'd seen, but his fears were confirmed by another flash of light. Except it wasn't lightning. A small ball of light floated out along the entrance path, showing at least three figures hurrying toward the house.

"Chaminda, bring him to Professor Graem. He'll be at the Singing Fish Tavern. Payment on delivery and one favor in the future at my discretion. Take him through the kitchen and out the side door. You were never here and saw no one, do you understand?"

"Professor Graem at the Singing Fish Tavern." Chaminda's demeanor changed completely as he answered. He stood ready with the stance of a soldier receiving orders. "I've been at home reading a book all night."

Anabella waved her wand toward the back of the house, and Orrin heard the sound of armor rattling. The house guards jogged into view a few moments later. She gestured in a fast shorthand sign language, and they ran in different directions.

"Orr— Casimir. Do behave at school and try to make some friends," Anabella said, glancing back out the window. "Find Professor Graem in the next few hours. He'll help you keep your head"—she paused and caught Orrin's eye with a smile—"above-water your first few days."

She reached for his arm and pulled him into a tight embrace. Her fingers found the back of his neck and touched the hidden collar. Orrin felt the same tingles run through him as she adjusted something in the slave collar. "Trust only Graem. You have six hours to find him and have him take control of the collar. If anyone else tries to tinker with it, you'll have a quick and explosive end. Tell him, 'The dragon sleeps while the tigers play.' He will watch over you."

"I'll do my best," Orrin answered. His face was too close, and he was acutely aware of his breath. He'd never noticed the green swirls in Anabella's eyes until this moment. "They're here for me, aren't they?"

Anabella ruffled his collar, playing at fixing his clothing. "I'll take care of it. Go learn something. Remember our Kala games."

Chaminda's eyes twitched in Orrin's direction, but he schooled his face. "Quickly now. Take my hand."

They passed the kitchen staff, who were pulling knives out of drawers that were too big to be used for cooking. The one who regularly brought Orrin his food pulled a crossbow down from above a cabinet. Everyone nodded at them as Chaminda pushed through the side door into the small garden used for herbs and a few vegetables.

"Have you teleported before?" Chaminda whispered.

Orrin nodded absentmindedly. He was still focused on the three intruders. How had Sanerris found out his first attempt to kill Orrin had failed so quickly? He should stay and help Anabella. He could use his buff spells. That would give everyone the edge. He wasn't even sure if there were only three. What if more people were coming up the path to the house as well? They could be fleeing a slaughter.

"Try to keep your feet. I'm bringing us into an alley not far from our destination, but we don't want to draw attention. I'll use [Teleport], on the count of three."

"I'll be fine," Orrin answered. He had [Teleport] and knew how it worked, but explaining that right now wasn't worth the time. Instead, Orrin took a step back toward the house. "I'm just going to tell Anabella one more thing."

"No, you'll stay right here. One." Chaminda grabbed his arm in a vise grip.

"Chaminda, you don't understand." Orrin tried to pull away. "I can help. I've got [Map]. There could be more of them than what she saw."

"Two."

Orrin ripped his arm away and pulled up [Map]. He was fully zoomed out. All the dots were too clumped to make out properly. One gray dot was at the base of the mountain path. *That's probably one of the guards. How did they get by him?*

Orrin zoomed in, refocusing on the house. Gray dots set up inside the house at different locations that Orrin could tell were windows and doors. Three dots were reaching the top of the path with no more behind them.

The three dots were also gray.

Enemies and monsters always show up as red. Why would—

"Three."

Orrin felt the twist of space that meant he was teleporting, but the drop in his stomach as they landed had nothing to do with the magic. Thoughts swirling in his head clicked together as he threw up on the cobblestones.

That was Daniel. They were coming to save me. I just ran from my own rescue.

Chapter 12

"Amateur children . . . never traveled beyond their own . . . all over my shoes . . ."

Orrin ignored Chaminda's grumbling. He wiped his mouth with the back of his sleeve as his mind reeled. The rain was a light drizzle in Mistlight, nothing compared to the torrential downpour they'd just left.

I should have recognized the light. That was Madi. I bet Daniel was right behind her, but I couldn't see them in the storm. Orrin berated himself, playing over a hundred what-ifs.

Slowly, a smile crept across his face. *They figured out I was not dead. They found me.*

He hadn't doubted . . . not really. Daniel was indomitable and Madi was clever. They also had the backing of Dey. At least, Orrin assumed Silas would give in to the demands of his only daughter and the [Hero]. Dey was relying on them to save everyone from the upcoming Horde.

"Stop smiling like a dimwit and come along," Chaminda demanded, grabbing Orrin's bicep and pulling him to the entrance of the alley they had landed in.

Orrin's last meal could barely be found among the detritus and substances in what Orrin assumed was a street-wide garbage can. "Why would you [Teleport] us into this filth?"

Chaminda tapped his finger to Orrin's head. "Use your noggin. Most buildings have teleportation wards set up. Sometimes I need to move about without people seeing me. Nobody notices the waste. If you need a quick escape or a place to hide, trash alleys are the safest bet. Now, step to."

Orrin's mind continued to second-guess his decisions. Anabella had been giving him so many commands over the past few days that he'd jumped when she told him to without a second thought. He watched Chaminda check the street before gesturing for him to follow.

Mistlight hadn't changed in the past week. Fewer people clogged the streets with the rain, and Orrin noticed a few people even had umbrellas. They approached a crosswalk, and Chaminda turned on his heel and threw an arm around Orrin's shoulder.

"I'm your drunk friend, support me," Chaminda whispered and began to stumble about. Orrin gripped his arm to keep the both of them from falling over.

"What are you ta—"

"You there, come help clean this mess up." A city guard, dressed in the colors of Lord Sanerris's house, rounded the corner. "Oh, is he drunk?"

". . . yes?" Orrin took a moment to answer. Luckily, Chaminda had more than one trick up his sleeve. The [Locationist] threw his body against the nearby building and bent double, dry heaving as he fell to his knees.

"Get him home," the guard sneered and turned. Waving his hand, he flagged down a set of adventurers and pointed around the corner. With fallen shoulders, the two men followed him.

Orrin took a peek. Two carts had collided just around the bend, spilling buckets of fish on the ground. The streets of Mistlight were nice-looking, but the sewage system wasn't exactly modern. A few inches of water had built up, and the fish were splashing around with a renewed sense of life.

The second cart had been carrying grain. Not as much had fallen off, but where the few bags had split open, the foodstuff had begun to absorb the water. Orrin watched one of the adventurers grab at a fish, only to have its tail hit him in the face. He fell back into the grainy water that stuck like oatmeal to his clothes.

"Quickly now, before they press us into service," Chaminda said as he tapped Orrin's shoulder. "We don't want to be late, and this will take a few hours to clean."

"Picking up fish won't take hours," Orrin argued back but followed Chaminda back up the street they'd come from.

"The fish also have to be delivered to the docks on time, along with whatever was in the second cart. Both axles were snapped on one of the carts. We'd have been hauling for the rest of the night."

Orrin reassessed his opinion of Chaminda. The man had appeared to eat out of Anabella's hand, but he'd seen a problem appear in front of him, analyzed it, and found a solution before Orrin knew what was going on. *He might be smarter than he acts.*

After backtracking, Chaminda led Orrin down a different street. Orrin could just make out the two carts in the distance. Multiple people were hoisting packages on their shoulders and walking in the opposite direction.

"The Singing Fish is just ahead," his guide muttered, more to himself than to Orrin. "I can be home with a good cup of tea and a warm blanket in ten minutes. The things I do for . . ." His voice petered out as he glanced back at Orrin. "Don't dawdle."

The tavern was easy to spot. A sign hanging above the door had the name scrawled across the standing fish cutout. He was holding a flute with his fins. *How is that a singing fish?*

"Delivered. Good luck at school, young one. Put in a good word for me, if you wouldn't mind. Jobs like this pay well. If you ever need a quick jaunt around, find me in the artists' quarter. Everyone knows me there." Chaminda held open the door and nodded his head inside.

For a moment, Orrin considered running. He'd thought about it a dozen times as they walked the streets of Mistlight, but the rub of metal on his neck kept him from following through. He had to meet Professor Graem and hope the guy made a mistake. If he could gain his trust, he might even be able to get the collar off.

With one last look into the rain, Orrin decided. Daniel had found him once. He'd do it again. This time he would stay put and wait. If he could get a message out, that would be best, but for now, observe and assess.

"Thank you, Chaminda. I'll let our mutual friend know how effortless the trip was," Orrin finally answered, holding out his hand.

"Glad to hear it," the man said, pumping Orrin's arm. "Graem will be the one with the walking stick. Never seen him without it. Now, get inside before you get sick. That rain is traveling our way. See you around."

Orrin waited for him to leave, but Chaminda forced a fake smile and pointed inside again. "I have to see you go inside."

With a sigh, Orrin entered the tavern, leaving his guide behind. He paused for a moment once inside, looking around the room.

A long bar was positioned along the left side of the room, with tables haphazardly situated everywhere else. Two barmaids carried food through a swinging door in the back, serving the customers waiting inside. It looked more like a regular restaurant than most Orrin had been to in this world.

Orrin noticed a man in his early thirties slumped on the bar, barely keeping his seat on the stool he was on. He held himself upright using a staff. Orrin counted five empty glasses, with one extra held gingerly between long fingers.

He made his way closer and sat down next to the man. "Excuse me, sir. Are you Professor Graem?"

"Na prosser her." The man slurred his words, sucking air as he tried to drink from his last glass. It remained a few inches away from his mouth. With an angry flare of his eyebrows, he heaved his face closer and bounced the corner of the cup against his teeth. "Ow. Thas hurt."

Orrin craned his neck, double-checking the rest of the room for anyone else with a walking stick or staff. He saw plenty of wands on hips, being openly carried, and even one man who had six strapped down his chest, but nobody else matched the description he'd been given.

"Sir, I think you're the man I was sent to find," Orrin tried again, leaning closer to the stink of stale alcohol. "Someone you know from work sent me?"

Orrin didn't know what he was supposed to say when he found the professor and cursed Anabella for not telling him more. He liked the way that felt, so he cursed her a few more times, using words in his mind that he'd never have the courage to say aloud.

"If yous don't mind, I'mma enjoining . . . enjoying my days off," maybe Graem mumbled into his glass. A drop of blood dripped from his busted lip and stained the clear liquid. "Shit."

"But you are Graem?" Orrin pressed, watching the man try to catch the dispersing red from his drink with his fingers.

"Of course, I'm Prosser . . . Profser . . . I'm Graem and teach school. This little red bit shouldn't be in here. It's really there, right?" Professor Graem turned to Orrin and blinked in confusion. "That's not really there."

Orrin almost fell back off his own stool as Graem reached for his face. Luckily, the man was drunk enough that his hand-eye coordination was thrown off. He fell forward with a loud thump.

The sounds of the tavern quieted as everyone turned to see what had caused the noise. Eyes landed on Orrin and traveled down to the moaning body under his feet.

In the eternal silence of that awkwardness, Graem's staff slipped off the counter as well. Orrin tried to grab it but only succeeded in altering its course. The gnarled top knot beaned Graem in the head.

Well, shit.

The tavern doubled as a small inn with only three rooms. Luckily, two of the rooms were currently unoccupied, and Orrin was able to convince the bartender to help him move the unconscious teacher to one of the rooms. It had cost him a gold piece, but Orrin didn't want the rest of the patrons below seeing what he was about to do.

Graem's frame was hidden under his robes, and the bartender had to have a cook from the back room come out to help carry him up the stairs. Orrin tried to help and felt the hard muscles under the robes. The bartender swatted him away.

One alone, a quick [Identify] relieved Orrin's final doubts that this was the right person. He took the snoring man's hand and placed it on his collar, hoping he would be able to deactivate it. No dice. *He must need to inject some of his mana into the collar to be able to affect it.*

Orrin ran over his options one more time before committing to his plan. First, he checked the profile that Anabella had given him. His name was Casimir Hale. The rest of the file was a list of names and dates that quickly lost meaning to Orrin. He was not going to be able to memorize this in a day, let alone however much time it took for his contact to wake up.

He almost decided to say fuck it and try to improv his backstory. Only a flash of inspiration stopped him from sending the paper up in flames. Taking a notebook from his [Dimension Hole], Orrin began to transcribe the important parts using [Through the Ages].

> **[Through the Ages]—A unique skill created to pass knowledge through the ages. Only those with the skill or those deemed the chosen target can read and write information using this skill.**

Orrin finished getting the names written down after only ten minutes. Anabella had created an entire family tree for him. *Overkill.*

Orrin used two fingers to open Graem's eyelid to see if he was awake, but the deep blue orb simply rolled up and away. The scruff on Graem's face hadn't been shaved in days, and he still smelled of stale beer. With a sigh, he began enacting his plan.

[Remetabolize] needed only one cast before the [Drunk] condition disappeared off Graem Balint. Orrin noted his level was fifty-six, making him one of the highest he'd seen. His class was more interesting.

> **[Librarian]**

A librarian runs the school?

Orrin considered waiting for Graem to wake up naturally, but he was on a timer. Anabella had made vague threats about what would happen if Graem didn't attune to his slave collar in time, and he had no intention of finding out if she was joking. He cast [Heal Small Wounds].

Graem continued to snore.

Orrin slapped him across the face.

"What? Where am I?"

Orrin waited for the man to sit back in the bed and take in his surroundings.

"Oh shit." Graem rubbed his hair back from his eyes and smiled sheepishly. "Did I get drunk again? Sean isn't going to let me back in. What time is it? Is it morning?"

Orrin tossed the man's staff back to him. He understood why Chaminda had called it a walking stick. It was less staff in the man's beefy hand and more twig. "It's only been a few minutes. I need you to listen. Anabella Sanerris sent me. You have to take this collar off me or we're both going to die."

Graem raised an eyebrow and reached toward Orrin. For a moment, he felt relief. He'd successfully bluffed the teacher and was going to be back in Dey within the hour.

Graem's hand lightly slapped Orrin's cheek. "Don't lie to your teachers. It's not good manners."

Orrin's head hung in defeat.

"You weren't supposed to be here until tomorrow night. I think. What day is it?" Graem stretched and leaned back in the bed. Orrin did not stare at the way the robes fell down his arms to show biceps bigger than his own legs. Definitely not. "If you're early, I can't take care of you. Classes start in two days. Come back tomorrow."

"I thought classes were supposed to start tomorrow," Orrin replied. "I'm not lying about dying. Anabella said my collar will kill me if you don't do something with it."

Graem narrowed his eyes and squinted in Orrin's direction. "She did a good job with the [Glamour]. I can barely make you out underneath it. The collar is good work. It's tough to alter the flow of magic to hide something that also alters the flow of magic. It's actually interesting. You know, the first person to figure out how to move magic that way ended up de—"

"As much fun as a history lesson would be," Orrin interrupted, "maybe after you make my collar not go boom?"

The man sighed and swung his feet to the side. "Come here."

Orrin approached cautiously. The hands that reached out slowly encircled him and touched the back of his neck. A tingle across his skin was all the hint he got that it was done.

"Done. Now you are mine. Want to tell me why you're still alive? I thought Lord Sanerris wanted you dead."

"How much did Anabella tell you?"

"She said to be ready to help a new student with some interesting magic with whatever you need but to keep you on a literal leash," Graem said, waving his hand at the collar he'd just claimed. "She didn't mention that you're the [Hero]'s party member who was executed a week or so ago."

"It's a long story."

Graem reached behind him and grabbed ahold of his staff. He pointed it at a chair near the door, which jumped into the air and floated to Orrin. It landed with a soft thump.

"Start from the beginning."

Chapter 13

"Start by explaining how I'm not drunk or hungover," Graem demanded, sitting forward in his chair. He leaned on his staff to keep himself from toppling over. "I remember drinking quite a lot."

Orrin had been trying to figure out where to start his story and was glad for the easy out. "I have a spell that changes toxins in the body. I just reduced the alcohol to nothing."

Graem squinted and snapped his fingers. "[Remetabolize]?"

"Yeah . . ."

"Don't get angry, I didn't scan your skills." Graem patted his chest and grunted. He stuck a hand into his robe pocket and sighed in relief as he drew out a pipe. "While I appreciate the lack of hangover, don't use that on me again without my consent. If I'm not at least a little hammered, I become difficult to be around. Or so I'm told."

He plucked a container from another pocket and took a pinch of whatever was inside. He let a few red and green crystals fall into the pipe. A flash of his hands and a small tamper was between his fingers. As Orrin watched the man in charge of running the Sanerris School pack his pipe with what were obviously drugs, he began to doubt Anabella's plan even more.

"Continue, then," Graem said as he took the first puff from the lit pipe. "Why are you here?"

"After my friends and I tried to save a prisoner from Lord Sanerris, I was captured. He wanted information from me and sent me to his mother's place," Orrin said, watching the puffs from Graem's pipe turn a multitude of colors before fading into regular white smoke. "She wants your help. I think she's planning a coup to—"

Graem struck his staff to the ground. It stuck where it landed, and a small burst of air went past Orrin. He didn't have time to react and fell out of his chair.

"Get up, it's just a sound barrier." Graem reached down and pulled Orrin to his feet like he was a toddler. The man was strong. "You shouldn't say things aloud that could get you killed. This is Mistlight, not whatever backwater town you come from."

Orrin ran his hand through his hair as he sat back down in the chair. The adrenaline from thinking he was about to be in a fight was making his hands shake. Orrin took a chance and flipped [Mind Bastion] on and off again. His breathing evened and his heart rate slowed back down.

"Impressive. Was that [Calm Thoughts]? Maybe [Calm Mind]?"

Orrin glared at the man. "Part of the information that Lord Sanerris wanted from me was what my skills are. Anabella knows enough, and if she didn't tell you my spells, I'm not going to, either."

Graem took another hit from his pipe and let the smoke curl from his nostrils. He tapped some dust from the pipe on the table next to them and slipped it away in his robes. "If Anabella knows, I'll find out eventually. Information is how she pays me. I'm trying to create the first compendium of all known skills and spells. Anabella has been my best source of data for years. But enough about that. She wants back in the game? How does she plan to . . ." He trailed off for a moment and snapped his fingers again. "A honeypot."

"A what?"

"You're a honeypot. It's a wonderful [Glamour], by the way. Did you do it or did she?"

"I'm not a honeypot," Orrin retorted, redness creeping up his neck. He'd thought the [Glamour] was a way to keep his identity a secret, but hearing the words out loud from Graem made him rethink what Anabella had done. He did look objectively better. A more chiseled jawline. A dimple to complement the slightly wider smile. Orrin didn't dislike the way he looked normally but even he could admit the current version of him was better equipped to seduce someone.

"Whatever you say." The man rested his chin on his fist, placing his elbow atop his staff. "She needs three votes to put her back in the Mistlight chancellor position, and her son won't be giving her his vote. That means she needs Tonsa or Madvarr's vote. Which one of the children are you supposed to sway? Anabella will already have Palmer's vote, and Wellan will have made plans to keep his daughter safe. You're supposed to befriend her, too, aren't you? How much did I get right?"

Orrin tried to keep his face neutral and rolled his eyes. "If she already told you the plan, why ask me?"

"She didn't tell me anything about the plan," Graem said with a smile. "My passion is learning about the system. It's why I'm a [Librarian]. However, as my late father used to say, I have a way of sniffing out the truth in social situations. He wanted me to be a politician or at least a [Lawyer], but people bore me to tears. Everyone is so predictable. The system isn't. Did you know that there are thirteen different ways to get [Remetabolize] that I've figured out so far? You don't have an amulet, so you aren't part of the Hospital. You don't strike me as a [Poisoner] or even an [Alchemist]. You'd have to be a pretty high-level [Alchemist] to get [Remetabolize]. This young and you went on a suicide run to try and kill Mistlight's ruler. So that means there is a fourteenth way to get the spell. Mind telling me now and saving us both a lot of trouble in the future?"

Orrin's palms were sweaty against his pants. He'd tried not to move a muscle during Graem's speech and was only now realizing that he might have left the frying pan that was Anabella's sharp mind only to fall into the fire that was Graem's inquisitiveness.

In other words, Orrin was fucked. He was a terrible liar, and if he tried to use [Mind Bastion], the logical thing might be to give the man some information. But Orrin had a hunch that the [Librarian] class might have a skill or two on finding a way to the right answer. Like a hunter in the forest trying to find his prey, Orrin could see

Graem's body primed and ready to dart forward and take what he wanted. Praying that what he was about to do wasn't the epitome of stupid, Orrin took a chance.

"Help me make friends with all three and I'll tell you where I got [Remetabolize]."

"You bought it in the store." Graem waved his hand. "I want to know what skill or spell you bought before that unlocked it. I do know your class name, but I've never heard of it. Do you know how you unlocked it or was it random? What other spells do you have? Are any of them class unique?"

Orrin sighed, watching his only hope go down in flames. "I'm beginning to see why people think you're difficult to be around. You ask a lot of questions."

Graem smirked but waved his hand for Orrin to continue. He told the man about his new name, Casimir Hale, and the genealogy he had to memorize. That had Graem rolling his eyes. "Leave it to Anabella to make this more complicated than it needs to be. Just tell everyone to keep their questions to themselves. You don't need to talk about family in school. Most are there to learn, not play at politics. And the ones that are here for less academic reasons aren't worth being around.

"My dreamwhisper will kick in soon. I'll be blissful and talk less. We should go register you for your classes before that happens. I'll figure out how you'll pay me for my help later."

"I've only picked four classes," Orrin told the beefy man as he snapped up his staff. The rush of wind coming back toward Graem didn't surprise him as much this time. "I need to take one more, preferably with Finley."

"Who?"

"Finley Madvarr."

"Oh, him. He'll take Battle Class. I don't know what others, but I doubt you'd be able to get into any of them." Graem continued to talk as he opened the door. "He's been here awhile, and you haven't taken any prerequisites. Come along."

Orrin argued a bit more, but Graem either chose to ignore him or his dreamwhisper, whatever that was, had kicked in. By the time they arrived in front of a large building on the far west side of Mistlight, Graem was barely standing up straight without the support of his staff. Orrin had a sneaking suspicion the man only had it to keep upright when he was intoxicated.

"Professor Graem, you're actually here for orientation," a woman's voice drifted through the second door that Graem knocked on. The first had been the back door of a restaurant across the street. "I'm not sure you've been on time for a decade."

"Wren, get this one into the classes he wants. I'm going to bed. Don't wake me up for two days," Graem said and pushed Orrin through the door. "I'm very serious. No wakey."

Orrin tried to apologize as he almost stumbled into a woman shorter than him. She pirouetted and caught his shoulder as he passed, keeping him from falling on his ass. "Graem, don't you dare. You have a class tomorrow afternoon. I will go to Lord Sanerris if you don't show up."

"Threats, threats, threats," Graem mocked her, moving his hand like a mouth. "I'll tell on you. You have to do what I say or I'll tell Mom. Really, Wren? Has it come to this?"

Graem blinked hard and yawned like he was waking up from a long nap. "Don't ever work with your siblings, Casimir. Wren, please get Mr. Hale settled up and I promise to be in attendance for my class. But I won't be at orientation."

Wren only stood up to Graem's shoulder, but the way she looked down on him made even Orrin shrink back. "If you do not show up for your class, I will have you stripped of library access for two weeks."

"I'm the [Librarian]." Graem's words started to slur as he argued back. "You cannoth take my booss . . . booo-k-s."

"Get upstairs. I'll deal with you later."

Orrin watched in shock as the mountain of a man drooped his head and stomped out of the room like an angry child. He glanced around and noticed the room they were in was actually a bedroom.

"I'm sorry, I didn't know where he was taking me—"

"Follow me, please. Casimir, was it?" Wren's voice had changed from the stern headmistress tone she used against her brother to a calming timbre that had Orrin on edge. People who talked like that always had a dark side they hid away, and Orrin suspected he'd just witnessed some of her authoritarian side with her brother. It was safer to be polite.

"Yes, ma'am. Casimir Hale." Orrin was proud of himself for getting the name right.

Orrin followed Wren out of the only other door in the room. He stopped for only a second when he realized he was standing at the front of a classroom.

"Professors have rooms and offices close to their classrooms. Most of us don't live here full-time, but it's nice to be able to sleep when we need to without walking across town," Wren explained with a quick glance at Orrin. "You're new and probably have some weird combination of skills my brother is interested in learning. Make him sweat it out . . . for me."

Orrin found himself smiling back. *Yep. She's the dangerous type who gets you with the friendly act.*

"The registrar's office won't be open this late, but I can fill in the paperwork for you. Do you know what sort of classes you want to take? Classes are expensive, but we have scholarships."

"I think I've been signed up for most of my classes already, but I need to take one more," Orrin answered and hurried to add, "My grandma wanted me to come here and chose for me."

"Family can be like that." Wren led him down a few more hallways before stopping in front of a closed door. She put her hand against the wood, and it clicked open. "What class do you want to sign up for?"

Orrin cursed Graem for abandoning him. He had wanted to scan the lists and see if Finley had signed up for any classes. He couldn't ask Wren. Anabella had been clear to only trust Graem, which Orrin was beginning to think was a huge mistake.

"I'm not actually sure," Orrin admitted slowly. "I was hoping to look at what was available to me."

Wren sighed and pushed the door open. The room was nothing more than a small study room with a single table in the middle. No chairs surrounded the table, but a single book was open on it. Against the far wall was a shelf of books. Maybe twenty in total.

"The books on the wall there have the classes that are available for students. Most have a minimum sign-up requirement, so it's best to get a few other friends to agree to the class. The blue one on the top left has most of the prerequisite classes for higher-level courses. As this is your first semester, you should look there."

"How do I know if any of the classes are available?" Orrin asked, genuinely curious. Maybe they had a magical book that changed the color of the ink or a quill that floated along and wrote the updates into each book.

"The registrar keeps track, but since she's not here—" Wren flipped the big book in the middle of the table around to face Orrin. "You can take a look in here. It's the main registry. Every student has to fill out their classes, and only once a class has been approved by the professor can it be written in here. Let me know what you want to do."

Orrin couldn't believe his luck. She was letting him read the book that held the classes that Finley was going to take. It couldn't be that easy, right?

Chapter 14

Wren turned the pages of the registrar's book, tilting her head to read upside down a little easier. "You should start your search at the beginning of this semester. We have about a hundred students this semester, so take your time. Do you have any questions for me? I have a few things to handle before the morning orientation."

Orrin let his eyes take in the writing below. Some of the scrawling was illegible, but the majority appeared to be in a flowing script that was easy enough to read. "When I'm done, where do I go?"

Wren shook her head. "Graem didn't even show you the dorms? I'll be back in half an hour to show you the way. Don't leave this room until I get back. Some of the professors have research rooms around this side of the building, and you do not want to stumble into the wrong one."

Orrin thanked her before she left. He turned the pages, searching for his alias. Each page contained about ten students and their selected classes. He found Casimir eight pages in.

Casimir Hale

1. Defensive Earth Magic—Professor Cade
2. Magical History of Asmea—Professor Quinn
3. Surviving Spell Attacks—Professor Hugh
4. Battle Class—Professor Galina
5. TBD

He felt the weight of the gold in his satchel as he flipped the page. The left page was full, but the right side, page ten, had only three students. The second-to-last name was Finley.

Finley Madvarr

1. **Battle Class—Professor Galina**
2. **Advanced Tactics for Magical Battles—Professor Foreman**
3. **Advanced Magical Combat—Professor Tallis**
4. **Mana Signatures—Professor Wren**
5. **Redacted—Professor Redmond**

Orrin grimaced. Nobody had told him that classes would be redacted. Anabella had told him he wouldn't be able to take some classes because prerequisites had to be taken first. She hadn't told him some classes would be secret.

It made sense, though. A super-expensive magical school wouldn't advertise the best classes to everyone. Even if somebody had the money to pay for the best magical education, Asmea was first and foremost a world designed to keep knowledge a secret. If everybody knew how to unlock the best class or spell, nobody would be left to fill the lower ranks of society. Orrin didn't like it, but he could understand it.

He checked the class names against the descriptions in the small library of books behind the table. Just as Anabella had warned, both the advanced classes that Finley was taking were out of Orrin's league. He found a few classes that Redmond taught, but nothing that matched up with a redacted class. Mana Signatures seemed interesting and it was even taught by Professor Wren, but the class wasn't in the blue prerequisite book she'd pointed out. Orrin opened two other books before he found the description.

> **Mana Signatures with Wren Balint. Study of magical changes in preset spells. Prerequisites: Sensing Magic and professor acceptance.**

Orrin whistled at the cost. Anabella had given him three hundred gold pieces for a single class and to live off for the next month.

She didn't know he had his own gold, but Mana Signatures cost four hundred and fifty gold. Anabella had said she'd cover the difference, but Orrin felt relieved he wasn't able to take the class. Spending that much on himself, even if it was someone else's money, would have left a bad taste in his mouth.

He returned to the beginner class book and opened it up. Sensing Magic cost fifty gold. From the description, Orrin thought it might be all about feeling the different mana in spells. Just like Anabella had made him do a few days ago. He noted it as a possibility.

He flipped through a few more pages, reading descriptions. Most of the other classes were on specific magical types, usually fire, air, or earth. Some were focused on combat, while a few appeared to be centered on specific professions. Revitalizing Fields was a class on using magic to keep farmers' lands producing at the maximum volume. Orrin lost himself reading about the different ways people had thought to use magic to improve the world around them.

Wren knocked on the door what felt like a few minutes later. Orrin, sitting on the floor, held a dark tome in his lap.

"What are you doing with the advanced class list? You can't take any of those classes."

Orrin used one hand on the table to pull himself up. "I . . . um . . . was planning what I want to take next semester."

In truth, Orrin had been reading every class description in the hopes of learning something more about space magic, time magic, or any other way he might get out of his own slave collar. He didn't know what he was looking for, exactly, but he had been reading everything in the hopes that something would stand out. His luck had run dry, though.

Wren raised an eyebrow at him. "What classes did you decide to take this semester?"

Orrin opened the book on the middle table and pointed. "These four are what I was signed up for already, and I think Sensing Magic might be good. I really want to take Mana Signatures. I've heard a little about it and—"

"Where did you hear about Mana Signatures? That's not a class just anyone is allowed to take. It can be very dangerous." Wren brushed a strand of her dark hair away from her face. "If this is a joke that Graem put you up to . . ."

The threat hung in the air.

Orrin's mind raced. Anabella had mentioned Mana Signatures, but she'd also told him to only trust Professor Graem. Wren was his sister, but Orrin wasn't about to take any chances. Luckily, he had his mysterious grandmother to fall back on as an excuse.

"Professor Graem didn't put me up to anything," Orrin said quickly, holding his hands up in surrender. "I think it must have been my grandma who mentioned it. I just know enough to see the different flavors of magic."

Wren tilted her head. "Flavors of magic . . . I like that description. Is that how your grandmother described it?"

Orrin shook his head. "She just told me to watch the mana as I cast the spell. It took me a bit before I figured it out, but by the end of the night, I could see the—"

"The end of the night?" Wren cut him off again, even quicker. She stepped closer to Orrin. "Graem did put you up to this. I'm of half a mind to throw you out the front door and strike your name from the records."

Orrin retreated around the table. "I didn't say it was easy. I've only done it with one spell. That's why I thought Sensing Magic might be a good start. If I can see all the different types of magic, I could probably figure out what someone is casting if I was quick, right?"

Wren's hand quivered in a fast flick. The wooden table elongated like putty and snapped around Orrin. It twisted around him and held him tight.

Orrin kept his emotions in check and tried to look as nonthreatening as possible. "I have no idea what I've said to upset you, but I apologize. I'll take any class you want, but you don't have to kill me."

"Kill you?" Wren's anger cooled enough for Orrin to notice she was shaking. "I'm not going to kill you. I'm just going to hold you until I get Graem down here to explain what is going on. You show up the night before classes, already signed up for most entry-level classes, but you know theories taught only in redacted classes. Who are you? Better yet, who is your grandmother?"

Orrin felt [Mind Bastion] trying to trigger. He thought about using [Calm Mind] on himself, but the way Wren was staring at him made him think any magic use might be his last. Instead, he blew out a breath before talking.

"My name is Casimir Hale. My great-grandmother worked on arrays, and my grandma raised me with stories of her magic use. I'm the first in my family to attend school here. I'm not trying to trick you, and I'm definitely not pulling a prank for your brother. I really just wanted your opinion on whether Sensing Magic was a good class to take. I have no idea why you're so mad at me."

The entire time he tried to talk his way out of whatever he'd landed himself in, Orrin's mind was racing in a different direction. Anabella had told him to try and see mana changing into the cast spell, but she'd been genuinely impressed when he was able to do it. Almost as if . . .

She didn't expect me to be able to do it.

The comments about being able to sense magic before taking the class had made Wren suspicious. He was the equivalent of a college freshman and shouldn't have known how to do it. Letting slip that he had been able to see the magic changes in one afternoon had set Wren off.

She didn't attack me until I mentioned using it defensively . . . which means that's probably possible. Orrin thought of the potential outcomes. *If I could see what someone was casting, I'd have an extra second or two to defend against it. Shit. I bet that's a higher class than Mana Signatures. If they're teaching people how to better fight others and I just happen to stumble in here acting like I already know . . . She thinks I'm spying on them or worse.*

"Can you change a . . . flavor of magic?"

The look of confusion on Orrin's face probably saved his life. "What?"

Wren moved from a readied position to a slightly more relaxed one. "Truly, you just happened to learn it in one day?"

Orrin felt the table stretch back and let him drop. He landed heavily on his feet but stayed standing. "Yeah, I promise. I didn't mean to offend you or anything."

Wren studied Orrin's eyes for a moment before pointing a finger at his face. "Tell me what you see."

Orrin complied, mostly because she was too close for him to run away without getting hit and too far away for him to attack her. He could feel in his bones that any spell he tried to cast wouldn't be quick enough in this situation.

He focused like he had in his prison room at Anabella's. Catching the flow of Wren's mana took him a few moments.

"If you are lying to—"

"Shh." Orrin shushed her. "I'm trying to concentrate. I don't do this all the time, you know."

He kept trying to slow his fast-beating heart and finally saw the tiniest wave of mana forming at Wren's fingertips. It was dripping and landing on the stone floor, but not like water. No, the way it was pooling at her feet and moving toward his own like . . .

"Metal?"

Wren snapped, and the mana activated, sending a dozen spikes of metal flying at Orrin. He raised his hands and cast [Ward], but the spikes disappeared before they struck.

"What the fuck?" Orrin cursed. He'd tried to be reasonable and calm, but a teacher had just tried to attack him. "You knew I wasn't lying and you still attacked me?"

"I let the magic die before it hit you. Get a grip. Do it again."

His eyes grew wide when Wren pointed at him again. "Are you crazy? No! I'll just take the four classes. Which way to the dorms?"

"Five. Four." Wren started to count down. "Three."

"Shit. Okay. Wait." Orrin tried to focus, but the surge of adrenaline from seeing those metal spikes flying at him kept his focus scrambled. He closed his eyes and used [Calm Mind].

"Two."

He opened his eyes and stared. The mana was holding at the base of her palm this time. It wasn't metal magic, but similar in some way. It also felt stronger and already primed. He ignored the sound of her voice as he watched it. The mana took form, and Orrin had time to shout, "Wood," before he had to duck.

A wooden baton appeared at his side and came down as he shouted. Even as he dodged, the magic was released again and the weapon disappeared.

"An actual prodigy," Wren said, smiling. "You really can see the flow. You'd be wasting your time with Sensing Magic. The exam is doing what you just did. I'll waive the requirement if you want to take my class. Mana Signatures is more advanced, but with the way you can see the flow—what kind of magic spells do you have? What is your class? If you can handle even two different types of magic, you'd be amazed at what . . ."

Orrin tuned her out. He'd thought he'd escaped the crazy sibling. It turned out that both Graem and Wren were missing a few screws.

Chapter 15

Orrin begged off as tired, getting Wren to show him to the dorms. She'd waved off his attempt to pay for the Mana Signatures class, scribbling the exemption next to his name in the registrar's book. Someone would come looking for the extra money, she assured him.

With the prices people paid for this school, Orrin was pleasantly surprised to find room and board were included with the price of one class. Wren led him up three flights of stairs, pointing out different hallways to classes, a dining hall and kitchen, teachers' offices, and the library on different floors. The top floor was dorms. They walked down multiple hallways, each with a board of names that Orrin didn't have time to read. Nearing the end of the hallway, Wren stopped before one that wasn't filled.

"Write your name here and slide the nameplate into any open spot. It will key the corresponding door to your mana. Nobody can enter your room without your permission." Wren handed him a piece of chalk. "Of course, you can pull someone into your room. We don't have rules against it, but it's better not to get involved with other students. It never ends well."

Orrin felt the exhaustion of his day hit him as he started to write his own name. A quick flourish changed the O into a C. "Anywhere is fine?"

The board had twenty spots, and over half were taken. He peered down the dimly lit hallway. Ten doors on either side and a dead end. He considered taking the room at the very end of the hall. That's what *Orrin* would have done. Do his best to avoid the group and try to study. Make sure to socialize the absolute bare minimum.

"Most of the rooms fill up quickly. You're lucky we have a smaller class this semester or you might have had to stay off campus. Don't worry if you don't get a room next semester. When a student drops out or dies, the empty dorm room goes up for grabs."

"Dies?"

"That hasn't happened in years," Wren assured him.

He groaned internally as he put his nameplate into the next open spot. Casimir would be rooming next to Ellis Glevrasker, whoever that was. A quick scan of the names showed none of his targets were on this floor.

"How will I know when and where my classes are tomorrow?" Orrin asked, hoisting the small satchel back up on his shoulder. He wanted to be away from Wren and her enthused teaching but had yet to see anyone else in the school. The rain was still pattering away at the nearby windows, but the darkness outside and his exhaustion made him think it was late at night. "Or later today?"

"It's still before midnight." Wren readjusted the stray nameplates on the table under the listed names. "We'll have orientation in the morning before breakfast. You'll receive your schedule then. I'll spoil you and tell you that our first class will be on the third day of classes. I look forward to seeing what you can do."

Orrin smiled politely and tried to escape. "I'll see you then. Thanks for all the help."

"If you have questions, feel free to stop by my classroom. You remember how to get there?"

Orrin didn't but was sure he could find his way back using [Map]. "Of course I do," he lied.

When the door shut behind him, he slumped against the wall. If Professor Wren was any hint of what was to come, Orrin's social batteries were going to be wiped out each day. He studied his new living quarters.

A step up from the dungeon, but not as nice as Anabella's house.

A desk was positioned under the single window in the room. Orrin glanced out the glass before he untied the drapes and covered the window from anyone looking up from outside. From what he'd been able to gather, the entire school was situated in a long rectangle, with a large courtyard of grass outside his window. He was on the northern side of the building, so his window wouldn't get much natural light but he'd be able to see the full run of the interior yard.

The bed was twin-size but with nice sheets and a pillow that rivaled anything he'd used recently. A small chest of drawers by the foot of the bed was the final piece of furniture. Against the wall above the bed was a shadow left behind from a removed frame. The nail still hung, and Orrin could make out the dimensions of whatever had been there before—the yellow paint of the walls was slightly brighter where the artwork had hung.

He really needed to plan a bit more. He had only let Wren coerce him into her class because Finley was in it as well. Anabella thought he needed more face time with him, as she'd mentioned he might be the hardest to get close to. Rhys was younger and thus, according to her logic, easier to manipulate. Maeve was socially awkward and would be elated to be the center of attention.

Orrin was beginning to seriously doubt Anabella's theories. The descriptions of the classes available here, which he'd been reading over, were things he hadn't even begun to discover in the books he'd read in Dey. Even the beginner classes had made mention of spell mechanics that Orrin was unsure of.

I have twenty-six days to figure it out. Learning is secondary here. I need to play Anabella as long as possible and figure out a way to get close to Rhys, Maeve, and Finley without getting too friendly. If it comes down to it, I'll let Anabella take over this stupid country. As long as she keeps her promise and gets me back to Dey. Orrin tossed his satchel with all his provisions on the floor. *Of course, if you want to move a little faster and save me before that, D, I wouldn't complain.*

With a sigh, Orrin grabbed the relic from the bag and jotted his required nightly note to Anabella, letting her know he'd arrived and convinced Wren to let him into Mana Signatures with Finley. Orrin wanted to ask about Daniel's attempted rescue but didn't want to tip her off that he knew. He tapped the stylus against his lip as he thought of how to word the question. He gave up trying to be clever and simply signed the missive with "I hope everyone is well."

He made the mistake of writing all this in bed, and by the time he finished, he was half-asleep. Orrin dropped the relic book on the floor and was out within minutes.

"Well done. I have sent an extra two hundred gold to make up the difference. You may keep the remainder for class essentials. Let me know if more is required. Trespassers retreated once you escaped. No casualties."

Orrin woke to the sound of doors opening and shutting down the hall. When he threw his legs off the bed, he'd almost stepped on the relic. Orrin frowned at the frustrating message in the Twin Book of Sending. He hadn't been worried about the price, as Anabella had told him she'd pay the difference, but it still irked him she didn't care.

"I think I deserve more than a 'well done' for bypassing an entire class," he muttered. He didn't know if it was common to be able to skip a prerequisite, but as his mysterious grandmother hadn't mentioned it as a possibility, he'd assumed she would be impressed more than she apparently was.

A knock on the door interrupted his dark mood. *I need coffee.*

"Is there someone in there? We have ten minutes to get to orientation." The male voice cracked on the last word. "Orientation," the boy repeated in a lower voice. "Hey, are you sure there's someone in this room?"

Orrin tucked the magical book into his storage skill and rubbed his hair down as he walked to the door. "Sorry, I got in late. I'll be—"

As Orrin opened the door, the boy on the other side fell back a step with wide eyes. Orrin instantly crouched and turned, ready for an attack.

"What . . ." Nothing was behind him.

"So—Sorry, I didn't mean to . . ." The kid, because Orrin couldn't really call him a man, was looking at the ground. He was younger than Orrin by a couple of years at least. "My name is Ellis. Ellis Glevrasker. I'm in the room next to yours."

"You looked like you saw a monster attacking," Orrin joked. "I thought I was dead before classes started. I'm . . . Casimir. Nice to meet you."

Orrin held out his hand, which the youngster took in both his own. He was getting the weirdest vibe from Ellis and couldn't put a finger on it.

"It's nice to meet you, Casimir. Did you arrive last night? I thought I was the last one to get here and pick a room the other day. Have you settled all right? If you need anything, let me know. I was going to head on down, but I can wait for you if you want. It's not a bother at all." Ellis still had Orrin's hand between his as he sputtered out his words.

Orrin wished the dorm room had a mirror, because Ellis was nervous. *Did Anabella's [Glamour] mess up while I slept or something? Did I grow horns?*

Orrin pulled his hand back gently and rubbed his fingers through his hair again. No horns.

"I—if you're not ready right now, I can save you a seat at orientation?"

Orrin put the problem away for later. "Yes, please. I just woke up and should put on something that doesn't smell," he said, pulling his collar up to sniff at it in an exaggerated fashion. "Do you know if they'll have coffee at orientation or even just breakfast?"

Ellis practically jumped. "I don't know, but I'll find out. I'll get you some."

"Wait, you don't . . ." He was too late. Ellis had fled. "Is it my breath?"

Orrin changed into one of the outfits packed for him, a black silk shirt with the slightest ruffle around the collar and black pants with a strip of green on the side. It wasn't exactly Orrin's style, but he noticed a lot of people shooting him glances as he made his way with the other stragglers down the stairs. An auditorium was situated on the western side of the campus. Orrin found Ellis waving from a row near the back, a cup gripped tightly in his other hand.

He made his way to the boy and smiled. "Thanks, Ellis. I needed this."

Ellis smiled widely back at him as he took the coffee. A groan of enjoyment slipped out at the first sip.

"I didn't know if you'd want cream or sugar, so I brought both." Ellis moved his books, pens, and two small containers from one of the seats. "You can sit here and then you can take what you want."

Orrin pointed at the mug. "Perfect as it is. Scoot over."

The two sat down. Orrin noticed more glances his way as the room began to fill. "Ellis, this is my first semester here. Do I have something in my teeth? People keep staring at me."

Ellis was trying to balance the milk and sugar containers on his books, which were barely staying on his folded knees. He didn't look at Orrin as he responded. "It's my first semester, too! Um . . . I didn't notice anything in your teeth."

Orrin grabbed the milk before it fell and put it under his own chair. "Weird."

Wren entered the room and slapped the podium at the front with her knuckles. "Sit down. Hurry up." She waited until the last person entered behind her and gestured toward the open door. "Professor Graem Balint would like to say a few words before the semester officially begins."

Graem entered the room, looking much better than the last time Orrin had seen him. He shook his sister's hand and straightened the podium. Graem rolled the sleeves of his robe up and rested his arms on the podium stand. He studied the dozens of students in front of him, watching and not saying a single word.

Someone coughed.

"You there, with the blue and green staff. You'll fail out within two weeks. You, up there, with the feathered hat, I give you two days. You with the ugly face, you might pass half your classes if you study hard."

Orrin watched in shock and terror as the professor pointed out nearly ten students and told them they would fail in some way. He waited for his own turn, the years of high school rushing back in a flood of bad memories, but Graem never turned his way.

"If I didn't call on you, good luck. Try not to die. I don't want to deal with the paperwork," Graem finished with a flourish and flipped off Wren as he strode out of the room.

Chapter 16

Wren's shoulders sagged as Graem left the room, but Orrin wasn't surprised when she turned back to them with a smile on her face. "Ignore him. You are all going to accomplish amazing things this year. Let's go over some basics for those of you who are new. Some of those I recognize from last term would do well to listen as well."

As she started giving an actual orientation speech to the students, Orrin realized he should have brought something to write all the information down. He nudged Ellis, who was trying to transcribe every word Wren spoke. "Can I borrow a pen and paper?"

Ellis pushed his notepad into Orrin's hands, along with the pen he was using. He dove into his bag and pulled out one of the many extras he'd brought. Orrin hadn't meant to take Ellis's notes, but the boy was already writing in a new journal before he could complain. Orrin started writing down what he thought was important to remember. It was awkward balancing his coffee in one hand, but he held the notes down with the cup between sips.

Wren explained that most classes would take place in the eastern wing of the school. Lists would be posted all around with class names, classroom numbers, start times, and rotating days. Classes ran for six days, with one day off each week. Each class was either a morning class or an afternoon class. The entire schedule had been crafted so that no one had an overlapping class. All classes were taught two times a week and ran between three and four hours.

"Your professors will tell you more about your individual classes." Wren took a step forward and swatted a student who was nodding off in the front row. He nearly fell out of his seat but was able to catch himself. Wren continued speaking as if nothing had happened. "Breakfast, lunch, and dinner are provided in the dining hall before and after classes. If you want to leave campus, there are multiple options for food around Mistlight. If you need to leave for longer than a few hours and you'll miss a class, please try and let staff know. I know that what I'm about to say is going to be ignored, but your professor has the final say on whether you pass a class or fail. Full stop. If they don't like you, too bad. I will not hear another complaint that you should have done better or your father will hear about this. The Sanerris School for Spells and Magical Learning does not care. I do not care."

Orrin smirked as he marked the times for classes and meals down. He would need to see how far off campus he could go with the collar. As far as he knew, Graem had keyed it to himself. *If Graem leaves campus and goes outside range, where does that leave me?*

He suddenly wanted this orientation to be over. Maybe Wren would point out Graem's room for him.

Standing at the front of the room, Wren noted the few school rules, which essentially came down to *don't try to steal from another student, don't go into rooms you aren't assigned to, and don't attack each other except in one particular circumstance.*

Orrin frowned as the professor explained.

"As we are all adults here, with classes of our own, the administration does not like to concern itself with petty squabbles between students. Konnor, if you touch him again, I will lock you in your chair for three days." A stout male in his twenties slid down his chair as he tried to become invisible. "As I was saying, if you have a problem with another student that you don't feel you can settle between yourselves, the courtyard is available every day after evening classes for a duel. In no circumstance are you allowed to attack each other outside of that time frame. To do so will result in the immediate expulsion of the aggressor. The rules for a duel are sacred and go back to the founding of our school."

Orrin watched the big guy up front who had just been reprimanded stretch his leg toward the smaller, older man sitting in front of him. He was writing furiously, trying to take down every word Wren said, just like Ellis.

Bully.

The word echoed around his head and Orrin cast a [Calm Mind] spell on himself. *You don't need to get involved, Orrin,* he chided himself. *Wren is watching and just threatened him. She'll see him and . . . ouch.* Orrin winced.

Luca, the man in his forties sitting in front of his tormenter, had been leaning forward in his seat hovering over his notes. Konnor had used the cover provided by the auditorium's configuration to push Luca's chair with his foot, tipping it over. Luca had stumbled toward Wren as he fell out of his chair. Windmilling his arms, he'd missed her only due to the professor's quick reflexes. Instead, he landed face-first against the wall.

Orrin expected Wren to bring down the hammer on Konnor. Instead, she shook her head and stepped around Luca's unconscious body.

"If you bring the challenge, the other party sets the parameters. Weapons only, limits to which spells are demonstrated or used to fight, or even what kind of liquid both parties have to submerge in for the duration of the duel." She smiled at the murmuring. "Yes, it doesn't have to be an actual fight. My personal favorite was when one young woman told her challenger they'd both be jumping from the roof. It's free entertainment available only to those attending our institute, and I suggest you attend. You might learn something. Once the parameters are set, the original challenger can call off the duel without repercussions but with the knowledge they cannot challenge again for two weeks. A professor must be present to adjudicate and declare a winner. Healing costs are not covered by the school. Any questions?"

Orrin had dozens of questions but kept them inside for now. Luca was on his hands and knees, shaking his head as he got his bearings. Others asked questions that he half listened to.

Part of him thought the demonstration between the two men had to be just that . . . a demonstration. Likely, it was a play put on to illustrate that while the rules were in place, the professors here didn't care enough to go out of their way to enforce justice. Orrin wasn't surprised. This world was brutal. Healers were thought of as second-class, because those classes couldn't help with taking down monsters or dungeons. Lord Catanzano's attitude toward Orrin had begun to change with Madi's reports on what he could do in battle and the help he brought to the entire team, but Orrin had no doubt the man would stack Madi with four other fighters if push came to shove.

Luca stayed half crouched, staring at something in his hands. Dejectedly, he turned and righted his chair, pushing it back into place between two other students. He collected his fallen notepad and trudged toward the back of the class, taking a seat behind Ellis and Orrin.

Orrin's fists clenched. *Do not get involved. It's not your problem to solve. You have to stay under the radar until Daniel finds you or you can fix Anabella's problem. Do not get involved.*

"That guy's a dick," Ellis said, turning around and handing Luca a spare pen. Orrin saw a broken one clenched in Luca's hand, ink staining his pants where he rested his fist. "I'm Ellis. You can borrow this until after class."

Luca's lip quivered as he nodded in thanks and started writing in his notepad again, but with less gusto than before. He had a red mark between his dark-brown eyes that he rubbed with a fist. The smudge of ink he left behind would probably be hidden by his long black hair unless he kept touching . . . He moved his hand to his face again.

"Don't touch it," Orrin sighed. "Can I cast a healing spell on you? I'm guessing you'll stop rubbing ink on your face if that goose egg is gone."

Luca's eyes darted up for a glance at Orrin. He dropped his gaze immediately. "I don't have the money for healing. I apologize."

Orrin took a deep breath in through his nose and let it pass out his lips before he responded. "On the house if you want it. I'm guessing that guy wasn't your friend?"

The suspicion that was directed at Orrin made him pull back momentarily, but he remembered that feeling. The hurt and embarrassment that came after you found yourself the butt of a joke or "prank." Orrin had lashed out more than once at Daniel. He smiled, putting every bit of gentleness his friend had ever shown him in it. "If you still don't want it, that's your choice, but at least try not to smear any more ink on your face. I think your pen is broken."

Orrin could see the scales of trust weighing against the possibility of being hurt again. He didn't turn away and waited for Luca to make his choice. Finally, he received a slow nod.

Orrin cast [Heal Small Wounds] at level one. The abrasion faded, leaving only the dash of ink across his face. Luca placed the broken pen on the ground and wiped his hand on his already-stained pants. He gingerly touched his forehead before giving Orrin a tight-lipped smile and a nod.

"Don't let the assholes get you down," Orrin whispered as he turned back around.

"You're a [Healer]?" Ellis murmured close to Orrin. "What are you doing here?"

Before Orrin could respond, a blonde girl sitting in front of them turned around, her ponytail flying over her shoulder as she did. Orrin could see her start to shush them both, but her eyes widened for a moment when she saw Orrin.

Fuck, is the [Glamour] failing?

"Hey, I haven't seen you around before." She turned fully, resting one arm over her chair. "Is it your first time to Triple S, or are you a returning student?"

"Triple S?"

"Sanerris School for Spells," Ellis told him, moving his chair a little closer as he did.

"Oh. That makes sense. First time." Orrin gave a polite smile and tried to focus back on the orientation.

Wren was answering the second student who had asked about changing room assignments. Orrin decided to never be on the receiving end of that glare.

"What's your name? I'm Willa Cohee. It's my second semester, so if you need any help with classes, let me know."

There are so many people trying to be helpful here, something is wrong. Orrin plastered a fake smile on and nodded politely. "Thank you, I'll keep that in mind. I'm Casimir Hale."

An agitated tic of the corner of her mouth made Orrin feel much better. She was mad at him. Whether for not noticing her pedigree or for brushing off her offer to help with classes, he didn't know. He'd listened in to enough of the other whispering before orientation started to know people were trying to make connections. The Sanerris School was more than just a place to learn about magic. It was a place for the younger generations to rub elbows with those outside their normal station.

"That was Cohee, as in Justice Cohee. She's my aunt."

"I'm sure she's very proud of you."

Ellis let out a squeak next to him. Willa's slow turn of attention toward his hall mate set Orrin's danger bells ringing.

"I wonder how many places there are close enough to school that are actually good to eat at?" Orrin sputtered, grabbing her concentration back from Ellis. "I'm sure your aunt has brought you to all the best places, right? Do you have any recommendations?"

Willa flicked her hair again as she answered. "Of course. I could show you at lunch today. We could be back before class starts this afternoon, or maybe even stay the night somewhere more private."

The reason for all his attention finally caught up to him. Orrin hadn't had people openly flirt with him. Sure, Garret had toyed with him, but the look on Ellis's face and even the predatory look in Willa's eyes made a lot more sense once Orrin remembered the [Glamour]. He was good-looking, as well as a new and mysterious figure in Mistlight. He swallowed. He might not have firsthand experience, but he'd watched Daniel's first crash-landing attempts at navigating the dating field. If he answered wrong, she might be offended. He didn't have time for that.

What would Daniel do?

A smile crept across Orrin's face. "We have to be back for afternoon class, but the three of us would love to grab lunch with you."

Orrin leaned back and pounded Luca's shoulder with one hand before wrapping his other arm around Ellis, who stiffened at the contact. "Where do you suggest we go?"

Chapter 17

"I don't get it," Ellis whispered to himself as he selected a plate of fish from the cafeteria's assortment of food. "Why would you want to get lunch with us over a Cohee?"

Orrin frowned at the plate of seafood before grabbing something meatier on the next shelf of protein options. He'd already piled his tray up with a small salad, a bowl of cut-up fruit he'd never seen before, and fries. At least he thought they were fries. He munched on one and coughed in surprise. It tasted like watermelon.

"Willa might be a Cohee, but her family is on the periphery," Luca said quietly. He picked three different meats, balancing a second tray on top of the first. "It was still a mistake to embarrass her like that. You flustered her in front of her friends. She'll retaliate."

Orrin sighed as he grabbed a jiggly dessert and turned around. The cafeteria was filled with traditional tables, each holding up to six seats. It could easily house three or four hundred students. He nodded his head to direct his new friends to one nearby and led the way as he thought about what he'd done.

Orrin planned to keep a low profile. He'd purposefully misunderstood a fellow student's invitation and invited along two classmates he'd already pegged as low on the social ladder. Ellis was a new student like him and followed him around like a puppy. The [Glamour] that Anabella had cast on Orrin made him attractive . . . to the point of distraction, in his opinion. Ellis was clearly smitten.

Luca placed his two trays of food on the table and dug in immediately.

"I didn't turn her down, which would have created more problems. I accidentally misunderstood her as inviting us all," Orrin said, pointing his fork at Luca. "She could have clarified she just wanted to go on a date with me, but she left in a huff. That's on her. She should know how to act in polite society."

Luca scoffed then began popping little sardines into his mouth, one after the other. "If you'd kept that smug look off your face, people might have believed you made a mistake, but you asked where she was going when she left. You made an enemy there."

Orrin scratched the back of his head, embarrassed. "I'll apologize to her next time I see her in class."

"She's not a novice like you two. She graduated most of her classes and is officially a second-term student. You won't see her in class." Luca spilled a bean soup across two pieces of bread and inhaled the sandwich.

Orrin glanced at Ellis. The younger boy poked his fish but watched them talk like a tennis match, his head bouncing back and forth.

"You realize the food is free," Orrin pointed out to Luca. "It's like you haven't eaten in days."

"I haven't. I had to save every copper for admission. Some of us have to pay our own way and don't have a rich aunt to pay for our classes."

Orrin took in Luca's worn clothes and remembered the way he'd clutched his broken pen in anguish. He was doubly glad he'd healed the man. Having an older friend who knew the ins and outs of the school would be invaluable.

"If you need some help, I'd—"

Luca put his fork down. He made no more noise than most of the students eating around them but the gesture was made with a finality that stopped Orrin in his tracks.

"I am not for sale. I neither need nor want a patron. Thank you for healing me and the conversation. I wish you luck at the Sanerris School. You'll likely need it." Without another word, Luca stood and returned his nearly empty trays.

He stopped at the exit and rushed back to Orrin and Ellis. He held Ellis's pen in his hand. "I almost forgot. Thank you for letting me borrow this. Here."

Ellis bit his lip in thought and tilted his head. "But the one I lent you was broken. I would like mine back, please."

Luca hesitated and gave a curt nod to Ellis. He dropped his broken pen on the table and left without another word.

"I'm so confused right now."

Ellis smiled after Luca's retreating form. "He's unbound." He noticed Orrin's face and explained further, "Someone who pays his own way to go here. He's not a novice like you and me. Some of the students spend months saving up the money for classes."

"Are you unbound?"

The smile faltered. "Partially. I'm taking four classes for someone and get to take one of my own. If I pass those four, I'll likely be back next semester."

"Why? Who would pay you to go to school?"

Ellis chewed slowly as he looked at Orrin. "You're unbound?"

"I'm here because my grandmother sent me, but I'm taking classes I want to." *At least that's what I have to say. Damn it, Anabella. You didn't tell me anything about this.*

"Sometimes a person wants to take a few classes but can't spend the time away from whatever responsibilities they have to attend. They pay a student to take classes for them. If I'm able to pass my classes, I'll spend a few months teaching my patron the specifics of the class. Then I'll come back and take the more advanced classes if they want to know more. If they don't, I can offer my services to someone else, but with the added step of having the base courses out of the way. Some of the people here are professional students."

Orrin considered that for only a minute before seeing holes. "Why would the school allow that? No offense, but you aren't going to be as good at teaching as the professors are. Plus, you could just teach anyone. Take a class one time and teach it over and over."

Ellis laughed. "That's not how it works. If I pass a class, I can only teach the person who paid for it. We have a contract. I can't teach anyone else unless I retake the class. The school looks down on that. They get a bunch of people who want to learn, the rich get the basics without having to spend weeks stuck on campus, and we bound students get to learn for free. If our employer isn't satisfied, we just stick around teaching them until they are."

Orrin took a sip of his juice. It was a weird setup, but Luca's response was disproportionate to his offer for help. "Why'd Luca react like that if it's a good gig?"

"If a bound student has an epiphany or creates something new, it belongs to the patron. It's sort of like I'm not really here. I'm just an expression of my patron's will. I figure I'll be taking only basic classes, so what's the harm right now. I want to take more advanced classes once I'm rich. I'll be a regular student then. Luca's been a student for a few semesters, I think. He's probably just wary. There are rumors of people catching students in contracts and stealing their inventions."

Orrin wanted to ask more questions, but he was already treading in dangerous territory. Too many more direct questions and Ellis would get over his crush and realize everyone who attended the school should know this shit.

"I'm lucky my grandma wanted me to attend. I don't even know how many semesters I'll be here, but I promise I won't steal even a pen from you," Orrin said, trying for a joke.

The flash of horror that crossed the young man's face told Orrin he'd failed. "You don't think that was stealing, do you? I have so many pens, I just thought it would be okay if one was broken."

"Hey, it's fine." Orrin grabbed Ellis's shaking hand. "I'll cover the pen. It's not a big deal. I need to get some of my own notebooks anyway. Let's check the schedule and hit the library. We can meet up again for dinner."

Ellis jabbered something affirmative and blushed the entire walk across campus.

He ran his finger over the class schedule posted near the library and sighed. Battle Class. Orrin's first class on the first day of school was a dumb fighting exercise.

He bought his books for his other four classes and dropped them off in his dorm. Ellis shadowed him and thanked him for his new pen. Orrin tossed the wrapped parcel containing his new notebooks, loose-leaf paper, and about ten writing utensils on his bed.

He glanced at the clothes he was wearing and decided not to change as he looked out his window. Battle Class was located at the southern end of the courtyard. A few students stood waiting already, even though class wouldn't start for another ten minutes.

Orrin was the second to last to arrive. Half the class wore robes, a quarter had on armor of some variation, and the remaining students were like Orrin, dressed in normal day clothes. Only one had a weapon strapped to his side, but Orrin saw plenty of wands and staffs.

The courtyard was several hundred yards long but only about a hundred or so yards wide. Nearby, a circle of sand marked out what Orrin guessed would be the fighting ring.

"I'm Professor Galina, and this is Battle Class. If you are not registered for this class, get off my pitch." A woman with short-cropped hair and the build of a weight lifter pushed her way to the front of the class. Two people left in a hurry and Orrin counted about twelve in total remaining. *For a school boasting under a hundred students, this must be a popular class.*

Professor Galina folded her arms, pushing out her impressive biceps. "This class is simple. We fight. You all get a chit."

An older student stepped out of the lineup and placed a basket filled with small golden squares on the ground. Galina nodded her thanks before she ordered, "Each of you take one now."

Orrin waited for most of the students to take a golden square before he moved. The guy who had been carrying the basket was near him, though, so he still beat the people at the other end of the line. A quick count confirmed his worry. Orrin snatched up his chit and moved back to the line.

The last two students realized at the same time there weren't as many chits as students. Both lunged for the last coin, but the girl was quicker.

The last guy frowned but turned to the teacher and pointed. "We need one more. I didn't get one."

Galina smiled. A faded white scar ran along her chin and up the corner of her mouth, giving her a bigger smile than normal. "The rules for this class are simple, as there are only two. Don't kill your opponent. That is the first and most important rule. If you haven't noticed, my assistant is a [Healer]. He'll be able to keep you from dying, but if you're squeamish about being injured, drop my class. You will get hurt. Don't worry about scars or permanent injuries. The infirmary is right there."

She pointed to the door directly behind the group. "The winner of any fight has the responsibility to get the loser healed. If you win a fight, you get another chit. If you lose a fight, you turn your chit over to me. If you don't have a chit at the end of the semester, you fail. The person with the most chits gets bragging rights. That young man in the back is the current champion."

Orrin and the class turned as one, and Orrin caught his first glimpse of Finley. He wore tight, dark fighting clothes with just the hint of armor underneath. Blond hair was tied back into a small bun, and he smiled and waved to the class. Orrin was surprised. He'd expected someone beefier from the way Anabella had described his fighting prowess, but Finley wasn't that much bigger than him.

"I don't have a chit," the student up front interrupted. He hadn't moved and stood a few steps in front of the other ten students. The teaching assistant took a step, but Galina held up a hand, waving him off.

"You get the honor of picking the first match. Everyone will watch. You must give one piece of advice to the loser on how to improve and remark on one thing the winner did wrong. I won't call on every one of you after each fight, but if I do and you don't satisfy me, I'll take a chit from you. You will fight at least once every class. Go ahead and pick someone. Introduce yourselves and get your asses into the circle there."

Everyone listened, and Orrin felt the hair on his neck stand up. *Don't pick me. Don't pick me.*

"I'll fight her." Orrin sighed in relief. A long finger pointed out the girl who had beaten him to the last chit.

The smaller girl walked forward. She wore a robe and was one of the few with a holstered wand on her hip. "Cora Ignacius. You said there are two rules, right? What's the second one?"

"Don't die."

Chapter 18

Cora Ignacius fought with wind magic. Puffs of air danced along her feet as she moved in quick bursts around the field. She fought exclusively with her magic and landed hit after hit against her opponent.

The man without a chit was Wilder Sigur. He dodged the first few attacks, but after one struck him, Wilder simply tanked the rest, clearly deciding it was easier to take the small hits. He clapped his hands together, and as he separated them slowly, a quarterstaff grew between his hands.

A skill like Daniel's that lets him summon a weapon. I wonder if it's a storage skill and that is a real weapon or if that staff is more like my [Ice Sword]. Orrin kept his eyes on the fight. Not getting called on to be in the first fight was lucky, but he knew the other shoe would drop soon. *I bet Galina calls on me first.*

As Orrin waited and tried to find something to say about either side, Cora continued her assault from a distance. She kept her feet close to the sand that marked the outer rim of the fighting ring. Wilder finished summoning his weapon and struck it into the ground in front of him.

Orrin heard someone nearby scoff. "Amateur."

A glance to his side confirmed the one who'd commented was Finley. His voice was softer than he'd have expected. Finley untied his hair and put it back up with sure fingers. Orrin noticed the dark, fitted clothes had several depressions molded into them. He stared for a moment too long, puzzled.

Finley caught him and frowned. "What are you looking at, newbie?"

Orrin hoped the [Glamour] hid his blush. Thankfully, he had a real reason for studying the rest of his classmates. "Checking out the competition. This won't be the last fight. You're missing something, aren't you?" He pointed.

Finley's frown turned into a smile. "Clever. I think this might be a good class this year." He turned to watch the fight as he ran a thumb over the divots, making them more pronounced as he touched them. "My knives strap up close to my clothes and are held in place by my molded armor underneath. It keeps them secure and in place so I always know where they are without having to look."

A knife fighter? Orrin watched the fight, too. Wilder was channeling magic through his quarterstaff but hadn't taken it out of the ground yet. *I thought he might be a close melee fighter, but he's here with no weapons.*

"No knives today?" Orrin stepped closer to Finley, leaving the seven students that weren't fighting and the teacher's assistant clumped together. Finley's reputation was working as a deterrent. "How do you plan to fight without your weapon?"

Finley's smile was open and inviting, as if they weren't talking about fighting. "If I'm wearing my knives, people die. This is sparring. I'll use one of the wooden practice daggers. They bring out a table of them after the first demonstration fight."

Orrin nodded. *Galina purposefully gives out fewer tokens than students to draw two people into a fight. She'll give us some more information about the class but throw us into the deep end.*

"What about you? I don't see a weapon. Mage or melee?" Finley asked. "He's won."

A moment later, Orrin felt a pulse of magic. The grass around Cora's feet grew and tangled her to her ankles. She used a pulse of wind magic to break free, but in the moment it took her to look down, Wilder had crossed the field. Cora panicked and cast three spells at him, each stronger than the last. Wilder dug his feet into the ground and sprinted through the wind. He swung his quarterstaff in a series of quick strikes. Orrin barely saw a hit to the thigh and one to Cora's opposite arm. He heard four distinct smacks, though. Cora was unconscious.

"Winner is Wilder Sigur. Go see Bellamy after you take care of Cora," Galina announced, pointing out her assistant. "Bellamy will be here if I'm not. His word goes if I'm absent. Do not give him a hard time or you'll answer to me."

"She's not kidding," Finlay whispered to Orrin. "Some idiot hit Bellamy a year ago when he told him to calm down. We never saw him again."

Orrin shivered at the implication. Galina could easily break him in two.

Within five minutes, Cora was standing in line with her fist clenching rhythmically.

Wilder had the good sense to position himself at the other end of the lineup.

"Finley, show the class what kind of advice we are looking for. Be as brutal as you want."

Orrin sighed in relief at not being picked.

Finley nodded as if he'd expected to be called on.

"Wilder, your spell took too long to cast and was too weak. You were able to stop Cora for a fraction of a second with that attack. You would have lost if Cora hadn't panicked and fought you on her own terms instead. You need to work on getting your casting time down and the actual effects stronger. If you have to summon a weapon during your fight, you've already lost. Have it ready before you begin next time, okay?" Finley spoke quickly with no judgment in his voice, just a recitation of facts as he saw the fight. Wilder didn't look angry at all at being torn down after winning and nodded along to Finley's criticism.

"Cora, you panicked at the end when Wilder came at you. Your strategy was sound. Wilder is bigger than you and you never engaged him directly. That was smart, especially against someone you've never fought before. You were chipping away at him from a distance, which gave you the best chance to win or run away when he came near you. Your wind spell hit a big area. We could feel it a few times all the way over here. Try finding a way to reduce the target area. If you could aim at Wilder's feet, you could have knocked him off balance and escaped easier. You might have been able to get in for a kill shot. Pick up a weapon next time. Always have a backup for your regular attacks."

Cora also nodded and Orrin saw the anger from her loss fade a tiny bit at having the undefeated champion of the previous semester praise her strategy. He saw why the professor had set up the class this way: the winner would be taken down a peg, focusing on what they could do better the next time. The loser would get a boost from what they did right, with some gentle advice on how to improve.

"I agree," Galina said, dragging a chest out from an open door. Orrin hadn't realized she'd left. "Part of this class will be drills with me or Bellamy. I'll take you aside after a fight and we'll work on basics, if you've never had the training, or I'll fix any mistakes you might be making. Cora, grab a weapon. You and Bellamy can work on finding something good for you. Maybe a spear or javelin, Bellamy? Something she can control midflight if she needs to throw it."

"Yes, ma'am."

"Any volunteers for the next fight? You cannot fight someone who just went, and you can't fight the same person twice in a class unless it's as part of a group."

Orrin watched the fights of the other students as Cora went through the chest of weapons. She settled on a chakram set, throwing the spinning blades with a precision that Orrin was nervous to face in the future, even if they were made out of blunted wood instead of sharpened metal.

"Heads up!"

One of the chakrams hit the ground five feet in front of Wilder, throwing dirt up at the man. His eyes widened.

"Sorry," Cora said with no sympathy in her voice as she retrieved the weapon.

Finley stifled a laugh next to Orrin.

They watched Arlo fight Peregrine next. Arlo's reach with his sword seemed to give him an early advance over Peregrine's shorter frame.

Even when Peregrine rolled away and was able to throw flames, Arlo used a skill that split the magic into two streams and rushed the middle. A burst of light made him turn his eyes away. When he blinked and saw Peregrine's summoned war hammer, he tried to correct his course but was too late. The fiery weapon swept his feet out from underneath him and set a small part of the field on fire. Peregrine won, and while they waited, the other students began to chat. Finley let them discuss the fight among themselves, only giving small feedback here and there. Orrin was impressed with his fighting insight.

After a discussion of Arlo and Peregrine's fight, other students faced off with magic. Leona and Sawyer both fought with summoned wooden weapons, but Leona also combined water magic to wear him down.

Finley requested two opponents. Hugo and Kyon knew each other from the previous semester and volunteered. To Orrin, the fight was astounding. Hugo used ice magic to create weapons in an instant. He hounded Finley with everything from swords to bows. He even made an ice shield that held up well against Finley's counterattacks. Finley used only his wooden daggers from the weapon chest.

Kyon waited at the perimeter, sending directed tremors through the ground to shake Finley's footing. He created puddles of mud for him to slip in, but Finley danced out of the danger zone each time. When Hugo overextended with an ice axe, Kyon twisted his hands and an entire portion of earth, still carrying Hugo, jumped back. Finley narrowly missed Hugo and laughed.

"That was great, Kyon."

The two worked well together, but the way Finley moved was precise and exacting. Every movement was deliberate and allowed Finley to attack in return. He pressed against Hugo, leading him back and forth across the field. After what seemed like forever—but couldn't have been more than a few minutes—Finley began using magic.

The fight was over within twenty seconds.

Finley's dual knives came down on a small buckler of ice. One careened off the slick surface, but the other stuck. Hugo used the opportunity and raised his free hand into the sky, summoning a longsword that he brought down at Finley's exposed side.

Orrin swore he saw Finley frown as he dodged. His hand came up and a small burst of wind, just like he'd described to Cora, knocked Hugo's legs out from behind him. Kyon used his magic to push Hugo and keep him up with the earth beneath him but wasn't able to get a shield up from himself. A second ball of air, so dense Orrin could see it, knocked Kyon out of the ring. Finley held his remaining knife at Hugo's neck.

"Yield?"

"Damn it, we almost had you. You had to use your wind magic, at least." Hugo spat some grass out of his mouth. "Yield."

Nobody in the class had anything to say about the fight, but Galina didn't chastise them. "These three have all taken this class at least once before. If they give you advice, listen to it. Same goes for Eloise. You're up next. Who else hasn't gone?"

Orrin raised his hand. "Casimir Hale."

The lanky woman in gray robes waved to him. "I'm Eloise Maki. Do you need a weapon?"

Orrin considered his options. If he used [Way of the Water], the fight would be easier. He trusted the skill enough to know he'd avoid most hits. He'd fought a dozen people in the caves below Mistlight's castle a week ago, just a few miles from where he stood. But he wanted to keep that a secret as long as he could. He could go with the tried-and-true method of decreasing Eloise's dexterity or strength until she couldn't move, but again, that would send signal flares into the sky. Spells like that weren't common, and the last thing he needed was Lord Sanerris hunting him down in the halls of a school he couldn't leave.

Orrin's [Ward] would stop him from taking too much damage, but playing turtle wasn't an option in this class. He'd need to fight back. His options were limited in the spell department, but he could always try to dazzle with his completely inept sword skills before using [Gust] to knock his opponent out of the ring. It wouldn't work more than once, but he thought he might be able to put enough mana into the spell to push another mage out of bounds.

Orrin used [Ice Sword] and [Fire Sword], bringing a weapon into both hands. He put on a layer of [Ward] and increased his own dexterity. *I'll play the role of wind mage for as long as I can.*

"I'm ready. Let's fight."

Chapter 19

Finley handed Eloise one of his wooden practice daggers. She balanced the blade along one of her long fingers and flipped it over to her other hand. With a nod of satisfaction, she walked to the fighting circle.

"Any advice?" Orrin joked with Finley before he moved into the ring. He needed to connect with him and was regretting not volunteering to fight against him. If he had pushed Finley out of the circle, maybe he'd gain his respect and they'd train together.

"Nope. I hate fighting Ellie."

Orrin joined his opponent on the grass, hoping he'd heard wrong. Finley was the champion of the ring, undefeated last semester. Why would he not like fighting Eloise? If she had magic that countered wind, which was what Finley had used and the main reason Orrin had decided to play up his [Gust] spell as a fake wind mage, he might have made a grave error already. He tried to figure out what would be the worst magic to fight against with wind but simply didn't have the knowledge base to tease out the answer. Trial by fire would be his teacher.

Eloise saluted Orrin with her dagger. He half-heartedly waved his ice sword. The fight began, and Orrin knew he'd already lost.

Eloise disappeared.

This wasn't [Camouflage] disappear. Orrin spent long nights focusing on himself in the mirror while using that spell in an attempt to better understand what it did. Daniel complained it hurt his eyes to look at him while [Camouflage] was running. Sometimes people didn't see him at all. He thought of his spell as an oil slick obscuring him from others' vision. They could see him if they focused, but he was blurry. Eloise wasn't blurry—she was gone.

His own hiding spell was the thing that saved Orrin from an embarrassingly quick defeat. Because some enemies could see through the spell, especially if they noticed any weird movement nearby, Orrin had trained himself to pick his steps carefully while being invisible. If he left a footprint in mud or snapped a twig, [Camouflage] lost most of its power.

Thankfully, the entire fighting circle was scarred with magic attacks, including a bunch of muddy puddles from Kyon's attempts to slow Finley down. Orrin moved into the relaxed position of Formless without realizing it while he studied the ground.

"Did she leave?" Orrin didn't turn to see who had asked the question. It was one of the men, but he had his back to the group.

"No, Arlo. She's a [Stalker]. Once she's invisible, there is no way to see her until she strikes. She doesn't hold back, either." Finley's voice was filled with glee at not being on the receiving end of an unseen dagger strike.

Orrin snapped his head to the left. A partial dent in the mud moved. He pointed his fire sword and threw a quarter of his mana into [Gust].

> **[Gust]—Push the wind toward your target. 1 MP cost minimum. Variable strength cost.**

His attack didn't strike her head-on, but Orrin knew he'd hit her. A flattening of grass showed where she'd rolled away in a hurry.

"That's what I'd do." Cora's voice drifted across the field. Orrin hadn't realized how quiet it was on the pitch, especially without the clang of weapons clashing. "Send attacks out in a pattern. She can't attack him if he keeps her pushed away. That was a huge spell, though. He should have kept the attack smaller."

Finley spoke again. "Interesting that we have so many wind users this year."

Orrin blocked out the chatter and let his vision go wide. He focused on nothing specific, waiting for any movement to snatch his attention.

His [Ward] blocked the first three attacks from her dagger—quick jabs at his kidneys that would have hurt like a bitch but felt like soft pokes from a stick with his magical protection. The dull thud of pressure snapped on the fourth hit, Orrin already swinging behind him. He caught a glimpse of Eloise before she disappeared again.

His swings hit nothing, but he continued to swipe in a crisscross pattern that he'd learned from Daniel's weapon teacher. He turned at random intervals, keeping his back to the sandy out-of-bounds line.

"Impressive constitution to tank four hits. He's going to be sore." Another voice caught his attention. Orrin glanced back to see Hugo standing by Kyon and Finley.

He knew it was a mistake halfway through the turn. He whipped his head back around just as something hit him dead center. Orrin glanced at the tree growing out of his stomach.

"Shit."

Something hard hit his back, ending with a slap against his head. He could only see the sky and couldn't understand what had happened. *I'm on my back?*

His status screen was blinking, and he checked his HP.

HP: 27/140

Damn. That hit like a truck.

Orrin reached a hand to where the pain was. It felt like something was sitting on his chest.

"Get out of the way. Eloise, you've won. Reverse the spell."

Is that a tree growing out of my chest? Orrin touched the wood, tracing the roots that he realized were still growing. They pulsed and dug deeper into his skin.

"It never hits that hard. I don't know why he could shrug off so many attacks but this is the one that takes him down. Bellamy, hold his shoulders down. I'm going to yank it out." Eloise stood over him, talking. Orrin's fingers grabbed a root and pulled, but the pain was exquisite.

HP: 25/140

"Don't touch it. I stopped the attack portion, but I'm going to have to excise the roots from your skin. I'm so, so sorry," Eloise said, wringing her hands. A strand of her hair hung down between her eyes until she blew it out of the way. "This is going to hurt, but Bellamy will keep healing you. Ready?"

She wasn't asking Orrin, because he wasn't ready. He thought he might be concussed. Strong hands pinned his arms to the ground, and Eloise took ahold of the small shoot growing out of his chest.

Orrin screamed and blissfully passed out. When he woke up, healing magic was already moving around inside him. *What?* He let [Mind Bastion] coat his mind in its protective coldness. *At least that stupid skill has stopped auto-activating.* He'd been working on that for months now.

He wrestled the mana away and used [Heal Small Wounds] to close the gap in his chest. Orrin blinked his eyes and saw Bellamy, Eloise, and Finley standing over him.

"Are you awake?" Bellamy asked, holding one hand and taking his pulse.

"Casimir, I'm sorry." Eloise wrung her hands and kept touching his chest as if making sure he was still alive. "I wasn't doing any damage to you and was frustrated. I thought you'd take the hit like you had the others."

Orrin checked his status. He was healed up but still had [Concussion] listed next to his name. He cast [Purify] on himself. He still felt woozy, but the abnormal status disappeared.

"I'm feeling better. I guess I didn't win, huh?"

The snort from Finley pulled Orrin's mouth into a grin. Eloise's attitude changed from terrified and repentant to irritated.

"Of course you didn't win. Are you another battle idiot like Fin? If so, I'll make sure to target your face next time. That way we can grow something between your ears to fill the void that's there right now," Eloise spat. She picked up a bag on the table behind her and stormed out of the room.

Orrin looked around. Finley and Bellamy were trying not to laugh, and an older woman with graying hair sat in the corner, ignoring them all. She had on the long robes with padded shoulders that Hospital [Healers] wore. The room was small, but Orrin guessed they didn't need much room for the Battle Class emergency room.

He tried to sit up, but Bellamy put his hand back on Orrin's shoulder. "You've likely got a concussion, so stay put. Alma was waiting for you to wake up before checking you over."

"I might have to make the lad wait," Alma said, turning in her chair. "I'm running low on mana and can't take another potion. If you don't feel well, Eloise can bring you to . . . Where did that fool girl go?"

Orrin didn't want to cause a scene. "She left after I confirmed I'm fine. No need for any more treatment. I appreciate you patching me up."

Alma waved her hands in the air and went back to reading a scroll on her desk. It was filled with small cubbies of rolled paper and some herbs. Orrin shivered when he noticed the hacksaw hanging near the window.

He checked his shredded shirt. There were no scars left after the healing and aside from the ache behind his eyes that told him he'd have a headache later, Orrin felt fine. He rubbed the back of his head and asked, "Can one of you help me back to class?"

Bellamy rolled his eyes. "He *is* a battle nut. Just like you, Fin. I'll go tell the professor he's alive. Are we still on for drinks tonight?"

"Yeah, I'll see you at eight," Finley said as he clasped the man's hand. "I'll get him to his room. Go on."

Bellamy shook his head and waved to Alma before leaving. Orrin immediately threw his legs off the small cot he was resting on and stood up. His bag was half-open on the table beside him, and he scooped it up.

"Going somewhere?" Finley stood in front of the only door, his arms crossed over his chest.

"Back to my room, I guess. Maybe the library." Orrin wanted to ask if he could go get drinks, too, but felt a weird vibe coming from Finley at the moment. "I have two classes tomorrow and I want to get a good star—"

"What happened in your fight?" Finley cut him off.

Orrin's mind raced. He didn't remember doing anything stupid. "Eloise turned invisible and then grew a fucking tree out of my chest. I think I hit my head when I fell backward and that's all I remember. Wait. I'm supposed to get feedback on how I did. Will that just happen next class or is that why you're still around?"

Finley's face twitched. "You wake up after being nearly killed in your first fight in Battle Class and the first question you ask is *did I win?* The second thing you want to know is what you did right and how you can improve . . ."

Orrin waited. Finley was suspicious, and anything he said was just going to be used against him. *If one of the people I'm supposed to befriend tries to run me out of the school on the first day, Anabella is literally going to kill me.*

Finley lost the battle and began to laugh, a grin splitting his face in two. "You're crazy, Casimir. I like it. Walk with me, I'll show you to the library."

Orrin followed Finley, who told him to call him Fin in the future, through the school. Fin pointed out the good things Orrin had done in his fight against Eloise, namely keeping to the sides and watching for her movement. "She's hard to spot. You either have to get her fast or hope she makes a mistake, but she learns quickly." He also pointed out things he should have done instead. "You used too much wind in one spot. Spread it out in small bursts until the grass doesn't sway behind her, then knock her out. How did you take so many hits?"

Orrin pulled [Ward] up and spun the screen to Finley. "I can negate some damage with this, but that tree spell knocked me back before I could reapply it. I think hitting my head also hurt me pretty bad. I had a concussion."

Finley grabbed Orrin's arm and began marching him back the way they'd come. "If you have a concussion, you need to have Alma take care of you. I've seen too many people never recover from head injuries. It would be a shame for you to die before we get to fight."

Orrin twisted his arm out of Finley's grip, using one of his forms. "I've got some healing spells and already took care of it. Honestly, Fin, I'm fine. Eloise surprised me, but she won't next time." A flash of inspiration hit Orrin. "We can fight anytime. How about tomorrow after classes?"

Finley rolled his eyes but his smile never left. "You are a battle junkie. We can't fight each other outside of Battle Class unless we have a real duel. Galina makes a big deal that there are only two rules, but there's a bunch more. I like your drive, though. What other classes are you taking, if you can tell?"

Orrin counted out his other classes. He had questioned Wren about the one redacted class Finley was taking—some classes were closed off and not supposed to be talked about unless you passed the right prerequisites. Talking about those classes to the wrong person could get you expelled if you were caught.

"Mana Signatures? You're going to hate it. We all do. Professor Wren is amazing, but it's tough. I failed it last year. You must have impressed someone if you got into her class as a novice. I don't think that's happened in . . . I don't know how long."

Orrin had a sudden urge to use an English accent and sneer, ". . . in a century." He resisted. Barely.

They finished walking, and Finley pointed out a set of double doors. "Here's the library. You can read as late as you want, but I suggest getting some sleep. The first week is brutal. The teachers try to prune the weak, and you're already starting off on the wrong side with losing your chit in the first fight. Not that you had a real chance against Eloise, to be honest. I'll see you in the next Battle Class."

As Fin walked away, Orrin felt like shit. He liked the guy. He was rough around the edges, but his heart was in the right place. He'd stuck around to make sure Orrin was okay and spoken to him like a human being instead of another target or obstacle.

He sighed and turned to the Triple S library. Maybe he could find some answers here. He had a plan. Now it was time to see if it was possible.

Chapter 20

Dinner started half an hour after afternoon classes ended. Since Professor Galina had ended the class after the final fight, Orrin had an hour to explore. He didn't have the time for a full investigation, but Orrin wanted to see the library before he began implementing his plan. He pushed through the double doors and looked around.

The library dwarfed the bookstores in Dey. Shelves lined the walls, with more running the length of the long room, making aisles to either side of Orrin. A single long table sat directly in front of the doors, with easily forty chairs on each side. Orrin craned his neck down one of the aisles and saw another table a dozen yards of books away in each direction. A raised desk lorded over the head of the table, where a bored-looking man in his thirties was seated. He didn't look up from the book he was reading, his legs propped up on the side of his desk.

Orrin waited to see if he'd been spotted. When the man scratched his long nose and turned the page in his book, Orrin crept to his right. He began searching aimlessly through the stacks, trying not to be suspicious. A set of stairs at the northern end of the library led to a higher floor. His foot touched the first step. *How many floors does the library cover?*

There was a forced cough behind him. "Students are allowed on the first floor but need a professor's permission to go upstairs."

The man from the front desk stood behind Orrin, still holding his book in one hand and reading. When Orrin hesitated, brown eyes lifted from the page to stare at him. "Do you have a permission slip?"

"I don't. Sorry, I didn't know." Orrin took a step back off the stairs. "I'm Casimir. I wanted to get a head start for my classes. I have Magical History and Surviving Spell Attacks tomorrow. I bought the books but wanted to see if there was anything else I should read to prepare."

The man sighed and slipped a finger up to touch a spot of his book. He glanced at Orrin, bored and uninterested. "Novice classes like those don't require second-floor access. You're snooping. If you want information on a specific topic, you can ask me, but you are wandering the library like you're casing it for a robbery. What are you looking for?"

Orrin wanted a few different things but doubted this librarian was going to help him find most of the topics he needed to investigate. He needed to surreptitiously find books on slaves and collars. Orrin hadn't given up on finding a way to free himself. He knew in his heart that Daniel would find a way to get to him, but if he could escape on his own, his friend wouldn't rub his kidnapping in his face quite as much. If he could figure out a way to attune the collar to himself or someone he trusted, he might have a chance at getting it off. Of course, that would require finding someone he could trust in this crazy country.

I could ask for books on time or space magic, but I bet those kind of things aren't exactly common knowledge or given to anyone. I need to figure out a way to stop Lord Sanerris if he attacks us again, and Daniel's space magic could use a boost. Orrin thought of the possibilities, trying to not fixate on the chance of finding a way home.

He also wanted to study a few odds and ends regarding his own skills. If he could find a book or two that broke down a better way to use [Analyze], he could find a way to drill down more on his own mana-production stats. While Orrin had succeeded in finding a way to display the maximum amount of mana he could run through in a day without killing himself, he knew there was way more. Somehow, Orrin had increased his maximum through exposure to extreme use. If he could use [Analyze] to figure out the formula or experience needed to increase his daily mana expenditure max, he could exploit the knowledge to the extreme. A never-ending river of magic to throw at enemies and monsters.

[Merge] and [Way of the Water] were two skills he definitely needed more information on, as well. How to find books on those skills without alerting anyone that he had them was going to be a trick. The way this librarian appeared behind him confirmed Orrin's fear that students were somehow tracked in here. While Orrin doubted a book on different combinations of magic spells to use [Merge] on was going to be conveniently placed on the first shelf he checked, he was going to keep his eyes open. He was very glad he hadn't grabbed the book *Mordinia's Favorite Fighting Skills* now that he was being interrogated.

Finally, Orrin wanted to find some books on healing. What he'd learned in Dey was different from what the elves said about the field. After feeling Bellamy's healing magic spread over his body, he was beginning to think this world's entire health magic system revolved around throwing as much mana at a problem as they could in the hopes that something fixed itself. It wasn't a terrible idea, but Orrin had some ideas from the not-so-insignificant amount of medical knowledge he'd picked up over the years from his mom.

None of those topics were safe to ask about. If this guy told Graem, Orrin was screwed. He was a [Librarian], so Orrin used his big brain to deduce he probably worked here in the library. Anything he researched using another library helper was going to be reported on.

"I just got my ass handed to me in Battle Class," Orrin started, feeling the kernel of truth morph into the lie he needed. "I wanted to see if there are any wind magic books that could help me get an edge."

"Section C, row eighteen has wind magic books. My name is Harvey. Please come ask before you waste your and my time." With that, Harvey walked off, holding his book in front of his face. Orrin watched him narrowly avoid the table and bookshelves as he made his way back to his desk.

Orrin was careful to stay in section C, row eighteen for the next hour. He read his way down the entire shelf, pulling three books that looked interesting and helpful from their titles. *Introduction to Blowing Away Your Enemies*, *Lift Up to the Sky*, and *Dartanan's Windstorm*. He sat down at the side table, out of sight of Harvey, and started reading through *Dartanan's Windstorm*.

To call this a book was generous, as Orrin counted no more than a hundred pages. The first dozen pages were filled with unconfirmed reports of classes that could gain the spell [Windstorm] or popular ways to unlock it. Unfortunately, Orrin didn't have the requisite spell, [Wind]. He flipped through the pages, but nothing else jumped out. He put it down and started the next book. *Lift Up to the Sky* contained a single sentence on [Gust].

An inferior version of [Wind], the variable cost is not worth the purchase.

Orrin pulled up [Wind] in the spell store.

[Wind]—Push a target with the wind. 5 MP. -3 AP

It took Orrin a minute to figure out the difference, as none of the books so far had said why [Wind] was better. *It can't be that [Wind] pushes a target and [Gust] pushes the wind. Semantics aside, that would be stupid.*

Orrin continued to read another few pages before giving up. He pushed the two books away and started *Introduction to Blowing Away Your Enemies*.

Finally.

The book was also a primer on [Wind] but had two chapters on [Gust] and the best ways to use it. Some of the things mentioned in the book, like increasing the magical vector's prime or focusing the apothem of mana into a cascading return made Orrin's head hurt. He didn't understand the phrases but got the general thrust. [Gust] could be used in attacks and in a lot of interesting ways, but it was so mana-intensive that most mages didn't explore it. [Wind] was better studied, better documented, and all around . . . better.

Not that Orrin cared. He'd bought [Gust] because it was cheap. In his next fight, he was going to equip a [Wind Ward] or [Fire Ward] or whatever ward he needed to dominate. It wasn't that he needed the chit or had to pass the class. Orrin for the first time in his life was strong and had the option to use it. Daniel wasn't here to protect him, and he was going to start using his wards to their full potential.

He snapped the books shut and returned them to their spots on the shelves. He waved at Harvey as he left, despite receiving no acknowledgment in return. His message to Anabella that night was short and to the point.

Lost in Battle Class but made first contact with Finley.

Orrin's second day at school started off low-key. The new students were still skittish, and the older students didn't try to stir the pot too much. He ate breakfast with Ellis, who was talking about his first class. Orrin listened to every other word.

Finley nodded to him as he passed with a tray of food.

"How do you know Finley Madvarr?" Ellis stopped talking about his class to stare. "Who are you, Casimir?"

"What do you mean?" Orrin put another scoop of the porridge in his mouth. On Earth, he'd eaten oatmeal, but the creamy breakfast was quickly becoming his favorite. He pinched a bit more brown sugar in. "We have a class together, that's all."

"Willa Cohee tries to get you on a date right after orientation. You get the acknowledgment of Madvarr," Ellis said, holding up two fingers. "You were shown to your room by Professor Wren before classes started."

Orrin choked on his porridge. He dropped his spoon into his bowl. "Are you spying on me, Ellis?"

The younger boy's eyes darted left then right. He leaned in. "I won't tell. How do you know so many powerful people?"

Orrin picked up his spoon and finished his breakfast. "Professor Wren was the only person awake when I arrived. Me and Madvarr are in Battle Class together, and he helped me after I got my ass kicked yesterday. I don't know or care about Willa Cohee. Does that answer your questions?"

Orrin could tell Ellis didn't fully believe him, but he dropped it. After breakfast, he hurried to his first class of the day, Magical History.

The less Orrin had to say about the class, the better.

Professor Quinn read from the assigned book. After two chapters, he put a bookmark in and walked out of the classroom without ever talking to the students.

Orrin was the only one surprised, as the other students were already up and moving out. The entire class was thirty minutes long.

"This class is a waste of time."

Orrin turned at the door. A woman in her early twenties was talking with a boy about Orrin's age. He was putting his copy of the class book into a bag and following after her.

"It's a prerequisite, Iona. I can't take any of the . . . Can I help you?" the man stopped talking to his friend and stared pointedly at Orrin, still blocking the doorway.

"Sorry," Orrin apologized, moving to the side. "I'm glad to hear I'm not the only one who thought that was a weird class. I'm Casimir. Nice to meet you."

The woman slid in front and crossed her arms. "My name is Iona. It was nice to meet you, Casimir, now leave."

"Iona, don't be rude," the man said, exasperated. "I apologize for Iona. She takes her job of protecting me too seriously. I'm Rhys. Are you also a novice? This class might be dreadful, but I'm told it unlocks many other classes we can take."

Orrin pushed his joy down, trying not to smile. Two for two. He'd already made contact with two of his targets already. How lucky was he? "Yeah, it's my first semester. No apology needed. Nice to meet you both."

Iona glared at him. If she was from Earth, Orrin would have pegged her as Indian, with her hair pulled back into a tight braid and winged makeup along her eyes. She hovered over Orrin like she'd attack if he tried to move in too close.

Rhys was not what Orrin had expected. When Anabella had described him, she'd given the impression of a weak boy kept prisoner by his mother. Rhys wasn't tall, but he was solid. His loose outfit couldn't hide the muscles rippling underneath, and his bright white smile stood out against his dark skin. Rhys's friendly demeanor and total confidence in talking with him made Orrin second-guess his plans for approaching this target. He needed to get away and rethink his strategy.

"We were going to go get some lunch around the corner, Casimir," Rhys called out as Orrin tried to make a quick escape. "Would you like to come with us?"

Orrin cursed. He wasn't sure how much leeway the collar gave him, but he wasn't going to test it out on the first full day of classes. He needed to find Graem and get a clear answer on how far from the school he could go.

"That would be amazing, but I have to meet a friend," Orrin answered and said a silent thanks to Ellis for making plans already. "How about after the next class?"

"It's a date." Rhys smiled. He had a really handsome smile.

Orrin beat a hasty retreat to the cafeteria.

Chapter 21

Orrin skipped lunch and searched for Graem. He tried Wren's room, but the door was locked. Orrin made his way to the library. Harvey the librarian still sat with his legs up, this time reading a different book. He shrugged at Orrin's question of how to get in touch with the professor.

Just as Orrin was about to give up and make his way to his next class, he turned a corner and saw the man approaching. He held two massive books under one arm and balanced another four stacked precariously in his other hand.

"Professor Graem, do you have a minute?" Orrin waved his hand.

Graem sighed and shook his head. "Go away. I don't have time for whatever it is you want."

Orrin trotted alongside him anyway. He needed answers.

"How far away from the campus can I safely go? I might need to go out into the city to socialize."

"I don't know or care. Figure it out." Graem's arm balancing the books swayed, but he kept them from toppling. "Now leave me alone or I'll have you expelled."

"If I send a letter saying how unhelpful you are to Anabella, what do you think would happen?"

Graem slowed to a stop.

Orrin wasn't stupid. He knew threatening the man was a massive risk, but while Graem knew some of what was going on, Orrin felt the man still had a healthy fear of the former leader of Mistlight. She scared the shit out of Orrin, and he barely knew anything about her.

Orrin's suspicion since their first meeting, that Graem wanted to pawn him off and stay far away from whatever was going on, grew. It made sense: plausible deniability that he was involved if everything went sideways. However, Orrin didn't give a shit. If they were going to play with his life and put him in danger, he was going to start demanding some answers.

"You're not sending any letters. You've been going to class." Graem's words were slow as if he was trying to convince himself. "Do you realize who you—"

"As of this morning, she told me that I was doing a great job so far," Orrin lied smoothly. Anabella's morning response to his nightly message had been two words long.

Work faster

"Hold these," Graem said, pushing the stack of books into Orrin's hands. As Orrin fumbled them against his chest, the professor reached out and tapped the back of Orrin's neck. "How far afield do you need to go? I would suggest staying away from the main defenses, any barracks, or the town square. Some people saw an uglier version of you die there recently."

Orrin pulled up his [Map] and zoomed out. The school was a few miles from Sanerris's house. He weighed the options of pushing Graem and making the entirety of Mistlight available to peruse, but the risk outweighed the benefits. He studied the man.

Gone was the drunk imbecile from before. As he adjusted something inside Orrin's collar, the concentration on his face was the same look Orrin's mom had when she was going over a particularly difficult patient's file. The stench of liquor was absent, and Graem was dressed like an actual respectable professor. The books in his hands had no labels on the spine, which Orrin was learning meant they were rare. He was doing his job and yet, here he was doing Orrin's bidding in an empty hallway near the library.

"Make it within walking distance. Maybe two miles or so? I don't need to go far," Orrin said, watching Graem nod in acceptance. "I'm going to need access to the second floor of the library as well."

Orrin held his breath.

"Two miles is fine, but you don't need access to the second floor. That's restricted to accepted students only. You don't have clearance."

"I'll have Anabella send a letter to you," Orrin said with a shrug. "I'm sure she'll love wasting her time."

Graem smirked as he snapped his fingers. The collar stung for a second, but the oppressive feeling of confinement that Orrin hadn't even realized was there lifted like the sun beating down after a cloud rolled away. "Go ahead. If you're actually in contact with her, let her know that I'd be delighted to give you free run of my entire collection if that is what *she* desires," Graem said, emphasizing the word. "You are playing a dangerous game with me, Casimir."

Orrin pushed the books back into the professor's arms. "It's all a dangerous game with me. My favorite part is I don't even know the rules."

Orrin left Professor Graem in the hall and ran to his next class.

He snuck into the back of the room just as Surviving Spell Attacks began. Orrin found a seat at the top of the auditorium-style classroom and sat. Roughly half of the forty students were sitting close to the front, with the rest spread across the back side of the room. In Orrin's experience in high school, the ones who sat near the front were the ass kissers or nerds who wanted to learn.

Of course, this was a magic class . . . Orrin wished he'd gotten here earlier to sit up front.

A door to the professor's office—and likely bedroom—sat to the left of the huge chalkboard. Orrin tried reading the multiple equations along the board and was excited to see a few that he recognized. He missed when the professor walked into the room, but when a deep, bestial voice growled and cleared its throat, Orrin almost cast [Ward].

Professor Hugh stood behind a lectern with the class textbook opened. He tried turning the pages, but his fingers were too big for the dainty book. Orrin could see frustration mounting in the narrowed eyes behind wide-rimmed glasses. The loud smack of the book being thrown against the wall quieted the last few hushed conversations going on in the room.

"Stupid book is useless anyway," the orc rumbled.

Professor Hugh was an orc. Orrin had seen a few around Dey, but they kept their distance and didn't interact much with other races. Madi's explanation was that they were scared that people might try to enslave them again. Orcs had been used as slave labor for centuries, with the mass liberation of their kind being a recent development. Especially here, in Odrana, where they'd been used as workhorses forever.

"My name is Professor Hugh." The orc started talking, moving from behind the small desk and nearly knocking it over. "This is my first class as a professor. Survive Attacks is important. There is math. There is thinking. Most important, there is pain. You must appreciate failure. I will administer tests each week. If you fail, you will be in pain. Pain motivates you to learn better than the hunger for power. Pay attention or don't. This week we will discuss the basics."

Orrin caught a glimpse of Rhys and Iona sitting near the front. She was whispering in his ear.

"I'm not going to learn magic from an orc," a prissy voice near Orrin spat. "The standards have dropped in Mistlight."

Professor Hugh laughed and pointed at the tall woman who had half stood to leave. A bolt of energy lifted her into the air and launched her bodily through the double doors at the back of the room. Nobody moved.

The orc slapped his hands together. "I am an orc. This is indisputable. I am proud to be an orc. This too is indisputable. If you wish to leave this class, you may. The school will reimburse you. However, if you plan to survive in the world, or if you plan to advance into the higher magics taught here, you will sit down and kindly not insult me. That will be my only warning."

Orrin could see the unconscious body of the woman through the still-swinging doors. She'd hit the ground and slid into the stone wall, which had probably saved her life, given the speed she was moving. A quick check on her status showed she was alive, but none of her friends moved to help her.

"We will begin with the formula that calculates the damage a spell can do based on your statistics. After that, we will discuss will and the role it plays in our mana pool. If you turn to the board here, you'll see . . ."

Orrin scratched notes as he watched the seven-and-a-half-foot-tall green man with arms thicker than Orrin's waist daintily draw charts and point to equations as he explained will, intelligence, and constitution. Orrin had figured out some of this on his own, but hearing the accepted explanations of this world smoothed out some edges.

For example, constitution played a large part in how much a spell could affect another person. Orrin knew this in theory from the time he'd spent the same mana healing a dwarf that he'd previously used on multiple humans. Professor Hugh explained the formulas for attacks against one another and the different factors that could change the outcome of a fight.

Someone in the front row raised their hand. Orrin could see the man's hand shaking.

"Hmm. A question?"

"Professor Hugh, you said that a higher constitution could override the deficits of a lower will, but I don't understand what that means. Wouldn't it be better to increase your will to increase the power of an attack?"

"Name?" Hugh crossed his arms but snapped the chalk he was holding as he did. He brushed white powder off his arm and picked another piece off the board.

"Hazel Jesup, sir."

"That's a good question, Jesup. Let's run a scenario. You have ten ability points to distribute. Your constitution, intelligence, and will are all at ten. How would you build out?"

Orrin sketched out the points on his paper and noticed a gaping hole in this question. If he was going to use a spell like [Lightstrike] that did a base set of damage, putting everything into will would make the most sense. He'd have a larger mana pool and could spam the casting of the attack more times. He had to remember that these magic users likely didn't have [Meditate] and therefore couldn't regenerate their spells each day.

However, if he was going to use a regular spell attack with a variable cost, like most of the regular mage builds had . . .

"I would keep my intelligence and will even, likely spending four points to each, to maximize the cost decrease from intelligence and the base damage output from will. The extra two points, I'd put in constitution to make myself harder to kill."

Orrin nodded. He'd only briefly paged through the Surviving Spell Attacks book last night, but it recommended the same slow but mostly even build of will and intelligence with constitution taking a back seat that he'd heard before. Tony had recommended it. Madi had recommended it. Orrin looked at his lopsided stats and grinned. *I'm terrible at taking advice.*

"That is the generally accepted route. What if we both have the same stats? Who would win in a fight?" Professor Hugh asked.

Orrin had had teachers like this before. Instead of teaching, they asked leading questions to make the student find the answer on their own. He hated it.

"Unless only one side had a mana potion or got lucky with a critical hit, they would likely run out of mana at the same time and exhaust themselves," Hazel answered. Orrin could see why the guy sat up front. He was smart but wanted to understand some small nuance of what the professor had said. Something that Orrin hadn't even caught or written down.

"If I put five points into constitution and the other five into whatever else, it doesn't matter what," Professor Hugh said while writing numbers on the board, "and instead of casting five [Firebolts] at the normal cost, I'd spend my entire pool on one or two shots."

Orrin looked at the equation for how much constitution could negate damage from an incoming attack. He'd thought constitution only equated to health points, but what Hugh was writing showed an impressive curve up. The more points someone put into constitution, the less damage an attack did in the first place. It wasn't much at fifteen, as Hugh's current scenario posited, but Orrin scratched a few equations out.

This wasn't math class with dumb questions about how many watermelons a soccer mom needed to buy to feed three hundred kids. This was min-maxing. This was finding ways to break the game.

"You wouldn't kill him, but he'd be a lot lower in health than you—" Hazel hesitated. "I think."

"You're right. The numbers only get better. You do need to keep in mind the mass that constitution increases on you. Eventually, a higher constitution base requires more strength to hold the body up, as well as more dexterity to keep the body moving in the first place, but it's an interesting mind exercise and shows why class scholars still debate the perfect loadout for classes. We're not even taking into account the damage to your own body you could do by pushing too much mana into one attack. A higher constitution could let you survive casting a spell larger than anyone else could. Keep that in mind as we move forward. You'll never know exactly who or what you are up against. The danger is always there. My job is to give you as many tools as I can . . . as much knowledge as I can . . . so that when you encounter something different, you don't die because you did something stupid."

Orrin realized the entire class was sitting forward, paying attention. He'd thought this was going to be a dumb class, but now . . . Orrin was excited to learn more.

Chapter 22

Orrin's mind raced as he sat through Surviving Spell Attacks. There was so much to unpack. Professor Hugh had taught him more in two hours than he'd learned since arriving here.

Beyond the basic formulas that Orrin already knew, Professor Hugh wrote multiple equations with different variables for them to study on his board. Equations for knowing exactly how much mana you needed to increase a variable spell to do a specific amount of damage. Each separate type of magic interacted differently against other types, so knowing if a [Fireball] spell was targeting a [Water Mage] or a [Wood Mage] was crucial. It was the difference between doing almost no damage and killing someone outright.

On top of that, a target's constitution made the math even messier. A higher base constitution gave a person more health points but also could bolster natural defenses against a contradictory magic type.

Orrin's thoughts ran deeper than just damage. *If I use [Identify] on a person and know their constitution, I can use those equations to figure out exactly how much mana I need to use to heal them.* He was almost out of class when he thought of [Analyze] as well.

[Analyze] was a mostly obsolete skill, according to most books and class builds that Orrin had read. However, Tony had made him get it long ago. The skill would tell Orrin what an object was in the most basic form. If he tried it on a cup, he'd be able to read "cup." The more he worked on the same object, the more descriptive it could become. The more he learned about the cup from outside sources, the more detailed the data would become. It could also be used on more than just people, including spells, status changes, and even the length of a person's foot.

Orrin had been bored one night. He measured a lot of stuff with [Analyze].

It was also how he'd built the little subskill indicator that told him how much mana he could blood cycle in a day before he died.

Orrin's combination of [Mind Bastion], [Blood Mana], [Meditate], and [Heal Small Wounds] gave him limitless mana. He could use his already-regenerating mana until it was nearly gone, use [Blood Mana] to sacrifice his health for more mana, and then cure himself using the same newly acquired mana while coming out net positive. The only drawback was once he turned off [Mind Bastion], he'd die.

He'd gotten lucky the first few times and drawn enough to get violently sick. Tony, a mage in Dey, had saved his life. He'd cautioned Orrin against overextending himself again, and Orrin was slowly learning.

But now . . . Orrin thought, writing down as much as he could. Professor Hugh was going on about how using this information against monsters was easy but harder against other people. Since monsters' stats were well-known and mostly static, a little research before a fight was invaluable.

Orrin really liked this teacher.

[Identify] would let Orrin find out the name of any monster he encountered, but with his upgraded version, he could also read most people's constitutions.

If I combined the two . . .

Orrin's thoughts were interrupted by the whispers around him. His fellow students were arguing among themselves, so much that the professor had to put down the chalk. He turned and stood silently, waiting for the loudest fights to simmer.

"I believe you have questions?"

Orrin noticed Rhys shake his head at Iona. An older man sitting on the opposite side of the room from Orrin stood up.

"Professor, you are advocating for a balanced approach to stat building with a constitution focus. Multiple texts on class leveling dispute the method. The Sanerris family disputes the method. What use do any of us have for more constitution when increasing my will would make my [Icebolt] do more damage? This class is supposed to be teaching us how to survive spell attacks and recognize basic threats, not tell us our planned routes to greatness are wrong." The man's robes moved as he waved his arms, getting more excited as his voice increased in volume the longer he spoke.

A few students nodded.

"I am teaching you the math, not advocating," Professor Hugh growled, crossing his arms again. "At this point in your life, you would be a fool to make changes from one class lecture. If you want to only know the basics, read the textbook. It has all the information you will need for the tests. If you want to learn to survive and be able to succeed in any situation, shut up and listen. Does anybody else have a comment?"

Professor Hugh's gaze landed on Orrin. A few students turned to look when he didn't turn or talk.

Orrin looked at his raised hand in terror. He'd had a question but didn't remember putting his hand in the air.

"Go ahead."

"What happens in the fourth equation when there is an equally high constitution between the target and you?" Orrin finally got the words out by reading the question he'd written down.

Professor Hugh's smile made two students scoot their chairs back from the front in alarm. Too many teeth. But then he started explaining, and Orrin sighed in relief. He wrote down the answer and put his offending hand in his pocket so it wouldn't try to ask any more questions.

Rhys sought him after class, and they made plans for lunch after their next history class. He wanted to bring Orrin somewhere fancy but relented to pick something local when Orrin objected to traveling too far from the schoolgrounds. Orrin ate dinner with a quiet Ellis and then ran back to the library.

His second night researching was another bust. He made his way back to his room and recapped his day in the Twin Book of Sending for Anabella. He also requested access to the second floor of the library again. He reasoned that Maeve had multiple years under her belt at the school and Orrin might need to impress her.

His eyes were closed before his head hit the pillow.

In the morning, he found Anabella had denied his request. She just told him again to work faster.

Orrin's first class of the day was Defensive Earth Magic. His table mate at the cafeteria was still just Ellis, although Luca would occasionally wave at them as he devoured multiple trays of food at another table. So, it was a surprise when Rhys and Iona sat down, making Ellis jump.

"Mind if we sit here?" Rhys asked with a smile, completely sure he would be welcomed. "My name is Rhys, and this is Iona. We have a few classes with Casimir. What's your name?"

"I—I'm . . ." Ellis floundered.

"This is Ellis," Orrin answered for him, holding his cup of coffee close. "His dorm is near mine."

"Well met, Ellis." Rhys smiled, those dazzling teeth disarming the poor boy. "What classes do you have today, Casimir?"

Alarm bells rang in Orrin's head for a moment. Rhys was too friendly. People didn't act like this unless they wanted something from you, and then you usually ended up in a trash can.

"Are you looking for someone?" Rhys asked, craning his neck around.

Orrin hadn't noticed he was trying to find Daniel. He'd always saved him from these situations at school.

Get a grip, Orrin, he chided himself. He hesitated between casting [Calm Mind] and [Mind Bastion]. In the end, he cast neither. *I need to get better at talking to these people. That's the entire reason I'm here.*

"Sorry, I thought I saw someone I know," Orrin lied and took a moment to sip his coffee again and think. "I've got an earth magic class this morning then Mana Signatures this afternoon."

Ellis dropped his fork. Iona stared.

"Mana Signatures as a novice?" Rhys raised an eyebrow. "That's . . . impressive."

Orrin heard the question Rhys wanted to ask but didn't voice. Instead of answering, he asked his own question. "What about you two?"

Rhys took a bite from his plate of food and nodded at Iona. She rolled her eyes but answered. "Our first class is Sensing Magic. He has Offensive Metal Magic this afternoon as well."

"Are you both [Metal Mages], then?" Orrin asked, curious. It was one of the last types of magic he hadn't bought a spell for. It cost too much to be properly useful to him, even though he'd seen one of the Dragoons use metal magic to destroy monsters.

"Mine is something like that," Rhys answered with a smile. "Iona has a different class, but she's being allowed to accompany me, even though she doesn't have all the requirements."

Orrin read between the lines. Rhys had a powerful class that he wasn't about to advertise, and Iona, his bodyguard, likewise wasn't going to tell her class to the new kid they'd just met. He could always cast [Identify], a spell he was learning was criminally underutilized by anyone but guards. Of course, Madi had warned him that it was impossible to know beforehand if someone had a skill that let them know they were being scanned. It wasn't worth the risk.

They exchanged more pleasantries, with Orrin drawing Ellis into the conversation. They parted ways, heading down different halls to their classes.

Orrin found his class on the ground floor. Two large doors were open on the far side of the classroom, opening to the center courtyard. Cairns of stone had been built, with more piles of rubble stacked up against the inner wall. An older professor was moving all the chairs and desks to the side of the room. Orrin helped, along with three other students who were a bit early. By the time the class filled out with all eight students, the classroom was a wide-open space leading to the outside.

Orrin spotted Maeve when she entered a few minutes after him. Her brown hair was parted in the middle and pulled back into a tight ponytail. Her eyes darted from corner to corner, noting everything before focusing solely on the professor. She wore a flowy yellow shirt with sleeves that hid her arms and a pair of rough canvas pants that were slightly too long for her.

She was also barefoot.

"I think this is everyone," the old man said, clapping his hands. His brown robe had a belt made out of rocks doing its best to hold together around a portly middle. His wispy hair would have been gray, but Orrin saw streaks of what he hoped was mud throughout his beard and on his head. "I'm Professor Cade. I hope you have all read chapter one. Please pair up and discuss it. In twenty minutes, you will attempt to block or evade an earth attack from your counterpart, so choose well."

Orrin kept his eyes forward for a moment too long on purpose. He tried to look confused when he turned as well, giving the other students time to pair up.

His report on Maeve was the most comprehensive of the three. She'd been a student at the Sanerris School for years. The notes about her physical description were accurate enough. The other students quickly paired off, leaving Orrin and Maeve as the last two to choose.

I guess the part about her being a bit of a social pariah is also true. Orrin smiled and waved her over. "I'm Casimir. What did you think about chapter one?"

The first chapter of Professor Cade's book, titled *Earth and You*, was a simple introduction to earth magic. It regaled the reader with how strong an [Earth Mage] could be with the proper training, becoming both the perfect offensive and defensive spellcaster. In other words, it was propaganda. Orrin had flipped through the next few chapters as well and noticed most of the book was about how much better earth magic was than any other type.

"It was droll, but since Cade wrote it, I guess I should say it was fascinating," Maeve answered but refused to look in Orrin's direction. She stepped by him and walked out the doors to the cairns. "Do you think he wants us to throw these at each other? What could we learn from that? A simple [Earthshield] would stop any form of thrown earth or stone attack. Perhaps he wants us to use different spells?"

She completely ignored him as she spoke. Orrin checked, but the rest of the students were talking with their backs to Maeve. Even the professor was doing his best to look busy and talk with other groups.

Orrin stepped out the door as well and hefted one of the stones from the top. "It is called Defensive Earth Magic. I bet we have to throw the stones at each other and test what the best defensive spell is. I'm sure he's got a favorite one, but . . . What was that for?"

Maeve had grabbed a stone from the pile and thrown it at Orrin. He hadn't been paying close enough attention, and she'd beaned him in the side.

"You didn't try to defend. Try again, but this time I'll throw harder." Maeve set up to pitch another stone, and Orrin felt the mana coalesce around her hand.

Chapter 23

"Hold on! Wait," Orrin yelled, crouching behind another stack of rocks. He waved a hand at Maeve. "We aren't supposed to do that yet. I didn't even get to talk about the first chapter."

Maeve lowered her stone, the magic fading from her fist. Orrin took this as a good sign and stepped out into the open again.

The other students were talking among themselves, but Orrin noticed the glances. Every person here knew who Maeve was, and they'd all paired up quickly. They were avoiding her.

Orrin felt equal parts anger and sadness. This is what it had been like for him at school when Daniel wasn't around. Maybe not as bad as this, but similar enough. People didn't actively avoid him, but Orrin thought he knew how Maeve had to feel. Unlike him, Maeve didn't have someone.

Fuck you, Anabella. I'm not going to use this woman for her friendship.

"Did you want to discuss something in particular? The first chapter was just Cade's analysis of why earth magic is best. His theory is well meaning but misses the point." Maeve gently placed the rock back on the top of the pile. "Earth magic isn't the best because it offers good offensive and defensive options. It's more than just fighting magic."

Orrin agreed that the first chapter of Professor Cade's book read like a child trying to argue his toy was the shiniest of all. The man's attempt at putting together a coherent argument boiled down to *my magic can beat your magic*. Maeve's last sentence gave him an idea for not getting his brains bashed in and for connecting a bit more with her.

"He's got a point about it being good for fighting, but the only earth magic spell I have is [Tilth]." Orrin moved fully away from the rocks and pointed to one of the small table-and-chair sets arranged next to the open doors. Orrin assumed they were there for later classes, so everyone would be comfortable watching each other beat each other up with rocks. He shivered. "I mean, I do have another spell that blocks earth magic, too. What would you say is the best spell?"

Maeve looked at Orrin directly for the first time. As their eyes met, hers widened before she turned away. She sat in one of the chairs. "Best spell for what? Widespread destruction or pinpoint accuracy? Offensive or defensive?"

Orrin thought back to Maeve's file and the few things Anabella had told him about his target. He sat down next to her. "It doesn't have to be anything about fighting. I'm not planning on using earth magic like that. I have to take this class to get into more of Professor Cade's higher-level earth magic classes. What about you? What other classes are you taking?"

Maeve's hand found a loose string on her sleeve. She pulled a small wooden wand no bigger than a pencil from behind her ear. She squeezed the wand with two fingers, running her hand down the length. It transformed into a knife. Maeve folded the string over the blade and pulled, cutting the thread away. She rolled the wand in her hands and returned it, back to normal, behind her ear. "I'm taking only two classes this semester, this and Rapid Agriculture. It was yesterday. Did you know that there is a spell unlocked by a [Berrymancer] that can create almost any Odrana wine vintage? You have to be level thirty-five before it unlocks, but the professor said most of our current supply isn't actually grown by hand anymore."

Orrin smiled. Jackpot. "That's pretty cool. Is that what you're into? Using magic to enhance food? I have a friend who makes coffee, but I don't think he uses magic for that. Maybe his dad does, now that I think about it. It's his shop. My friend's dad, I mean."

Maeve pushed her feet into the grass beneath the table, digging some of the dirt up. "It's fascinating but not my particular area of expertise. I need one of the professors to accept me as a thesis student before I can get access to some books I want to read. If my theory is correct, I might . . . No. My dad says I shouldn't get my hopes up or tell people about what I want to try. Sorry. It has to do with growing things, but Professor Juniper doesn't like me after I told him that his [Growth] spell was weak. If he'd just get out of his own head, he'd see that the . . . I'm doing it again. Sorry. My dad says I talk too much sometimes when I get excited about something. Basically, Professor Cade is my last chance to get an earth magic adviser."

Orrin shrugged. "Don't apologize. I know next to nothing about earth magic beyond my one spell, so anything you tell me is new and exciting. How do you convince that old fart to be your adviser?"

Maeve giggled. Orrin had met a few kids who were homeschooled when he and Daniel entered high school. A bunch of parents were running a homeschool program that was shut down for illegally using state money for something or another, and the kids were enrolled last minute at their high school. Most of them integrated with only a few hiccups. But a few of them reminded Orrin of Maeve. She didn't have a filter, either. Something that probably kept her from gaining friends. Friends who could point out the social cues and rules you could only learn from being bullied and fighting back in public school.

"If I pass this class, he'll give me a meeting. If he doesn't like my idea, then I'll have to find another way. I'm sure I can find the information I need somewhere else, but the problem is the Sanerris library has some of the rarest and oldest books in Asmea. Oh, Cade is coming over."

Orrin saw the professor heading their way, too. He made a quick decision and waited until Cade was within earshot. "What you said about the first chapter makes a lot more sense. I didn't really understand it until you put it like that. Thanks, Maeve."

"What?" Maeve tilted her head to the side, confused.

"Hi, Professor Cade." Orrin tried to act surprised as the man rolled by. "Maeve just convinced me I need to focus more of my spells in earth magic. She made some good points. I'm going to have to reread that first chapter."

"I've heard good things about Maeve's magical prowess, so it's not surprising to hear. She does take after her mother," Cade said with a gentle smile. He turned back to the open doors and bellowed into the room, "Everyone outside for our first demonstrations."

Orrin turned back in his chair and smiled at Maeve. An odd look was plastered on her face. "Are you okay?"

"You made up a story. Why?"

"I was trying to make you look good in front of him. Teachers love it when you make them feel smart. Plus, I didn't make up a story. You really did help me understand his book a bit better. You made some good points, too, just not about what I implied to him," Orrin explained. "He should be your mentor and let you read those books. I'll help."

"Why?"

"We're partners. I don't know many people here at school. Why wouldn't I help?"

Maeve didn't push again. They stood and joined the class spreading out in the field. Orrin could see other classes working outside—flashes of fire on one end and something that shimmered in the air at the other. *Was that water or air magic?*

Cade split the groups, directing one person to throw rocks at another with a gentle underarm toss. The point wasn't to harm the person but to test what kind of spells they could use for defensive purposes. He explained that unenchanted earth was the easiest thing for earth magic to defend against and directed them to begin.

Orrin was first up and threw the rock short the first few times, trying to get the distance correct. When one rock finally appeared to be on track, he sighed in relief. His aim was on target and would hit Maeve's leg if she didn't block it.

Around them, the other students defended themselves with various levels of success. A small wall formed out of the ground in front of two different students, while another waved her hand to make dirt jump from the ground like fish.

Maeve gestured, and the stone rocketed back at Orrin. He narrowly dodged the missile that shattered against the stone wall behind him.

"What was that? You almost hit me!" Orrin yelled from the ground. He'd thrown himself to the side and landed hard on his knee.

"I'm sorry," Maeve muttered, looking off in the distance.

Orrin brushed his legs and stood up just as Cade ordered them to switch sides.

Orrin groaned.

Orrin left the infirmary after class and quickly made his way to the cafeteria for lunch. He could have healed himself, but a few other students had been bruised as well. He figured being part of the group was better than standing out.

He was the only one who had an injury worse than a few scrapes, though. One of Maeve's throws had broken Orrin's pinkie and ring finger on his right hand. He'd used [Earth Ward] to protect himself and made a mistake.

> **[Earth Ward]—Create a ward around yourself and your party within 50 feet that protects against earth magic for MP maximum. 20 MP.**

A thrown rock wasn't earth magic. He'd used a regular [Ward] after that first throw, cradling his hand until Cade dismissed them.

Ellis waved as Orrin entered the room. He grabbed some more food and made his way to the table.

"Hey, Ellis. How are your classes going?" Orrin asked, sitting down.

"All my regular classes are fine," the young man answered, moving his fork around the half-devoured fish on his plate. "Have you heard the news, Casimir?"

Orrin put a bite in his mouth and chewed. He'd thought he'd gotten chicken, but it was fried fish. He swallowed before answering. "I don't think so. What's up?"

Ellis leaned forward and beckoned Orrin in. His curiosity piqued, Orrin glanced around and noticed many close and whispered conversations were happening all over the cafeteria.

"A [Hero] pushed back two regiments of the army and Lord Sanerris was forced to pull back from the border. The elves helped and might invade Odrana."

Orrin felt his stomach drop to his feet. He pushed his plate away. "When? Did anyone get hurt?"

Ellis was a ball of nervous energy. "Two days ago. We're only getting the information now because Lord Sanerris left the city to help the fight. The [Hero] got away but both sides had a few casualties. Not Lord Sanerris, of course. He's already back in the city and calling for the other lords to send more troops. My benefactor fought for me to stay here. I got a dispensation and won't be drafted into the fight, but if the elves try to push too far east into our lands, I'll do my part and join up."

Orrin didn't respond, filtering out the obvious propaganda. Daniel had attacked Odrana and won. He didn't know if he was relieved or scared for his friend. He checked his Quest, but the Stop the War Quest was still active. Ellis kept talking, but Orrin wasn't listening.

". . . I'm sure you'll be fine, Casimir. Only two or three people are being drafted or leaving school to fight. I doubt you'll have to go." Ellis placed his hand on Orrin's but quickly pulled back with a blush.

Orrin doubted Anabella would allow him to be drafted. He wasn't worried about that. "Who got drafted?"

"A girl in my class broke down in tears when she got a letter. Deanne, I think. And another novice that I don't have classes with," Ellis counted on his fingers. "Oh, and Finley Madvarr, of course. He's the one who volunteered. He left this morning."

Chapter 24

Orrin tried to not run as he made his way back to his room. He locked the door and pulled out the secret message book that Anabella had given him. Pulling out the stylus, he scratched a message.

Emergency. Finley left school. Daniel pushed your son's army back to the border and Arvin's throwing a hissy fit. People are getting drafted.

Orrin sat on the edge of his small bed, willing Anabella to write back. It wasn't the right time, but she had to know. He needed to know what to do.

He went over his options for the hundredth time. Orrin wasn't dumb enough to try and run with the collar on. He needed it off before he could escape. His hopes of finding some way to do that had hinged on the library, but each late night so far had been a bust. He'd spent hours poring over any book that might have a chance at containing that kind of information. The last message's request to get into the second floor was a desperate attempt in what Orrin was beginning to think was a hopeless quest.

If I can't get the collar off, I can try to contact Daniel. He'd already written three letters and dropped them off in different mail-collector boxes around town. He didn't know if he was being watched. He didn't know how long it would take for mail to reach Lord Catanzano in Dey. He didn't even know if Silas would read the letter.

Each one was the same: *I'm alive at school. —O.*

Orrin cast [Calm Mind] on himself when his hands started to shake. There were another twenty minutes before his next class, but Orrin considered lying down and taking a nap. He couldn't remember the last time he'd slept a full night. His next class, Mana Signatures, was supposed to be a second chance to connect with Finley. There was no reason for him to go if his target was out hunting his friends.

He reopened the book to the same message, laughing at him. He slammed the book shut and shoved it back into [Dimension Hole].

I will find a way out. He worried he was lying to himself.

Daniel and Madi were probably fighting along the border of Odrana right now. Ellis's report had mentioned elves fighting with them. Orrin wondered how Daniel had convinced them to leave the forest.

Orrin let himself wallow for five minutes and then gathered his things. "If you trap me here, I'll get as strong as I can. Don't underestimate me."

"Mana Signatures will be a lot like Sensing Magic but with more practical application," Professor Wren announced as she entered the room, pushing a cart loaded with blocks of colored metal. The six students, including Orrin, quieted immediately. "Kieran, be a dear and grab the other cart right outside the door."

The guy sitting near Orrin jumped up and disappeared out the door. He was the only one who'd introduced himself to Orrin when he entered the room. The rest of the class knew each other from the prerequisite course they'd all finished a few weeks before, but Kieran was a repeat student—he hadn't passed Mana Signatures the last time he'd taken it.

Kieran struggled to push the other cart in. It held a diverse array of objects. A glass bottle with something green floating in the middle. A blackened claw suspended in an open container of clear liquid that bubbled. A small bonsai tree. A solid metal box with no holes or clasps.

Kieran was short but stout. Orrin had heard one of the other students call him *the dwarf*. He'd met an actual dwarf. Kieran was human. He wasn't a little person, either. Just a shorter man. The cart placed, Kieran rubbed the top of his close-shaved head and made his way back to his seat. A half dozen small desks were set up in a semicircle. He sat back down next to Orrin.

"What is all that?" Orrin whispered as Wren began moving objects off the carts. She placed them one after another down the long table that ran the length of her room.

"Same as she used for the last class," Kieran muttered back. "Magical items charged with different types of mana. I'm just glad she didn't try to bring in live animals again. She made me clean up the droppings last time."

Orrin shook his head as Professor Wren took to her lectern.

"If you are here, you can see the flow of magic. Congratulations. You are already better than nine out of ten idiots in the world. This class is about doing more than seeing. It's about understanding. Each of you was able to pinpoint a flavor of magic in our last class." Wren stopped and smirked at Orrin. "That won't be enough in this class. You will learn to recognize every type of magic I can throw at you. You will learn to manipulate those you are proficient in. You will never speak of the things you learn here outside this classroom, or I will hunt you down myself. Are we understood?"

Orrin was a moment delayed on the quick "Yes, Professor Wren" that the other students recited in harmony. He could feel Kieran hold his breath next to him.

"Casimir here wasn't in your class last semester. He received a special dispensation to skip Sensing Magic. Since he is better at this than all of you, we should make him go first, yes?"

Orrin regretted not skipping class as he felt the other students staring daggers into his back. A few grumbled. It wasn't his fault. Wren was the one who'd let him skip the prerequisite.

"Casimir, come up front." Wren smiled and waved him forward. "You should all feel lucky. You are taking this class with an actual prodigy. Casimir learned to read the magic after only one hard day of work."

The grumbling got louder. Kieran's eyes were downcast.

"That's not true," Orrin said as he shuffled around the side of the desk. "It took me a few hours one night."

Orrin's plan to be quiet and not draw attention to himself was pointless if Finley wasn't here. He didn't know what kind of game Wren was playing at, but he could guess. She wanted him to be the class target. The person who was naturally good at the subject that the teacher would point to and say, "Why can't you all be as good as Timothy?"

Most of these students were college-aged or older, but none of them had had to endure the torture of modern-day education. None of them had had a different teacher every year of their lives until middle school. None of them had had to survive the fresh hell that was the changing teachers, teaching styles, and grading systems that arrived with sixth grade and lasted until high school graduation.

Orrin almost felt sorry for the five men and women in front of him. The first teacher who'd used this method of comparison teaching on Orrin was Mr. Loubet. Seventh-grade math shouldn't be a competition. It shouldn't have a list of grades from top place to last posted over half the blackboard. Orrin usually hovered near the middle of the list, but those at the top pulled some underhanded crap on each other to try and be number one. Those on the bottom . . . well . . . Orrin was glad he was good enough at math to not be a target.

Until they'd moved to pre-algebraic equations. Orrin's mind found the puzzles easier to grasp. He'd moved up the chart in a frightening hurry. Mr. Loubet had even pointed him out as an example of what you could do if properly motivated.

Thankfully, Daniel had come looking for him when he didn't show up for the bus. He'd listened through the thin metal of the locker as Orrin told him the lock combination and opened the door. He'd tried to get Orrin to report the other kids to the school, but Orrin went a different route. He purposefully tanked his scores for that section and moved back to the middle of the field. *Shining too brightly gets you shoved in a locker.*

Orrin knew Wren's reasoning for teaching this way. Competition bred greatness. If even one person excelled due to wanting to one-up

Orrin, she would count it as a successful class. If Finley was still here, Orrin would duck his head and be bashful. He would let one of the other students—probably the girl with the bangs who'd called Kieran a dwarf—bully him a little. It would be different in this sophisticated setting, he was sure. More verbal slings than the fists, lockers, and trash cans of Orrin's past. He could engineer the situation to happen in front of Finley, too. He'd seemed like a noble kind of guy.

Except there was no reason for Orrin to go through that. He was in a foreign land, surrounded by people who were going off to fight his friends, and unable to do what he wanted or even what he'd been ordered to do. In short, Professor Wren had picked him on the wrong day.

It was disappointing. She'd been reactive and volatile during their first meeting but mostly compassionate compared to her brother during orientation.

"False bravado only gets you so far, my dear." Wren smiled at the rest of the class. "Let's see if you can tell me what kind of magic is coming from that small tree."

The other mistake Wren made was not knowing Orrin better before picking him. He'd grown out of the stage from Mr. Loubet's class of keeping his head down and purposefully tanking himself. Nobody in his high school would call him the best student, but he studied. He did the homework.

Anabella had opened his eyes to the different flavors of magic almost a week ago. He'd been practicing.

Orrin stepped close to the tree. The obvious answer of wood or earth magic was too simple. He put a hand up, feeling the aura of magic. His hand warmed. Not like the fire magic of his [Fire Sword], but like the gentle light of one of Madi's butterflies. He smiled as he remembered the feel of her magic.

"Light magic."

Professor Wren hesitated before pointing at one of the rocks on the table. "That one next."

"Ice."

She moved him through several items, growing more agitated. "Sit down, Casimir."

"Yes, Professor." Orrin bowed his head and nudged his way back behind Kieran.

To her credit, Wren began teaching instead of pushing more. She described the waves of mana that came off all spells or magically infused items, along with multiple ways people learned to sense them. She drew a long strand of shapes in a helix down one side of her board.

"This is the core magic equation. Almost every known spell can be traced back to here, and those that cannot . . . we just haven't figured it out yet."

Wren began drawing more symbols off from different points of the original strip, pointing out the different elemental magics before moving to a few more that certain students in the class had.

She also drew complicated equations that supposedly showed how each mana signature of magic interacted with others. She talked for nearly an hour until the board was full of scribbles so small, Orrin was having trouble making them out.

One of the students, a guy who could be Orrin's grandfather, raised a hand. After a moment, he coughed politely. Wren turned around.

"Yes, Noor?"

The man stood and clasped his hands behind his back before he spoke. "Professor, if these mana signatures all derive from the same core, is that not proof of an original magic? Something more powerful than all the rest?"

Wren's smile was positively devilish. "And what magic would you call the core magic? Certainly not your light magic, Noor. I've already shown you where it fits in." She tapped the board, where a line of math that made Orrin's head hurt stood.

"I do not know what it is, only that it must exist for all the other spells to exist around it."

Orrin could tell there was some other argument being made underneath the spoken words here, but he didn't know the context.

"We can discuss that later. This next question is for anyone other than Kieran, who has so graciously agreed to retake my class. What is the common thread here?"

Orrin glanced around but only saw confused faces. Kieran's fists were clenched under the table. *She's kind of a bitch.*

"Kieran, I suppose this is your moment to shine," Wren said, walking up to the small desk and tapping the wood.

"Each equation is a derivative of the core magic." Kieran's eyes were closed as if he was reading from his memory. His voice sounded like he was reciting from a book. "If a caster knows the equation, the variables can be changed upon casting. While the core magic cannot be obtained, various fluctuations and deviations can be achieved through careful manipulation of the mana signatures."

What does that mean? Orrin wrote down what Kieran said and tapped his pencil on the paper. *Various fluctuations and deviations . . . huh?*

"Professor, how do you manipulate a mana signature?"

Wren waved a hand at the woman with bangs. "You probably can't. It takes near-perfect understanding of a specific mana signature before you can try. It's dangerous and not the core subject of this class. If you show me you have a deep understanding of one type of magic's signature, I'll graduate you from this class. Next semester, you'll be able to take a redacted class."

Orrin raised his hand and waited for Wren to nod in his direction. "Manipulate a mana signature. Is that like changing the spell?"

Wren grabbed a wooden staff from behind her lectern and held it above her head. "[Woodbolt] is not commonly considered powerful."

She peered down the staff like sighting on a gun and pointed it over the students' heads. A blast from the end of the staff erupted, and a clanging noise sounded behind them.

Orrin turned and noticed a hanging metal circle was rocking. A piece of wood no bigger than his pencil clattered to the ground underneath it.

"However, once a mage understands the magic's mana signature and learns to manipulate it . . ." Wren cast another spell.

No. It's the same spell, Orrin realized as a piece of wood as thick as his forearm speared through the metal circle and pierced the wall behind it.

"You can change the spell in new ways. It's dangerous. It's unpredictable. But it makes our magic more powerful than you can ever dream."

Chapter 25

I'm looking into it. Keep on target. Status report?

Anabella's message was waiting for Orrin after he returned from his Mana Signatures class.

Orrin punched his mattress. What did she expect him to do?

He skipped dinner. He started to respond multiple times, coming up with sarcastic quips, stinging rebukes, and even a plea to let him go, but in the end, Orrin simply reported on his progress with the two remaining targets, Maeve and Rhys.

Dropping the relic back into his [Dimension Hole], Orrin plotted.

He was exhausted from the first three days of classes and glad Anabella had decided to make him take only five classes. He'd already heard grumbling from other students taking six classes about the long days.

These people would never survive high school on Earth. Orrin smirked as he dropped on his bed. *There isn't even homework.*

Orrin's schedule was straightforward: on the first and fourth days of each week, he had Battle Class in the afternoons. The second and fifth days were split between Magical History and Surviving Spell Attacks. Defensive Earth Magic and Mana Signatures were on days three and six. Everyone had the seventh day off. Tomorrow would restart his three days of classes.

Despite Orrin's message to Anabella, he was not that worried about Finley leaving. He'd started putting his mini-plans into motion. Using the girl from orientation, Willa, as an excuse, Orrin got Graem to loosen his reins. Access to more of Mistlight was risky but gave him the opportunity to start a few other tactics.

The letters to Silas were a long shot. Orrin considered sending more, maybe even to Amir or the Guild of Dey, but rejected the thought. Involving his friend would only paint a target on his back, and Orrin didn't know enough about the Guild's politics to risk including them. Not to mention, there was no guarantee someone friendly would even receive a letter.

The library was turning out to be a dead end, too. Orrin spent most of his off time and nights researching, but either slave collars were a higher-level magic kept on the second floor or it was a specialized field of magic that he wouldn't find a book on at all.

During class, Orrin tried to keep the facade of Casimir going. He acted charming, which meant imitating Daniel. He made quick progress on actual assignments, mostly because he was learning the lack of earlier standardized education slowed down many of the other students. As long as Orrin was forced to be here, he would milk the school for every bit of knowledge he could.

Orrin sighed and sat up on his bed. He pulled up his status, changing the configuration around a bit to avoid descriptions of his spells.

Orrin	Utility Warder Level 18 (2,786/9,000)	Ability Points: 15 Administrator Points: 24
HP: 140/140	MP: 380/380	
Strength: 9	Constitution: 14	Dexterity: 11
Will: 28	Intelligence: 11	
Abilities: [Mind Bastion] [Dimension Hole] [Identify] [Blood Mana] [Map]—[Party View]; [Monster View]; [Trap View]; [Zoom]	Spells: [Calm Mind] [Purify] [Heal Small Wounds] Level 3 (10,000/10,000) [Camouflage] Level 2 (6,480/10,000)	[Increase Strength] Level 3 (7,255/10,000) [Increase Dexterity] Level 3 (7,315/10,000) [Increase Will] Level 3 (10,000/10,000)

[Side Steps] Level 3 (52/300) [Mana Pool] [Through the Ages] [Analyze] [Meditate] [Obscure] [Way of the Water] [Merge] [Diagnose] [Boost]—(Spell Modifier) [Split Spell]—(Spell Modifier)	[Lightstrikes] [Lightstrike] [Ward] [Inverse] [Utility Ward] [Tilth] [Gust] [Ice Sword] [Fire Sword] [Teleport] Level 2 (1,525/10,000) [Ice Ward] [Remetabolize] (1,000/1,000) [Water Ward] [Water Reservoir] [Toxic Touch] [Poison Ward] [Fire Ward] [Wind Ward] [Earth Ward] [Plant Ward] [Camouflage Ward] [Light Ward]	[Increase Intelligence] Level 3 (8,275/10,000) [Decrease Strength] Level 1 (50/1,000) [Decrease Dexterity] Level 1 (50/1,000) [Decrease Will] Level 1 (10/1,000) [Decrease Intelligence] Level 1 (20/1,000)

He had fifteen ability points left and so many options for potential purchases, but the thing he needed most was a way to escape. He'd been able to use [Toxic Touch] to burn through Brandt's collar when they rescued him, but Anabella's threat that the same trick wouldn't work again scared him. He'd avoided trying the most obvious way out of the collar: [Merge].

The power to combine spells and skills to make new ones was rare and dangerous, according to Madi. Anything he created would be added to the store, making it something others could unlock as well.

Orrin still spent a few minutes confirming his theory. Even though he couldn't use [Toxic Touch] as a spell, he could place it in [Merge] and get results close enough that it would probably work. The problem was the promise of an explosion if the collar was tampered with. While a [Ward] or even [Fire Ward] would stop some of the magical backlash, the exploding metal and concussive force in such a small area would likely still kill him. His spells protected against magical damage, not the aftereffects of a confined explosion near his spine and brain.

Orrin felt through the illusion of a necklace and touched the cold metal. Using [Meditate], he ran his fingers against the collar until he found the small portion that housed whatever controlled the magic inside. Orrin's library search was a dead end unless he could get access to the more restricted areas or ask for help . . . something that would spell disaster if word got back to the wrong ears. Instead, he took deep breaths through his nose and pushed the air out his mouth, feeling his body relax.

It's just like in class. Feel the mana.

The mana signature was there, almost too easy to find. It took twenty minutes to figure out the real problem.

Orrin's own mana was powering the collar. It acted as a block, not letting him see beneath the hood. Orrin spent two hours in a trance trying to find a way in but failed to make any progress. Too tired to continue, he crawled under the blanket and tried to sleep.

At breakfast the next morning with Ellis, Orrin asked about the free day. "What does everyone do when there are no classes?"

Ellis was reading a book with one hand and trying to shovel food into his mouth with the other. "I have to finish this chapter before class starts. Talk to me later. Sorry."

Orrin shrugged and cleared the empty trays for both of them as Ellis walked off, still with his nose in the book. Rhys and Iona were in class this morning, and Orrin didn't know what Maeve got up to outside her few classes. He wasn't actually sure he'd seen her in the cafeteria once.

He tried one last time to search the library for information about slave collars, but his one free period rushed by without his luck changing.

He left for lunch in a bad mood. Ellis skipped or was trying to finish a book . . . Orrin didn't know for sure. He contemplated skipping Battle Class but decided to go.

"Casimir, you and Hugo are fighting today," the professor announced as they entered the room. They were the fourth set to fight.

Orrin watched Hugo as he talked with Wilder. The bigger man kept his quarterstaff and summoned the entire class now. He elbowed Hugo and pointed at Orrin. He turned and tried to act like he was watching Peregrine and Cora's fight.

"Casimir, right?" the shadow to his side asked.

"Good afternoon, Hugo," Orrin said, wincing as Cora's chakram landed against Peregrine's head. He was still standing but obviously dazed. The weapon the TA, Bellamy, had assigned her was perfect for her fighting style.

"You're mostly a distance spell slinger, aren't you? I know you summoned those swords for your last fight with Eloise, but you didn't even get a hit in with them. Sorry, that sounded unkind. I mean, you don't seem trained in swords." Hugo's voice was lower than Orrin expected.

"I'll be fine." Like the others with summoned weapons, Orrin's two swords were already out and stabbed into the ground behind him. Bellamy was going to do an introductory weapon training after the battles today. He'd also mentioned the possibility of buying private lessons for more intensive walkthroughs, which was something Orrin would not be doing.

Hugo crossed his arms and rubbed his elbows. "Sorry, that sounded mean again. I want to know because I'm working on my distance weapons more and wanted to try using a bow, but if you'd prefer to keep it up close, we can do that."

Orrin remembered Hugo's fight against Finley. He was the one summoning different types of ice weapons, from shield to spear, in rapid succession. "I think the point of the class is to win, right? Shouldn't you use the skills you're best at to win?"

Hugo's hands moved up and down, rubbing the opposite arm as if warming himself up. "I'm not worried about losing to you. With these early fights, most of us try to keep to the basics and not show off our better spells. It's easy to come up with a strategy against someone who goes all out each week. I need the practice and thought I'd ask."

Orrin closed his eyes in frustration. Another secret edge that nobody had shared with him. It made sense: in a class where earning wins was the goal, going all out before the final battle only shared your strengths and weaknesses with the group. "Thank you, Hugo. I hadn't considered that. We can fight long-range if you want, but if you are just shooting arrows at me, it's going to be a long fight."

Hugo smiled and nodded. "Maybe not so long if I hit you."

Two minutes later, Peregrine took another hit to the head and didn't recover in time. Cora hit him with a follow-up wind attack, concentrated on his legs, and he went down.

"Hugo and Casimir." Galina nodded at them once everyone gave some advice and criticism. "Get in there."

Orrin pulled his two swords from the ground, even though he wouldn't need them. A few rounds of [Increase Dexterity] and [Increase Will] made him faster and with a much larger mana pool. He cast a [Ward] and [Ice Ward] on himself as well.

I'll only use [Gust]. It doesn't matter if I win these fights right now. I'll wait to see if Finley comes back before I try anything new.

"Fight."

Hugo stayed true to his word and summoned a bow and arrow of clear ice. Orrin easily dodged the arrows, which splashed down, turning into water as they missed. Unlike his own attacks, Hugo's weapons lasted only as long as he needed them.

Orrin's own wind attacks back clipped Hugo a few times but never hard enough to turn the tide of the battle. It dragged on, and

Orrin was considering charging in a bit closer when Hugo smiled and let the bow disappear.

Orrin hadn't been hit one time.

"I win," Hugo announced. "Look at the ground around you. Do you surrender?"

Orrin realized with dread the arrows hadn't been the attack. Rather, Hugo's aim wasn't to hit Orrin but to soak the ground around him with water. Water that Orrin knew without a doubt Hugo could control with his ice magic at the snap of a finger. The smile on his face confirmed it.

Orrin should have surrendered and shrugged it off, but the frustration of everything crashed against him. The futility of trying to escape, the injustice of Lord Sanerris and his mother keeping him from his friends, and the stupid little games these adults were playing while his friend was fighting in a war.

Orrin gave no warning. His dexterity was only in the fifties, but another few casts maxed it out. Orrin ran directly at Hugo.

The first step was free. He moved so fast that Hugo reacted a split second too late. The second footfall turned Orrin's ankle as spikes of ice formed and shot out all around him. He kept his footing and continued closing the distance.

He only soaked a few more feet.

Orrin brought his foot down between two growing ice pillars and jumped forward, clearing most of the rest of the wet ground. He kept charging, watching Hugo's eyes widen as his plan failed. A dark glee shot into Orrin's heart at finally getting a win.

Hugo summoned a shield of ice. A full tower shield that blocked Orrin's view. He reached into the air behind Hugo and pulled, using [Inverse] on [Gust]. It was one of those secret attacks he'd thought of. Pulling the wind instead of pushing it. Something he hadn't done on the field yet.

The roaring wind behind Hugo pushed the shield to the ground, nearly toppling the bigger man forward. His eyes moved back up from his fallen shield just as Orrin punched him with a regular [Gust]. He directed the wind at a forty-five-degree angle from the ground, right into Hugo's gut.

Hugo was knocked off his feet and launched into the air. He careened ten feet and landed outside the circle with a crunch of something breaking.

"Oh, shit," Orrin yelled and ran to the man's unmoving body. "Shit. Shit. I'm sorry. Are you okay?"

"That wasn't ranged at all," Hugo grumbled. "Did you punch me?"

"Casimir wins. Get Hugo to the infirmary and then back for debrief," Professor Galina called from the other side of the fighting circle. "Next up is . . ."

"It was a spell. Can you walk?" Orrin asked, ignoring the two classmates moving into the circle behind him.

"I might have broken my leg when I landed."

Orrin used [Identify].

Hugo Barclay	**[Hecaton of Ice] Level 29**	**Status: fibular fracture; tibial fracture**

"Two broken bones," Orrin read quietly. He reached to heal but was able to stop himself from revealing even more of his secrets. "Let's get you fixed up. Good fight."

Hugo grunted but let himself be pulled up. A few of the students who'd previously ignored Orrin gave him a nod as he helped the man limp past them. He'd won a fight and would get a chit. Any other student in Battle Class would be ecstatic, so why did Orrin feel terrible?

Chapter 26

"Casimir took too long," Eloise admonished. "He could have used the backward windblast earlier in the fight and taken Hugo out."

"I disagree." Cora spun one of her chakrams around on her index finger. She was more comfortable with the new weapon every class. "He timed it perfectly. He drew Hugo into complacency before using his trump card. Most of us have to time our attacks to the second with skill and accuracy."

Orrin flinched. It was no secret that Eloise's ability to go invisible was her greatest strength and one that most of Battle Class had no recourse against. Cora's insinuation against Eloise wasn't lost on anybody.

Orrin listened to the criticism with an open mind but did not expect anything that would actually help him. He was hiding half of his real attacks, not to mention his ability to render any of his classmates a crawling invalid with a few casts of [Decrease Dexterity] or [Decrease Strength]. He'd never used [Gust] in a real battle before, as far as he could remember, and only had purchased the spell to get [Wind Ward].

Any new spell that Orrin took had the chance of giving him the corresponding magic type as a warding defense spell. He figured it was part of his class [Utility Warder] and had gathered as many different types of wards as he could. His spell [Ward] soaked damage, while the other types, including [Ice Ward], [Fire Ward], and [Water Ward], could stack and absorb each specific magic type. As long as he knew what kind of monster or opponent he was facing, Orrin could tank a few hundred points of magic damage. He'd worked hard to get most types of ward spells, with only metal magic being the current outlier.

The class finished their critique of Orrin's fight and gave Hugo praise for what he'd done right. Some of the older students picked on him a bit for only using an ice bow, commenting that he would have won if he'd simply charged Casimir in the beginning.

Orrin felt a hand land on his shoulder.

Professor Galina frowned down at him. "Come with me."

The rest of the students didn't pay attention as Orrin followed her through the door that she came out of each day. The class met on the battlegrounds, the circle they'd fight in. Battle Class didn't have a classroom.

Orrin was surprised to find a small office, filled with chests overfilled with practice weapons. Galina moved around these with ease and sat behind a desk. A suspicious stain ran along half the top, and a stack of papers haphazardly covered the rest. Some of the papers were nailed to the wood with a knife. The chair was too small for her muscular build, and she squirmed for a minute, trying to get comfortable.

"Please sit," she said, waving her arm at the small stool in front of Orrin.

Orrin grimaced as he pulled the stool closer, making it scream against the floor as he dragged one leg. He sat on the edge of the seat, fingers clenched on his legs. The woman in front of him oozed danger in a way that only a few people on Asmea did.

"Was there a problem with my fight, Professor?" Orrin took a guess.

There's no way she knows I'm spying for Anabella. Orrin prayed he was right.

"Yes. You're holding back." Galina rubbed the top of her head with one callused hand. "The children out there focused on the wind spell you inverted and missed your increased speed. Why aren't you using that to your advantage?"

Orrin let out a breath. "I'm saving my speed for when I need to win. I don't know who I'll be up against ne—"

"Cut the bullshit," Galina said, crossing her arms. "You don't have to tell me what you're hiding, but don't lie to me. That's worse. It doesn't matter, anyways. After class, Bellamy will give you a task. Do it and report back to me after our next class. Here is your chit for winning."

The small golden square landed on the table. Orrin reached for it, but as his fingers closed over the token, Galina's hand darted out and grabbed him.

"If you don't use your full speed in every fight from now on, I will disqualify you. This is school, but we practice for real combat. There is a war going on. In a real fight, you use everything you have. Hit the enemy and keep hitting until they don't get up. Being smart is good, but opponents rarely cooperate with your plans."

This close, Orrin couldn't risk casting a spell. She'd feel the mana pooling. He needed to use [Calm Mind] but had to settle for [Mind Bastion].

"If I'm ever in a real fight, I won't hold back." Orrin ran the pros and cons of casting a few [Increase Strength] spells and setting the teacher straight. Continued anonymity outweighed momentary gratification and immediate safety.

Professor Galina smiled. "Good. I'll make sure you have a real fight next time. Go back to class, Casimir."

Two of his classmates were fighting, but Orrin paid them no attention. His heart was beating fast.

"Casimir, the professor asked me to talk with you." Bellamy scooted between a few of his classmates to stand near Orrin. He leaned in close and whispered, "You have a boosting skill?"

Orrin closed his eyes in frustration and in the hope that nobody nearby had heard. A sentence like that could get back to Lord Sanerris and make life very difficult . . . or very over.

"I have a spell that increases my dexterity, yes."

Bellamy nodded and handed Orrin a slip of paper. "Meet me here after dinner. Wear comfortable shoes."

Class ended without incident, and Orrin spent dinner with Ellis. Luca sat near them but spoke little. He'd stopped shoveling food in his mouth at every meal and now ate at a more regular pace. Orrin saw his friends off before heading to the room written on the paper.

He stood outside the first-floor room on the eastern side of the school. He was closer to his dorm than Battle Class. Orrin knocked and tried the door. It was open.

"Bellamy?" Orrin squinted into the darkness, trying to hurry his dark vision along. "Are you in here?"

"I'm behind you, Casimir."

Orrin jumped, falling against the door. It swung open, and he rolled backward into the room.

"Sorry," Bellamy said without emotion as he stepped over Orrin. He carried a steamer trunk with him. "I'll be set up in a minute."

Orrin dusted his pants off and stood. The room was narrow and long. Two small walls separated the room into long alleys, like for bowling . . . or like a shooting range. The end of the middle lane held a paper target.

"You'll be standing at the end down there," Bellamy directed, pointing down the lanes. He pulled a softball-size rubber ball out of the trunk and tossed it in the air once. He set it down and pulled out ten more. "I'll be throwing these at you while you try and avoid them. We're going to build up your dexterity tolerance. Do you know what that . . ." Bellamy trailed off as he looked up at the room. "Those idiots are supposed to reset the room. One second."

The man set the last ball down and shook out his robes. Kneeling, he muttered as mana gathered at his fingers. Orrin watched the two walls making up the alleys sink into the ground. Now a larger area spread out, wide enough to fit a soccer goal.

"You're going to throw balls at me?" Orrin said, full of dread. "This is what Professor Galina wanted me to do?"

"You're going to use your spell or skill and avoid the balls. The more you move under the influence of a higher dexterity, the faster your body will acclimate to it. That is dexterity tolerance. You'll be able to move quicker, utilizing the full potential of your skill."

"Spell," Orrin corrected again. "Why are you throwing balls at me, though? Can't I just run laps or something?"

Orrin was having flashbacks to Little League baseball and getting hit every time he went up to bat.

"Pain is a good motivator." Bellamy tossed a ball in the air again. "We've got an hour every night until the next class. Let's begin."

Magical History passed quickly the next day, even if Orrin was a bit sore from being pelted with softballs. Orrin decided Professor Quinn ranked high on the list of worst teachers he'd ever had. The awful droning of his voice stopped only when he finished a chapter. Two chapters a class and he left the classroom without a word. A typical semester ran for eight weeks, but the book for the class only had thirty chapters, which meant the man would run out of reading material before the class ended. Orrin would bet gold the professor wouldn't show up for the remaining sessions.

"We can read the book and continue training," Iona said as she walked by Orrin, Rhys at her side. "He doesn't teach. I told you I didn't need to read the assigned chapters."

"That's not the point, Iona," Rhys grumbled before noticing Orrin. "Casimir, good to see you. You didn't forget about our lunch today, did you?"

Orrin had forgotten completely.

"As long as we're back for the next block—I'm not going to risk pissing off Professor Hugh."

Rhys frowned. "Are you in Surviving Spell Attacks? I didn't see you last class."

Iona had seen him, of that Orrin was sure.

"I sat in the back."

They made small talk as they walked to the restaurant Rhys had picked. Iona followed a step behind, watching every shadow. Rhys included her in the conversation, but once Orrin was around, she rarely said more than a few words in response.

Orrin tried to steer the conversation to Rhys and his family, but the young man was adroit in turning things back on Orrin. Every sentence that Orrin was able to get Rhys to say cost three well-crafted lies about his background. Orrin started blurring the lines, telling stories about the trouble he and his friend David would get into growing up.

The restaurant was intimate, with only a dozen or so small tables. Iona pulled a chair against the back wall out for Rhys and sat at his side. Orrin's back remained to the door.

By the time they ordered food, Orrin knew he was in trouble. Anabella's dossier had noted Rhys Tonsa's mother was intelligent and shrewd in her business ventures. She'd turned around the mining operation in eastern Odrana after taking over. Rhys was every bit his mother's son.

"What other classes are you taking, Casimir?"

It was a simple question but one that Orrin couldn't lie about. If Rhys could access the master registrar, he'd know immediately Orrin was in classes with the other children of the Odranan chancellors.

"A few different classes, but one I'm not sure I'm allowed to talk about," Orrin falsely bragged, taking a sip of his water and hoping he could throw Rhys off. "Professor Wren herself placed me in it and let me skip a prereq. What about you? Anything good?"

"We have two classes together," Rhys answered as a waiter brought out the food. Orrin got chicken soup, while Rhys's dish consisted of small vegetables and rabbit. Iona nibbled on some bread and fruit. "I'm taking four more. Two classes related to my magic, although one of those is more of an independent study with Professor Wren. I'm taking one class with Iona, since she would never ask for herself. I mostly sleep in it."

Iona gently nudged her body against Rhys, who smiled in return.

"Iona and I grew up together. She took a job as my bodyguard but forgets that we were friends first." Rhys's smile caught her and she rolled her eyes.

Orrin smiled, too. He hated that he was forced to befriend Rhys under false pretenses. He might be a year younger than Orrin, but he carried himself as a much older force. He was someone Orrin and Daniel would have been friends with on Earth.

"What about your sixth class?" Orrin counted the classes up. "You said you're in six but only mentioned five."

"Did I?" Rhys dug into his rabbit and started eating. "I don't remember. What do you make of Professor Hugh? We have some orcs back home, but he's one of the first I've met as educated."

Lunch continued like that, courting small conversations back and forth. Rhys demanded he be allowed to pay, and Orrin gave in after a timid refusal. He couldn't figure out why Rhys had invited him to lunch after meeting him once but figured any face time with the target was good.

Orrin left at the school gate to grab his notebooks for Surviving Spell Attacks. He climbed the stairs two at a time. They'd run late, and there was just enough time to get to his room and back before Professor Hugh threw him out.

Orrin rounded the corner just as Ellis closed the door to Orrin's room. The younger man tested the handle and turned. He let out a squeak.

"Casimir . . . It's not what it looks like."

Chapter 27

Ellis scanned the empty hallway as Orrin approached. He looked like a rabbit about to make a run for it, wiping his hands on his pants in a nervous gesture.

Orrin held his palms up in a placating manner. He kept his voice quiet and calm as he asked, "What does it look like, Ellis?"

He pushed down the devastation at finding someone he'd begun to see as a friend spying on him. Orrin heard rumors in the cafeteria daily about fights and people being caught performing some extracurricular espionage but had thought his own relative anonymity would keep him clear of the spy games the different houses and aristocrats played at the school.

The young man's shoulders drooped. "It looks like I'm leaving after messing up your room and going through your things. I promise, Casimir, I would never do that. The door was ajar when I came up to my room, and I knocked. I called out for you and opened the door when nobody answered. I didn't put it there. I was about to go report it and find you."

Orrin was never so happy for [Dimension Hole] as he was right now. He didn't know if he believed Ellis, but there was nothing in his room to be stolen or found. He kept Anabella's relic in his storage, along with a few other precious items. "Nobody was inside?"

Tears brimmed in Ellis's eyes as he shook his head. "I swear. It wasn't me."

"Wait." Orrin paused as Ellis's words caught up with him. "What did you find in there?"

Ellis finally lost his composure and ran down the hall. Orrin let him go. He'd been caught red-handed at the door. If Orrin, as Casimir, made a formal report about someone breaking into his dorm room, there wasn't anywhere the boy could go unless he gave up his chance to attend the school.

Orrin opened the door and entered.

His desk was upside down in the center of the room, each drawer removed and smashed to pieces. The knife used to tear the mattress to pieces stuck from the nearest banister of the bed frame, feathers coating the room from the once-plush pillow. The chest that Orrin didn't use had been opened.

The mess from his room being turned inside out wasn't bad. The item that had spooked Ellis was another matter.

The drapes were drawn and Orrin's window was open. A rope hung from the bar atop the window. It swung taut in the breeze, the end tied off around the neck of a dead animal. It was half skinned, the blood still leaking into a puddle on the floor below. The near-silent drip of blood caught his eye, a tiny splash of red jumping from the puddle on the ground, hitting the yellow wall under the window.

"Casimir?"

Orrin pulled his eyes away from the gruesome sight to find Professor Graem squatting above him. He couldn't remember sitting down against the wall in his room.

"Let's get you out of here." The man spoke with a gentle voice, his eyes betraying his concern. "We'll get this cleaned up."

Orrin took the proffered hand and pulled himself up. Belatedly, he realized he was late to Professor Hugh's class. He wasn't one to skip classes.

"I have to get to class."

Graem kept his hand on Orrin's shoulder as they walked out of the room, his staff clicking on the ground. He gestured, and three men in guard uniforms moved in. Orrin saw a few faces sneaking peeks out of doorways. Curious students looking for ammunition in the newest rumor.

"I'll talk with your teacher. You're in shock."

Orrin let himself slip into [Mind Bastion]. He analyzed his situation logically. There was no reason he should be in shock. He'd been through much worse in his time in Dey. This wasn't anything to break down about. He'd killed people, fought monsters, been kidnapped, and lived with lies that could end his and his friends' lives for months now.

"I'm not a [Healer], but I know a good one if you want to talk with somebody." Graem continued talking, but Orrin stopped listening. The anxious and racing thoughts subsided as he cast [Calm Mind].

"I'm fine now, thank you." Orrin slipped out of Graem's grip and stopped on the stairs. "Ellis said the door was already open when he got there. I thought the doors were magically locked to our mana, right?"

Graem sighed and sat on the steps. He tapped his staff on the ground, and Orrin felt a bubble of air encompass them.

"Ellis Glevrasker? He's the one who notified us of the incident," Graem said, shaking his head. "Casimir, those doors can be bypassed by anyone with half-decent mana manipulation skills. I'm less worried with the how and more about the why."

A flask appeared in his hands, and the professor took a long swig before offering the small container to Orrin. "Did you piss somebody off in the first week?"

Orrin considered taking the drink for longer than he wanted to admit but shook his head. "I don't think so. I've been trying to be friendly. I won a match in Battle Class, but I don't think Hugo would do something like this." He snapped his fingers. "I turned down an advance from some girl. Her aunt is a judge or something. I don't remember her name. We only met at orientation."

A door below opened, and two women climbed the stairs toward them. They stopped talking when they saw Professor Graem sitting on the steps talking with Orrin. He made a shooing motion, and they retreated the way they'd come.

"Neither of those are reasons to skin a possum in your room," Graem said when the door closed again. "Did you tell anyone the reason you're here?"

Orrin rolled his eyes. "I'm not an idiot."

"We will try to figure out who did it, but the chances of finding the culprit are low. If you don't have any idea who it could be, we don't have a lot of clues to go on." He put the flask back in his pocket and stood, grabbing his staff. "I'll have your things moved to another room as soon as we're done investigating. Do you want one in a different wing?"

The smart thing to do would be to leave the school completely and never return. Someone wanted to send a message. Orrin didn't care to find out what the message was. Unfortunately, that wasn't a choice.

Orrin closed his eyes to think. He could hear his mom's tired voice repeating her favorite saying, *When life gives you lemons, make lemonade.* He hated that mantra, but his mom would say it every time he had a shitty day. Orrin joked with Daniel once that his mom had the saying wrong after a shitty day of school. *When life gives you lemons, throw those lemons at your enemies.*

"Can I stay in the same room?"

Graem's teeth showed as his face split into a vulpine smile. "What do you have in mind?"

Orrin went to Surviving Spell Attacks even though he was late and Graem advised against it. He was nearly an hour late after discussing his plan with Graem, but he wanted to apologize to Professor Hugh and maybe catch some of the lecture.

He was surprised to see an active demonstration happening.

"Attack the candle, not the person. How many times must I repeat this?" Professor Hugh yelled as he bodily tossed one of the students up the narrow stair path between the tables. "Who is next? You, at the door . . . you are late."

The man in his forties dusted his robes as he stood up and pointed at Professor Hugh in anger. "You made a mistake doing that, orc."

Hugh smiled toothily. "Please. Attack me."

Orrin thought the man might actually do it, but a quick glance at the dozens of students in the auditorium stole his confidence. He pushed by Orrin, muttering as he left.

"Come down. You can go next."

Orrin turned from watching the man rush down the hallway to see the thirtyish remaining students staring at him, including Rhys and Iona. "I'm sorry I'm late, Professor. There was . . . I was detained by Professor Graem."

"Not interested. Your turn."

Orrin had no choice but to walk down the stairs. He'd turned off [Mind Bastion] with ease. The skill responded to his wishes without much of a fight with his higher level, but Orrin knew it was all too easy to rely on it. He wanted to fall into the cold, logical feeling again instead of having the warm eyes of everyone in the class on him.

"You stand there. Attack my candle. Defend your own." Hugh stood tall behind one stool, making it seem smaller than it was.

Two stools sat on opposite ends of the teaching area, with a thick candle stuck to the seat of each one. A box of matches sat near Orrin's side, while Professor Hugh's candle was aflame already. He moved around to the back of the chair and glanced askance at Hugh.

"Light the candle. Any spell to attack."

Orrin rubbed his eyes. Maybe Graem was right and he should have skipped class. He'd come looking for theory and math to distract him from what just happened. Orrin was not in the mood for whatever this was.

"Do I just have to blow out your candle? Is that the test?"

Hugh grinned. "Easy, right?"

Orrin used the match and cupped his hand to let the wick catch. His mind still raced with ideas of who could have done that to his room. Was it a threat or a cover for trying to steal something? If someone knew Anabella had loaned him a relic, maybe that was the goal? Or maybe someone knew he was a spy for her and wanted to find generic correspondence?

The candle flitted to life.

"You first."

Orrin liked this class. Professor Hugh taught in a manner that Orrin got—lectures and information he could write down to study more later on his own. This demonstration shit was the opposite of that.

He threw a blast of [Gust] at the candle. Hugh snapped his fingers, and a spark of lightning jumped from his hand. Orrin couldn't see what happened, but the blast of air brushed the chalkboard.

Hugh rerouted his attack.

"Notice how air magic responds to lightning shields." Hugh turned and talked to the class. "Air magic moves along direct paths. Lightning is ever-moving. Direct hit against a moving target redirects away. How much stronger should his attack be to break minor lightning shield?"

Surprisingly, Iona raised her hand to answer. Hugh nodded in her direction.

"Casimir would need to compress the air by a magnitude of three to bypass the inherent weakness against lightning."

"Correct. Two point eight, to be precise. Try again. I will use the same level of defense."

Rhys smiled and patted Iona's shoulder.

Orrin's first spell cost ten MP. Using Hugh's instructions, he rounded up the next attack to thirty MP.

The lightning shield shattered as Orrin's [Gust] burst against the candle. The flame went out.

"Questions?"

Orrin raised his hand, waiting for the orc to notice. The eyes of the class were on him again. "If I cast three spells at ten mana instead, would that be different than a single thirty-mana blast?"

Iona whispered something to Rhys as Professor Hugh chuckled. "Do you have mana left to try?"

Orrin smirked and nodded. Hugh held the wick of the candle between two fingers. When he removed his hand, the flame was back.

Orrin's first spell hit the lightning shield and ricocheted into the class. It almost hit a woman sitting in the front row, but a larger lightning shield caught it. His second spell fizzled against the roof. The third broke through and guttered the fire again.

"Results?" Hugh asked, looking to the class for the answer again.

Orrin hated to admit the exercise was better than he'd thought.

"It works the same," said a man with short dark hair, sitting in the back of the room. "Except it's more dangerous for everyone around you."

He got a few scattered chuckles.

Hugh clapped his massive hands once to regain everyone's attention. "In battle, he still kills enemies but might kill comrades with extra deflected attacks. This is why we learn. Better to take down the enemy with one attack than risk hurting friends."

Professor Hugh dismissed Orrin and called another student. Everyone took multiple turns defending the candle as well as attacking. Orrin learned a lot, but the smell of copper never left his nose.

Chapter 28

Orrin bounced his foot as Professor Hugh dismissed the class. He'd learned more in the last hour about the use of air magic than . . . well, ever.

Surviving Spell Attacks had started off as a theoretical class, but this entire last session was practical application. The wildly intelligent orc teacher took each student through both offensive and defensive exercises. He organized the entire thing as a game, engaging the class with questions, advice, and pointers for better use of their magic.

Professor Hugh also gave the students waiting a job, namely, asking questions. When a student using primarily fire magic took a turn, half the class quieted. Fire magic was one of the most predominant classes of magic. They asked questions that gave Orrin insight into the use of his own [Fire Sword], something he realized he was underutilizing quite a lot.

Based on that first student using fire after Orrin's arrival, he came up with a new way to use the skill. He'd need to test it, but Orrin was confident that he could temporarily make the sword grow a few inches to a foot longer. It wouldn't be useful enough to keep running nonstop, but if it worked, Orrin theorized he could bypass even Daniel for a strike or two during swordplay.

The problem was the limited magic types in the class. Since half the students used fire magic, the majority of Professor Hugh's advice related to their magic. The orc would occasionally whisper something to a student using a different magic type. Only thirty-two students were left in the class. By Orrin's count, about seventeen used fire magic. Three students used water and four others used air magic, but the remaining students had nobody to ask questions on their behalf. Those students also appeared too shy to ask questions of their own.

Orrin was the same, waiting for the last of the students to leave before approaching the orc. "Professor? Do you have a minute?"

"Class ended. I have hours. Grab that." A massive hand waved at the stool holding the candle. Orrin grabbed it and ran to keep up as Hugh carried his own chair to the corner of the room.

"I wanted to ask about different magic types not discussed in class. Specifically, about light, ice, and poison magic. How would the matrices be different when—"

"Next class—" Professor Hugh turned and cut Orrin off using his strongly accented voice, "we will discuss each student's magic type and what is weakest or strongest against it. You have wind magic, yes?"

Orrin hesitated for only a breath, having already committed to revealing a bit more to Professor Hugh. It was a calculated risk. From what he'd been able to learn, the orc was a new teacher and not a political animal. He was the safest bet that Orrin had to find a way out of his collar.

"I use wind magic, yes," Orrin stated but sped up his next words as Hugh started to walk away. "But I also use a wide variety of other magics, including the ones I just mentioned."

Hugh paused and peered over his shoulder. "Your class allows multiple types like this? Poison and light are . . ." He trailed off, trying to find the right word. "Incompatible."

Orrin nodded. "My class lets me use almost any type of magic. The rest of our class doesn't cover my full repertoire, so I thought I'd ask you after class instead of wasting time for everyone."

Hugh finally faced Orrin fully. Orrin craned his neck to meet his eyes. The orc was close to eight feet tall.

"Prove your words."

Orrin summoned an [Ice Sword] and [Fire Sword], something he'd already shown off in Battle Class. He dropped them and moved back to the corner where Hugh had pushed all the class supplies.

Orrin found what he'd been looking for and grabbed the empty bucket. He placed the bucket at Hugh's feet and used [Water Reservoir] to fill it.

"I can't really use my poison magic in here," Orrin lied, not trusting the teacher with the knowledge that he'd been collared. "I can use [Lightstrike] if you want."

Hugh frowned for a minute and then held his fingers close. A spark jumped and grew into a circular shape, becoming a full buckler within a few seconds. "Attack."

Orrin complied, sending the weak attack at the teacher. Hugh caught it with ease against his lightning shield.

"You are interesting. Ask your questions."

Orrin smiled. *Finally, some progress.*

The next day, Orrin was the source of all gossip. While fights between students still broke out despite the rule against it, nobody had gone so far as to break into another student's room. The dead possum was mentioned only in whispers.

Professor Graem had come by during dinner the night before to tell Orrin his room was cleared out. When Orrin complained that he should get a new room, Graem shut him down, dressing down the haughty Casimir in front of most of the school.

"If you can't be bothered to shut your own door, it's your own fault some animal got loose in your room. The school will not cover the cost of replacing your items or relocating you."

Orrin held his breath, letting his face get red as the man walked away, pounding his staff on the ground with every other step.

He wouldn't know if anyone bought the act for a while, but it was out of his hands now.

Orrin's classes for the day were Defensive Earth Magic and Mana Signatures. He spent the first class dodging rocks again with Maeve. Every attempt to talk with her ended with a new bruise, even with an [Earth Ward] running. He was beginning to see why Professor Cade was Maeve's last choice for adviser. The man was inept and taught them next to nothing that wasn't in the class book.

Orrin was looking forward to learning more in Mana Signatures but a scrap of paper was taped to Professor Wren's classroom door.

The paper read, *Class Canceled Today*.

Noor, a student from the class, muttered something and walked off as Orrin approached. Kieran, the shorter man who sat next to Orrin, stood near the door with a clipboard in his hand.

"Casimir, right?" Kieran asked with a sad lilt in his voice. "Professor Wren asked me to wait here until everyone has shown up."

Orrin frowned. "What if someone tells their friends and they never show up?"

Kieran raised his eyes from the clipboard. "I'll be waiting until the end of the period, then."

"Do you know where she is?" Orrin asked, feeling bad for the man. He was repeating Mana Signatures and Wren seemed to have it out for him for some reason. "Is she sick?"

Kieran shrugged. "She said she'd be gone for a few days but would be back before our next class. My guess is she got called to the front line. I heard a [Hero] showed up along the border where the elves were attacking. It must be an elf lover, because the [Hero] fought off, like, half the main conscripted forces before Lord Sanerris arrived. Professor Wren is an expert in trap magic . . . what with her metal and wood abilities. My guess is she's been called to the front to set a trap for this [Hero] of the elves."

Orrin squeezed his fingers tightly into a fist. Daniel was fighting and he couldn't do a thing. "I thought [Heroes] were supposed to be the good guys? Why would he fight for the elves?" Orrin's voice dripped with disdain, trying to sell his false story as a loyal Odranan.

Kieran waved to another student as they came by to read the note, marking another tick on his sheet. He waited until they were relatively alone to answer. "My guess is the elves got to him. Not all [Heroes] are good. If you see June, can you send her my way? She's the only one who didn't show up."

Orrin promised to keep an eye out, but he couldn't remember who June was. He hadn't been paying attention to the other students, even in his smallest class. He walked back to his dorm to drop off his school supplies. As Orrin climbed the final stairs and walked down the hallway, Ellis rounded the corner.

"Ellis," Orrin said, nodding his head at the young man. He hadn't ruled him out of vandalizing his room, but he was at the bottom of a list of suspects in his mind. "No class?"

Ellis, for his part, didn't balk at seeing Orrin. The kicked-puppy look in his eyes could have been an act, but he smiled slightly at Orrin acknowledging him. "Canceled. A lot of classes were today. I think more people were drafted for emergency services."

Orrin gave a tight-lipped smile and kept walking.

"Casimir?" The boy's small voice broke at the end of the name. "I'm sorry that happened to you. If you find out who did it, let me know. I'll help."

Orrin crooked his head to the side. "Help what?"

Ellis shrugged. "Get revenge. I don't have many friends here, but you were kind to me. I get why you don't trust me, but the professors are on it. They'll figure out who broke into your room. When they do, I'll take care of them for you. Then you'll see it wasn't me."

Orrin studied the way Ellis stood, shoulders slumped and head down. He remembered a time when nobody believed in him. When he was acting out in school because his dad had disappeared out of nowhere and his mom had fallen into a depressed spiral. Daniel had found Orrin with his hand on the fire alarm, ready to pull it.

"What are you doing, O?" Daniel had asked. Orrin couldn't remember why they both were in the empty hallway between classes. He just remembered Daniel's words.

"Nobody cares, Daniel. My dad is gone. My mom won't talk to me. Nobody cares. It'll be funny, you'll see." Orrin knew it wouldn't be funny. He knew it would cause more pain for his mom, but some small part of him thought if he got in real trouble, maybe his dad would come back and everything would be normal again.

"I care. Orrin, you're not alone. You've still got me."

Orrin saw Ellis and remembered Daniel, holding his hand out to his friend about to go down the wrong path.

"I've got to throw my stuff in my room really quick," Orrin finally said to Ellis. "Where are you off to?"

Ellis lit up but tried to keep it cool after a second, settling into an attempted nonchalant smile that was slightly too wide. "I'm going to see if I can get a spot for the dungeon run tomorrow. I thought it might be worth it if I can gain a level or two."

"What are you talking about?"

"Mistlight's dungeon? Usually you have to pay a lot of gold to enter, and even then, the wait list is months out, but it's blocked off just for our use on our free day. You know, tomorrow?"

Orrin sputtered. "Let me get this straight. There is a dungeon that only the students get to use once a week?"

"Only during the semester and only for the first ten floors, unless you get special permission from Professor Graem. How did you not know about this? It's half the reason some students come here."

Orrin ignored Ellis's question. "Can we make our own parties and go?"

Ellis shook his head. "No, parties are limited to five groups a week. Each group has to be approved by the professor in charge. Are you interested?"

Orrin considered his choices. He'd need to go to Graem and make sure he could even get into a party with the collar on, but if he could level even once, that would give him access to some spells he'd been looking at last night.

"Let me go talk with Professor Graem. I might want to take on more than ten floors."

Chapter 29

"Not a chance," Graem said, trying to push his office door shut. Orrin could smell pungent smoke wafting through the air.

"I'm going to sign up, and when someone tries to invite me to a party, what is going to happen?" Orrin countered, shoving his foot into the path of the closing door. "If I'm stuck here doing her bidding, I want to have some sort of payment."

Orrin's request for Graem to change the magical restraints of his slave collar once again was not going well. After Ellis informed him that the school allowed students to enter the Mistlight dungeon on their off day each week, Orrin's plans evolved again.

Every solution to his current problem relied on using his skills, spells, or Administrator powers to solve his predicament. Orrin's dilemma came from not knowing how to get the collar off without being killed. He was stuck on campus, with a limited amount of freedom to move about town. The one missing element was gaining more experience. Whatever solution he came up with could fail, and that would stick Orrin with useless skills and no ability to make further attempts to gain his freedom.

There was also one major hope as well.

Obtain Level 20
Reward: [Hero Kit Level 3]

When Orrin completed the last Quest, Obtain Level 10, the system had given him an error regarding the reward. [Hero Kit] appeared to be class-specific and Orrin wasn't allowed to have it. However, the system had let him choose a reward. Orrin didn't realize it at the time, but it was his Administrator power letting him manipulate the blue-box Quest.

The knowledge that he might be able to gain experience and get to level twenty made Orrin remember the way the system had responded to his thoughts about a reward. Maybe he could gain an ability to control the slave collar or even just take it off. He could escape the dungeon, [Teleport] back to Dey, and be done with the entire charade in just a level and a half.

Orrin	Utility Warder Level 18 (2,786/9,000)

According to Ellis, only five groups containing five students each were selected each week. While the students were restricted to the first ten levels, Orrin hoped he could make up the six thousand points he needed to get to level nineteen. He would need to cheat his party members out of as much experience as he could safely steal, but that was only if Graem let him go in the first place.

"Any payment issues are between you and Anabella." Graem kicked Orrin's foot out of the doorway and stepped into the hall. He closed his door and blinked heavily in the sudden brightness. "My job is to keep you on mission and safe. There is no reason for you to go. As far as I know, none of your new friends are jumping at the chance to go play dungeon diver."

Orrin chewed the inside of his lip. It was a flaw in his plan: the students who did go into the dungeon were mostly the lower-leveled ones from poorer families. Being restricted to the first ten levels meant less experience than a noble could get with an outfitted party designed to keep them safe while keeping monsters distracted. Someone like Finley or Maeve had a high enough level already that such gains were a waste of time. Orrin had tried to find Rhys, hoping to convince him to go, but he hadn't been able to locate him or his shadow, Iona.

Orrin tried the last card he had. "When Finley gets back, I need to be stronger. I'm nearing level twenty and could use a few extra stat points. If I can show rapid improvement while he's away, I might be able to get closer to him."

Graem squinted his bloodshot eyes at Orrin. "Casimir, that is a weak argument."

"If you don't let me go into the dungeon, I'll find monsters outside the wall. I have to level. I'm not good enough to take him on as I am."

"You won't be able to take on young Madvarr in your lifetime. He's been trained since he could walk. I don't have the brainpower to waste on this. I already let you stay in your room and created a scene in front of everyone like you asked. Why let you risk everything for some meager experience points?" Graem rubbed his brow in frustration. "If you are selected, come back and visit me. I'll open your connection up for one invite. If you try and join a party other than the one assigned to you for the dive, I will end you. You will have no freedom to move around, no matter how it hampers your assignment. Do you understand?"

Orrin nodded, worried to say anything in case Graem changed his mind.

"Now get out of my sight, I'm trying to relax. I find my days extra stressful of late."

Signing up for the dungeon was as simple as writing down his fake name on a ledger. Of the roughly hundred students who started the semester, approximately a quarter had gone to fight against Daniel and the elven army that was ravaging the countryside. It took all his strength to keep quiet about the misinformation and obvious propaganda he heard in these rumors.

A little fewer than half of the remaining students signed their names on the list. Orrin was number thirty-three.

Next, he prepared. Orrin went to the library and simply asked for books on the Mistlight dungeon. He was told the only one was checked out but due back in an hour. Another student was likely reading it in their room. However, he had to wait his turn, with three other students queued up for the book before him.

Orrin gave up and went back to his room, where he sent another message to Anabella.

I'm going into the dungeon to get stronger. Maybe you can help me get selected. I think it might help impress Finley if he ever comes back. No progress with Maeve, as class was canceled. More delays because of your son's war. Rhys is getting friendlier. We had a nice lunch together.

Orrin kept the stylus pressed against the final period. A dozen insults careened through his mind. He wanted to rage against his captor, for the powerless feeling he had every morning when he woke up, and for the fear that his friend was fighting miles away.

With a shaky hand, Orrin closed the relic sending book and put it away. He sat at the desk watching the last of the sun fade across the school's edifice, meditating and wishing for something to hit.

Orrin woke to another short and direct message.

A great victory will be announced in five days and all new recruits will be sent home. Permission for entry to Mistwater Lanterns will be granted. This opportunity came at a great cost. Do not squander it.

"What is Mistwater Lanterns?" Orrin muttered, figuring it out even as he said it. "Oh, it must be the dungeon name."

Orrin cleaned up and put on some new clothes, making sure to check the inventory for potions he kept hidden in [Dimension Hole].

If he was selected, Orrin would be going straight into the dungeon, as only this day was set aside for the students. He didn't know how multiple groups in a dungeon worked, but Ellis didn't seem to be worried about it, so neither would he. The boy hadn't gained his trust back, and Orrin was still suspicious, but until his other plan came to fruition, he was giving Ellis the benefit of the doubt.

Orrin considered his plan for the dungeon. He was going to cast increase-stat spells on himself before using a level-two [Utility

Ward]. It would lock in his stats at a higher maximum and, if done before a party invite was sent, would work only on him.

The trouble would be making his speed seem normal, but the maxed intelligence and will would make his spells hit harder and for less mana. That was the real trick. He could hunt monsters for as long as it took.

At breakfast, a list was already up with the names of the selected students. Ellis sat dejected. Orrin didn't approach the board and instead picked up some food.

"You didn't make the cut?" Orrin asked, sliding into the seat next to him with a plate of eggs and ham. He wanted to be full for the hunt.

"I'm on the reserve list, the ones who didn't get into a group this week. I'll be first next week," Ellis said, apparently trying not to whine too much. "I saw your name. Congratulations."

Orrin sighed. "I hadn't checked it yet. I don't even know what I'm doing. Any advice?"

He had three reasons for sitting with Ellis before checking the list. The first was simple: he knew his name would be on it. Anabella had told him as much in her message. The second was to comfort a friend, even if he ended up being the prey of Orrin's other hunt. The third reason was information. Orrin needed to know what to expect below.

"It's simple. They'll explain it." Ellis pushed a small roasted potato around on his plate.

"I'd rather hear it from someone I trust." Orrin thought he'd laid it on too thick when Ellis didn't respond right away. A moment later, to his horror, he saw tears. "Ellis? Are you—"

"I didn't do it, and I know I'm innocent. Everyone else talks about how it had to be me, but you still talk to me like a friend. I'm probably going to lose my sponsorship, but you sit next to me, making everyone more confused."

Orrin let him ramble for a minute before reaching out and patting the crying boy on the shoulder. "Hey, if I thought you killed something in my room, I would have already thrown you out the window." Ellis laughed and coughed at the same time. "Don't worry,

I'm sure Professor Graem will catch whoever broke into my room and everyone will see they were wrong."

Orrin prayed he was right and Ellis wasn't the culprit. If he was, the boy was also an amazing actor. "Talk to me and take your mind off it. Why five groups only? Why not everyone who wants to go in? How do five groups go into the dungeon in the first place? Won't it get crowded?"

Ellis wiped angrily at his eyes and shook his head before explaining. "Mistwater Lanterns is one of the oldest known dungeons, and part of the lords' job is keeping it culled. The first ten floors have turned into huge ecosystems that can take days to travel if you don't know where you are going. The Sanerris house keeps watch to make sure nobody tries to destroy it, as the dungeon is used for training as well. Even though we get to use the dungeon as students, we are limited to one day. We still have to get to classes tomorrow." Ellis smirked. "Each group will enter an hour after the last. If you see another group, your protocol is to leave and head in the opposite direction. If more than five groups enter, it makes it harder to train . . . I think. I'm not sure the exact reason why only five groups of five students are allowed, but it's been that way for decades."

Orrin processed all the information and asked a few more questions about the makeup of the dungeon. The most important aspect was that the dungeon used water and light magic.

"Light magic is weak but can amplify other types of magic. The lighted areas under the Lanterns are danger zones, with stronger monsters."

"Why only ten levels? Why not try and defeat the entire dungeon?"

Ellis laughed, finally regaining some of his normal mirth. "I think the dungeon is over a hundred levels deep. It's not possible to defeat it. The ten-level maximum is to let us spread out. There are maps in the library of how to get to each floor as quickly as possible. I think most groups prefer floors two to four, since they are the easiest to get to and have some good monsters to fight, but nothing crazy like floors five and seven. Nobody ever goes beyond floor six."

Orrin noticed two people enter the cafeteria and move to the wall. He'd never seen them there before and suddenly felt a pit in his stomach, remembering Anabella's words about an opportunity.

"I'm going to check on which group I'm in," Orrin said, standing up and leaving his plate behind.

He made his way up behind the dwindling group and found his name. Just as he'd feared, two of the five names were unknown. The other two stood next to him. Rhys and Iona.

"Tell me again why we are training in the dungeon?" Iona queried.

Rhys stared at Orrin as he answered. "It's an order from home. A new potential prospect."

Chapter 30

"Casimir, it appears we are in the same group." Rhys smiled, shushing Iona. "I received an urgent message from my mother that I needed to train in the dungeon as soon as possible. Imagine my surprise to find you assigned to the same party. You wouldn't know anything about that, would you?"

Orrin was impressed with Rhys's boldness. The young man certainly suspected Orrin was a spy of some sort, which was why he'd invited him to lunch the other day. That night, Orrin had dozed off before the pieces fell together: Rhys talked with no one else in the class except his shadow, Iona. The questions about Casimir's past were probing for hints of where he was from as if to pinpoint who'd sent him.

He thought back to Anabella's comments about the shrewdness of Lady Tonsa, Rhys's mother. *It seems like the son takes after his mom.* Of course, now that he thought about it, Anabella's note had mentioned an opportunity. He didn't know how she'd done it, but that spider made even the matriarch of the Tonsa family jump.

Orrin decided to play it safe and tell the truth. "I just found out about the dungeon last night. I don't remember seeing your name on it. I also didn't know you were in my group until I just read it."

Rhys was good, but he was young still. The last few months for Orrin had been a constant exercise in lying and watching people's reactions. So, when Rhys's lips tightened quickly, Orrin knew he was marginally safe.

"We entered our names this morning," Rhys said, gesturing to the wall with the dungeon divers broken out into five groups. "Do you know the other two students in our party?"

Orrin read the names: Hamish and Sloane. He didn't remember either from his classes. He shook his head.

"Not in any of my classes. How about you?"

Rhys exchanged a look with Iona. She shrugged.

"Sloane is in a class with me," he admitted slowly. "We've never talked before."

"About time we did, eh?" A brunette woman in her forties came up from behind Iona. The bodyguard for Rhys fell into a crouch and moved to block an attack that never came. "Don't get all twisted up, girlie. We're all in the same party. I'm Sloane Katra. How many of you have been in a dungeon? Scratch that. How many of you three have been into Mistwater Lanterns? We have second shift, so we go in an hour and a half. We'll have as much time as we want, but I recommend no more than eight hours of experience hunting. We don't want to be exhausted for class tomorrow, do we, Rhys?"

Rhys placed a hand on Iona's shoulder and she stepped beyond him again. "We have never been to this dungeon but have experience in them in general. I've also studied the first thirty floors in sufficient detail. What about you?"

Sloane ignored Rhys's question and turned to Orrin, her brown eyes crinkling in delight as Rhys stiffened from being passed over. "How about you, hon? Ever been in a dungeon?"

"I've never been into Mistwater Lanterns," he answered simply. He studied Sloane, trying to figure her out. She was built like a mage but carried herself like a fighter. A smaller frame than Iona, but she moved with efficiency. She'd also snuck up on them without much effort. If she was from Earth, Orrin would have thought she was Japanese, but she talked slightly different than everyone else from Odrana.

"Veskar scum," Iona muttered, too quietly for Sloane to hear.

"Do you know where our last member is?" Rhys tried to regain control of the conversation. "I've never had the pleasure of meeting Hamish."

"Hamish is one of those guys you have to meet to really know, ya know?" Sloane's smile told them what she thought about the current situation. She was in charge and everyone knew it. "He won't want to be party leader, though. If it's all the same, I'll take the lead. As the only two who have been in Mistwater, I can tell you now, it can be deadly."

Orrin watched the Rhys and Sloane standoff and sighed to himself. *Why am I always surrounded by posturing idiots?*

He snuck away while they continued to argue and made his way to Professor Graem's office. Orrin needed the collar adjusted so he could join the party. He was lucky Sloane and Rhys both wanted to be party leader or he would have had some explaining to do.

Orrin knocked on the door and waited. A minute passed with no response, and he knocked again.

"Go away."

"Professor Graem, it's Casimir."

Orrin muttered a curse under his breath a minute later when the door remained closed. He made a fist and pounded on the door.

"Go away or else I'll expel you from this school!"

Orrin continued to pound on the door, pausing only to wave at a group of students walking down the hall.

The door jerked open and a bleary-eyed Graem swung at Orrin. With his stats increased it was almost too easy for Orrin to flick his hand out and redirect Graem's punch into the door frame.

"Fuck! Ow. I'm going to—"

Orrin pushed the man into the room and closed the door. "I don't have a lot of time. My group goes into the Mistwater Lanterns in just over an hour. Are you sober enough to fix the collar?"

He was pushing his luck with this man again, but something about Graem's inability to get through a day without some sort of substance abuse was grating on Orrin's nerves. This was the person who was supposed to be watching out for him, but at every turn, Orrin was dealing with problems that were well beyond his means to fix.

Through the haze of whatever hangover he had, Graem was coming to a realization, too: Casimir was in his private quarters and demanding things once again.

A staff jumped from the bedside and flew into his outstretched hand. Graem raised his arm high and . . .

A stupefied look spread on the professor's face. The annoying student spy Casimir was gripping his elbow, preventing him from slamming his staff down.

"Professor Graem, I'm going to sober you up before you attack me again," Orrin said slowly. He was suddenly very glad he'd increased his strength. Graem was a lot stronger than he looked.

Orrin spent a few minutes healing and using [Remetabolize] on Graem.

"I apologize for attacking you, but I'm quite sure I told you not to do that again," Graem said as he put on a shirt. Orrin turned to give the man some privacy. He didn't really need to turn as he'd already caught an eyeful of the man in next to nothing, but giving some dignity back to the teacher seemed like a good idea.

"You asked me not to take away your buzz," Orrin retorted. "You were hungover and incoherent. Plus, neither of us has the time for you to sober up naturally."

Graem moved toward Orrin, placing his hand on the collar. Orrin felt the magic weave into the metal and tried to study it again, but Graem was quick. "You have one hour to enter a party. I'm warning you, don't try anything funny. I've set the collar as a tracker, so I can find you anywhere. Don't make me hunt you. Neither of us will like that."

Orrin wisely kept his insult in his mind. He had bigger fish to fry than a washed-up drunk. However, as he moved to leave, Graem reached out a hand and caught his shoulder. The strength in those fingers stopped Orrin cold.

"Who is in your party?"

"Sloane and Hamish," Orrin rattled off, trying to duck out of the iron grip and failing. "I don't know them. Rhys and Iona are in—ouch—let go of my shoulder."

"Rhys Tonsa? Fuck." Graem threw his staff on the bed. He moved back to his wardrobe and pulled out his teacher robes. "Nobody tells me anything that is going on around here."

Orrin was lost. "You ignored me banging down your door. Who else would be dumb enough to do that to you? What's the big deal?"

"The Tonsa whelp is going into the dungeon with you and I wasn't informed. An attack or warning was sent to you and I can't find a motive or clue about who it was." Graem threw an arm through his robe and gestured wildly at Orrin. "All of this . . . I can't say it's surprising, but it is bold."

Orrin folded his arms and waited.

"You don't see it?" Graem picked up his staff from the bed. "It's an assassination attempt. You're the patsy. Sloane and Hamish are the other members of your party? I think I've heard of Sloane. I don't know Hamish. He'll have information or evidence that puts Rhys in your room. You'll either be killed or Rhys's death will be pinned on you."

"What?"

Graem used the end of his staff to nudge Orrin away from the door. "It's easier to kill someone in a dungeon."

"No, wait. Why do you think I'm the patsy? You said you didn't know who broke into my room. That might not be related to Rhys at all. We had a plan to catch them."

Graem rolled his eyes. "I was fine to go along with your little trap until it involved the scion of one of the most powerful and richest families in Odrana. Spy games and subtle manipulation are allowed. Murder is not."

"What are you going to do?" Orrin needed that experience.

"Cancel the entire dungeon run," Graem said as he put his hand on the door. "I can't risk a Tonsa dying on my watch."

Orrin grabbed the door handle, making Graem give him a dangerous look. "I'm pretty sure Anabella got Rhys to go to the dungeon in an attempt for me to spend time with him. What if I can promise I'll keep him safe?"

"Explain." Graem threw up his anti-listening spell, covering the room in that protective layer again.

Orrin let [Mind Bastion] spin up in his head. He ordered his thoughts and started talking. "I got . . . a letter from Anabella that the dungeon was an opportunity for me, and Rhys got ordered in by his mom at the same time. There is no proof that any of the other members of my party are involved in what happened in my room or that it's connected to Rhys in any way. There are five parties going into the dungeon, and from what I've heard, we're supposed to go to different floors and avoid each other. It sounds to me that even if this was a hit attempt, there are over twenty other people you need to suspect. Not to mention, if you cancel the entire thing, you're just letting the bad guys know you're on to them. Wouldn't it be better to play it safe and maybe expose whatever is going on at the same time? Also, I can let him know up front. If he wants to pull out, there is an entire wait list of other students to take his place."

Orrin was proud of himself for spinning such a compelling argument on the fly. At the same time, he was analyzing his past meetings with Rhys and trying to figure out if any other classmates had seemed jealous of them talking or overly watchful of the young heir to the Tonsa line. Even with his mind clear, he couldn't find a lead.

"You want to use Rhys as bait," Graem pointed out. "The target you were sent to befriend."

"What better way to make friends than by saving his life . . . if you're right and he agrees to it." Orrin let go of the door handle, as Graem wasn't actively trying to leave anymore. "It could just be a coincidence that someone trashed my room. Nobody knew we would be in the same group. Wait. Actually, who assigns the groups?"

Graem gave Orrin a dark look and rubbed his hand over his face. "My sister."

There was no good response to that, so Orrin kept his mouth shut. He was learning.

"We are going to go talk with her and make sure everything is aboveboard," Graem said with finality. "That will decide if you get to go into the dungeon or not."

Chapter 31

"Wren doesn't know about my deal with Anabella, so keep your mouth shut," Graem instructed as they walked together. "In fact, you should go back to your room and wait. I'll come get you unless she agrees to call off the entire dungeon raid this week."

Orrin shook his head. "I'm not stupid. You'll have her cancel it and never tell her my plan so you can go drink."

Graem stopped and put his hand over his heart, feigning disbelief. "How could you make such an accusation?"

Orrin chuckled as he kept walking. When the two men arrived, Graem knocked once and pushed the door open. "Sis? Are you in?"

"Graem, you cannot barge into my office. What if I—" Wren stopped talking as Orrin hovered in the doorway. She was sitting behind her desk, stacks of reports littering the top. "Come in, Casimir. What is this about?"

"Casimir is scheduled to go into the Mistwater Lanterns later today . . ." Graem paused dramatically. "With Rhys Tonsa."

"I know. I assigned the party." Wren signed something and picked up another sheaf of papers to read. "What's the problem, Graem?"

"Casimir's room was recently broken into and vandalized. My sources have informed me that multiple high-level players are gathering in secret. Enough puzzle pieces are clear to see, Wren. Someone is going after the Tonsa boy. I want you to cancel the dungeon today."

Wren signed another paper and finally glanced up at her brother. "Is that all? I already know about his incident. I signed the paperwork for the cleanup myself. Although why I continue to do all your work is beyond me. I'm not worried about Rhys Tonsa."

Orrin bounced on the balls of his feet and jumped in as she took a breath to berate her brother. "Professor Wren? I'm with you on this. I told Graem we should use this as an opportunity. We can tell Rhys our suspicions and set a trap to—"

"You are not to tell Tonsa anything. Protect him if something comes at him, but that shouldn't be necessary. The dungeon run proceeds as planned, and if I'm correct, you are due at the entrance with your party in just under an hour, Casimir." Wren pulled a new stack of papers close and sighed heavily. "If that's all, you can see yourself out. Brother, take that stack to Mindy for filing. Thank you."

Graem put his hand on Orrin's shoulder. "Step outside for a moment."

The general joviality of his voice was gone, and Orrin hesitated for only a moment before complying. The door shut behind him. Two minutes later, the tall man opened it again. A scowl marred his face.

"Walk with me." Graem's hand fell on Orrin's shoulder again, steering him down a series of hallways. They passed several teachers and students, but all found something else to look at as Graem glowered down at them.

Orrin hopped forward a step when Graem pushed him into an empty classroom, putting a few feet between them. "What was—"

Graem's staff landed on the stone floor and his sound-bubble spell spread out. "Don't talk. Listen. There are more pieces moving here than you know, and I have no way to contact Anabella quickly enough to figure out if she knows what is happening. You mentioned you have a way to contact her. I need you to tell her what is going on. She likely knows everything already. She taught me most of what I know about information gathering. But in case she doesn't . . . tell her my sister put you in Tonsa's party at his mother's request. I have actionable intel that someone was hired to enter the dungeon to take out someone, but I can't find out who it is. They might be a holdover group or a single person. I don't think the elder Tonsa is trying to take out her own son, and there is no reason for Anabella to take out a target that she's invested time in recruiting, because I'm sure that's what you are here doing. Tell her my sister is not actively working against her, please?"

Graem's speech gathered steam until he was speaking so quickly at the end that Orrin had to concentrate hard to understand each word. He almost pulled the relic out and sent a message based on Graem's anxiety alone but remembered Anabella's warning to keep it hidden.

"What did your sister say that rattled you so much?"

Graem realized he was holding Orrin's shoulders and backed away. "She doesn't know I'm working for Lady Sanerris. She was paid to put your group together and not ask questions. If Anabella is the spider who controls the country from the shadows, Lady Tonsa is the fox that keeps the wolves at bay. Wren doesn't realize she's in a game between the two of them, and everything I've found shows your bedroom incident has nothing to do with either of them. Which means a third party. When titans like those two women fight, good people die. I can't let my sister be swept into that."

Orrin couldn't let the man's worry for his sister's safety continue. "I'll let her know your sister isn't trying to get in her way. And I'll make sure Rhys is safe. I can heal more than hangovers."

Sharing that extra bit was giving the man more data points for whatever strange analysis he ran in his head, but Orrin wasn't about to let him worry more than necessary. He'd been helpful so far, giving Orrin more of a lead than he'd thought he'd get while a slave to Anabella's machinations.

Graem scratched the side of his cheek. "You are going to have to tell me all about your class one of these days."

Orrin reached up and tugged on the fake necklace illusion that was his slave collar. "Right after you take this off."

Graem grabbed his staff, and with a pop the sound barrier dissipated. "We need to hurry. You have a dungeon to raid and an assassination to prevent."

The entrance to the dungeon was located in a building half a mile from Mistlight. Graem commandeered a carriage and got Orrin to the entrance within ten minutes.

"This is a dungeon?"

A short stone building sat in the middle of a field. Orrin could see the walls of Mistlight behind them, shining in the morning sun. Multiple embankments had been built around the squat building, making it appear as if it had fallen to the ground and rippled the earth around it.

"You need to stop acting like a foreigner. Everyone knows what Mistwater Lanterns looks like. It is one of the reasons Mistlight was built here in the first place," Graem said, stepping down out of the carriage. He pointed to the small hills as they walked closer. "These are built for defense in the case of a dungeon break. A single [Earth Mage] can raise walls in concentric rings, giving us time to defend. Of course, we haven't had an outbreak from the Lanterns in a century or more. The main entrance is inside and guarded well."

Orrin took it all in as they arrived at the heavy wooden doors guarded by a single watchman. He nodded lazily at Graem and let them enter.

The inside was barren and unassuming. Another guard sat on a stool, whittling a block of wood into something that could have been a dog, a horse, or some four-legged animal Orrin wasn't familiar with.

About a dozen students waited around a hole in the ground, with a teacher that Orrin didn't know holding a clipboard.

"Professor Graem, what are you doing here?" The younger teacher ran up at spotting him. Orrin snuck away before getting involved in another conversation.

"Casimir! Over here."

Orrin sighed as his social batteries were forced to turn back on. Rhys waved at him, holding a big spear. *No, that's a glaive.* Orrin remembered Brandt forcing them to try using the heavier spear-like weapon. It wasn't as popular as a plain spear due to cost but gave the option to slash an enemy with its longer, curved blade in addition to the traditional thrust of a spear. Rhys held it with a casual familiarity.

The faces surrounding Rhys soured at the sight of Orrin. Iona glowered as usual, but Orrin was surprised to see Hamish giving him an ugly look as well. Only Sloane gave him a polite but tight-lipped nod. She carried a long quarterstaff. Hamish rested a battle-ax over his shoulder. Iona's sword was strapped to her side but she also carried a few wands.

They stood close to the hole, which Orrin recognized as another set of stairs going into the ground. A few steps down, a haze covered everything, making it impossible to see farther.

"Sorry I'm late," Orrin said as he approached. "Professor Graem needed to talk with me."

Rhys's eyes shot to the teacher but swiftly returned to Orrin. "Not a problem. We were just going over our strategy. You're a sort of [Wind Mage], right?"

Orrin's Battle Class strategy was paying off. "Of a sort, yes."

"Sloane is an [Assimilator] and Hamish is a [Bruiser]. Both of them will be our front line." Rhys gestured, pointing out the two other members of the party. "You and I will be the back line. Iona can fill any gaps as needed between the two positions."

"How much weight can you push with your wind, Casimir?" Sloane asked, stepping in front of Rhys. Orrin sighed internally at the two still fighting over leadership.

"I've never measured it, but at least a human? Maybe more if I have to," Orrin answered truthfully. He didn't use [Gust] enough to know for sure, but he could always use [Boost]. The spell modifier would likely make his spell strong enough to knock over even this building if he poured his entire mana pool into it. Not that he would admit that to these people.

"We're still debating going to floor six or nine," Sloane said, holding up a hand to cut off Rhys. "Tonsa wants to go to floor six. Easier experience, large groups of enemies for farming, and an easy climate."

"Sounds good," Orrin answered, catching a smile and nod from Rhys. "Why not go there?"

Sloane smiled. "Floor nine has single enemies that are worth more alone than we could get in an hour of farming on six."

"What she didn't say is that the entirety of floor nine is a ledge along a lava field that would take us three hours of running to get to in the first place. We would have only two hours to farm, and those monsters aren't a guaranteed sighting," Rhys said, leaning against his glaive's shaft. He looked comfortable in his loose, light-colored clothing, which only highlighted his dark skin. "While I am all for taking a risk, the payoff isn't worth the work involved. Not to mention the danger of floor nine."

"The danger?"

"There's a monster from a lower level that moved into the ninth floor a decade ago. It sleeps in the lava fields and only rarely comes up to attack," Sloane added quickly. "The chances of it waking up and attacking us are slim to none."

Orrin's mind had been weighing the pros and cons of both attacks until Sloane said that. "Floor six it is."

"Wait! As the tiebreaker, you should know exactly what you'd be—"

Orrin cut her off. "Sloane, it would have been a fair argument until you jinxed it. Floor nine is cursed now."

Iona finally spoke up. "What do you mean?"

"If we were to go to floor nine after Sloane said it was completely safe, whatever that monster is would attack us. That's just how my luck works. I'm not going there."

Sloane made a few more attempts, but a beaming Rhys shut her down. Finally, it was their turn to enter. Rhys let Sloane go first, followed closely by the silent Hamish. The Tonsa heir took the middle, and Orrin followed behind Iona. The entire time he'd known the pair, she was never more than two steps from him.

As Orrin climbed down the stairs, he saw a familiar message and smiled.

Welcome to Mistwater Lanterns!

It was time to get some experience.

Chapter 32

Orrin squinted against the sunlight beating down. He shaded his eyes and glanced back the way he'd come.

I'm in a dungeon, right?

"Hurry up, slowpoke," Sloane yelled from in front of him. "The path to the lower floors is over this way."

What Orrin had expected was more of the enclosed spaces or maybe large rooms he'd encountered in dungeons before. The first floor of Mistwater Lanterns left him in awe.

He was on a new planet.

For as far as he could see in every direction, grassy knolls crested over pristine ponds. The sun above warmed his skin. Birds whistled in the distant trees, swooping above his head. A rabbit sprinted away from Sloane as she trampled the tall grass. Hamish and Rhys were close behind, with Iona struggling to carry a pack Orrin hadn't noticed before.

"You're sure this is the way?" Rhys asked Sloane as she moved between the small pools of water. Orrin leaned over, trying to see into the clear water, but saw nothing. The ponds seemed empty but were much deeper than he'd originally thought. The sun shining above couldn't illuminate the dark bottom.

"The correct pool is marked. I'll give you Odranan fucks one compliment. You keep your dungeon well managed."

Orrin saw Iona whisper something to Rhys, but he shook his head.

"Did you all join up as a party yet?" Orrin asked, trudging along behind.

"Oh, I'll invite you," Rhys said, looking into the air for a moment. "There we go."

Rhys Has Invited You to a Party
Yes or No?

"Got it," Orrin said, accepting the invite.

Usually, a person's name appeared to the group when they were invited to a party. Orrin waited for something bad to happen, but Rhys kept walking. He checked the party log and found Casimir Hale listed under Rhys Tonsa. The collar must be keyed to his fake identity somehow. Anabella really thought of everything.

"Iona, do you want me to carry the bag for you?" Orrin offered, trying to build a rapport with the cold girl. "I didn't think we would need supplies for a day trip."

She ignored him and kept struggling through the muck. The path they were on wasn't the obvious one. That award went to the paved road that moved away from the entrance to the dungeon. Instead, they veered to the right, following the grass crumpled by the last group to enter.

"Iona insisted on bringing some bandages and potions, as well as food in case we end up stuck. You never know what we might encounter," Rhys answered in her place. "Thank you for the offer, but she takes protecting me and my possessions very seriously."

"Stop," Sloane said as she knelt and held a fist in the air. "Three monsters ahead. We need to go around that pond and get to the one on the far right."

"Why is the entrance to the next floor so close?" Orrin asked. "And why can't we just take those three monsters out?"

Hamish answered his first question, speaking in a low, slow voice. "This dungeon has been excavated over the years. There are multiple spots where we have broken through to the next floor. It makes it easier for dungeon-raiding teams to return to the lower floors and keep us safe by culling the strongest monsters."

"And the monsters?" Orrin pried as they started walking in a crouch along the water's edge. "We can take three on the first level, right?"

"The first floor is filled with thousands of Sunny Bunnies," Rhys whispered as if that explained everything.

Orrin sighed. Everyone else had done their research, it seemed. He was behind Iona, trailing the group. He surreptitiously pulled his dungeon monster encyclopedia from his pocket dimension and turned to the back.

Sunny Bunny is one of the weakest monsters known. A single Bunny can be taken down with a child's arrow; however, be wary, as the resulting explosion of their body after death can do minimal light damage. These explosions alert Bunnies in the vicinity. Larger groups can be time-consuming for the well prepared and deadly for those caught unaware.

(alone *** in groups)*

"Are you reading a book right now?" Iona hissed, speaking to Orrin for perhaps the first time since they'd met.

Orrin closed the pages and waved the book at her. "Just a bit of light reading to pass the time."

She scoffed. Orrin waited until she turned away to push the book back into his [Dimension Hole].

Orrin wondered how much damage the explosion of a Sunny Bunny would cause him. If he could use a [Light Ward] to protect himself, he could run around and gather a bunch of them up for some easy experience. He might need to try that. Even if he received only a few points per rabbit, he could farm the first floor.

He considered accidentally getting the attention of one of the monsters and giving up his warding magic secret to the group. It would be easy experience, but he didn't know these people well enough to trust them with that kind of information. He'd use a [Ward] on Rhys if he had to, but Orrin wanted to keep as many cards close to his chest as he could.

It took only twenty minutes to reach the right pool from the starting point of the dungeon, but Sloane had them stop and wait in a crouched position for so long that Orrin's legs cramped up a bit. He finally noticed the small stack of rocks, painted red, that marked this pool as special.

"Rope?" Sloane held out her hand.

Iona glanced at Rhys but complied when he nodded again. She set her pack down and pulled out a coil of rope, handing it to Sloane.

"Everyone grab on and don't let go. It can be scary the first time, but you only have to hold your breath for a few seconds. Try and enjoy it." Sloane wrapped the end of the rope around her fist and grabbed her quarterstaff tight in the other. "We go on three."

Hamish took hold a few feet behind Sloane. Iona and Rhys took the middle, and Rhys handed the end to Orrin.

"Three."

Orrin gripped his end of the rope. "Are we jumping into the pond?"

"Two."

Rhys rolled his eyes. "Did you not learn anything about the Lanterns?"

"One." Sloane jumped. The rest followed, with Orrin being pulled in with them.

Because he hadn't jumped, Orrin went into the pond face-first. Water stung his eyes and went up his nose. As he coughed, he realized he was already through a curtain of wetness and was sliding . . . fast.

It's a water slide!

The tube was pitch-black, so Orrin couldn't see anything. He felt the pull of his party members on the rope he still held. Questions raced through his mind as fast as they were traveling. Was he sliding on rock? How did the small amount of water under him keep flowing? Who created this?

In an instant, though, the ride ended. The other four members of the team slid to a stop, using their hands and feet to slow themselves. Orrin, sliding on his belly, only went faster, and he knocked into Rhys just as the young man started to stand up.

Orrin and Rhys ended in a tangle of arms and legs. Rhys laughed first, with Orrin joining in. The danger of the dungeon was temporarily off their minds after the fun of the water slide.

"Remove yourself." A blade touched Orrin's chest, pushing hard enough to hurt but not to draw blood. He went still.

"Iona, back away now. It wasn't intentional." Rhys's voice was hard and commanding, at odds with the usual cheeky tone he used. Iona obeyed instantly.

Rhys put out his hand and helped Orrin to his feet. He frowned as he checked over Orrin. "Do you not use any armor or weapons?"

Orrin thought back to his abandoned armor at Anabella's cottage with a pang of nostalgia. He shook his head. "I have summoned weapons, but I'll attack from a distance."

"I'd be more worried about Iona," Rhys joked . . . or so Orrin hoped.

The second floor was another large landmass with a frozen lake in the middle. Each floor felt like a world in and of itself, but Sloane explained to Orrin that after years of exploration, the first thirty floors were well mapped out. Each floor contained a different way of getting down to the next floor: stone stairs, a hole with a ladder, and a spiral staircase that would have been at home in a castle. It took them two hours to get to the fifth floor and only ten minutes from there to find the stairs carved into the side of a bluff.

"The only downside of using the shortcuts is there are no safe rooms between floors," Sloane continued to explain to Orrin as they hugged the cliffside and descended. "We can always fight our way through a floor like normal to rest or camp out if it's a safer floor."

"Is floor six a safer floor?" Orrin asked, trying not to look at the void to his left. Hamish had picked up Iona's bag despite her protests and taken the lead. Rhys's bodyguard was holding the back of her ward's shirt as they shuffled slowly together behind everyone else.

"No. We will work our way back to the safe room between five and six. It should take an hour, but we can fall back and exit the Lanterns if we get overwhelmed."

Orrin was about to ask another question when Hamish disappeared on the next step.

"Floor six is after this step," Sloane called back. "Be ready to fight."

She disappeared.

"Fight what?" Orrin asked the empty space. He turned back to ask Rhys, "What are we fighting?"

Rhys reached Orrin. He held his glaive in one hand and gave Orrin a tiny push with his free arm. "Get going. She doesn't like heights."

"Rhys, you guys didn't tell me what we're up against on the sixth floor."

"Skylight Anglers. Flying fish. Just try to hit them and keep them scattered. I'll take care of the rest."

Orrin opened his mouth to argue, but Iona pointed a wand over Rhys's shoulder. He put his hands up and stepped back into the next floor.

When the haze parted, Orrin saw Hamish and Sloane already fighting. When Rhys said *flying fish,* Orrin had imagined small fish jumping out of the water. He had some experience with fighting monsters like that.

What he did not expect to see was a horror from the ocean deep floating in the air. A monstrosity the size of an elephant, with an elongated jaw, razor-sharp teeth, and a dangly appendage hanging from between its eyes with a light. A light that spat out darts of magic that splashed on the two tanks.

"Casimir, attack the fin ray," Rhys yelled, running by him. Orrin realized he was standing still, watching the fight.

"What's a fin ray?" Orrin shouted back, throwing a [Gust] at the monster. He also used [Identify].

Skylight Angler—345/400 HP

"The thing on its head, you idiot," Sloane said, pointing her quarterstaff. The fish ducked through the air and rammed into Sloane. She vibrated and twirled, tapping her weapon against the side of the Angler. Sloane seemed unharmed, but the space she touched on the monster caved in as if it was hit much harder.

Orrin moved up to stand beside Rhys and Iona. He used another [Gust] on the fin ray, causing it to spin up and over the fish's body. The light magic attacks stopped for the moment, and Hamish, finally able to focus on something besides dodging, ran in close. His axe raised high and cleaved through the underside of the Angler.

Rhys swiped his glaive in the air, throwing afterimages of his weapon at the monster. *No,* Orrin realized. *He's throwing metal blades out of the glaive head.*

Iona's wand pointed at the ground, and jagged spikes of earth shot out from under the Angler. Two stuck deep, halting its escape.

The monster was dead in another few attacks. Orrin kept the light away from the tanks and threw a summoned [Fire Sword] at the monster to do some damage before it died.

Experience Gained: 100 XP

Orrin looked at his status and frowned. The fight hadn't taken long, but he would need sixty-two more Anglers to hit level nineteen. Hamish and Sloane were resting, having used a lot of stamina in the fight. Rhys and Iona seemed fine for now, but they wouldn't have the mana needed to fight as long as he could.

If only he could go off on his own and fight unrestricted, Orrin was sure he could take one of the flying fish down alone. He just needed to wait for the right opportunity while also keeping an eye out for the supposed assassination attempt on Rhys.

Orrin checked his [Map]. The sixth floor was massive. In his zoomed-in phase, he could see twenty to thirty more red dots signifying more Anglers. He panned out, and the number tripled with each subsequent zoom. This was going to be a lot of work.

Chapter 33

"The exit is that way," Sloane said, pointing away from the dead fish. "Let's set up a half mile out from it and figure the best setup for the time we have left."

Orrin considered pointing out the least crowded way to the floor's gate door but decided against it for now. With [Map], he could watch for monster attacks. The monsters of both the dungeons and the world above appeared as red. Everyone in his party was a blue dot on the [Map]. Anyone else would be gray until they attacked. Or maybe it was when they decided to attack. He didn't have a solid idea.

The only other colors that regularly showed up on his [Map] were white for animals and yellow for traps. Orrin never found much in ability books about [Map] or the various extra functions he'd unlocked. In a world that valued quickly attacking and killing monsters, the utility spells and skills were not heavily researched.

Instead of being obvious and giving directions, Orrin walked slightly to the left of the group and waved them over to ask questions as they walked. They still ran into Skylight Anglers, but not nearly as many as they would have if Sloane had been allowed to barrel ahead. Still, each attack after the first one involved three of the flying fish at minimum.

Orrin continued to use [Gust] to push the Anglers around. He tried to keep two or three occupied while Sloane and Hamish hammered them into fish food one at a time. Rhys and Iona used their magic to great effect as well. The four hundred hit points melted away off each target, giving Orrin time to push one fish out of the grouping he'd created for the next assault.

He played with [Gust], figuring out the smallest amount of mana he could use to push an Angler away, change its direction, and even keep it at a standstill. The last move took a bit of learning. He had to use [Inverse] to push and pull with the air, keeping the fish from escaping its new windy prison.

In total, the group took down seventeen Anglers on their trek to the campsite. A stone door frame stood in a small grove of trees. Iona and Rhys sat down and even Hamish leaned against a tree.

"Rest for ten minutes and then we'll send someone out to scout and pull back a few of the critters at a time," Sloane instructed. "I'm going to complain when we get out. Floor six shouldn't have this many monsters. Somebody is slacking off." She squatted and stretched her leg in front of her. "If you need to take a mana potion do it now, youngsters. This might be a quick trip for all of us if we get swarmed."

Iona and Rhys were sweating, but not to the point that Orrin thought they were low on mana already. Sloane kept them moving at a brisk pace. He wasn't quite sure who was the actual party leader, as Rhys still gave directions during fights from time to time.

Instead of worrying, Orrin checked his status.

Experience Gained: 1,700 XP (100 XP x 17)

According to Sloane, spending more than eight to ten hours inside the Mistwater Lanterns would risk their sleep and performance in class the following day. It had taken just over two hours to get to the sixth floor and another two hours to fight their way to this location. Sloane's earlier estimate didn't take into account the increased spawn rate of the Anglers. By Orrin's math, they could spend another five to seven hours farming experience. He was at 4,586 out of 9,000 experience points needed to get to level nineteen. The team would need to kill another forty-five Anglers for him to reach the next level . . . unless . . .

Orrin joined Sloane where she was stretching.

"Sloane, I can run pretty fast with my wind magic. I could do some scouting and pull a few giant fish back each time. How many do you think we could take out?"

Sloane responded without looking up. "We struggled when Hamish caught that group of five. With you playing around in the back and not attacking them, the rest of us have to spend twice as long killing them. I think four is safe, but three is better." She was doing some sort of yoga but with only one hand on the ground.

Orrin wanted to argue that his doing more damage to one Angler wouldn't have helped if he allowed all the fish to converge on the party at once. It was the same argument he'd had with Madi in the beginning. Everyone's attraction to dealing the most damage was ingrained into their culture. Madi came around after multiple fights, but Orrin thought a part of her was still happy it was Orrin that did crowd control, healing, and the other "useless" tasks. Sloane wasn't worth the time it would take to convince her.

"I can bring in groups of three." He kept his response curt.

"Ask His Highness if he's recovered. Hamish and I could keep fighting until we need to leave, but once the three of you run out of mana, we'll have to pull back." Sloane shifted her foot to the ground and bent over, creating a bridge with her body. "If we can get another three or four groups of three taken down, it's still a good haul for a day's work, though."

Orrin nodded and walked away before he said something. Sloane's attitude had been funny when directed at Rhys, but her casual disregard for their abilities was more grating when directed at him.

"Rhys, how are you and Iona? I'm going to do a bit of scouting and try to kite a few Anglers this way."

Rhys let the water bag he was drinking from down. "We're ready for another fight or two. Can I ask you a question before you leave?"

Orrin shrugged in response.

"Why do you throw [Fire Swords]? Don't you have something better to attack with? I thought after seeing you use so much mana in class, you might be holding something back."

The question wasn't considered outright rude, as Rhys didn't ask for a specific skill or spell, but it still walked the border of polite talk. Orrin didn't care and would have talked about his buff spells if he trusted this group a bit more, but with the collar on and what he was currently trying to do, he wasn't about to share.

"I have a few tricks up my sleeve, but I'm fine doing what I'm doing. Do you think the Anglers are just waiting patiently to attack one at a time? I've been keeping them penned up so we can attack them. While I'm not doing as much damage that way, we all stay safer. Slow and steady wins the race."

"Slow doesn't win races, Casimir."

In a world with magic, a story about a tortoise and hare racing probably wouldn't have the same moral. "It means playing it safe is the smarter choice. I could run in and attack with a sword, but that would let the Anglers attack all at once. If each of us takes one on our own, we could probably survive, but the experience would be distributed weird and someone could get unlucky."

"You'll never get far if you aren't powerful enough to hold your own against something as weak as a Skylight Angler," Iona chimed in. The dismissive look in her eyes gave Orrin another pang. He missed his friends.

"I didn't say I couldn't take one out," Orrin said, trying to keep his composure. "I'm not going to waste my time explaining it more. If you want, I can bring back three and we can do it your way."

Iona shoved a bottle back inside her bag. Orrin noticed the markings of a mana potion. She must have been closer to running out than they'd thought. "We would appreciate that. We can handle these small groups."

Orrin saluted sarcastically and turned away. He started a light jog and waved to Sloane on the way out.

Survive. Stay together. Get home. Orrin repeated his rules in his mind. He pulled up [Map] and found a group of four Anglers moving about two miles away. His feet began to eat the ground, taking larger steps and moving faster. His increased dexterity training seemed to be paying off, as he left the group behind within minutes.

Once he was out of sight, Orrin pulled his monster book out of [Dimension Hole].

Skylight Anglers use light magic to swim through the air. They use their light appendage to throw attacks of magic, but their main attack consists of using long teeth to tear flesh. While relatively simple on a singular basis, Anglers spawn at high rates and attack in pods.

*(** alone **** in groups)*

Orrin thought of a few different ways he could fight the monsters alone. He could use [Decrease Strength] until they couldn't carry the weight of their own bodies. He could use [Way of the Water]. He could kite them, attacking from a distance and running. Even a larger group would go down with enough [Lightstrikes]. As he approached the four fish in the distance, he used [Calm Mind] to shed the anxiety and stress he'd been under constantly for the last few weeks.

If he was going to release some tension, Orrin was going to go all out.

The four Anglers floated along without noticing him. Once he was close, Orrin used [Camouflage]. The training with Bellamy to increase his output potential was paying off as well. Orrin closed the fifty yards in a flash. He stabbed a [Fire Sword] directly into the softball-size eye and twisted before letting the blade go. One quick jab with his increased strength to the hilt of the sword pushed the blade through the Angler completely. It fell lifeless to the ground.

Before it bounced, Orrin was on the second Angler. The four monsters stood no chance against the combined speed and strength of a fully juiced-up Orrin. Using [Way of the Water], he dodged the few counterattacks of the remaining three fish. Once there was only one, Orrin experimented.

"Three casts of [Decrease Strength] to bring you down, huh? You must be strong." Orrin raised his foot over the fish's eye. The book didn't say that was the weak spot, but from the dozens of punches and kicks he'd just delivered, he would need to remember to add that in as a footnote.

Orrin stomped three times before the head caved in.

Experience Gained: 2,000 XP (500 XP x 4)

"That's more like it."

Orrin's fight had lasted two minutes. The party had fought each group of monsters for upward of five to ten minutes. He knew that he'd grown, but this was insane. The maxed-out stats were starting to show their full potential, and Orrin knew from his training he was only tapping a small part of his total potential.

He found another group of three fish and hit them all with [Lightstrikes]. Falling back, he dodged their thrown light attacks and kept them moving toward the party. He moved slower than he could, as he wasn't sure when he would come into their view.

"Take the one on the left, we'll go right." Sloane's voice came from behind him. "Casimir, take out the center one, or at least keep it tied up until we can help you."

Orrin used [Gust] again to separate the fish and make it easier for them to attack. Hamish and Sloane made quick work of the right-most Angler before moving to attack the one Orrin was half-heartedly throwing [Fire Swords] at. They didn't quite finish it off before Iona and Rhys joined in.

Experience Gained: 432 XP (100 XP x 1; 166 x 2)

"Not bad," Sloane said, huffing as she leaned on her quarterstaff. "Try and be a little quicker bringing the next set back?"

Orrin smiled and saluted her again. Iona let out a single chuckle, which he ignored. Turning his back on the party, he ran back into the depths of the dungeon.

Chapter 34

Orrin repeated his strategy again: he searched the floor until he found a small group of Skylight Anglers and experimented with his spells, earning the lion's share of experience for himself.

One of the topics Professor Hugh had mentioned in class was how certain types of magic could exacerbate their corresponding spells. For instance, when fire magic and ice magic mixed, people could sometimes create icy fog or boiling steam depending on the mana output, spell level, personal power, and a multitude of other uncontrollable factors. The core of the reading for Surviving Spell Attacks was a simple explanation of what types of mages you should avoid as a different type of mage.

Orrin's questions had been on using your own magics in combination. While it was rare for a mage to use two conflicting types of magic, it wasn't unheard-of, according to Hugh. Orrin kept his specific magic spells to himself, but he was able to come up with two new ways to attack using his summoned swords. Usually, he threw the cheap weapons at monsters to get the underlying requirement of damage on a creature to earn a portion of its experience. He studied the Anglers as they approached.

"Let's do this."

In his right hand, Orrin held a [Fire Sword]. Pointing the sword at the group of three monsters, he cast [Gust], focused not out in front of his body but through his hand. He let the mana coalesce and soak itself in the fire mana escaping as heat along the summoned blade before letting it loose.

The result was a hair-dryer effect. The air still pushed the three monsters back, but a quick check with [Identify] showed Orrin that he had done no damage to the fish.

He dodged multiple light attacks with his increased dexterity. With his speed, the fish couldn't hope to bite him and instead spread out in an attempt to hit him with their ranged attack.

It took Orrin three attempts before he found a way to ignite the sword's fire mana and intertwine it with the air magic from [Gust]. A shimmer of heated air blasted out in a cone in front of him, burning a hole through the forehead of one Angler. It dipped drunkenly to the side, hurt and blinded but still alive.

Using the summoned sword in this way made it crumble away to nothingness. However, in his left hand, Orrin held his second experiment: an [Ice Sword]. He repeated the attack using all he'd learned.

A breeze cooled the creature's burned skin.

"What?" Orrin shouted in frustration. "That should have worked. Whoa—"

He dived to the side. He'd been so focused on the one half-dead Angler that he'd turned from the other two. They'd swum through the air to get close and almost got his leg and arm.

He summoned another [Fire Sword] and finished off the first Angler. With only two circling him, Orrin spent five minutes trying to get a combined ice and air attack to trigger but couldn't figure out what he was doing wrong.

In frustration, he slowed both Anglers down with [Decrease Dexterity] and approached the closer one.

"Why won't this work?" At the last word, Orrin swung the icy sword down on the fish. So used to combining his [Gust] at the same time from his earlier attempts, Orrin did the same on reflex.

Where Orrin hit, ice rapidly crept along the Angler's body. Over half the fish was covered in scaly ice. Orrin's sword disintegrated.

Orrin snorted a huff of air, half in laughter and half in disbelief. He summoned another [Ice Sword] and walked behind the half-frozen fish before hitting its back fins. This time he focused on the magic.

With the [Fire Sword], he used the air magic to grasp the fire magic. The fire rode the air magic toward the target, creating an attack from a distance. With the [Ice Sword], the ice magic was too heavy. Only when he used it during a point of contact could the air and ice form along the given path of the enemy's body.

"Fire and air for ranged attacks," Orrin said as he blasted another [Fire Sword] apart to hit the monster a third time, blowing it to pieces. He approached the final Angler. The fish quivered mightily, trying to move. "Ice and air for close-up melee."

Orrin used four [Ice Swords] to kill the last fish.

Experience Gained: 1,500 XP (500 XP x 3)

He smiled at the broken bodies of the giant fish in front of him. The questions he'd asked Professor Hugh about different magic types and how each could change when combined had paid off.

Orrin checked his [Map] and saw a group of four monsters between him and his party. He lured them back to the entrance to the sixth floor of Mistwater Lanterns. He split his attention between his recent finds and keeping two of the fish battered around.

He chuckled to himself. *Battered fish.*

Experience Gained: 400 XP (100 XP x 4)

The fights he did on his own used more mana, but he still had enough to go out for another round. Unfortunately, it didn't seem as though his party was in the same shape.

Sloane and Hamish appeared to want more fights, but sweat had covered Iona's forehead before the fight began. She fought mostly with her sword, but when one of the Anglers moved toward Rhys, she used magic to spike it from underneath. It stopped the monster in its tracks, but she'd fainted almost immediately.

Orrin felt a twinge of sympathy for her. He remembered how terrible he felt with mana exhaustion, even if it hadn't happened to him in a long time.

He checked his status while waiting for Rhys to check on her and for Sloane to give the order to go back out.

Orrin	Utility Warder Level 18 (8,918/9,000)	Ability Points: 15 Administrator Points: 24
HP: 140/140	MP: 694/1,100	
Strength: 9 (100)	Constitution: 14	Dexterity: 11 (100)
Will: 28 (100)	Intelligence: 11 (100)	

So close to leveling. They're not going to want to stick around for another few hours, though, Orrin thought, watching Rhys kneel and whisper with his bodyguard. Hamish muttered something to Sloane, who shrugged.

"That might be all we can take today," Rhys said, standing up beside his bodyguard. "Iona can't take another mana potion."

Orrin hesitated. He had a few regen potions. *Iona must have a small mana pool if she's already flagging. We have three hours left before we should head out. I wonder if she'd even trust me enough to drink one?*

"She can wait by the exit. Hamish and I are going to hunt a bit more. Do you two want to join us?" Sloane answered with her arms crossed. Hamish stood to her side and slightly behind.

"We're a party. Nobody is getting left behind, and we leave as a group. That is the rule for the dungeon."

"Casimir? Can you find only groups of two and three for us?" Sloane turned away from Rhys.

Orrin saw Rhys's fists clench around his weapon. He ignored Sloane and put his hand on Rhys's shoulder. "Can I talk with you for a minute?"

Orrin walked back to where Iona was lying. She had both eyes closed and looked green.

"Casimir, there is a reason for the rul—"

"If Iona could keep going, would you want to fight more?" Orrin interrupted him. He put his hand in his pocket and fingered the small vial that appeared in his palm.

"She's out of mana. She pushed too much and didn't listen when I told her to keep to physical attacks," Rhys said, directing his voice at the woman between them. "There's a reason we're not supposed to overuse mana potions, isn't there, Iona?"

She groaned at the word *potion* and turned in the grass. For a minute, Orrin thought she was going to puke on his feet.

Orrin considered what he knew about Rhys. The man was slightly younger than him and obviously well educated. He appeared to have inherited his mother's brains and seemed socially outgoing. However, his bodyguard and friend, Iona, never left his side. From Anabella's files, Orrin knew attending school was his first foray into the real world.

The worry Rhys had for Iona was real. She wasn't going to die from a little mana exhaustion, but as a fellow mage, he had to know how uncomfortable it was. *If I help her feel better, he'll trust me more.* Orrin felt like shit as soon as the thought crossed his mind. Still, he was on a mission, and until a better choice came along . . .

"I have a way she can slowly regain her mana, but you have to trust me, and you can't ask me about it."

Rhys tilted his head as he stared at Orrin. "Do you have a mana transfer skill?"

Orrin jumped on the possible excuse. "Something like that. I have a potion that can let her move about and regain her mana like she was resting. If I give it to you, though, don't tell the others. I don't have a lot of them."

"Can I see one?" Rhys put out his hand.

Orrin weighed his options. He needed Rhys to trust him so he could make Anabella happy, but he also wanted to get more experience. He didn't think he was going to have time to get thousands more experience points to get to level twenty, but even the extra ability points from hitting one more level could open up a few options. Plus, he could try and sneak back in on his own.

He handed the small regen bottle over.

"This looks poorly made," Rhys complained as he studied the glass. He held it up to the fake sky and used the light to look through it. "I'd rather not risk it. I like you, Casimir, but I don't trust without verification."

Orrin pulled another regen bottle out of his pocket using [Dimension Hole]. "Take both and pick one. I'll drink whichever one you pick before she drinks the other. You have no reason to trust me, Rhys. You seem nice, and I'm trusting you with one of my secrets. I'm close to leveling, so this isn't me being altruistic. Worst-case scenario, it's poison and you have to rush her out of here to a [Healer], but why would I poison the bodyguard over you?"

Rhys slowly took the second bottle without breaking eye contact with Orrin. Not for the first time, Orrin saw steel behind the boy's . . . no, the man's eyes. Rhys was clever.

He handed one of the bottles back to Orrin. "Drink it."

Orrin popped the top and tilted the bottle so Rhys could clearly see the liquid splash into his mouth. He checked his status and saw his normal rate of mana regeneration had grown exponentially. He'd be back at full mana in no time. *Maybe I should try for five Anglers before I bring some back?*

"If this harms her, there is nowhere you can hide from me," he said quietly before kneeling back down to Iona. "Iona, I have something for you to drink. It's not a mana potion but will make you feel better."

Orrin walked back to Hamish and Sloane. "We'll keep going in a few minutes."

"What was that about?" Sloane peered over Orrin's shoulder, trying to catch a glimpse of Rhys and Iona. "Did you convince her to take another potion? I think she's already taken three."

"No, I used a skill. She'll be fine to go before I head out."

"Then get going," Sloane said with a shrug. "If she's going to be useless, tell her to not hit our targets. The same goes for you and Rhys. The two of us want to make this trip worth it. Bring at least two for us and you three can take whatever is left over."

Orrin didn't answer and went back to make sure Iona was doing fine. In two minutes, she'd already regained some color and was sitting up on her own.

"I'm going back out. Sloane and Hamish requested two Anglers for themselves. The three of us are to stay out of their way," Orrin explained. A desire to use [Identify] and make sure Iona's mana was regenerating crept up, but he pushed it away. He didn't need to make himself more mysterious.

"We can handle two as well," Iona said with a weak voice. "I'll show them."

Orrin kept the smile off his face at her gumption. "I'll bring back four, then. Be ready."

He stood up and brushed his knees with his hands.

"Casimir?"

Orrin turned back to Rhys with his hand out.

"Thank you."

"You'd have done the same," Orrin answered him, gripping the man's hand. "I'll be right back."

Chapter 35

Orrin's mana recovered at an astronomical rate while using the regen potion. His [Meditate] skill let him recover one mana point a minute. While only sixty mana points regenerating over an hour seemed like a small amount, the majority of people in this world had to wait for sleep or use a mana potion to recover their used mana.

When he'd given a regen potion to Iona, she'd effectively learned to use [Meditate] for an hour. When Orrin drank his potion, it increased his mana growth from one point a minute to one point every second. That meant that over the next hour, Orrin would recover thirty-six hundred points of mana. He would need to throw mana around with abandon if he was to make even a dent in his rapidly climbing mana bar.

As he rushed away from the group, he gauged how much mana was already filling his mana pool. His maximum mana was set at eleven hundred, and the few hundred he had used throughout the day was rapidly refilling.

He summoned a [Fire Sword] and [Ice Sword] and went to work.

Orrin spent much of his time being cautious. He tested and theorized because if he didn't do it, Daniel surely wouldn't. He spent so much of his time worried about refilling his party's [Wards], healing injuries, and buffing that he forgot the simple fact that he was using magic.

As Orrin approached the first set of three Anglers, he did something new. He let loose.

Orrin didn't reduce their stats. He spun through the three targets using [Way of the Water], narrowly avoiding splatters of light magic and teeth alike. However, he never worried about getting hit. His own speed guaranteed the monsters' attacks were always a second behind. He sent blasts of [Gust] up through each sword, burning with each thrust and freezing with each slash. In short, Orrin had fun playing with his magic.

This is how Daniel feels when he fights up close with Gertrude. Orrin ducked under one of the floating fish, using its body to shield against the other two's light spell attacks. *All the adrenaline of a fight.*

With his intelligence and will increased to the max, each spell cost next to nothing.

One of the Anglers backed away as Orrin summoned another [Fire Sword] to his hand.

"Oh no, you don't," Orrin said and pointed the [Fire Sword] at the retreating monster.

Without thinking about it, Orrin used [Boost] on his [Gust] spell as he replayed his new trick of sending the air magic into the [Fire Sword]. His mana was nearly full in the under ten minutes it had taken him to find this group of monsters and dart about within their defenses. He threw a minute's worth of mana into the [Boost] spell modifier.

> **[Boost]—(Spell Modifier) Modify a spell to perform additional effect based on MP**

The spell didn't increase the amount of fire magic that [Gust] was able to steal from [Fire Sword] before it disintegrated in Orrin's hand. It did manage to launch the Angler through the air in an arc. It landed hard on the ground a few hundred yards away and didn't move.

> **Experience Gained: 500 XP**
> **Level 19 Obtained!**
> **+10 AP**

Orrin laughed as he rushed to the other two bags of experience waiting to die.

Experience Gained: 1,000 XP (500 x 2)

He closed his eyes for a moment, breathing heavily with the exertion of dodging the last desperate attempts of the Anglers to hurt him. Having watched Hamish and Sloane fighting close up with the fish, he knew his feat of killing them three at a time by himself was impressive. It wasn't something he was going to advertise, but he'd gained a level, improved his spell selection a bit, and gained some fighting experience. The thought of experience made him open his eyes and his status box.

Orrin	Utility Warder Level 19 (1,418/10,000)	Ability Points: 25

The entire fight had taken him only a few minutes, but he really didn't have the time to spare for another fight. Orrin contemplated waiting to be the last one through the exit. He could simply stay here and farm Anglers until he hit diminishing returns. At five hundred experience points a fish, that wasn't going to be anytime soon.

Each additional fight of three to four fish would be fifteen hundred to two thousand experience. In five more fights, he could hit twenty and would complete the Quest. He was hoping at that point his weird Administrator powers would let him take off this damn collar.

He pulled up his [Map] to find another group of three. Since Sloane wanted two for her and Hamish, Orrin planned to bring only one for Iona and Rhys. Neither of them was a front-line fighter, so Orrin would either need to control one with precision use of [Gust] or use his fighting style to distract the monster. He wasn't ready to give that secret up yet.

The Anglers were piling up in larger groups closer to him. The school of fish must have some way to tell their numbers were being thinned out. Orrin settled on a group of four and used [Boost] and [Gust] to knock one far away. He kept the three moving in a zigzag pattern around other groups until the fourth fish gave up chasing them and turned to join another cluster of monsters.

Pulling close to his party, Orrin saw Sloane and Rhys standing far apart. Each had their shadow posted next to them. He brought the three Anglers close to Sloane and let her hit two. Using [Gust], Orrin pushed the third toward Rhys and Iona.

Orrin watched Sloane step into the melee between the two fish, once again wondering what her class build was all about. She'd called herself an [Assimilator], but all Orrin had seen her do was hit with her stick. The hits did seem to pack more of a punch than his own sword attacks would without his strength buff. Orrin wasn't sure what her level was, but either some magical hijinks were going on or she'd devoted too many points to her strength. Hamish spun his axe, leaving deep, bleeding furrows wherever he attacked.

Rhys used his glaive like an actual weapon, forcing Iona behind him. The single Angler challenged the two of them, but Orrin could see they had it under control. Whenever Rhys moved to one side, Iona dashed in to attack before skipping back.

Everything was going to plan.

Orrin shivered at the thought and quickly checked his [Map]. The red dots that denoted the Skylight Anglers continued to group up in larger groups away from them. *Was Graem wrong about the assassination attempt?*

Rhys stabbed out the Angler's left eye, which gave Iona the breathing space needed to rush in for the kill. Their single monster went down. Since Orrin didn't harm the thing, he received no credit for the kill. The downside of being a utility caster in a world of attackers.

"Casimir, you forgot to attack this one," Rhys said, stabbing the fallen monster to make his point. "You should hurry up and do some damage to one of Sloane's Anglers before she . . . well, there goes the first one."

Orrin looked over his shoulder at the woman with the quarterstaff. The first Angler was a broken mess on the ground. Hamish was hammering away at the second, keeping it at bay with large sweeps of his blade. The last beast went down in only a few more minutes once they both targeted the same one.

"I thought you wanted to gain experience?" Rhys said, scaring Orrin. He hadn't noticed the younger man walk up behind him.

Orrin waved a hand. "I gained a level already. A few hundred extra points aren't going to make the next level come any quicker. How's Iona holding up?"

They both turned to look at Iona. She was poking the fish with her sword, testing for weak spots.

"She's much better. I don't know who your [Alchemist] is, but I'd pay them well for that recipe."

Orrin hesitated. Rhys didn't need to know he was the one with the recipe. "It's dangerous to use too much and expensive to make. I'm not supposed to give them out like that, either. She'd kill me if I brought you to her door."

Rhys gave his toothy smile. "I could protect you. She might like my offer."

"I'll think about it. They only last an hour, so she should still be careful."

"Can you take another group or are you all too weak to keep going?" Sloane asked without preamble. She walked toward the three of them, leaving Hamish behind. He was dragging the corpses to the small pile of dead fish they'd accumulated near the floor door.

Orrin deferred to Rhys by glancing at him. Crossing his arms with his glaive tucked into his elbow shouldn't look so cool.

"I think we should head back. We've gained enough experience for a day's work."

Sloane sneered. Her attitude became worse the longer they were in the dungeon. "I'll tell Hamish."

"She's been fun," Orrin muttered as she walked away. "Is there a way to request not being on someone's team for the future?"

Rhys uncrossed his arms. "You can request it, but unless you have a full party of five, it's supposed to be random."

"Which means I can probably pay for it to not be random, right?" Orrin watched Rhys for his reaction.

Rhys laughed. "My mother would say gold solves all." He reached back and rubbed his shoulder. "You did better than I would have thought today. I wouldn't be against doing this again with you. You are a bit unorthodox, but it works."

"We could find another two people and make our own party."

Rhys smiled and then sighed. "She's walking in the wrong direction. Sloane? The exit is this way."

Iona's head snapped to the side at Rhys's yell. She left the dead fish and came to stand by Orrin and Rhys.

Sloane and Hamish were walking back toward the field where Orrin kept disappearing to bring back monsters. They didn't turn back as Rhys yelled.

"Are they leaving us to go fight some more?" Orrin asked. He wasn't going to stop them if they were, but it seemed like a stupid idea.

"No. I'm party leader and we are going back right now," Rhys said with steel in his voice. He sucked in air and yelled, "Sloane and Hamish, come back."

Hamish raised a middle finger in the air.

"We tried. It's not worth getting into a fight over. Let's go." Orrin had that feeling again and checked his [Map]. Nothing new appeared, but Sloane and Hamish were walking toward a group of about ten Anglers. "Damn it. Stay here."

"Wait, wh—"

Orrin was running already. He closed the distance to the other two members of his party in just a few seconds. "Hey, assholes. You can go kill yourselves if you want, but there's a group of ten . . . Actually, all the groups are bigger now. Everything I can see for a few miles out."

Sloane glared at him. "You can tell us whatever lies you want, but we can handle ourselves. Anglers don't travel in schools that large unless it's a dungeon break. We've cleared enough of them out that's not a possibility. Go back with His Highness, Casimir. You aren't strong enough to force us back, and Hamish and I both need a few more kills."

It wasn't the first time that Orrin wished he could share his [Map] view. The skill wouldn't let anyone else see it, though. "I'm not lying, Sloane. If Iona was at full mana, I'd still recommend we leave. Something isn't right. The monster groups are clustering. Come back to the door and I'll find a way to bring a few more back for you two."

"She said no," Hamish drawled, bringing his axe off his shoulder and holding it across his body. "We know what we're about. We don't want to babysit anymore today."

Orrin raised his hands and took a step back. "If you head north, there's a group of six. That's the smallest one I can see. Just be safe."

Sloane and Hamish walked off in the same direction, ignoring his advice. Orrin moved back to Iona and Rhys.

"They'll get in trouble for leaving their party, but it's not uncommon," Rhys responded after Orrin told them of the conversation. "We should head back."

Orrin gave one last look back at the small figures retreating from view. He didn't like Sloane, but he would be worried about ten Anglers. That would be a lot of mana to slow each of them down, not to mention actually hitting them all before they closed the distance.

"We can make a report when we get back. The school or the guard might send someone in to drag them out," Iona added, seeing Orrin's hesitation. "We did everything we could."

Orrin kept his [Map] up as they approached the floor door. This was the door that people would normally use to travel from the fifth to the sixth floor, but retreating into it would bring them straight to the exit.

Sloane and Hamish were moving closer to one of the larger pods of Anglers.

"I'll go first," Iona stated. "Rhys will follow directly behind me. Understand?"

Orrin nodded, paying her only half his attention.

Just as Iona took a step toward the stone door, a new dot appeared on Orrin's [Map].

"Iona, get back." Orrin threw himself forward without thought.

A cloaked man stepped out, entering the floor.

"Oh, sorry. We're just heading ou—"

The man fell toward Iona with a dagger already drawn, but Orrin used [Gust] to shove him back. He flew backward, his arms flailing. Orrin angled the wind so the man fell directly back into the open doorway, but the assailant had time to drop two items on the ground as he went through.

"He tried to attack me," Iona said in a confused voice. "Where did he come from?"

"Iona! Casimir! Get down!"

Orrin dropped, pulling Iona to the ground with him. A dome of metal materialized over the doorway, just as Orrin felt a flash of magic explode. Something rushed by him, but a quick check of his status showed no damage.

"Rhys! Are you all right?" Iona scrambled from Orrin's grip. Orrin turned and let out a gasp at the sight. Rhys was covered in metal from head to toe. As Orrin watched, metal cascaded away in layers. It flowed to his wrist until Rhys was standing there again.

Rhys whispered something to Iona, and she went on high alert. Her sword was drawn, and she scrutinized every direction. Rhys walked toward Orrin.

"You saved Iona's life. How did you react so fast?"

"I've been using [Map] to watch those two fools and saw someone stepping through the door. I saw the knife and reacted." Orrin told the truth, mostly. He might have had some foreknowledge that someone was coming after Rhys, but that attack had been for Iona. "What did he drop?"

"Spell canisters. A [Scribe] writes down a spell on a sheet of paper and it gets activated when it hits the ground."

"Luckily, you covered it in time." Orrin waved a hand at the metal dome covering the doorway still.

"I didn't get both," Rhys whispered. "I moved too slow. I'm sure that I blocked one attack, but the other got through before my [Steel Turtle] activated. Whatever it was didn't do any damage to me, but I'm keeping the door covered just in case someone else comes along."

"Shit." Orrin checked his [Map].

"What is it now?"

"I think it was some sort of aggro spell. Every Angler on the floor is headed right at us."

Chapter 36

Orrin waited two long heartbeats for Rhys to give an order, make a plan, or lead in some way. Instead, the young man continued to stare at the ten-foot-tall metal dome that covered the exit to the dungeon.

"Rhys, I think you need to drop the turtle spell so we can escape, bud."

Iona moved up to her ward and jostled him when he didn't respond.

"That . . . if I take it down, I can't cast it again. It's all that's protecting us from another attack."

Orrin took note of Rhys's shallow breathing and dilated eyes. His rapid, jerky movements at the slightest sounds broke his normal veneer of a calm and collected heir to the family's lordship.

He's in shock. Orrin couldn't blame him. He could feel [Mind Bastion] nipping at his brain, trying to make him take the most logical approach and simply flee.

Orrin cast [Calm Mind] on himself instead and took another look at his [Map].

Guesstimating the speed at which the Skylight Anglers were traveling toward them, Orrin figured he had two to three minutes to make a plan to save himself, Iona, and Rhys. The other members of their party had removed themselves from his consideration by leaving them behind. *If they survived, good for them.*

Still . . . Orrin noted Sloane and Hamish's location. They were slightly to their east, and the majority of the incoming monsters were located in the northern part of his [Map]. It might make sense to use the two of them as a meat shield if no better plan arose.

Despite the calming balm of his antianxiety spell, Orrin surrendered over to [Mind Bastion]. He needed the quicker processing speed that came with discounting the emotional aspects of himself. His best plan was to try and use [Tilth] to dig a hole under the steel dome hiding the door.

"Rhys, I'm going to use a spell on you. It's called [Calm Mind], do you know it?" Orrin let his [Map] fall away for a moment as he approached the duo. "Iona, can you use your magic to make a hole under his dome? We need to get out of here now. I'll help protect Rhys once we are through to the exit, but we can't fight the hundreds of Anglers that are about to be here."

Giving Iona credit after her earlier hesitation, she grasped the situation better this time. She nodded and turned her back to them both, focusing her outstretched hands on her new target.

Rhys held his glaive up as Orrin approached him. "How do I know you aren't a part of this? I know it's you. You work for Lady Sanerris. She'd be happy to see me dead as revenge against my mother."

Orrin with emotions would have talked to Rhys, but he didn't have time for that, and he was letting [Mind Bastion] dull his normal empathy at Rhys's confused situation. He pointed and cast the spell three times for good measure.

Rhys's breathing evened out, but he kept the weapon pointed at Orrin.

"We can talk about whatever problems you have with me later, but right now I want to live. Get that shield down."

Rhys risked a glance at Iona, who was using the last of her mana to tunnel under his steel. Except every time she made a hole, the metal reacted and flowed into the empty space between its lip and the newly formed lowest point.

"We can make it out without your help," Rhys countered, quickly reasserting himself between Iona and Orrin. "Iona, stop doing that. It won't work and you're wasting your mana."

"Rhys, we don't have a choice. The exit to the seventh floor is two hours away if we run, and I can't protect you against that many Anglers."

Orrin felt a twinge of surprise that she was voting for trusting him. She'd never warmed up to him before. He pushed on her heels. "I promise you. I don't want to hurt you guys. I am not a part of this and will protect you both. Please, take that down now."

Rhys teetered, torn between his choices. With a grunt of annoyance, he flicked his hand and the metal collapsed into a molten pool that evaporated into the air.

Where the stone door used to stand was a crater the exact size of the dome that just disappeared.

"I'm going to take a wild guess and say that wasn't your spell." Orrin broke the silence as they stared at their lost opportunity for escape. "I think the second canister was an attack meant to take us out if the assassin failed. Your quick thinking might have saved our lives. I owe you one, Rhys. Thank you."

Orrin spoke aloud as he processed the scene before him. He hadn't even known a floor door could be destroyed. Did that mean the entire sixth floor was now unreachable the normal way? Had somebody else taken out the entrance to the seventh floor? His mind raced along different possible ways out.

His compliment to Rhys at the end had been meaningful. It was true and he'd meant his words, but Orrin said them aloud now for a reason. He needed Rhys back to his collected self. If they had a chance of escaping this alive, Orrin had to be able to count on him.

"What do we do now?" Iona whispered. "I think the seventh-floor entrance is to the north, right?"

Rhys walked to the edge of the burned and broken ground and nudged a piece of dirt into the hole. "Yes. The door to the seventh floor is two to two and a half hours north-northeast without any battles. You can avoid the Skylight Anglers by sending magic flares. They will move toward bright lights."

He recited the words as if reading them, and Orrin felt another surge of emotion through [Mind Bastion]. *Someone else who studies ahead!*

The Anglers reached Hamish and Sloane. The two dots on his [Map] moved quickly among the first ten, and Orrin watched one red light blink out. He shut it off.

"We have a minute or two before the monsters arrive. I'm going to use a spell on the three of us. It is not [Invisibility] but is similar to it. If we don't attack anything and stay close to one another, we might be able to make it to the next floor. We can rest in the room between floors or try to go to the next floor and exit from there. Does anyone have a better plan?"

Orrin asked because he hoped one of them had an ace up their sleeve. [Camouflage Ward] would let him cast [Camouflage] on his party, but only at the first level. If the monsters on this floor could see through his spell, they would be fucked. If Rhys or Iona lost their nerve and attacked, they were dead.

"I could build a stone barricade around us and we could wait for a rescue," Iona ventured. "The door won't rebuild itself for a week, but when Rhys doesn't show up for class in a few hours, the school will send someone looking for him."

"Unless someone is in on that hit attempt," Orrin said with a little hesitation. He didn't want to implicate Graem or even Wren, but there was too much unknown still. The timing of the attack was too perfect. Either Hamish or Sloane . . . or maybe both of them . . . were in on this, and Wren had created the party. Graem had known something was happening and tried to stop the entire dungeon run, but as the person in charge of the school, he'd let Orrin play hero a little too easily. The cloaked figure's attack was too coordinated for it to be a coincidence.

Orrin checked his pockets for anything unusual. Even with [Dimension Hole], he could still place objects in a regular pocket. He turned out the inside of his pants and patted his shirt. "Do either of you have anything that could be tracked on you? Something that someone gave you recently?"

Rhys shook his head and nodded at his glaive. "This is all I brought with me. Iona has my potions and some basic supplies only."

Iona picked up the bag she had dropped earlier and rummaged inside. A wooden box came out first, followed by a smaller canvas bag. She threw out waterskins, two blankets, a rope, a clump of metal the size of Orrin's fist, and a sleeping roll. Reaching inside, she turned the bag upside down and shook it.

A coin rolled along the trampled grass before falling to its side.

"That's not mine."

Rhys moved to pick up the silver piece, but Orrin grabbed his hand. "Give me a second."

"You said we don't have a lot of time. I can tell a lot about a piece of metal from touching it." Rhys stared back into Orrin's gaze with a semblance of his old self.

"You aren't the only one with tricks," Orrin muttered as he studied the coin. It didn't look different from any other silver piece he'd seen. "You're sure that this isn't yours?"

"I packed this bag myself, and no money was ever put inside."

Orrin used [Analyze].

Silver coin

He tried again, focusing hard for any tell of magic. Orrin nearly gave up after the seventh attempt gave him the same result.

One more and then Rhys can try.

Silver coin—proximity enchantment

"It has a proximity enchantment. I don't know that magic. Do either of you?"

"We need to leave," Iona said with worry in her voice. "I can see them coming."

Orrin turned and looked for himself but had to check on [Map] to figure out how close the monsters were. Iona likely had a skill like Daniel's [Telescope], letting her see far into the distance.

Rhys picked it up and slipped it into his pocket. "I'll study it later. Who had access to your bag outside of our group, Iona?"

The woman slipped the items back into the bag as she kept her eyes on the ground. "I packed it this morning as soon as we knew we were coming here. The other students waiting around us or the professors, maybe? Hamish was near me at one point. Casimir offered to carry it. Sloane sat on it once after a fight. I'm sorry I failed you."

"You didn't fail anyone." Orrin cut Rhys off before he said anything more. He reached down and grabbed Iona's rope before she repacked it. "It's going to be hard to see each other when I cast this spell. Hold tight to this. Hopefully, the Anglers don't see it. If you get separated and still can't see your hands well, sit down and wait. I'll find you. We are going to travel fast but carefully. Do not attack unless I give the order."

"When did you get put in charge?" Rhys fought back, standing close to Orrin. "You might be leading us into another trap."

Orrin clenched his fist. It might be easier for him to knock them both out and try to carry them. His strength was high, and neither Rhys nor Iona appeared particularly heavy.

"There isn't a better option," he said instead. "Make your choice, because I'm leaving either way."

Rhys's helplessness at the situation was blossoming into anger and stubbornness. Orrin could tell this might have been the first real danger he'd encountered in his life. All his privileged upbringing and smooth talking wasn't helping in this messed-up scenario.

"If you trust me now, I'll answer any questions you have once we escape," Orrin offered, holding the rope out. "You can take point as well. I don't know where we need to go."

Rhys snatched the rope from his hand. "Every question."

Orrin nodded. He cast [Ward], [Light Ward], and [Water Ward] on all three of them. If they didn't take damage, the other two might never know about the spells. If they did get hit and noticed something weird . . . Orrin would cross that bridge if he reached it.

"Lead the way," Orrin said, taking the end of the rope. Rhys walked up front, and Iona posted herself in the middle. Orrin cast [Camouflage Ward] and watched both of his party members go hazy just as the first Anglers came into view.

Chapter 37

Orrin held his breath as the first giant floating fish from hell swam through the air nearby. Smaller schools of Skylight Anglers started to group as they pecked at the blasted ground where the exit to the dungeon once stood.

"They're not attacking us," Iona whispered from between Orrin and Rhys. They continued to make their way north toward the door to the next floor. "Is it working?"

"I think it is," Orrin responded quietly. "Keep moving."

Orrin kept his [Map] open to avoid the larger groups as best he could with whispered instructions to Iona. A brief splash of blue against all the red surprised him.

"Either Sloane or Hamish is alive," Orrin called out in a soft voice. "I see one of them on the edge of my [Map]."

Orrin didn't suggest going to meet up. As cold-blooded as it sounded, he'd written them off when they'd left before the attack. After finding the coin in Iona's pack, he trusted neither of them.

Orrin noticed Rhys had stopped walking when the rope went slack between them. Two shimmering figures waited a few steps in front of him, but Orrin avoided staring. Daniel was right. It hurt to look directly at [Camouflage].

"Why are we stopping? We aren't clear of this yet," Orrin said as he got close.

"Sloane and Hamish are the most likely suspects to have sold me out," Rhys said, his voice still tinged with anger. "If they're alive, we should—"

"Ignore them completely and get to safety," Orrin cut him off. "Name one good reason why we shouldn't escape first and let somebody else deal with capturing them."

"They tried to kill Iona and me." Rhys paused for a moment before adding, "And you. They should be dealt with here in the dungeon. It'll be easier than outside, where somebody can save them or pay to have them disappeared."

Orrin's estimation of Rhys dropped a little at the casual suggestion of murder.

"I only saw one marker," Orrin explained. "One of them could be dead already. We don't have enough information. It's safer to get back to school first."

"But—"

"You're assuming it was Hamish and Sloane. What if it was only one of them? What if Hamish is innocent in all of this and just wanted some extra experience? What if we find him but Sloane died in the tsunami of monster fish that whoever attacked you summoned to one place? I'm surprised either of them is alive, to be honest. If I set up that attack, I'd have used it as an opportunity to take out the entire team, not just you. If nobody is alive, this entire thing would be written off as bad luck in the dungeon."

Rhys didn't respond, but Iona finally added her voice. "Rhys, he's right. My priority is getting you to safety."

"What else?" Rhys's voice had taken the steely cold timbre again as he questioned Orrin. "What else would you do if you'd set this up, Casimir? Since you've given it so much thought."

"I'd have somebody waiting on this floor near the next door as well. I'd have somebody else at the seventh floor's entrance. Maybe even back at the dungeon entrance. As many contingencies as I could afford, in case you made it through," Orrin answered truthfully, having already tried to think of anything else they might encounter. "I'm not seeing anyone else on this floor right now, but I'm keeping an eye out for it. If Hamish or Sloane is partnered up with whoever wants you two dead, I think we should be running for the exit and not wasting time arguing. We know where they are, but they can't see us. They can't find us. You've seen how fast I can run, Rhys. If I wanted to kill you, all I'd need to do is leave you."

No further words were exchanged. The rope pulled taut, and Orrin continued to bring up the rear.

After another twenty minutes, the incoming swarms of monsters began to thin out. Orrin estimated between two to three hundred Anglers were now swarming the spot where the assassin's aggro spell went off.

He reapplied [Camouflage Ward] when it ran out every five minutes. His only warning that the time was up was the sudden appearance of Iona and Rhys in front of him. The sixth time it ran out, two Anglers noticed them and changed direction.

Iona dropped her bag and stood in front of Rhys. "Take Rhys and run. I'll hold them off."

"We can take them," Rhys said, his face drawn. He'd recovered a bit from the shock of the attack, but Orrin knew that kind of sudden trauma was lurking just beneath the surface.

Iona shook her head. "It would take too long. More will come to the sounds of . . . What are they doing?"

Orrin dropped his hand as he finished casting [Decrease Strength] on both multiple times. His mana regen potion finally wore off, and he swore as he saw his mana pool not recovering as fast. "Can they track us if we disappear again?"

Iona turned her body so she stood between Rhys and Orrin.

"For fuck's sake. I'm not here to hurt you. This isn't the time for a heart-to-heart. Answer the question."

"I'm not sure," Rhys said as he gently pushed Iona to the side. "What kind of spell did you cast?"

"Go kill the one on the left. I'll take the right." Orrin walked away, ignoring the question. He used a newly summoned [Ice Sword] to hack the Angler to pieces.

Experience Gained: 500 XP

"Could you do that to them the entire time we've been here?" Iona asked as they regrouped, leaving the sashimi pieces covering the grass behind them.

"It costs a lot of mana," Orrin lied, handing them the rope. "Let's try and avoid any more fights."

Orrin continued to watch his mana go down over the next hour. He knew [Mind Bastion] helped him think logically but found another fun trick—it helped him keep time by counting. It wasn't perfect, but without a watch, Orrin improvised as best he could. Every three hundred count, he had his camo ward ready to go. He didn't see another blue dot on his [Map], despite keeping it running most of the time. Either Sloane and Hamish were dead or they were keeping out of their path.

"I need a break," Iona finally said, piercing the silence around them. Only a few random Anglers had passed them over the last ten minutes.

Orrin watched as a hole appeared in the ground, pushing dirt up into a hillock. Within a minute, an entrance down into the once-pristine grass appeared.

"Neat trick," Orrin said, looking into the dark cave she'd created. It reminded him of a computer game he'd played for a while with square blocks. He always went exploring too far from his base and made small, covered dirt houses to avoid the nightly monster attacks. Orrin sighed. He missed video games.

The trio moved inside and Iona closed the entrance, leaving them in darkness. Orrin heard rustling sounds as Iona went through her backpack, and the sudden burst of light surprised him.

A light cube, Orrin figured. The clump of metal she'd had in her bag was like his heater cube.

"I told you this would come in handy," Iona bragged as shadows flickered off the tight hole in the ground. She'd shaped a small circular room with the compacted dirt and even left a raised seat along the edges for them to sit. Everyone's feet touched, but it was still comfortable enough to rid Orrin of the stress of constantly watching for an attack.

Orrin noticed something else. Iona wasn't tired. Rhys's robe, on the other hand, was soaked in sweat. He leaned his head back against the wall and took deep breaths.

Orrin felt bad for not noticing earlier. His own stats were buffed up, with a quick top-off here and there as needed. Iona gave the impression of a hybrid fighter and mage build, with enough strength to carry that big pack around. Thinking back now, Orrin realized Rhys was using his glaive as a staff and leaning on it more.

"Are you okay, Rhys?"

"I'm fine," the man snapped back in the darkness. The light of the cube was only a little better than a fire, and something about being underground made it seem darker.

Orrin grunted in frustration. He was not going to let Rhys exhaust himself and die after saving him. "You're not fine, and if you don't communicate with your party, you'll slow us down. Are we pushing too hard? We can rest until you're recovered."

Rhys said nothing but settled back a little more. Iona nodded thankfully toward Orrin.

Keeping one eye on [Map], Orrin kept playing with [Merge], as he had been doing for days. There had to be some combination of spells that he already had that would help him get out of the collar. He had twenty-five ability points to spend. He had twenty-four administrator points to spend.

After a few minutes, Orrin groaned in frustration and rubbed his temples.

"Thank you for that," Iona breathed into Orrin's ear.

He jumped and felt the confinement of the space. Rhys's chin was on his chest, and a light snore echoed in the room. Orrin turned toward Iona. She'd moved closer to him, giving Rhys a few extra inches to stretch out.

"For what?" Orrin tried to see where the exit to the tiny space was and failed.

"Talking back to him and making him rest. Nobody gets away with challenging him back home. He does whatever he thinks is best.

It's one of his greatest flaws. His mother gives him everything but someone to contest him. He doesn't listen to me when I do speak up, and I worry he'll do something pigheaded one day while I'm not around that gets him killed."

Iona rarely spoke more than a couple of words around Rhys. Now that he was resting after pushing himself to keep up with them, she opened up to Orrin. He'd known she was attractive, but with her sitting so close, he couldn't help but notice it again. Her deep brown eyes drew him in as the shadows continued to dance on the wall.

"What do you think our chances are? Of surviving, I mean." Iona's voice was close to breaking.

[Mind Bastion] was still on. Orrin kept it running the entire time to be safe. He couldn't afford to break down in a stressful situation like this. He knew it was a crutch, but it was convenient and useful. A darker part of his mind told him to use this opportunity.

Iona was scared and confiding in him. With her walls down, she appeared much younger. Orrin forgot that both of them weren't that far off from his own age. They kept up the act of being adults well.

Tell her "I'll protect you" and she'll be a great ally. She could be my way in with Rhys. Orrin felt disgust flare, even through [Mind Bastion].

He let the skill go and felt the fear and uncertainty of the situation fully for the first time in hours.

"I think if we work together, we have a chance. I'll do my best to help you keep Rhys safe. I have a few tricks up my sleeve still. We need you recharged, though. Get some rest. I'll keep watch until he wakes up." Orrin told her the truth. He didn't want to lie or give her false hope.

She blinked hard twice and nodded. She turned to move but hesitated. Looking back, Iona rested a hand on Orrin's shoulder. "Thank you. No matter the outcome, you helped us, and I'm in your debt."

"Friends don't keep count of that stuff. Buy me a cup of coffee when we get out of here and we'll be good," Orrin joked.

"Oh, I can do better than that," Iona exclaimed, grabbing her pack. "This might not be good after sitting all day and I don't have any cream to go with it, but . . ."

Iona pulled a waterskin from her bag and offered it to him.

"I already had some water earlier," Orrin said with a smile. "Thanks, though."

"It's coffee."

Orrin seized the skin before she changed her mind. "I can't believe you've been holding out on me."

Chapter 38

Orrin wasn't sure if the Twin Book of Sending worked in the dungeon. He waited until Iona fell asleep against Rhys before taking it out of his [Dimension Hole] and scribbling a quick message to Anabella.

Orrin woke both Rhys and Iona up after two hours. By his best guess, they were a few hours late for a normal check-in after the dungeon run. The school administration would wait a few more hours before worrying about them. Orrin didn't know if Anabella would read his note or be able to react in time.

He also hoped that Graem might attempt a rescue earlier given his prediction of an attack on Rhys but decided not to trust in either of them. He was going to do this on his own.

Rhys groaned as he woke from his short nap. His age and privilege showed the longer he was inconvenienced. He demanded they wait and eat before heading out, which Orrin didn't mind. He made Orrin and Iona leave the hidey-hole first so he could go to the bathroom in it, which Orrin found disgusting.

When he told Iona to close up the newly dubbed bathroom with her magic, Orrin stepped in. "That's enough. She shouldn't waste her mana on something so trivial. Go outside like everyone else next time."

Rhys might have argued, but Orrin used his magic and everyone disappeared from view.

The Skylight Anglers decreased in number and patrols as they got closer to their target. After the [Camouflage Ward] wore off the fifth time, Orrin crouched and tugged the rope they all held. Iona ducked down as well, but Rhys stood over them, one hand in his pocket and the other holding his glaive like a walking stick.

"There aren't any Anglers nearby, so I'm going to save some mana for now," Orrin explained. He ripped some grass from a thinned-out area and used his hand to smooth a portion of the ground out. Drawing a rough map on the ground, he marked where the entrance had been before it was destroyed and their current location. "Rhys, do you know if we're still going in the right direction? I think it's been about two hours."

Rhys's robe was dirtied with blood from the Anglers, grass, and the dirt he'd napped on, but standing there over him, Orrin admitted he was regal. As if it was a favor to Orrin, Rhys sighed and dropped to his eye level. Keeping ahold of his glaive with one hand, he took his other hand out of his pocket and pointed at the map.

"There is supposed to be a small pond in this direction. From there, we should be able to see a lantern to the north. Sometimes a variant of the Skylight Angler will spawn near the lantern. Regular Anglers are stronger under its light. The exit to the safe room and the seventh floor is there."

"Would it be safer to go back the way we came?" Orrin asked. "We could try making our way back to the fifth floor and climb back up those stairs on the cliff."

Rhys shook his head. "Even if we wanted to, the shortcuts are one way. Something about the magic of the dungeons lets us go down through the cracks we find but not back up. I'll admit that your [Map] skill is more useful than I ever thought it could be. I've never heard of making a trek over an entire floor like this without multiple fights."

Orrin's [Map] zoomed out as he searched for the pond. "I think there's some water a few miles to the east. There are a few Anglers around it."

Rhys stood up. "I'm going to suggest having a member with [Map] in all my future parties. The time saved not wandering around offsets the lack of attack power you bring."

Orrin wiped the dirt off his hand using his pants as he straightened up. "I do fine on attack power, but I agree. There is too much emphasis on taking down monsters fast instead of smart."

"Explain that," Rhys demanded as they began to walk.

Orrin ignored the way he asked and launched into the same argument he'd brought up with Madi multiple times. Current parties were usually built around having five damage dealers. Taking down monsters quickly worked well . . . until the monsters were too strong. Specialized teams made more sense in Orrin's opinion. If a [Healer] was around, fatalities would decrease. Having someone specialized in crowd control would take the pressure off the damage dealers, letting them take their time killing monsters in waves. A [Cartographer] could avoid groups too large.

"Of course, knowing what you're walking into is the most important thing. Take this floor, for example. The fish are mostly light and water magic. A group of fire users should never come here. Sharing the knowledge about what each floor contains and using waves of our own specialized teams, I don't see why Odrana couldn't destroy the entire dungeon." Orrin waved his arms in a wide gesture. "As pretty as this is, imagine how bad it would be if there was ever a dungeon break. It's not worth keeping this so near the city. Three Anglers coming from the south."

They lay down in the grass and waited for Orrin to give the all clear again.

"The longer it takes to kill a beast, the more stamina or mana a person would use," Iona whispered, giving the same argument Madi routinely did. "When one person isn't attacking, the others have to pick up the slack."

Orrin smiled at her through the grass. "Give a [Healer] a spear and let them poke holes in the target. I'm not saying they need to stay away from battle."

"Do we have an extra spear to give Casimir?" Rhys grumbled. He didn't like how much sense Orrin was making.

Orrin ignored the barb. He didn't need to prove anything to Rhys. The fish swam through the air a couple of hundred feet away, not catching sight of them and moving out of range a few minutes later. "Let's go."

Orrin had angled their path, so they'd overshot the pond. After another twenty minutes, Iona pointed to the ceiling.

"Lantern."

Orrin squinted against the light. The entire "sky" was bright, but an intense haze in one spot was obvious once pointed out.

"That's a lantern?"

"Some floors have more," Rhys explained as they walked. He looked better after his rest. "The monsters travel to them daily."

"Why?"

Rhys rolled his eyes. "Who knows? Does it matter?"

Orrin could think of a few reasons it might. If the lantern was a source of nourishment or refreshment and he destroyed it, would the monsters of the entire floor become weak? Would they all die immediately? Maybe destroying it would make all the Anglers stronger.

Another question nobody seems to care to know the answer to.

Orrin could see the pond to their south without his [Map] now. It was far enough away that the few Anglers circling in the air were out of range to attack them but close enough that Orrin could see the water moving. *That's weird. I wonder why a pond has waves?*

He also realized the lantern they were approaching created a wide dome. It didn't seem that large from a distance, but as they entered its range, Orrin peered left and right. It covered a large area of the dungeon floor.

"Has anyone tried to attack a lantern before . . ." Orrin trailed off as something caught his eye. "Get down!"

Orrin had kept [Map] up to the side for most of their trek and had only seen the red dots of the Skylight Anglers until now. A blue dot now stood out on the edge of his screen.

"Sloane or Hamish is near the door," Orrin whispered when Rhys and Iona army crawled to him. "Wait here, I'm going to go and check who it is."

"We can all go," Iona said with a raging fury in her voice. "I have some questions for whoever survived."

Orrin knew a dead party member would remain in the party until the leader removed them. The names *Hamish* and *Sloane* continued to sit above his own on the party tab of his status box. "I can escape if I need to. If they attack, you need to get Rhys through to the next floor and then escape. Find Professor Graem."

"We are not going to let you fight alone," Rhys said as Iona nodded along. "You saved us. Either we all go or none of us go."

Orrin wanted to sneak up and incapacitate whoever was waiting by the door. Rhys and Iona couldn't know how often he could cast his debuff spells or they might start asking questions. His execution wasn't that long ago and the wrong rumors going about could tip off Lord Sanerris that Anabella was not doing as requested. He was about to argue more when Iona reached out and put her hand on his in the grass.

"Casimir, I don't know you well. Lady Tonsa told us to join this dungeon raid. She received information that someone with powerful connections would be here."

"Iona!"

"Shut up, Rhys. It's obviously him," Iona said as she squeezed Orrin's hand. "We're here for you. I don't know who you know or why it was important to Lady Tonsa that we connect with you, but you saved my life. You saved Rhys's life, even if he won't admit it. Even after the attack, you stuck with us. I don't care about your connections. Rhys and his mother do, but at this point, with more danger in front of us, let me be the one to stand in front. If you get the chance, push Rhys through the door and go back to Goldenhall with him."

Orrin tried to process the information Iona had just dropped on him. He felt the cold creep of his skill trying to turn back on and pushed it down. *Anabella said she set up an opportunity at great cost. I thought she meant getting me into the dungeon, but what if she put Rhys in my party for us to get closer?*

He rubbed his temples. This was why Daniel hated riddles. What cost would she pay to get Rhys and him in the same group?

Was he just supposed to fight alongside Rhys? Anabella knew Orrin had fought against her son and survived. She knew a little about his skills and spells. Had she known that an assassination attempt was coming, too? *Maybe I was sent to keep Rhys alive.*

"We will not leave you behind," Rhys said passionately. "The three of us can take down one person."

"Enough," Orrin said holding up a hand. "I'm thinking."

Orrin waited for them to argue and felt silly when they both stood quietly waiting. "Damn, now I lost my train of thought. It doesn't matter. We all get through this. We can sneak by whoever it is. We don't need to take down anyone."

"Leaving an enemy behind us is asking for death," Iona pointed out. "Can you use that slowdown spell you used on the Anglers?"

Orrin ignored her probe and asked a question in return. "What did you learn about that coin, Rhys?"

The young man had spent the walk with one hand in his pocket. It didn't take a genius to figure out he was holding on to the silver coin that tracked them.

"I've been able to interpret the receiving magic."

Orrin raised an eyebrow. "What the fuck does that mean?"

Iona blew a short chuckle of air through her nose.

"The coin is a tracker. Another item is keyed to receive the signal sent from the coin. When the two get close, I should be able to exchange the magic in both so the coin becomes the receiver. Then whoever is holding the original receiver will have a very bad day."

Orrin's mouth went dry at the depth of hatred in Rhys's eyes. Someone had come after him and Iona, and the young man was ready for revenge.

"It's not here in the dungeon, though?" Orrin confirmed. Rhys shook his head. "Good. Here's the plan. We move forward until we see who it is. I'm guessing Iona will see them first. We'll backtrack and figure out what to do from there. The last thing we need is to attack someone who might be a friend. Even if it turns out one of them was the one who set this up, they might have another spell that could take out the gate. We need to avoid that at all costs. I don't want to live here for days."

Rhys grumbled but agreed. Orrin cast [Camouflage Ward] and made sure his stats were still buffed. They didn't know what they were walking into.

Hamish or Sloane?

Friend or enemy?

Chapter 39

At Iona's suggestion, they swung wide so as to approach from the northern side of the floor exit door. Orrin admitted her idea made sense. Either Hamish or Sloane's blue dot on his [Map] confirmed one of them was waiting a few dozen yards from the exit. Since it was the last remaining way out of the dungeon, keeping watch from nearby was smart. Orrin's secrecy regarding his own skills, specifically [Map], gave them a slight edge. Without it, the betrayer would have the upper hand on their unsuspecting victims.

"They haven't moved once," Orrin whispered, almost to himself. "Is there a good ambush point near the door?"

"There shouldn't be anywhere to hide near the exit," Rhys responded. "As far as I know, neither of them has any spells for invisibility, either, but I didn't know you could do this. It seems my information sources need updating."

"You had me investigated?" Orrin asked as they turned and began to backtrack. He knew he shouldn't be surprised that Rhys had tried to dig up information on him. It was just a new experience to be interesting enough to warrant that kind of attention.

"Of course," Rhys answered, tugging on the rope that connected them. They moved slower and closer to the ground as they approached, the tether that kept them from wandering off in one hand while they held their weapons in the other. Orrin didn't summon a sword yet and kept to the back. "You arrived at the Sanerris School with no known backers, bypassed the required classes to gain entry into a highly sought-after magical theory class, and an unknown party entered your room to leave a dead animal hanging there. Half of the reason I'm even taking classes here is to make good connections for my family and my future. You switch between being someone worth knowing and someone to avoid. With the way the teachers talk about your genius, I thought it was worth getting to know you. When you had the incident in your room, I thought you might leave. You didn't, and it made me more curious. When my mother sent her missive that we should join the dungeon raid, my money was on it being you who showed up."

"Someone broke into my room and it just made you curious?" Orrin moved to a standstill, causing the rope in Iona's hand to pull her to a stop as well. "I guess I should add you to the list of suspects."

Orrin's spell timed out, and Rhys's visage came into view. Looks of confusion and anger crossed his face in a flash before he realized he was visible. The young lord calmed his emotions and moved back toward Orrin.

"You stayed and even kept the same room." Iona kept herself between the two young men, but Rhys's stress must have finally reached the breaking point. "You obviously know who broke into your room and took care of them. The only alternative would be you aren't scared of whoever it is and are sending a message by staying in school. Professor Graem wasn't bluffing during orientation. People die here. Sometimes it's a failed experiment, but assassinations aren't off the table, as you've just seen firsthand. It's why Iona was sent with me. It's why we have the security set up at our dorms, for all the good that seems to have done. If I was a suspect, you never would have agreed to go into this dungeon with us. What possible reason could I have to do that?"

Orrin wanted to tell him off and explain the plan he and Graem had put together, but movement on his [Map] drew his attention away from their little spat. The entire discussion had been whispered, but sound carried on the plains. His immediate fear of an attack from their lost party member faded quickly, as the blue dot sat exactly where it had been.

"Shh," Orrin hushed Rhys and put a new [Camouflage Ward] up. "Monsters incoming."

During the entire trek, Orrin had maneuvered them around the roaming Skylight Anglers, keeping them from having to enter any fights. The frame of the floor exit was in the distance, just a few hundred yards away. Their potential saboteur was positioned another hundred feet or so to the south. At the far edge of his [Map] sat the pond that broke the monotonous waves of grass.

Six Anglers were traveling away from the pond and toward the door. One of the Anglers trailed a little behind the others, but all six would be upon the blue dot that marked their teammate in a few minutes.

The original plan to recon who was nearby and then figure out what to do was dead in the water. Iona would follow whatever Rhys decided, and he wasn't in the best frame of mind for making sound decisions. He wanted revenge. Orrin wanted answers.

"Six of them are traveling right toward Hamish or Sloane. We aren't going to have time to talk about this. I'm going to grab whoever it is and drag them through to the break room. Get in there and wait for me." Orrin let go of the rope. "Or go ahead and get back to safety. I'll find you later and tell you what I find out."

"Why should we trust you?" Rhys asked, making Orrin flinch at the volume of his voice. "This could all be part of your elaborate trap."

Orrin wasted precious seconds sneaking close to Rhys. It wasn't hard to do, even though he was semi-invisible. The bent grass under his feet hadn't shifted since Orrin cast his spell.

"Just get Iona out of here safely, you idiot. If you don't trust me by now, you never will," Orrin whispered, making Rhys step backward. Then he ran.

Orrin ate up the three hundred yards to the door with barely time to ponder on how much he used to hate running. The more he got used to the increased dexterity, the more he was beginning to enjoy stretching his legs. It didn't hurt that he was moving as fast as a car.

Checking the [Map], he frowned at seeing only five Anglers. He pushed his bad counting skills out of his mind and came to a stop near a tangle in the tall grass.

"Hi again, Sloane," Orrin said as he began pulling the braided grass apart. The woman had somehow twisted the long blades into braids that covered her from head to toe. It was almost a burial shroud, and once he pulled the first few apart, he realized why.

Sloane was fucked up.

Her left foot was gone, bitten cleanly away by an Angler. Above the missing foot but below her knee, the leg bone was broken, splintering off at the wrong angle. A multitude of cuts scarred her torso, and burns from the light magic attacks covered her arms. Her face was soaked in her own blood, multiple open lacerations oozing. One eye was closed with a gash running through the middle. Orrin couldn't see if the eye was gone.

"Sloane, can you hear me?" Orrin glanced in the distance and could see the Anglers barreling toward him. Except now there were only three of them and something bigger chasing behind. "Oh shit."

Orrin made sure Sloane was breathing and checked on her with [Identify]. Her HP was low. Low enough that Orrin cast a [Heal Small Wounds]. Sloane moaned as she regained semiconsciousness.

Now that he was close, Orrin could see the trail of blood and the divots in the ground where she had used her quarterstaff as a cane. She must have walked and fought her way to the exit, only to collapse from blood loss this close to escape.

Her constitution was high enough but even with Orrin's boosted healing powers, she would need professional attention. He could simply dump more mana at the problem, but keeping her docile until he got answers would make asking the questions easier.

He tried to be gentle as he picked her up, but despite his increased strength, Orrin wasn't skilled in firefighter-carrying the dead weight of another person. He noticed her quarterstaff in the dirt beneath her and almost dropped her as he swiftly put it in his [Dimension Hole].

Orrin sprinted toward the exit as he checked his [Map]. The other blue spots that marked Iona and Rhys were gone, meaning they'd entered the doorway. The stone frame doorway that was so close. He heard a cry of pain from an Angler, a sound he hadn't known they could make.

Later, he would blame his inquisitive nature. He was only three steps from the door when he turned to look. During all their fights, the Anglers had never moved fast enough that he was worried they could catch up with him.

They'd also never been running from their only natural predator before. Two Anglers remained and Orrin caught a glimpse of the behemoth that swallowed one of them as he scrambled backward. He practically fell through the doorway, not having time to use an [Identify] but knowing this was not something he wanted to fight.

He was still carrying Sloane as he entered the break room between floors. Orrin caught himself before he tumbled and cursed aloud.

"That thing is terrifying," he muttered to himself. "Did you guys see . . ."

Orrin trailed off when he realized he was alone.

Fuck. Orrin really thought they'd have waited, but either Rhys was still shaken up or Iona had pushed her ward out to the seventh floor. They'd be able to turn right around and leave. *At least they're alive.*

He did a closer investigation of Sloane. The number of broken bones, bites to her flesh, and shredded skin were nothing compared to the amount of internal bleeding and the concussion she'd suffered. Orrin wasn't sure if she'd used a health potion and gently set her down before sitting cross-legged near her.

Slowly, Orrin healed her. He practiced the new technique he'd picked up after his fight in Battle Class to target specific areas of her body. He used only level-one healing, as he wanted to study the way the mana moved around at the most basic intensity. Closing the worst of her bleeding wounds was easy. He could see the problem and willed the mana to stay in that area until it returned to normal.

He encountered more difficulty in fixing the internal bleeding. Through his mana, her insides looked like they'd been through an earthquake, all shaken and shattered. Her health fell slowly but steadily between healings until he simply layered the mana on those injuries and let her body do the work instead. It took more mana that way, but if there was anything he had to spare, it was his mana pool.

Sloane groaned as the mana made its way into her head and cleared up some of the concussion. The scars on her face remained, but she'd been lucky to not lose an eye.

"Sloane, can you hear me?"

"Where am I?" Sloane reached up and rubbed her eye. Flakes of blood crusted and fell. His healing didn't clean her up, so she was still covered in blood and dirt. "Am I dead? Nope. I can't feel my toes. That sucks. How'd I survive?"

Orrin explained where he'd found her and brought her through the door to the exit room. He mentioned the larger monster that was chasing the Anglers and eating them, too. Sloane's eyes became clearer as he talked, and he helped her sit up against the wall.

"I also was able to grab your staff. I know how you fighters get about your weapons," Orrin said, pointing to the corner where he'd left it. "It's yours if you can answer a few questions about what happened in there."

Sloane stiffened at the change in tone. Until now, Orrin hadn't mentioned Rhys or Hamish, but as they were the only two left from their party, it was obvious what he wanted.

"Is Hamish alive?" Orrin asked what he thought was the easy question first.

Tears welled up in Sloane's deep brown eyes. "I had to do it. I didn't want to, but he made me."

Orrin clenched a fist but kept his face calm. "Who made you? Do you know why?"

"I don't know why. He said we could get more experience taking down a few more beasties on our own. After that explosion, I tried to go back to check on everyone, but that's when he attacked me."

Orrin's hand released. "Hamish attacked you?"

"Yeah, I thought that you knew and that's why you asked. We fought, and then more Anglers than I've ever seen swarmed all over us. Hamish was torn clean in two, but I dived headfirst into one of them bastards. I killed it from the inside and escaped. I couldn't see the doorway anymore, and it was covered with the fish, so I assumed every one of you was dead or escaped. I made my way to the seventh-floor door but had to fight the entire time. I lost my foot trying to kick one Angler while another struck me from behind. I was so close when I felt my body give out. I barely was able to cover myself with the grass. I gave myself even odds of never waking up again. How'd you even find me?"

Orrin didn't have a lie-detector skill, which, now that he thought about it, would be a really handy thing to get later; however, he believed her story so far.

"Did you see the person try to kill Iona?"

"What?" Either Sloane was an amazing actress or that was genuine concern on her face. "Did she escape? What about Rhys?"

"They're both fine, I think." Orrin stood and paced the floor. The resting room between dungeon floors was bare and not huge, but he made sure to keep out of quick reach of Sloane as well as between her and the doorway. "Did you put a coin in Iona's bag?"

"What are you talking about?" Sloane pushed her way off the wall and stood on one leg to face Orrin. "Casimir, are you accusing me of something?"

"I'm asking questions after an assassination attempt where two of our party members left shortly before the ambush. From what you've said about Hamish attacking you, I'm leaning toward him being the traitor. I don't know why he would attack you, and you could be lying." Orrin rubbed his eyes. "I don't really have any authority to arrest you or anything, Sloane, but you have to admit it's suspicious."

"I wanted more experience, you know? I've been in here before with Hamish. We fought well together in the past. After his first attack"—Sloane touched her side, where Orrin had healed a cut that might have been from an axe—"I tried to back away and talk to him. He kept coming at me and just said he was sorry it had to be this way. I don't know what is going on."

Orrin saw her eyes dart to the door to the next floor. "If you try to run, you won't get away. Let's return together and you can tell your story to Professor Graem. I'm sure Rhys already gathered some people near the exit."

Orrin readied himself to attack. She spun a good story, but if she tried anything . . .

"I'm innocent, but I'm not scared of a healer with wind magic. You have the weirdest class I've ever heard of, Casimir. Don't you worry your pretty little head. We'll get this all sorted." Sloane made a fist and hit the wall. The stone rippled as a shock wave hit her quarterstaff, launching it into the air.

Orrin was halfway to casting a [Decrease Dexterity] when she caught the staff and placed it under her arm as an improvised crutch. "Let's go, then."

Orrin sighed as he followed her to the doorway. They stepped out onto the seventh floor. Orrin heard a bird call in the distance and saw the splashing waves of a beach off to his left but ignored it as he took Sloane's arm and pulled her out of the dungeon.

Chapter 40

Hands seized Orrin the moment he appeared in the building that housed the entrance to the Mistwater Lanterns. Using [Way of the Water], he disengaged from the grasp of two different people and rolled to his side. His [Ward] was still active, and his twin fire and ice swords materialized in his grip.

"Casimir, stand down."

Graem's voice called out from behind a dozen guards, but Orrin couldn't see him. Two of the guards pinned Sloane to the ground. She kept still and didn't resist.

"Professor Graem? What's going on?" Orrin risked a glance at his [Map]. Sloane appeared as gray again, meaning that Rhys must have dissolved the party when he got back. "Why are these guys attacking me?"

"Nobody is attacking you," Graem said, stepping out from behind two of the bigger guards standing by the door leading out of the building. "We didn't know who would be coming through. Every group is being detained as they leave until we get to the bottom of the Tonsa incident."

"Did Rhys and Iona make it out?"

A flash of emotions battled on Graem's usually bored face. "They're alive."

Orrin dropped the point of his swords and relaxed a bit. "Someone tried to kill Iona and the rest of us. I went back to save Sloane after we—"

"You can give your report in a more secure location. We are removing everyone from the dungeon and bringing them in for questioning. That includes you two. Drop the summoned swords, Casimir. You have nothing to fear from us."

Orrin felt something off in Graem's words but no pointed hostility. The guards standing near him held a relaxed stance. Only two held cudgels out, and nobody drew steel. He slowly placed his swords on the ground and kicked them away. "What do we do now?"

Orrin followed Graem's directions as they were marched out of the squat building. The guards loaded Sloane into a covered wagon with bars on the door. Orrin was moving to step on as well when Graem touched his elbow and shook his head.

"You'll come with me."

Within the hour, Orrin sat in a plush seat in Graem's office. Graem poured a drink from a decanter and threw it back before filling two more glasses. He placed the drink in front of Orrin before sitting down across from him. "Tell me everything that happened."

Orrin complied, telling Graem about the normal parts of the dungeon and fighting the Skylight Anglers. He left out how many he'd taken out himself but kept mostly to the truth. He recounted how Sloane and Hamish left them and the subsequent attack on Iona. He told Graem about Rhys's attitude after being saved and finding Sloane half-dead. As he rehashed Sloane's story, Graem held up his hand.

"That's enough." Graem finished his drink and pointed at Orrin's untouched glass. "Do you mind?"

"You don't care what she said? If you are interrogating her, you should know what she told me. You can check for inconsistencies." Orrin watched as the liquor disappeared down Graem's throat. "It was probably Hamish who slipped the coin into Iona's bag. She said he died, but he might have made it out, too."

"He won't . . . didn't . . . oh, fuck it. Hamish is dead no matter what," Graem said, rubbing his hand through his hair in frustration. "Stay away from this. You're lucky to be alive, Casimir. You made it out. Go to class. Tell people . . . nothing. Just say you've been told not to discuss anything that happened in the dungeon."

"You know something," Orrin accused the man.

Graem sighed and reached over the back of his chair, grabbing the amber bottle. "Drop it."

Orrin didn't like being ignored. He was tired. He'd risked his life for experience, but he was used to that after the past few months. He'd also risked his life for his new friends and was finding that didn't bother him as much, either.

However, he'd also risked his life to bring back Sloane. He knew a part of himself had done that for good reasons, but a larger piece just wanted answers. Graem's hypothesis that someone was going to try and kill Rhys had been right. If he didn't care to know the particulars of Sloane's story, it could only mean one of two things: either Graem already knew what she'd say or it didn't matter what she said.

"Is Sloane still alive?"

Graem took a pull from the liquor bottle. Orrin snapped his fingers so Graem knew it was him. The headmaster of the most powerful mage school in the world spat liquid from his mouth. "What did you do to my whiskey?"

"Removed all the impurities until it was water. Answer my question, Graem."

Orrin's collar burned and he choked as he was pulled back off his chair by an invisible hand around his neck. His feet knocked the chair over as he flew through the air and landed hard against the stone wall behind him. Orrin reached for his throat and scratched at the metal, his feet trying to find a grip on the ground inches below him.

[Mind Bastion] roared into force, grabbing at his options. Graem's use of the collar was unexpected in the moment but not something Orrin hadn't considered. His fingers tore the skin around the metal as he dug for purchase. If he could grab underneath and pull, his increased strength might be enough to break the metal. It was risky, but any attempt to fully attack Graem would likely end in Orrin's death.

His nuclear option wouldn't help him in this situation. He could buy another Administrator skill and take away Graem's class or abilities, but he didn't know what would happen after. When he used

Assign Class on Amir, his friend had accepted the change. What if he took away Graem's class but not his levels? What if he was wrong about what Reset Class did? Even if he survived the moment, Graem would still wield the authority of the school. Resetting his class might mean that Graem lost the ability to even remove his collar.

His only real option was groveling for mercy, but Orrin would rather risk the collar exploding and taking them both out. His [Ward] was up, along with every variation of the spell he had. If anyone would survive, it would be him. It was an option he'd considered for a while but never thought to actually try until now.

Orrin's left pointer finger slid under the metal.

"No, stop!" Graem yelled, dropping his hand. Orrin slid down the wall and landed in a crumpled pile of limbs on the floor. "I shouldn't have done that. Don't kill yourself."

Orrin got two fingers of his right hand under the collar as well and began to pull.

"I'll answer your questions, you idiot. Don't be stupid. I made a mistake." Graem reached up and tried to pull Orrin's hands down. "What is this? How are you so strong?"

Orrin shouldered Graem away, keeping his fingers under the collar. "I can break it. I don't know what it'll do, but I can do it. I've played this game for too long. Take it off or I'll take the chance."

"Calm down. I'll tell you what I know and you can decide what you want to do. It might be better if I take that collar off you and let you disappear anyway. I don't want to kill anyone tonight."

Orrin stopped pulling on the metal. Despite his threat, he wasn't sure he could pull the collar apart with his strength. It was magically reinforced. He could feel the magic strengthening the substance under his fingers.

"Are you going to kill Sloane? Even though you know she isn't the one who attacked Rhys?" Orrin took a step back and kept his hands up, ready to try again.

"Officially, Sloane tried to escape after confessing to the attempted murder of Rhys Tonsa and his party inside the dungeon. She is likely dead or will be dead shortly." Graem picked up the diluted whiskey and growled before throwing it at the opposite wall. He went behind his desk and started ruffling through his drawers. "You are to be cleared of any involvement, with lots of tedious paperwork confirming you saved the young man's life. Lady Tonsa and your mysterious benefactor are going to meet to discuss a reward, at which point, your mission regarding the Tonsa boy is complete."

Orrin plopped down in the chair. "She's innocent, Graem. It was Hamish. There was someone else on floor five. They waited until we were close to the doorway and popped out to attack. If we can find them—"

"You naive child," Graem said, slamming his top drawer shut and moving to another. He sighed in relief and pulled out another bottle, this one with a reddish hue. He drank half the contents and sat in his desk chair. "Hamish isn't from Veskar. Sloane is . . . was. Her attack against Rhys and your attempts to keep him safe will push Lady Tonsa straight into Anabella's trap. With a common enemy in Veskar, the people of Mistlight will turn their attention away from the elves to the West. An international incident like this might make the other families evaluate their stance regarding which Sanerris is on top."

Orrin's mind raced as he followed Graem's explanation. "But Sloane was almost dead. I brought her back. If I hadn't, there would be no body, no proof."

Graem shook his head. "No, it didn't matter what happened. Once you entered that dungeon, any outcome was a win for Anabella. Sloane was one scapegoat. If you or Iona died, evidence could be planted. Double agents, working for Lord Sanerris. If Rhys died, it would be her son's fault. Anabella secured the Tonsa vote tonight. You got lucky. According to Sloane, Hamish died in the dungeon, which wraps up that loose end. Sloane is the easier one to pin everything on. Mostly because you are controllable. Even if you started shouting from the streets what happened, nobody would believe a first-year student. Not that you'd be able to. With the collar on, I'm supposed to control you."

"Try it." Orrin clenched his fingers around the armrests.

Graem held up his hands. "Like I said, I'm not killing anyone tonight, and I'm not pushing you when you are so obviously on edge. Go sleep. Skip your classes today. Nobody will blame you."

"If Anabella planned all this, she's not going to let me go. Why are you telling me all this?" Orrin felt a pit in his stomach even as he asked. "Insurance."

"She did say you were smart." Graem pulled another long drink from his bottle and frowned when he found it empty. "Damn it."

"She won't kill you. You're her helper."

"I know things. If asked to stand in front of a tribunal and a [Mind Mage] or [Reader] is brought up, I'm fucked and so is she. I'm not protected like one of the big families. I'd have to let them in, and once they read my mind, she'd be screwed. I didn't know everything until you were already inside the dungeon, but that won't matter. I'd be executed for plotting against the Tonsa family."

Orrin was still unsure about a few issues. "You knew someone was trying to assassinate Rhys and told your sister. She set the party. She works for Anabella, too."

Graem moved to his bookshelf and took a thick book off. Throwing it on the table, he pulled a few more from the same row out until a small hatch was revealed. Flicking the latch, he pulled out a small pipe and some leaves. Orrin watched as he began to fill the pipe.

"I reached that conclusion with faulty data." Graem lit the pipe and took a puff. "While you were in the dungeon, our little plan worked. Your vandal went back. It was a local second-story worker . . . a thief. He gave up his client, Willa Cohee. She's a classmate that you pissed off somehow. When I confronted her, she confessed almost immediately. She seemed proud, actually. It was momentarily enjoyable to expel her. But she wasn't involved in trying to kill Rhys. She knew nothing beyond not liking you."

Graem smiled languidly as his drugs kicked in. "I started to think I was wrong about someone being after Rhys and went back to my sister. Turns out various people had paid for group selections this month. I can't prove it yet, but I'm sure Anabella positioned it so Hamish and Sloane wouldn't have a full party, so when Rhys joined, they were the only front-line fighters left. For some reason, Lady Tonsa wanted her son in your party. I don't know why, but she paid Wren to connect you."

Orrin rubbed his eyes. He'd kept watch for the few hours Rhys and Iona slept and it was early morning now. "Rhys was ordered to join the dungeon run and make friends with me. He knows I work for Anabella, but his mom told him to connect with me for some reason. Anabella said something about this dungeon run costing her something. Maybe I'm the something."

"This is going to cost everybody a lot more now. If Lady Sanerris is trying to start a war with Veskar, that isn't something I want to be a part of, no matter the intelligence she gives me."

Orrin wanted to ask what kind of information she could offer him that he couldn't find in his library, but pounding on the door interrupted him before he could ask.

"Professor Graem, the prisoner escaped. She died trying to breach the city walls," the voice on the other side of the door yelled.

Graem closed his eyes and inhaled deeply on his pipe. "You better get back to your dorm, Casimir. It's going to be an interesting next few days."

Chapter 41

According to Anabella's last message in the sending book, a victory on the elven war front was imminent in the next four days—or at least something along those lines would be announced to the general public. Orrin sat on his bed, his feet hanging off the edge. He double-checked the sending book again, but after his report to Anabella in the dungeon, no responses had appeared. He cleared the message and thought about what to write.

She risked my life and Rhys's life for a chance to get her power back. Orrin hesitated with the stylus over the page. He made himself close the book and put it back in his storage. *She planned for every scenario. Graem is scared enough that he's telling me his inner thoughts in the hope it keeps the noose off his neck. I should keep her as uninformed as possible from here on out.*

Graem's offer to take the collar off might be his way out of this mess. The guards had called him to come to inspect the death of a student, even if she was a prisoner of the state for her supposed attempt to kill Rhys. Orrin would need to see if the man was serious about removing his collar. From what he remembered, Anabella paid him in information for his loyalty. Specifically, Graem had mentioned he wanted to make a list of all spells and skills.

Orrin had a slight advantage there. From what Madi had told him, people's access to the store included only a few dozen stock options and then the specific spells or skills related to their class and level. Orrin's store list was extensive, outpacing even Daniel's list . . . and he was a [Hero].

Whether that was due to Orrin's class as a [Utility Warder] or something to do with his Administrator access, he didn't know. The downside to giving more information to Graem was Orrin's lack of knowledge regarding the world at large. He could accidentally give Graem the tools he needed to unlock some horrific spells.

The alternative was trusting that Anabella would honor her end of the bargain. From what he gathered, the Tonsa family was now back on Lady Sanerris's side. Anabella thought she could get Maeve's father to her side, and the only remaining person that Orrin was supposed to befriend wasn't even at the school anymore. In his opinion, he'd completed his mission. He flopped back on his bed and stared at the ceiling.

Orrin briefly thought about Willa, the woman who'd asked him on a date during orientation. The glamour that made him look so good and made people open up to him more had worked against him there. He'd tried to turn down her advances by playing oblivious and inviting along friends to their date. When she never followed up with him, Orrin had thought the entire mess was behind him. He'd never suspected her of hiring someone to break into his room and leave a dead animal behind.

Who does that?

He rolled out of bed and checked that his windows were shut and locked. Using his still-increased strength, he bent the metal clasp so it wouldn't open again. *If I want fresh air, I'll go outside.*

Crawling back into his bed, Orrin checked on the blinking notifications in his status. [Increase Intelligence] was finally maxed out. His strength and dexterity buffs lagged behind, but his first debuff had reached the next cap as well.

[Decrease Dexterity] Level 1 (1,000/1,000) !
Upgrade available. -2 AP
[Increase Intelligence] Level 3 (10,000/10,000) !
(2/4 Completed)

He had twenty-five ability points and felt rich. Putting aside his doubts, Orrin purchased the upgrade. It cost only two points. He was interested to see what happened when all the increase buffs were maxed out.

Orrin completed his nightly ritual of using his entire mana pool to the point he could feel a headache coming. His morning block was a free period, and Battle Class wouldn't start until well over twelve hours from now. *I'll see how I feel when I wake up*, Orrin thought as he drifted off to sleep.

Orrin missed Battle Class. He'd been pushing himself so hard that when he woke, the sun was already low in the sky. Through his window, he could see the group of students at the other end fighting, but instead of joining them, Orrin listened to the crying out of his stomach and went in search of food.

In the cafeteria, a few students were grabbing an early dinner or between-meals snack, but the majority of the school was in class. He saw one or two familiar faces but nobody he knew well enough to eat with. He slapped a few pieces of meat and cheese between some toast and made his way back to his room.

Even without talking to anyone, Orrin felt the tension around the school as he walked through the hallways chewing. Graem was absent, with no summons to discuss his current circumstances. Extra guards were posted in the streets outside. Fewer people in the hallways and everyone talking in hushed and hurried whispers. Orrin swallowed the last bite of his dinner and locked the door behind him.

With classes tomorrow, the smart thing to do would be to hit the library or go through the store again. Each time he searched for spells, Orrin would have an idea for a combination in [Merge] and have to stop himself from spending his points without thinking. Instead, he got comfortable on his bed and opened up [Way of the Water].

[Way of the Water] 35% 7/20 completed.
Continue?

Orrin bowed to Styx upon entering. The fighting teacher made of water sloshed back at him and sat on the ground, as he had a few training sessions ago. He raised his hands and the familiar drop of water emerged between his palms.

"This again?" Orrin complained but sat down. Every time he increased the percentage of [Way of the Water], he gained a better understanding of the fighting style. It was still mostly a way to avoid damage, but that meant it was perfect for him. He'd bitch about it, but if Styx had him stand on his head for an hour in a waterfall, he knew he'd do it.

Styx waited until Orrin was comfortable and in place. Once he mirrored the watery figure in front of him, Orrin called his own non-magical water bead into being. Styx pulled his hands apart in a slow and exaggerated fashion, and Orrin watched the small drop of water grow into a needle-thin line. Styx shoved his hands back, and the line coalesced into a drop again.

Orrin waited to make sure Styx wasn't going to add another step before looking away. He felt bad that he hadn't practiced with the summoned water outside of these trainings, but without a clear purpose of what he was doing, Orrin didn't understand the use.

Instead of beginning right away with the useless-looking exercise, Orrin recounted to Styx all that had happened. Talking to his best friend was an impossibility, but at least Orrin had Styx to complain to.

"I feel bad that she's probably dead, but I can't save everyone," Orrin finished. The watery figure hadn't moved an inch. "What? No advice?"

Styx's shoulders moved such an infinitesimal amount that Orrin wasn't sure if he actually shrugged or not. With a sigh, he tried to pull his hands apart like Styx, only for the water drop to dissipate into nothing. Orrin pulled his lips tight and rolled his eyes at Styx. "Any advice on what to do?"

"BECOME."

"Super helpful," Orrin muttered. He summoned and retried multiple times. It didn't matter how fast or slow he moved his hands; the water bead would evaporate as soon as it left the sweet spot directly between his palms. He spent an hour trying and getting more frustrated.

"I can already summon water and push it around," Orrin said in a huff, standing and using [Water Reservoir] to splash the ground between himself and Styx.

His teacher didn't respond but sat patiently as Orrin stomped around throwing a fit. He vented and screamed, letting out the frustration he'd kept bottled inside for the past few days. The entire hidden-spy-in-a-school-of-mages thing was not for him. This was some [Hero] shit. Speaking of that asshole, why hadn't he come to rescue him already? Surely Daniel knew where Orrin was by now. He used a few more spells, throwing magic into the walls of the training room.

After he spent his anger, Orrin collapsed back into the same spot and glared at Styx. "I'm not having a good day. Can you be a bit more specific?"

"BECOME."

Orrin closed his eyes and thought happy thoughts. Driving a [Ice Sword] through Styx wouldn't kill him, right? He might have some weakness to ice magic. Professor Hugh's lessons were clear that ice magic worked well against wat—

Orrin's eyes shot open. He stared at his hands and summoned the drop. He ignored everything around him and let the magic around him flood his mind. Using the same techniques he had in class, Orrin felt for the water mana that had to be . . .

The water mana in the water . . .

It wasn't water mana.

Orrin frowned. The drop of water that was suspended between his fingers wasn't made of water mana like he'd thought. He'd known for a while that it was different, since his collar had blocked mana use in the past before Graem allowed him more access, but what he felt now confused him. The bead of water felt like an extension of himself. The longer Orrin stared at it, the more he felt connected.

Orrin pulled his hands, and instead of dropping, the ball expanded slightly for the briefest moment. In his excitement, Orrin took his eyes off the ball, literally, and it splashed on his crossed legs.

It took another twenty tries, but eventually, Orrin could drag the water into a thread. He felt the achievement of progress but ignored it. "Styx, is the water part of me? Like my soul or something?"

"NO."

Orrin scowled at Styx's tone. He might as well have called him an idiot. It was a good guess. In the fantasy books he read on Earth, some types of magic used the soul to do extraordinary things. He didn't know what Styx was teaching him, but it was way ahead of anything he'd learned at magic school.

[Way of the Water] 40% 8/20 completed.
Continue?

"I'll be back later," Orrin promised. He'd spent only three hours in the skill's simulation training. It was nearing nightfall, and he was famished again. A quick trip to the cafeteria to refuel and he returned to his room. His lucky streak of avoiding anyone was holding.

Orrin sat cross-legged on his bed and retrieved the sending book from his inventory. His orders were to check in every night. He sent Anabella a bullshit question about what next steps he should take, expecting no response. His expectations were on point when he woke up the next day to no new update from his jailer.

He had Magical History and Surviving Spell Attacks, but after taking a quick glance in Professor Quinn's classroom and not seeing Rhys, Orrin skipped. He went to the library and made a beeline for the profession skills sections. An entire row of books dedicated to the different professions and related skills. The bookcases underwent normal upkeep procedures but still gave off an abandoned atmosphere. Orrin found one book on alchemy and another on distillery and alcohol processing. With everything going on, this was his chance to look into another possibility of escaping without multiple eyes watching his every move.

When Orrin had tried to use [Merge] once before, two of his skills gave the option of [Create Poison]. Despite his best searches, he couldn't find books on the [Poisoner] class, which he'd hoped might point him in the right direction. Orrin could care less about poison. He could already use [Toxic Touch], which was an amazing—if scary—spell. What he wanted to find was something between an alchemy potion and a poison. Orrin wanted to create acids.

He figured [Alchemy] was a good start, but at twelve ability points, buying the skill outright was too expensive. The store didn't show a specific skill like [Acid Maker], either. If he could create a new skill that combined the destroying nature of his [Toxic Touch] with, say, the ability to create alcohol, he might be able to break the collar enough to slip out of it.

Orrin settled into a corner of the room and began to read.

Chapter 42

Orrin skipped dinner, too engrossed in reading the books on alchemy and distilling alcohol. They confirmed the starter prices for profession skills were on the higher side, usually between eight and fifteen ability points. [Alchemy] cost twelve AP, and [Brew] cost ten. Both skills were customizable, with their respective books discussing the need for a mentor or teacher to show the budding [Alchemist] or [Distiller] the best way down any particular path. Actual details were sparse. Reading between the lines, Orrin figured that profession skills were kept secret. Likely to control the supply and demand for produced products.

[Brew] was only the starting point. [Distill] and [Focused Fermentation] were mentioned as two paths for more specific specialization. Multiple cooking-adjacent spells were needed, and the alcohol book discussed the costs and benefits of using engineered containers of different makes for beer, wine, or liquor.

[Alchemy] had more applications than Orrin had originally thought. While [Potions] were mentioned, the book noted various guilds to approach if interested in other uses. The skill had applications in farming, engineering, building materials, blacksmithing, tanning, and more.

Orrin put his head down on the table. There were elements of what he needed in both skills, but his knowledge was lacking. He knew some basic high school chemistry and biology, but not enough to make acid. From what he gathered, he could make low-grade liquor easily. Turning it into something that would eat through metal was a different story.

He still needed to deal with the collar's little quirk of exploding as well. In the alchemy book, Orrin found a potion that gave him hope. A recipe for a warmth potion promised to stave off cold and block some types of ice magic. If Orrin could reverse engineer the spell and change it to a cold potion, he might be able to block some damage from the exploding collar when he eventually ripped it off.

The problem was that would take time and there was no guarantee it would work.

I need to convince Graem to take it off, Orrin thought, his finger hooked into the collar. To the few people left in the library this late, it would appear as if he was playing with his necklace. *Or I have to chance it, use [Merge], and hope poison is close enough to acids for it to work.*

Putting the books on the return cart, Orrin headed back to his room, only to stop at the corner before his hallway.

Someone was sitting on the floor beside his door.

Orrin prepared to cast [Camouflage] when he realized it was Ellis. He relaxed as he approached the boy.

Ellis jumped up as Orrin rounded the corner with a smile across his face. "Casimir! I'm so happy you're okay. I heard you had some trouble in the dungeon, but I couldn't find you today. Did you hear that it was Willa who hired someone to destroy your things for rejecting her advances? It's all anyone is talking about. The rumor is that her aunt is ostracizing her and demanding the entire family do the same."

Orrin closed his eyes in frustration. Another enemy was exactly what he did not need. "Did you wait long? Sorry. I was in the library."

Ellis moved to the side so Orrin could open his door. "Not too long. I wanted to make sure you were safe. I heard from one girl at lunch that your party died in the dungeon, but I knew that couldn't be true. A lot of people were worried, though. You were missing and so is Rhys Tonsa. He was in your party, too, right?"

"I think Rhys went home. I haven't seen him since I left the dungeon." Orrin didn't lie, but he wasn't about to get into the entire conspiracy with Ellis. He unlocked his door but used [Map] to make sure nobody was waiting on the other side. A new habit for sure, but one that he was learning was necessary. "How are you? Is everything fine with your backer now that the real culprit has been caught?"

Ellis flinched but kept the smile plastered on his face. "Yes, everything is fine. I was even granted another semester's tuition for the trouble. I mean, I'll still have to take some classes outside my area, but it's a great deal."

Orrin pushed his door open and stood in the doorway of his room. "That's great, Ellis. Did you need anything else? I'm going to turn in."

Ellis shuffled his feet. "No, that's it. I'm glad you made it through the dungeon. See you tomorrow for breakfast?"

Orrin agreed and closed the door with Ellis bouncing around outside. The boy's elation at being seen as innocent was obvious, but Orrin could tell something was still bothering him.

It's not my problem, Orrin told himself. *I can't fix everything.*

He sat down on the foot of his bed and pulled up [Merge].

"But I can be prepared just in case."

> **Merge: [Water Reservoir] and [Toxic Touch]?**
> **Compatibility: 30% to 100%**
> **Chance of original spell loss: 0% to 35%**
> **Variations: 2**
> **Cooldown: 2 hours to 6 days**
> **Review Choices**

Using [Merge] cost nothing more than a few days of the skill's cooldown. The chance of losing [Toxic Touch] scared him, but he couldn't use it anyway, with the collar keeping the skill locked down. He figured Anabella kept the spell sealed so Orrin wouldn't have an easy way to accidentally kill himself.

Orrin held his breath. *And here I am making myself a new way to do just that.*

He scrolled to his second option and clicked yes.

[Create Poison]—Learn basic poisons
Original spell [Toxic Touch] retained.

Orrin let out a sigh of relief. He'd beaten the odds. Pulling up the new skill, he studied the new interface.

[Create Poison]:
(Known Recipes)
(Craft)

His new skill was set up similar to how [Brew] was supposed to appear. He clicked (Known Recipes), expecting nothing, and was pleasantly surprised.

(Known Recipes)
Slow Poison—A weak poison that must be ingested. Causes the victim to become dizzy. See ingredients. (10 MP)
Weak Poison—A weak poison that must be ingested. Causes the victim to become fatigued. See ingredients. (10 MP)

Orrin clicked the list that included a few different plant names. If he was right, all he had to do was use the system's (Craft) selection while having the ingredients nearby and he'd have a poison. He needed a glass jar to contain the poison as well. He was going to need to go shopping.

Orrin saw another blinking exclamation point near the bottom of the screen and mentally selected it.

New Subskills Unlocked for [Create Poison]:
[Create Corrosive]—Learn basic corrosives. -4 AP
[Create Poison]—Learn advanced poisons -5 AP

[Create Solvent]—Learn basic solvents. -4 AP
[Create Toxin]—Learn basic toxins. -4 AP

Orrin stared at the list in front of him and nearly let out a cry of joy.

A ray of sunlight snuck through the curtains that Orrin had forgotten to close all the way, brushing his face with warmth. Orrin shoved his head under his pillow and grumbled into his mattress.

He'd stayed up entirely too late after buying [Create Corrosive] and playing with his new skill. The (Craft) skill was more than simply pushing the ingredients together. He could mix and match different ingredients to make his own poisons or corrosives. Although, without any materials to work with, Orrin was going simply on theory.

Without the needed plants, bases, chemicals, or metals needed for his poisons, he couldn't do much. Orrin had even checked the store, and while he could buy the ingredients for ability points, there wasn't a Big Book of Poisons that he could purchase. Which sucked, because the [Create Corrosive] subskill he'd purchased came with only one option.

Acid—Create basic acid. (10 MP)

Orrin rolled out of bed and began his daily routine. After getting dressed and using the bathroom, he made his way to breakfast. He had no intention of going to his Magical History class and left the grounds with a piece of toasted bread with berries in it. Stopping along the way for a coffee, Orrin stood in front of an apothecary.

He'd picked the store that was most off the beaten path of the main stores but not down a dark alley he might get mugged in.

I need to walk the line between respectable establishments that will have what I need but not so respectable they don't have the more questionable items I want. That was his thought process, but in truth, he was still worried. A few of the items he needed for his poisons were downright scary-sounding. He didn't want to make any poisons, but even the acid needed something called unspoiled sheep bile.

For all his worry, the old man behind the counter didn't look up from a book as Orrin grabbed handfuls of leaves and placed them in the wicker basket he'd picked up from the entrance. When Orrin asked for sheep bile and ogre tears, the shopkeeper closed his book with a sigh and returned from the back room with small bottles of cloudy liquids. Orrin double-checked with [Analyze] to make sure he wasn't getting swindled, but everything ended up being . . . boringly normal. A few more bottles and glass vials from a shelf and Orrin left two gold pieces lighter.

He made his way back to the school. Nobody cared that he'd skipped his morning class. Graem hadn't been by to see him, and Anabella's lack of messaging to him was now beyond suspicious.

Laying the ingredients out in his room, Orrin anticlimactically made his first acid. He held the clear liquid up in a flask no bigger than his pointer finger and let the midday light shine through it.

Orrin cast [Ward] on himself, along with a few other spells, and held his breath. Tipping the acid on the collar, he suppressed a scream as the liquid dribbled off the edge and caught his neck.

After a round of healing himself, Orrin yanked on the metal, but the collar stayed where it was.

It was all a waste of time.

Orrin went to Surviving Spell Attacks to distract himself. Professor Hugh went over more mathematical equations, but Orrin's head wasn't in class. He hadn't felt this depressed since his dad disappeared on them.

He fumbled his spells during the practical aspect of the class and left with a few bruises from being knocked across the room. Without [Calm Mind], Orrin wasn't sure he'd have made it through dinner. Ellis tried to talk with him, but after moving his food around on his plate, Orrin went back to bed.

The bright light of the morning was the world laughing at him. He'd tossed all night and barely slept. Every time he almost fell asleep, Orrin would wake with a new thought and search the store, reread the description on one of his spells, and once he even returned to the training world with Styx to ask a question. The watery teacher gave no help.

Orrin still wore the same clothes as yesterday. He decided it was time to go to Graem. He took the few items he'd collected from around the room and stuffed them into his [Dimension Hole]. *I'm not coming back.*

It was still early enough that only a few people were in the halls, and Orrin made it to Graem's room quickly. Opening the door, he walked in unannounced. He slammed the door behind him, uncaring why it was unlocked in the first place.

"Graem, I'm done. Take this thing off me right now. I did what she wanted and helped with Rhys, but I can't be here ano—"

Orrin tripped over Graem's body on the floor. A trail of vomit leaked out of his mouth, and the man was not breathing.

Orrin's brain froze. He'd seen death multiple times in this world, but mostly from monsters or actual attacks. Graem's immediate appearance screamed *overdose,* and the man's history would back that up—if not for their conversation only days ago. If Graem was dead, Anabella would be coming after Orrin next. She wasn't responding to his messages, which meant she was coming. He needed to escape.

"Graem? Are you still sulking? I need your help with one of the vendors. He's trying to raise the contract prices. Are you in there?" Wren's voice preceded the heavy knocking. "Let me in, you idiot."

Orrin noticed the lock had relatched when he shut the door. The only thing standing between him and the dead teacher's sister was an inch of metal.

Chapter 43

Before Orrin could make a plan, the lock twisted and Graem's door opened. Wren stepped through the door frame, and her eyes landed on the still body of her brother.

Orrin hoped his cast of [Camouflage] had been quick enough. He slowly backed away from the man's unmoving form as a cascade of emotions filtered over Wren's face.

"Graem? This isn't a funny joke. Get up." Her voice quivered. "I'm serious. I've told you that I would kill you if you ever did this again."

Orrin's confusion spiked. Was Graem pulling a prank?

He used [Identify] on the body.

Graem Balint	Librarian Level 56	Status: Intoxicated; Poisoned; Comatose
HP: 18/270	MP: 5/190	
Strength: 13	Constitution: 27	Dexterity: 13
Will: 19	Intelligence: 32	

"Oh shit, he's alive," Orrin said in his surprise.

The armoire behind him twisted and struck through him in three differrent places, pinning him to the ground.

"Drop the spell, assassin," Wren hissed, standing over her brother's body in a defensive pose. "What did you do to him?"

"Professor, it's me, Or— Casimir," Orrin gasped through the pain. Two long branches stuck through his left leg, and the larger shaft of wood had pierced his right shoulder, pushing him down into an awkward half bow. He dropped his [Camouflage] spell. "Graem is alive. You have to let me up so I can save him."

"Don't lie. What are you doing in his room? What did you do to him? If he dies, I'll keep you alive for weeks." Spit hit his face as the feral scorn in Wren's voice deepened. "Who sent you?"

Orrin's health dropped again when she melted the doorknob, shaped it into a long spike, and sent it into the center of his back. Orrin screamed in pain, and [Mind Bastion] kicked in.

Ignoring the twisting and burning metal digging into his spine, Orrin cast [Decrease Will] on Wren five times. He didn't have time to use [Identify] or do math. He reacted to save his life, because there was no doubt in his mind that the teacher meant to kill him.

Wren grabbed her head in both hands and screamed in pain. The iron nail stopped digging its way into Orrin's back, and the branches growing from the furniture stopped pulsating with life. Orrin summoned a [Fire Sword] and cut away at the wood holding him down. He was able to yank the larger piece out of his shoulder and was working on the two in his leg when Wren started crying and fumbling her hands into her pockets.

"I'll kill you. I'll kill every one of you. You promised he'd be safe. I'll hammer you to a tree and let your blood feed the roots for a year. I'll shave your flesh from your body and braid it into a lash to beat you with." She continued making increasingly deranged threats as she pulled a vial from a pocket and downed what was obviously a mana potion.

Orrin pulled his leg free, healing himself as much as he dared. One part of him was already casting [Decrease Strength], but he stopped himself. She'd still be able to cast spells unless he drained her mana again.

There wasn't time to fight. Another check on Graem showed the man's health had dropped another five points. Orrin cast [Heal Small Wounds].

"NO!" Wren screamed and pulled the wooden floor up into a barrier that covered Graem. The teacher of Mana Signatures could see the mana moving toward her brother and moved to defend him. "Leave him alone. Fight me."

"Professor, he's dying. I need to heal him." Orrin tried to circle around her and the half-raised cocoon that blocked his view of Graem. Even in the middle of a fight, a small part of his brain registered he needed line of sight to heal. "His health is dropping and he's poisoned . . . and comatose, whatever that means. I can save him."

"You're the one trying to kill him," Wren said as she bent and touched the wooden floor. As she stood, a staff grew with her hand, like she was drawing putty from the ground. A makeshift spear spun in Orrin's direction. "Leave now and you might live."

Orrin watched as she began pulling things out of her other pockets and dropping them on the floor. Small wooden carvings, a knife, and an empty vial she scowled at before throwing it to the ground. She was searching for something.

"What can I do to convince you?" Orrin pleaded. Graem's health was down to the single digits now. "I'll give you a health potion. He's got less than ten points of health left."

"I'll not feed my brother your poison," Wren screeched and threw the next something in her pocket at Orrin. A ball of thread bounced off his chest.

"I'm sorry. I tried being reasonable." Orrin used [Decrease Strength], [Decrease Intelligence], and [Decrease Dexterity] on Wren. A small pout on her lips was all she managed before she fell to the side, immobile.

Orrin scrambled his way to Graem and began using [Heal Small Wounds]. Once his health was a little higher, he used [Purify] as well. Graem's comatose and intoxicated statuses went away, and his eyes flickered open.

"Casimir? What?" Graem's confusion turned to pain as he grabbed his stomach. "Fuck, this is not a good trip. That hurts."

Orrin checked Graem over. The poison status was still there. "Professor, you're poisoned. I can't heal it."

"Get me up," Graem said, putting his hand on Orrin's shoulder and trying to stand. "Wait, why is my sister sleeping on the floor?"

Orrin explained how Wren had found them and assumed the worst. He left out the particulars of how he'd taken her down. "Graem, I need to get you down to the infirmary. They can figure out a cure for the poison."

"I'd rather know how you defeated one of the best mages in the world while taking only a few scrapes," Graem said, looking at Orrin with a slightly scared but mostly intrigued look. "She's going to want to kill you—I hope you know that."

"She might have said that a few times." Orrin ducked under Graem's arm and half carried him out of the room. "You can smooth it all over later."

He waited until they'd left the room before adding in a whisper, "Of course, you could take this collar off and I'll disappear. You should, too. Someone tried to kill you."

Graem was silent during the walk. Multiple people rushed up to ask if he needed help, but Graem simply sent one student ahead to warn Alma that he was poisoned and would need an antidote.

Orrin didn't push Graem for an answer. He could see the man was scared from his brush with death and going over his options. When they reached the infirmary, the old healer, Alma, was already waiting with a frothing liquid that seemed more like cement than something Graem should actually drink. She directed Orrin to drop Graem off in a small room with a curtain for a door to one side of her larger workspace. She waited for Graem to grumble and get settled before handing over the concoction.

The man downed the entire glass in one go and winked at Alma when he was done. "Not the best drink I've ever, had but top ten for sure."

"Go flirt with someone your own age, Balint. I'm old enough to be your grandmother," Alma retorted and swatted his arm, but as she left, Orrin saw a smile on her lips.

"Are you sure you're okay? I can heal you some more," Orrin offered as soon as Alma closed the curtain.

"Alma's the best at this. The poison is already working its way out of my system, and I'll be fine after a bit of sleep. Tell me everything that happened. Oh, wait." Graem spread his arms, and his sound bubble spread around the room. "Go ahead."

Orrin told him about knocking on the door and finding him on the floor. He sheepishly explained how he'd thought Graem was dead and hadn't thought to check until Wren was in the room.

Graem laughed.

"If I'd been a few minutes later . . ." Orrin trailed off.

"My sister would have found me and forced a potion down my throat before dragging my ass down to Alma," Graem said, waving off the near-death experience with aplomb. "The timing was too precise. It was a warning."

Orrin stared pointedly at the sweaty mess of a man in front of him.

"I told you when we first met that people are predictable. I've made sure to be around people I trust or have them on their way to me every twenty minutes since we spoke last. This is part of the game at this level. You've already dealt with it, too. How many times have people tried to kill you in Odrana? And I'm talking about Casimir."

Orrin frowned. "You still didn't answer my question."

"Hmm. Which question?"

"Will you take my collar off?"

"No."

Orrin closed his eyes and counted to three. "Why. not?"

"My job is to help you get your honeypot on. I just survived a poison attempt for being ancillary. I'm not going to go out of my way to help you escape."

Orrin was on borrowed time. The decrease-debuff spells only lasted five minutes, so now Wren was on her way to murder him for sure. "Will you at least take the explosive murder trap off? I can't sleep at night worrying I'm going to turn the wrong way and make it go off."

Graem gave Orrin a look that said plainly, *we both know that's a lie*. After rolling his eyes, he shrugged and reached over, tapping the collar. Orrin felt the magic twist in the metal, a roaring tiger going to sleep. "I owe you for saving my life. Please try not to escape today. I'll talk to Wren. She might even let you stay in her class."

Orrin shivered, remembering the threats she'd used. He'd seen behind the curtain of her rage and now wasn't sure whom he was escaping from.

"Alma, where is my brother?" As if on cue, Wren's voice cut through the infirmary.

Orrin used [Camouflage] and ran.

Orrin almost went back to his dorm room but decided to wander the halls instead. If he saw Wren approaching, he could run again.

He considered ducking into an unused classroom and ripping the metal off. Whatever game Graem was playing with Anabella, he wanted no part of it. If he did increase his strength and rip the metal right off his neck, the [Glamour] would end. Hiding in the school for another day from Graem wouldn't be an option.

Orrin walked by his Defensive Earth Magic classroom and took a peek inside. The students had moved on from throwing chunks of dirt at each other. Instead, each was using their magic to cover a dummy. Professor Cade had explained it at the end of the last class. It was a test of sorts for each student. Cade would send different types of magic at the earthen armor in an attempt to break it.

Maeve was the only one sitting down, every other student performing minute changes to cover cracks or thicken magical matrices.

Orrin felt bad. He liked Maeve. She was an oddball and the kind of person he would have spent time with on his own initiative. From their few classes, it didn't seem like she was impressing Professor Cade enough to convince him to be her adviser.

On an impulse, Orrin sent an [Earth Ward] and regular [Ward] toward her dummy.

Orrin smiled as he watched Professor Cade, who had destroyed each of his classmates' defenses in two to three attacks, spend a minute testing his powers against Maeve's target. It took eight attempts to shatter the stone suit she'd created. Maeve's feet swung shoeless from her bench as she watched with a slight frown on her face.

"There you are."

Orrin ran. He didn't glance back, as Wren's voice was distinct enough that he had no doubt he'd been found already. Orrin noticed an open door ahead and dashed inside.

Sorry, Graem, I can't wait anymore, Orrin thought as he placed his hands on either side of the collar and began to pull as he increased his strength.

Instead of breaking, the metal of the collar hardened and stretched into multiple thin bands. Orrin tried to keep his fingers underneath but had to slip them out before the pressure cut them off.

A shadow crossed the door. Orrin turned with dread to find Wren standing with her hand stretched out toward him.

"You have some explaining to do."

Chapter 44

Orrin choked as the collar–turned–bands of metal cut off his breath. He looked around the room for anything or anyone to help, but the doorway he'd run through in his haste to get away led to an empty classroom. Other than a few loose chairs pushed against the far wall, the room was empty.

Wren stalked up to him, her hand raised in the air. Orrin could feel her mana twisting through the metal bands. He raised his fingers up to his neck and found blood from where he'd already been cut. He had seconds to react. Taking her down last time had been easy, so if he just—

Wren twisted her fingers, and the collar yanked him to the tips of his toes.

"Wait," he gasped. "I can't breathe."

"You won't, either, until you tell me what you did and how you did it. You tore through my defenses like paper. I find you invisible in my brother's room with him dying at your feet. He makes up a story that you saved him and work for him, but too many things don't add up. Put your hands behind your back, now."

Orrin's lungs began to burn as he tried to suck in more air. He hovered on the edge of consciousness as Wren pulled his hands back. He couldn't fight back in any way, showing once again how little power he had even with all his levels. Something circled his wrists, and he heard a distinct click before the bands around his neck loosened. He fell to the floor in a heap and gulped in the air.

"Now." Wren's voice sounded throughout the room with a quiet but fierce tone. "Let's chat."

The door slammed on its own accord, and one of the chairs screeched as it pulled its way to them. Wren sat down with Orrin at her feet.

"Tell me who you are."

"... and then I brought him to Alma," Orrin finished his tale. He hadn't held back, telling Wren his real name, his capture and subsequent deal with Anabella, the assassination attempt, and his own mission that Graem refused to let him escape from. "I swear to you, I never tried to poison Graem. In fact, I've cured his hangovers and detoxed his body of drugs so many times, you could call me his doctor."

Wren's eyes were focused on Orrin, and he knew without a doubt she was searching him for any use of magic. Orrin wasn't worried about his health depleting, even with the cuts on his neck. Wren's magic had reattached the collar into one piece, making him question if she could deactivate it completely. He leaned into the captured and helpless act, hoping against hope that the sister would free him where the brother wouldn't.

"Why you? You present like a [Wind Mage], but you used spells I've never heard of on me. Why would Lady Sanerris send you to entice these targets? They aren't even the ones making the decisions. You could probably incapacitate any one of them separately, but there are easier ways and places to pull a kidnapping."

Orrin had thought the same thing himself multiple times. Rhys's mother was known to be as smart as Anabella, and Rhys didn't hold that kind of sway over his mother, even if they'd become best friends instead of the clusterfuck of maybe-enemy/maybe-savior relationship they had. From what he knew, Maeve's family would vote for Anabella as long as she was safe. Finley was even more of an outlier. "She promised not to hurt their parents, but maybe just the threat of me would be enough. Imagine Rhys is your kid and Anabella comes up to you and points out how close I got to him as a friend. A veiled threat might work well enough for whatever she has planned."

Wren rolled her eyes. "If Lady Sanerris makes a veiled threat to you, you're already dead."

They sat there in silence.

"You have to teach class in a bit. Are you going to kill me or let me go?" Orrin tried to sound sure of the answer.

"It would be easier."

"What would be easier?" Orrin felt sweat roll down the back of his neck . . . or maybe it was blood.

"My job is to protect the students here," Wren said while standing and pacing in front of him. "You might not realize it, but you are a danger to at least three of those students."

"Two aren't even at the school anymore, and I wouldn't hurt any of them, anyway."

Wren glared down at Orrin, and he shut his mouth.

"You admitted that you are a member of the [Hero]'s party and tried to usurp justice in Odrana. Being associated with you could be a death sentence for most of the students here. On the other hand, you saved Rhys and his bodyguard. My brother feels indebted to you. You are doing a decent job keeping yourself alive and haven't killed anyone that I know of . . ." She trailed off, giving him a significant look.

"And I don't plan on it, either. Take the collar off me and I'll leave, never to be seen again."

"If only it was that simple. My brother, in his infinite stupidity, is working for Lady Sanerris. I haven't tied myself to any house but work more as a freelance agent for a few. Thankfully, none of them have given me a direct request to find a spy in the school. Now that I know Graem is linked to you, I have to move carefully. If I free you and let you run away, Graem is implicated. If I kill you, he might face Lady Sanerris's wrath for failing her in some scheme you're a part of. You'll have to stay for now, but if and when he tells you to leave, you should hope to never meet me again."

"Professor Wren, I mean it when I say I just want to get home. I don't want to be a part of this and never did. I don't know what is going on half the time, and I feel like I'm waiting for the other shoe to drop."

Wren stopped pacing and walked behind Orrin. She grabbed the handcuffs she'd secured on him and took them off. "Not everyone was cut out for the political affairs of Odrana. Get as much of an education as you can in the next few weeks. I doubt we'll see each other again after that. Now, get to class before I change my mind."

Orrin scrambled to his feet and began to exit the room.

"Oh, and Casimir," Wren called out as he placed his hand on the doorknob. "Thank you for saving my brother."

Orrin decided that skipping Mana Signatures would be a bad idea. Showing up a few minutes after him, Wren gave no indication they'd fought that morning and taught the class as she normally did.

"Now, the best way to sense a mana signature and exclude it from the environmental mana around it is to let the system pull the spell from you like normal and focus. Once you begin to see your own mana being changed into a certain flavor of magic on a regular basis, you can begin to understand it better."

Orrin thought about what he'd done in the dungeon. Using [Fire Sword] and [Gust], he'd manipulated the mana of both to create new spells. He remembered Wren's presentation with increasing the output of her [Woodbolt] and frowned. That wasn't what he'd done.

All around him, the other students were casting various spells, using targets, buckets of dirt or water, and even a shaft of light coming through a window. His frown deepened as he thought about his own magic spells.

For the most part, Orrin was using [Gust] to keep up the facade of being a wind magic user at school. But if the mana signature of any spell could be read and understood, what about his increase-stat spells?

Orrin used [Increase Will] at the lowest setting on himself, trying to drag the spell out as long as possible to have more time to study the mana flowing out of himself. The first two casts resulted in nothing. His frown deepened. Every other spell he'd cast, Orrin had been able to find some glimmer to focus on. After two more casts, he finally found it.

"What are you smiling about, Casimir? What spell are you casting?" Wren asked, standing in front of his desk.

"I . . . um . . . it's a spell to increase my stats temporarily." Orrin spoke softly. Kieran was the closest person, but he was engrossed in casting his own spell over and over. "It took me a few times to find the mana signature, but—"

"Cast it again," she demanded, not caring to keep her voice low. "Not on me," she quickly added.

Orrin didn't comment and pointedly ignored the flash of fear that crossed her face. He used the spell again.

"That . . . do it again."

Orrin cast his spell three more times before Wren waved her hand. "That's enough. Don't waste all your mana."

Orrin stopped. Wren's head was tilted to the side as she studied him again. Orrin couldn't read her expression. Part fear? Part excitement?

"You can see it, too, right?"

"Yes, it took a few tries to find it, but it doesn't really match any of the magic types we went over."

Wren nodded frantically. "Do you see any similarities in how it would fall into the core magic equation?"

Orrin turned his notebook, finding the page full of scribbles from the first day of class. "It doesn't quite fit the equation for light magic, but this part connects, I think. There is also a little bit of that tangle at the end over here in the earth magic equation, but again, it doesn't fit completely."

"Stop looking at the various pieces," Wren demanded. "Step back."

It took him a minute to gather what she was saying, but Orrin's notes from the first day were pretty thorough. Ignoring the individual parts of his spell, he focused on the entirety of the swirls and angles of his buffing spell crawling all over the page.

"It looks a lot like the core magic equation itself."

"Professor?" Noor, the old man who was using the light from the window to study his own light magic, called out. "I believe I'm seeing it. I have a few questions regarding the calculi I want to apply to the spectrum."

Orrin could see Wren wanted nothing more than to ignore Noor and stay asking him questions, but she did her job. "Stay after class," she demanded before walking over to the hunched elder.

Orrin tried mapping the differences between his [Increase Will] spell and the core equation as he'd copied it from the board. There were noticeable differences between the two, but the way his spell's mana signature spun and moved was closer to the original than any other type of magic Wren had taught them.

Orrin was about to cast [Increase Will] as well when the door to the room opened and a new face walked in.

Well, an old face that Orrin hadn't seen in a week.

Finley Madvarr.

Finley paused at the door and waved at Orrin. Orrin raised his hand to wave back when he realized Finley was in reality waving to Kieran.

That's right, Finley said he'd taken this class. He failed it with Kieran.

"Mr. Madvarr, take a seat. I didn't realize you'd be back today." Wren hurried to the front of the room to greet her newly returned student. "Grab a seat. We're studying our own mana signatures today. If you are too tired from your . . . recent activities, you can rest instead."

Orrin raised his eyebrows in surprise. He had never seen the bootlicker side of Professor Wren.

"Actually, I'm not here for class today, Professor," Finley said with a smile. He swept his hair back in a practiced motion, tying it up behind his head. "I need to have a word with Casimir."

"With Casimir? What? Why?" Wren sputtered, surprise and fear crossing her face.

"That's classified," Finley answered. Orrin noticed for the first time that Finley's knives were all lined up against his armor. One of his hands rested casually across the hilt of one of the weapons. "Casimir Hale, please follow me."

Chapter 45

Orrin awkwardly gathered his books as he stepped out into the hallway with Finley. He took his time, trying to get a read on Finley's mood. He'd told Professor Wren he needed to talk with Orrin for a classified matter but retained the same relaxed pose he showed on the Battle Class field before a fight. Orrin noticed a pack stuffed to overflowing sitting against the wall next to the classroom door.

"Did you just get back?" Orrin asked, pointedly staring at Finley's sock that had fallen out of the bag. "I heard you went to the front lines of the war with the elves."

Finley snapped his fingers and walked away, expecting Orrin to follow. He left his things behind, glancing around but ignoring Orrin.

Orrin walked slowly behind him. Finley's boots left flakes of dirt with each step. Three of Finley's daggers were missing, and the clothes he wore over his armor were ripped in places, letting Orrin see the hard leather he kept hidden underneath.

He returned from the war front and the first thing he does is stop to talk to me. This isn't good.

Finley rummaged in his pocket and took out a key. He scanned up and down the hallway with wary eyes before using the key on a nearby door and shouldering it open. "Get in."

Orrin hesitated until Finley's eyebrows pushed together. He stepped in and made sure to put on every version of ward he had. He was close to getting away and was not going to get into another fight. If Finley attacked him, he was going to down him as fast as he could and run.

The door clicked shut behind him.

The classroom hadn't been used anytime recently, if the dust covering the seats and desks was any clue. Curtains choked off most of the evening light, but Finley solved that by yanking them open. Light streamed into the room, and Orrin raised his hands as Finley approached him.

"What is going on, Finley? This is a little too cloak-and-dagger for my taste."

Finley raised his open hand above his head, fingers splayed. He made a fist, squeezing his fingers shut. "We need to talk quickly. I'm not supposed to be back until tomorrow. I had to pay a [Locationist] a lot of gold to break protocol. Even if she hasn't reported me by now, too many people saw me arrive."

Orrin's ears popped as the air around them condensed into a familiar feeling. Finley had cast a version of whatever spell Graem used when he wanted to talk in private. He stepped back, holding his hands up. "Still being a little scary there, buddy."

Finley noticed his free hand was tapping the hilt of one of his knives. "Sorry, I'm still a bit jumpy. Your friend is a right bastard in a fight, and if Madeleine wasn't there, I'm not sure I would have made it out."

Orrin froze at hearing Madi's full name for only a moment, but Finley was watching for it.

"It is you, then. You don't look exactly like who she described, but when she talked about who you are as a person, I knew. You're Orrin, right? The party member of the [Hero] of Dey who was executed for trying to kill Lord Sanerris?"

Orrin briefly considered lying, but at this point he had nothing to lose. "We didn't try to kill him. He was torturing our friend and we rescued him. I got stuck behind and they locked me up with this." Orrin tugged on the collar around his neck. "It's a slave collar. There's also a [Glamour] on me so I look different."

Finley kept his hands away from his weapons, which was the only reason Orrin was talking instead of hitting him with a few [Decrease Strength] spells and running away.

Finley cursed. "Is it true that the elves aren't attacking us and Odrana pushed the aggression first?"

"From what the elves told me and Madi, yes. They just want to be left alone. Lord Sanerris attacked Daniel . . . the [Hero] . . . in their forest. How are my friends doing?"

Finley turned away from Orrin's gaze. "It hasn't been easy on anyone on the border. Madeleine has always been strong, but your friend's eyes . . . We've been taking lots of losses wherever he attacks or defends."

Orrin's heart broke for Daniel. They'd known that Odrana would throw their superior numbers at the elves, but that was only theory. Daniel was defending the innocent from an aggressor, but killing people took a toll.

"You fought him?" Orrin asked. "I've seen you fight. Is he okay?"

Finley let out a strangled laugh. "Is *he* okay? I almost died. If Madeleine hadn't stepped between us, I would be dead. I didn't expect to see her on the battlefield, and when she told me to take my regiment and retreat, I thought it was a joke. She kept the [Hero] back while he raged and tried to goad me into attacking again."

The man began to pick at his hair bun, idly pulling it loose. "I was ordered to hold a line along our border for the first few days, but when we were sent on more and more scouting missions, I realized we were capturing new land and holding it. My family keeps good maps. We protect the border with Veskar. I might not spend much time in Idrisid, but I know the major land markers near where I was stationed. Madeleine confirmed my fears. I was ready to pull my men back and confront Lord Palmer. Then Daniel asked me something strange. He wanted to know if I knew where Lady Sanerris was hiding."

"What?"

"That's what I said." Finley pulled a chair out from a desk and sat down. "I'm exhausted. Sit down or stand, it's fine."

Finley kept his hands in plain sight, obviously trying to show that he wasn't a threat. "He asked like I should know, but I didn't. Why would I? Lady Sanerris handed over the rule of Mistlight to her son and retired. I've met her all of three times in my life. I told him that I might have heard my parents mention she lived by the sea once. He cursed, and that's when Madeleine said Lady Sanerris had captured their friend. They raided her villa by the sea but arrived too late. There were only a few guards, who they overpowered. They found a dead body that looked like their friend, and Daniel almost lost it. Luckily, Madeleine's grown in her magic and saw through the illusion, because she hinted he wanted to attack Mistlight directly. We talked for a few more minutes as I made my troops fall back, and the more they talked about you, the more I was suspicious."

Orrin remembered the man he'd killed in self-defense. *Did Anabella use a [Glamour] on him so he'd look like me?* How many people looked like him in death now? Two?

"How did they know I was alive? Did you tell them about me?" Orrin had stayed standing and unconsciously walked closer to Finley. "Are they on their way?"

Finley shook his head. "I didn't want to get their hopes up. I thought I should make sure first. I guess Daniel never believed you were dead. They paid some people to try and free you before the execution, but that didn't work. They retrieved your body from the ocean after your execution, which I have to say is damn impressive. From what I gathered, the fact that so much effort was taken to make it seem like you were dead is what kept them both going on the hunt. It's funny to me. When you arrived, I thought you were just a random noble's kid, but the way you fought, I thought this kid had training. I looked into you but couldn't find anything. Why are you here?"

For what felt like the hundredth time, Orrin explained his capture, imprisonment, and forced servitude into the political world of Odrana. Finley's look of disgust caught him off guard. "It's not like I had a choice. My plan was always to tell you, Maeve, and Rhys everything before I escaped. I'm not a fan of either Sanerris."

"I'm not blaming you. You did what you had to in order to stay alive. I'm embarrassed that our country played you like this." Finley stood and stuck his hand out. "Casi . . . no, Orrin. I apologize on behalf of Odrana. I'll get that slave collar off you, get you back to the front line, and help you sneak over to your friends."

Orrin shook Finley's hand, letting out a sigh that quickly choked into a sob. He cast [Calm Mind] on himself before the tears pushed out. "Thank you, Finley."

"Grab your things. I'll see if my [Locationist] can get us back tonight."

Orrin imagined Daniel's face when he snuck up on him. His friend who was fighting a war . . .

"What about the war? Why were you being sent back?"

Finley smiled sheepishly. "I'm being court-martialed for not following orders. When I got back with my regiment, I demanded to know why we were pushing into the elven territory. Lord Palmer is lazy and doesn't do anything that doesn't benefit himself. He told me I had my orders and to go back out immediately. I refused, and he became aggressive. Taking a swing at me was a mistake." Finley shrugged with a wide smile on his face.

Orrin frowned. "Why would he swing at you? I'm sure he had other people that could go out in your place."

Orrin thought about what he knew. Anabella had said that a great victory would be announced in five days, which would be tomorrow. Finley had rejected his orders to go back out to fight. A cold shiver ran down his spine as he pieced together that Anabella hadn't meant a great victory for Odrana.

"You were supposed to die tomorrow."

"What?" Finley's hand moved to his dagger, and his eyes narrowed. "That's not a threat, is it?"

Orrin pulled out the Twin Book of Sending and showed it to Finley, telling him what Anabella's last message had said. It was long cleared, but his own messages to her were still there. "I think you were supposed to die. I'll bet you were in the southern part of Idrisid, near the border with Veskar."

Finley paled. "I thought they kept me there because I know the lands down there a little better."

Orrin told Finley about the recent attempt on Rhys's life. "I think Anabella wanted you two to die so your parents would move to attack Veskar and vote her back into power."

"Why would she send you to cozy up to us, then?" Finley asked, trying to poke holes in Orrin's theory.

"Plausible deniability. She can point to me if anything goes wrong and say she was trying to keep you safe."

Finley did pull a dagger now and glanced at the door. "If I knew where she was . . ." He trailed off. "What do we do, then? I slipped a few guards, but I was supposed to be brought back here to Mistlight. My dad would have the charges dropped and I'd return home for a year or two, but now I think you're right and someone would have attacked me."

Orrin hated what he was about to say. He wasn't political or smart enough to outwit Anabella. But with the right people around him . . .

"I have a terrible idea that might get me killed."

Finley blew a stray hair out of his face and began to tie his hair back again, the dagger held between two fingers as he worked a small thread back around the bun. "That sounds like something we should avoid."

"But it might also end one war and stop another from starting."

Orrin explained his thoughts to Finley.

"That's not a plan," Finley complained. "That's suicide."

Orrin smiled. "Not if we time it right."

Finley rolled his neck and stretched his arms above his head. "You realize this is going to end with a fight?"

"I'm counting on it."

Chapter 46

Orrin's plan was simple in theory: get all the players in one room and hit them with the truth, that Lord Sanerris, the current ruler, was forcing them into an unwanted fight with the elves because he wanted more power. His mother, Anabella Sanerris, wanted her old job back and had recruited Orrin to befriend the other ruling members' kids. She might have also tried to kick off a war against Veskar.

Orrin would gather Maeve and Wren, while Finley would contact his father and Rhys's family. Orrin contemplated trying to get in touch with Lord Palmer as well but decided against it after hearing about Finley's recent encounter with the man. From what Anabella had told him, Lord Palmer was her man through and through. He'd voted against her son taking over but lost the vote. Orin had also considered bringing Graem into the mess, but he reported to Anabella, so there was an even chance that he'd notify her right away.

If they were lucky, they'd get everyone on his side, but Orrin figured having Finley by himself was enough. Once he told his family about the games the Sanerris family was playing with their country, they'd surely want to do the right thing and vote them out of power. The way Finley talked about his parents, they had as much integrity as he did.

Orrin hoped he was right.

It was dinnertime, and Orrin didn't want anyone to stop him. He cast [Camouflage] on himself as he split up from Finley. Orrin watched Finley grab his pack and put his hood up over his blond hair before heading down the hall.

Orrin considered his options as he went invisible. Wren would be easy to find in her office, but Maeve was another matter. Orrin had no idea where her dorm room was or if the heir to the Wellan family even stayed on campus. He searched the school, making sure to avoid people returning from dinner. He even used [Map] to check around corners and avoid walking into anyone with only a quick peek to make sure Maeve wasn't around.

Now that he thought about it, Orrin couldn't remember seeing Maeve outside of class. Retracing his steps from earlier, Orrin found himself outside the classroom for Defensive Earth Magic. The door was partially open, and he could hear muttering inside.

"I don't know why it worked so well before, Professor. I can only replicate what I did so many times. Are you sure that you used your full power earlier on my first spell?" Maeve's clueless voice carried well, although Orrin flinched at her unintended insult at the professor.

Orrin crouched closer to the door to hear the response.

"Ms. Wellan, are you insinuating that I cannot cast a simple [Earthbolt] with precision and accuracy? If you cannot explain how your [Earth Manipulation] spell rebuffed my spells during class, then I will count this as a failure on your part," Professor Cade threatened. "Try again or leave my classroom."

Orrin touched the wood of the door and gently pressed it. The door moved a few inches wider, and he crept into the room. He could wait until Professor Cade left or threw Maeve out.

"I'll see you next week then, Professor," Maeve countered with her normal nonchalance. She gathered up her books from her desk. "I'll try and find the anomaly during—"

"You won't return to my class next week. You've failed. Good luck in your future attempts at a mentorship, Ms. Wellan. I do believe you've exhausted your options at the Sanerris School."

Orrin couldn't believe what he was hearing. His help to make Maeve's dummy stronger earlier that day had backfired. Professor Cade was kicking her out of his class, and it sounded like he was declining to be her mentor as well.

That's the only reason she took this boring class.

Orrin couldn't even help her. If he somehow did communicate with her that he'd cast a [Ward] spell on the target earlier, she wouldn't want him to do it again. Maeve's no-nonsense attitude was refreshing, but she was not one for subterfuge.

If I'd only arrived a few minutes earlier, Orrin thought but then dismissed the fantasy. It wouldn't have helped. Both Maeve and Cade would notice the spell while studying the target so intensely. He could sneak back out of the room and reenter. Tell Professor Cade that he'd been the one to bolster Maeve's homework. That might keep her from getting dismissed from the class.

"Just as well," Maeve said with irritation in her voice. "The more you taught, the more I realized I won't learn what I want through you. I'll find another way to get to the books I want. Good night, Professor."

Scratch that idea, Orrin said to himself as he watched the old man have a conniption. His face turned red, but he had no response to Maeve's statements. Maeve spun on her heel and moved for the door.

Orrin moved fast, trying to beat her out. He didn't know if she would close the door behind her, and he didn't want to get stuck inside with Cade. He was closer, so it wasn't much of a problem, but he did catch the tail of his shirt on a splinter as he moved a little quicker on the way out.

The slightest tug and the splinter broke off. He stood against the wall directly outside and waited for Maeve to exit. He planned on following her a little before revealing himself. Nobody liked a snoop.

Maeve closed the door behind her, and Orrin heard the sound of a table being thrown in the classroom. Cade was having a temper tantrum. She was barefoot as always, but after closing the door, Maeve didn't move. She glanced up and down the hallway before turning around.

"Hello, Casimir. What are you doing here?"

Orrin froze.

His spell wasn't true invisibility, but Orrin had found the spell was stronger since he'd leveled it up. Despite no mention of changes beyond [Camouflage] lasting a little longer and not being dismissed by attacking, he'd realized it was harder for people to spot him while using it. He'd kept to the shadows and stayed out of her direct sight.

"You brushed against the door on your way out, and I can feel your movements through the ground. I know you are here still because I couldn't feel you running away," she explained as if hearing his thoughts. "One of my teachers growing up played a similar game with me. I find it helps keep me safe, although I'm not sure that was her intention. Are you going to talk, or are you doing something important? Should I not have told you I knew you were here?"

Orrin dropped his spell. "You're scary perceptive. Sorry about that. I was looking for you but didn't want to attract attention. I'm avoiding everybody at the moment."

Maeve nodded like he was explaining the sun was bright in summer. "Sometimes I think about trying to find a spell to help me avoid people as well."

An awkward silence—for Orrin—fell between them.

"You were looking for me?" Maeve prompted, shifting her books in her hands. "I'm not sure I'll be any help. I failed Professor Cade's class and won't be returning, so if you need my notes, I can give them to you."

"I don't care about his class," Orrin said, waving his hand and dismissing the class. He'd learned next to nothing from Professor Cade, who spent the class extolling the virtues of his own magic while belittling all other types. "I need you to come with me. We need to talk with Professor Wren."

Maeve tilted her head. "Is this about another attack? I heard that Rhys left school for the rest of the semester while they investigated, but nobody has come close to attacking me . . . except for you, I guess. But I don't think you'd hurt me. You're kind."

Orrin was thrown momentarily, blushing at the sudden compliment. He and Maeve spoke enough during class that he knew she meant well with her words but didn't either think or care about how things would be perceived. He forced a quick smile. "It'll be easier to explain to everyone all at once, but Finley Madvarr will be there, too. I think we can save a lot of lives and stop Odrana from plunging headfirst into another war."

Maeve studied Orrin for a long few heartbeats. "Do you promise that coming with you will save lives?"

Orrin opened his mouth to hastily promise but stopped himself. Maeve was intelligent. She wasn't asking for his opinion; she wanted a promise that he thought this was a good course of action for her as a powerful figure in Odrana.

"I think the Sanerris family is starting wars and sending people to die in a power struggle between mother and son. I want you and your father to help me stop them."

Maeve nodded and turned her back, walking away from him. "Let's go, then. Tell me everything as we walk. I'll help as much as I can, and I'm sure Dad will as well."

Orrin scrambled to keep up. He talked in a quiet whisper, explaining the same things he'd told Finley. *So much for explaining only once.* He shook his head as they left the hallway and entered the other side of the school.

Finley was standing outside Wren's door, waiting with someone with a cloak covering their head. Orrin waved as they approached, trying to get a glimpse under the hood.

"Did you get in touch with your family?" Orrin asked. "Who is that with you?"

"You don't recognize me?" Iona turned to face him, letting the torchlight flicker across her face. "I'm hurt. I thought I'd made an impression."

"It's great to see you, Iona, but what are you doing here?" Orrin went to shake her hand, but she grabbed him, pulling him close for a hug.

"I never got to thank you properly for saving us. Lady Tonsa sends her regards and says you will always be welcome in Goldenhall," Iona whispered before releasing him. "Madvarr here claims you have some important news for us?"

Orrin felt like all he was doing lately was blushing. "Yes, we should see if Professor Wren is here and then I'll tell you all. Fin?"

Finley leaned against the wall, smirking at Orrin. "I sent messages to my father and Goldenhall. Iona teleported in a few minutes ago. I also received a message to proceed with his authority, so whatever we decide, he'll back us."

Orrin was surprised that Finley was trusted with that kind of proxy power, but it made sense that the lord of Ronden couldn't leave for meetings while protecting the borders of Odrana. "Let's get Wren on board and see about saving some lives."

Orrin knocked on the door. Wren opened it before his hand hit a second time.

"Maybe the next time you plan a coup, keep your voices down?" Wren scowled. "Get inside, all of you."

Shuffling into her office behind the others, Orrin leaned toward the teacher. "What have you heard?"

Wren huffed as she closed the door and shook her head. She lightly pushed Orrin out of the way as she made her way to a bookshelf. Wren carefully took a box down from a higher shelf and laid it gently on her desk. Orrin peered over her shoulder at what was inside.

A dozen circular grooves were carved into the bottom of the box, and seven glass orbs rested inside. Before Orrin could ask what they were, Wren palmed one and threw it at the door.

A familiar pop of his ears answered his unasked question.

"Now that we can talk without uninvited guests overhearing everything we say, I want to thank you all. I've enjoyed my position as a teacher here for years and always knew that my students would be the death of me."

Maeve, innocent as ever, said. "We didn't come to kill you, Professor." Then she turned quickly to Orrin. "Did we?"

Orrin put his palm over his face. What had he gotten himself into?

Chapter 47

Orrin propped himself up against Wren's desk, studying the group around him. Maeve, the socially awkward daughter of Lord Wellan, the ruler of Ceraun, stood close, watching his every move. Her father managed the breadbasket of Odrana, keeping the people fed. Anabella's report had stated that the only reason Lord Wellan had voted to oust her in favor of her son was a concern for the safety of his daughter.

If I can keep her safe, Lord Wellan will likely help.

Finley, fresh from the front lines of a war with the elves, stood to his left, near the bookshelf full of curios. He stared at a long knife held aloft by an ornate wooden stand, but as he reached out to touch it, Professor Wren slapped his hand.

Finley Madvarr was one of the best fighters Orrin had met in this world. He was also honorable and believed Orrin's words. He hadn't taken the story at face value but used analytic thinking and his own knowledge to accept an uncomfortable truth. Namely, that his country was instigating wars. If his father had truly given him the power to decide the direction that Ronden would throw their weight behind, Orrin thought he had another of the provinces of Odrana on his side. Which brought Orrin to his last hope.

Iona, the bodyguard of Rhys Tonsa, kept her eyes on everything. She stayed closest to the door, acting like she was studying the large map of Odrana on the wall but really watching the others in the room. Orrin was happy to see her and glad she was alive after the fiasco in the dungeon, but she was just a bodyguard. It made sense that Rhys's mother wouldn't make her way to Mistlight at Finley's request, but he'd work with what he had. Wren worked with Rhys's mother from time to time, so maybe she could help convince Lady Tonsa to back Orrin's big play.

"We are not here to kill each other," Orrin announced, much to Finley's amusement. "Before I tell you all my story, I want to apologize for misleading you. My name isn't Casimir. I'm Orrin."

"What?" Iona stepped closer to the door, putting her hand on her sword handle. "What do you mean?"

"I was captured while rescuing my friend from the dungeons below Lord Sanerris's home and sent to his mother for some reason. She placed a slave collar on my neck and forced me to come here to school," Orrin explained, lifting the collar up to make his point. "She also put a [Glamour] on me, so you can't see that I'm wearing it. I guess this just looks like a necklace."

"Professor Wren, is this some sort of joke?" Iona demanded. "You allowed a spy to be placed in the school and put him in the same party as Rhys?"

Wren paled slightly as she answered, placing her hands on her desk to steady herself. "I recently learned about Casimir's . . . Orrin's mission. I did not know when I placed him in Lord Tonsa's party—at his mother's request, by the way—or I would have questioned the situation more."

"The boy who was beheaded before term for attacking Lord Sanerris?" Maeve chimed in. "That was you?"

Orrin glanced back before hopping up to sit on Wren's desk. "It was someone else that they pretended was me. We only fought Lord Sanerris when he tried to kill us. It's a whole story, but he was torturing my friend and everyone got out but me. After Anabella gave me a chance to come here, I thought I would have a better chance of escaping if I complied. I never would have put any of you in danger, though. That's why I brought you all together—I think you're all in danger. Iona, somebody already tried to kill Rhys. I bet you were told Sloane was the one who set up Rhys in the dungeon. That's not true.

I saved her, and then they killed her because she was from Veskar." Orrin's voice filled with rage, and he took a deep breath to calm himself before continuing. "Fin, I already told you my theory, but for everyone else's sake . . . He was going to be killed in battle tomorrow. Likely by someone who looked like they were from Veskar. They had him stationed near the border."

"He's telling the truth. Lord Palmer was not happy when I told him I was pulling my men back. It seemed odd, but now, knowing what Orrin told me, I realize how cagey his answers to my questions were," Finley said, reinforcing Orrin's story. "I also met the [Hero] of Dey."

"What does that have to do—"

"Here?"

"When did you—"

The other three people in the room began asking questions at the same time, and Finley winked at Orrin. "Enough. Maeve, I know you've met Madeleine Catanzano. She fights by his side. She also spoke highly of Orrin, although I didn't know it was the same man we know as Casimir at the time."

Orrin finally had the attention of the room. He told them of the plan to befriend the three heirs and even his own failed attempts at escaping. He explained everything . . . again.

"I think Anabella wants you three dead so that your parents will vote her back into power. She's using Veskar as a fall guy to regain her position."

Finley spoke first. "I can have an army of three thousand on the borders of Mistlight in twenty hours."

Orrin cringed at the thought of a full civil war breaking out. A small part of him wondered if that would fulfill the Stop the War Quest, but he shoved that thought aside. "The point is to keep the general population safe, Fin. We don't need to start another war. That's what they want."

"Why not tell the lords and ladies of Odrana about Lady Sanerris's plot?" Iona asked. She'd finally moved closer to the group. "If they know what she's trying to do, they won't vote for her over her son."

"Her son who is currently waging a war against a group of people who just want to be left alone?" Orrin asked sarcastically. "Lord Sanerris is as bad as his mother. I know I'm not exactly the person you should come to for advice, but maybe vote the Sanerris family out?"

Silence filled the room, more so than before.

"Orrin, a member of the Sanerris family has ruled in Mistlight since the founding of Odrana. The only families that are older are the Wellan and Ibarra families, but only the Wellans have kept their hold as lords." Wren moved to the side of her desk, closer to Orrin. "What you just said is essentially treason."

"Is it not treason for them to throw your people into a war because they want more power?" Orrin asked, waiting for Wren to look away from his glare. He stole a quick peek at the glass orbs behind him.

"I agree with Orrin," Maeve said as she broke from the circle they'd created and began to roam Wren's office. "My dad doesn't trust Arvin. Plus, I'm tired of killing the people trying to kill me."

Wren slipped off the edge of her desk and landed hard on the floor. "Killing people? Not here at school, right?"

Maeve ran her finger down the spines of a few books on one of Wren's shelves. "Do you have any books on the intersection of plant and earth magic?"

Orrin reached back and slid one of the glass silencing balls into his sleeve. It was the size of a small peach, and he used the motion of hopping off Wren's desk to close the box. "Maeve, you're scaring Professor Wren. Who tried to kill you?"

"I didn't ask their names," Maeve said as she pulled a book off the shelf and started to flip through the pages. "There wasn't much time for talking."

Orrin shivered at the casualness of her revelation. Maeve might have killed someone one day before coming to class and battling him with earth magic. "When did it happen?"

"The first attempt was a few days ago," Maeve answered slowly. She was reading the book in earnest now. "Someone tried to attack me as I walked to my apartment. The man tried to stab me as he passed. Yesterday, someone else tried to sneak up on me when I cut across the courtyard after class."

Wren gasped, and Maeve finally tore her eyes away from the book.

"Don't worry, I buried them deep enough nobody will ever find them. I even regrew the grass in the courtyard so nobody will find a bare spot."

"In the courtyard . . ." Wren whispered in shock.

"That doesn't add up," Finley said as he helped Wren stand. He gently pushed her into her chair. "Why would someone try to kill Maeve at school? There's no connection to Veskar, and her father was always a strong supporter of Lady Sanerris in the past."

"He did vote her out in favor of her son," Orrin commented. "Revenge, maybe?"

Wren seemed to gather her strength and shook her head. "That's not her way. Lady Sanerris never does something without a backup plan. Maeve, put that book back. It's restricted."

"That's the least of our worries right now," Orrin grumbled. He shoved his hands into his pockets, depositing the glass sphere in his dimensional space for later use. "I think Iona and Finley need to go see what their families want to do. I'm not going to betray anyone here, but I want to leave Odrana. This isn't my fight."

Maeve placed the book back on the shelf. "You will go back to Dey?"

"I'll find my friends and try to keep the elves away from the borders for a few days. That should give you time to fix your problems. Wren, you can take off my collar, right?"

The professor looked lost, and Orrin momentarily felt bad for her. As Graem had said, she'd played the game and had been caught between the powerful families of Odrana. No matter how this shook out, she wasn't coming out unscathed.

"Iona, the reason that Lady Tonsa wanted Casimir . . . Orrin placed in your party was because she wanted to poach him as a potential asset, correct?"

Iona met Orrin's eyes before nodding.

"Take him back with you."

"Hey, I'm not going anywhere. Take this collar off. I'm not a slave."

Wren ignored him. "Have him explain everything again to her. Maeve and Finley can teleport home as well. Let the lords figure out the timing. Work with Orrin to give them both what they want."

"I'm not doing anything unless this collar comes off," Orrin nearly shouted. Everyone was looking at him. "I could have killed you all and trusted Anabella to remove it. I'll help you to a point, but trust goes both ways."

Finley crossed his arms and tilted his chin up at Wren. "This man has committed no crime worthy of slavery. Remove the collar, Professor Wren, on the authority of the Madvarr family."

Wren stood shakily and approached Orrin. She touched the metal around his neck. He heard a click, and the ring of metal fell to the ground.

I'm free. Orrin could hardly believe it. He'd worked so hard and planned so much, only for Finley to order Wren to remove it. Part of him screamed to run from the room and [Teleport] back to Daniel. A more bloodthirsty part of him wanted to find Lord and Lady Sanerris and take them out himself. *What would Daniel do?*

"You look better without the collar on." Maeve broke his train of thought. "More natural and less perfected by magic. I like it."

Orrin blushed at the sudden compliment. He'd forgotten he would lose the benefits of the [Glamour] without the collar.

"Watch out, Orrin," Finley said with a smile and a poke at his side. "That's the highest compliment I've ever heard Maeve give someone. Her father might try to arrange a marriage."

"Now, will you agree to go with Iona?" Wren was practically wringing her hands. "Lady Tonsa will be able to come up with a solution, I'm sure of it. I'll pay the price of the [Locationist]."

Orrin ignored Finley. "I'm not going to put myself in a place where someone else can control me again, but I'll do what I can to support you all. Fin, where did you fight with Daniel?"

He crossed the room and had Finley point out a location near the southwestern part of Odrana. Orrin would [Teleport] part of the way and then run. He hoped Daniel would still be there. If not, he could always [Teleport] to the elves.

"You aren't going to help?" Wren said dejectedly. "Lady Sanerris will kill me for letting you go. I'll still pay for a [Locationist] to bring you to the border."

Orrin looked at the people around him. Finley, Maeve, and Iona gave no indication of what they were thinking.

"I can use [Teleport]. Fin, you can come back with me if you want. We can talk with Madi. She's better at knowing what to do in these situations than me."

"I'll come, too," Maeve said. "I'd like to meet the [Hero]."

"That's too dangerous. We shouldn't have you all together," Orrin said, a terrible thought occurring to him. "Anabella has failed at each step. She'll need to kill you both for her plan to work."

"Lady Sanerris's plans have contingencies for success, even in failure. She's not someone we can win against alone. We need to talk with Lady Tonsa," Wren said, again trying to convince him.

"I'm not promising anything, but if Madi agrees it's safe, we can meet outside the Mistwater Lanterns in an hour," Orrin said. "If you and Iona can convince Rhys's mom to come, then great. Maeve, can you get your dad to come for a meeting, too?"

Maeve frowned a bit at being excluded. "If that's what you think is best, Orrin. We are still friends, right?"

Orrin smiled. "Yes. Definitely."

"What are you going to do about Lady Sanerris?" Iona asked as Orrin invited Finley to his party.

Orrin glanced at the map. If Anabella had left her seaside cottage, there was no telling where she would be holed up. He scratched at his neck. "I'll burn that bridge when I get to it."

Chapter 48

Orrin's [Teleport] required that he know the area he wanted to travel to. In their mad dash to rescue Brandt from Lord Sanerris, he'd seen some of the country of Odrana, but not well enough to pinpoint the area they needed to go to. Finley convinced Orrin to use his [Locationist] to travel back to the front lines of the war. Orrin figured in the worst-case scenario, he could [Teleport] himself away.

The trio popped into a bustling camp with people running around and shouting, even this late at night. Seeing a [Locationist] appearing, two officers rushed in and started issuing demands. Finley took Orrin's hand and quietly crept from view.

"I thought your camp was supposed to be disbanded," Orrin whispered. A group of soldiers lined up as a woman with a sword almost as big as Daniel's began shouting orders. Orrin did a double take. The soldiers wore broken armor and mostly held spears. Most of them were younger than he was or old enough to be his grandparents. One old lady was holding on to her spear like it was the only thing keeping her upright.

"I disbanded my men. These are conscripts that they pulled in after I left." Finley's fist clenched over and over as they walked. "The faster we find the [Hero], the faster we can get these folks back home."

Orrin and Finley moved through the chaos without getting stopped. The tents at the edge of the camp were abandoned, which made sneaking out easier than he'd hoped.

"How far away is the place you saw my friends?" Orrin whispered as they crouched behind one of the tents. The canvas was cut and flapping hard in the wind. "I can try to send them a party invite if they're close enough."

"About five miles to the west, there is a small forest outcropping disconnected from the elves' main stronghold. I was tasked with patrolling it and setting up a permanent presence there if possible. That's where we need to go," Finley said, his eyes glinting in the moonlight. His head moved slowly but consistently, watching everything. "How long can you run before you need a break?"

Orrin thought back to what his answer would have been before arriving in Asmea. A minute or two? "I can keep up with you. Let's go."

Orrin reveled in the feel of the wind rushing against his face in the dark. He increased his dexterity enough to make Finley work to keep up and focused on using [Map] to avoid any dangers. Twice, he circled back and tapped Finley's shoulder to avoid patrols from either Odrana or elven forces. It took less than an hour to get to their destination, with Finley being the anchor slowing them down.

The forest outcropping was nothing more than thirty or forty trees within sight of the elven forest. Thick bramble covered most of the floor under the trees, making it hard to see inside, especially in the dark. Orrin slowed as they approached and tugged Finley's sleeve, crouching near a large boulder.

"Someone is hiding in there," Orrin whispered, zooming in on his [Map]. "Only one person, and they've posted up on the northern side of the tree line, closer to the elven forest."

Finley nodded, and his hands gestured through a complicated arrangement of movements. He waited a few seconds and sighed. "You don't know hand language, do you?"

"Nope." Orrin smiled. "Other than this." He flipped Finley off.

"I'll go around and move in from the west back toward our position. Give me five minutes and then you come in as well. You don't need to move fast, just approach and try talking to whoever it is. If they attack you, I'll retaliate from their blind spot," Finley explained, ignoring Orrin's middle finger.

Orrin could try to use [Camouflage] to approach, but that would require both leaving Finley behind and hoping the person didn't notice him. He liked Finley, but he wasn't about to start casting even more spells in front of him, so he nodded.

The man unsheathed two of his daggers and crept off into the night.

Instead of waiting five minutes, Orrin watched on his [Map]. It was a good thing he did.

Finley made it to the other side of the trees by going south and around. He was a few hundred yards away from where Orrin would have stopped in his position when more dots appeared on Orrin's [Map].

"Shit."

Orrin ran straight toward Finley. Instead of wasting time going around, he cast [Teleport], using his line of sight through the small batch of trees to jump the distance directly.

Four people, not including the original target, were dashing at Finley, who had yet to notice them. They were too far away to see clearly, but the one out front carried a sword that looked familiar.

"Daniel?" Orrin yelled as his feet hit the ground on the other side of the forest. "Is that you?"

The charging figure slid to a halt, and the sword in his hand pointed in Orrin's direction. There was a hushed demand to the person nearest him, and Orrin shielded his eyes when a flash of light blossomed above his head.

"Orrin?"

That's Madi's voice. Orrin smiled and waved. "Hey, guys, where have you been?"

Orrin was tackled to the ground. He never saw Daniel move, but his friend had him in a bear hug. His beard was trimmed but full, and tears were rolling down his face as he laughed.

"I knew you weren't dead. I told Madi over and over," Daniel said as he let Orrin go. He picked up his friend with ease and gave him another hug. "Didn't I, Madi? Orrin's too smart to get killed by those pricks."

Madeleine Catanzano approached with balls of light hovering around her. Each orb gave off a slight hint of different shades of red, blue, and yellow. She hovered at a safe distance.

"Daniel, are you sure it's him? We just captured Finley Madvarr over here. It's too coincidental."

She thinks Finley took the information they gave and made a doppelgänger of me? Orrin was impressed at how distrusting she was being. He was a touch proud.

"Madi, it's me. Fin helped me. There's a bunch of stuff going on and—"

"She has a point," Daniel interrupted him with his sword pointed at his face. He'd gotten quicker. "Tell me something that only the real Orrin would know."

"You suck at *Mario Kart*. Toad is a terrible choice to pick."

Daniel tackle-hugged him again. "It's him."

"I'll never understand you two," Madi said, shaking her head and letting the majority of her floaty balls of light disappear. "Finley is with you?"

"Yeah, he is. Fin helped me a lot." Orrin smiled and waved at Fin as they approached the rest of the people they'd almost fought. Madvarr sat on the ground with his hands behind his head. "We've got a lot to tell you."

Daniel and Madi introduced their strike team.

Tem was a [Locationist] offshoot called a [Mapmaker]. He spent most of his time exploring the world and mapping it out but could return to spots with ease. While his [Mapmaker] class allowed him to use [Teleport] for cheaper mana costs than a [Locationist], he rarely worked in the field, preferring to be alone. Lord Silas Catanzano was paying him an astronomical fee to keep Madi safe with a quick escape option.

Reyhana was an elf, loaned out to help by Arandir. Neither he nor Reyhana would explain what her class was, but she could hide them in plain sight, even in the middle of the day.

Orrin recognized the fifth member and pushed Daniel's arm off his shoulder to shake the man's hand.

"Good to see you, Brandt."

The tall [Knight] took Orrin's offered hand and pulled him in for another hug.

"Everybody is really touch-feely today," Orrin complained as Brandt tried his best to crack his ribs. "I missed you, too, big guy."

Brandt held Orrin's shoulders and studied him for any injuries. "You've saved my life too many times to count and Lady Catanzano's as well. I'll never be able to thank you. I'm relieved you are alive."

Orrin tried not to blush and changed the topic. "Tell me what you guys are doing here."

Madi started explaining, with interjections from Daniel. The five of them had been moving through the border of Odrana and the elven forest, keeping Odrana's stronger forces on their toes. They raided smaller parties, trying to gain information from them. Sometimes Reyhana would sit out as bait, using a cloaking spell to keep the rest of them from being seen. If they were discovered by a force too large, they'd run.

"Most of the time we run," Brandt chimed in. "The elves fight only when people enter the forest, so we've been working as more of a deterrent than anything. Except a few times . . ."

"He's talking about me," Daniel said with a sigh. "We raided Sanerris's mom's place and fought our way through a few guards. Madi bought some information from a broker that you were being held there."

Daniel blinked and glanced at the moon. "Someone left a dead body that looked just like you. If Madi hadn't figured out it was a trick . . ."

"He was angry that we'd gotten bad information and took it out on the next few patrols we came across," Madi explained.

"I was there," Orrin said after a pause. "Lord Sanerris sent some thugs to kill me, or maybe Anabella—that's his mom—set me up. I don't know. There's a lot of moving pieces. That's why we came here. There's a power play going on between Lord Sanerris and his mother, who used to rule. They're provoking wars with the elves and Veskar to gather support for themselves. They're even trying to kill Fin and some other friends I made at school."

Daniel wiped at his face and turned an incredulous eye at Orrin. "School?"

Orrin smirked and told them his story, from waking up under Sanerris's control to moving to his mom's villa. He explained what Anabella had sold him as his mission and what he'd come to believe it actually was—a distraction.

"I'm still stuck on the school part." Daniel smirked. "Did they teach you magical algebra?"

Finley, who sat on the ground patiently being ignored, spoke up. "What's algebra?"

"It's math," Daniel answered before he saw who asked the question. "Are we sure this guy is on our side? He almost killed me last time."

Orrin laughed. For the first time in weeks, he felt free and right with the world. Daniel was being an ass, Madi was moving between Daniel and Fin, ready to defuse a fight, and Brandt stood by, undecided on what he should be doing. It wasn't Earth and it wasn't home, but this situation was what he'd been dreaming of.

"I trust him," Orrin said, noticing everyone was giving him weird looks. "Don't give me shit, I needed a laugh. I've been a prisoner for weeks. Do you know how hard it is to keep a fake story about where you're from straight?"

"I thought his name was Casimir when we last met," Finley added. "But when Madi was talking about your quiet friend who asks questions and watches out for everyone, I had my suspicions. I arrived back at the Sanerris School to find that Orrin had recently saved the life of Rhys Tonsa. Someone tried to kill Maeve as well. We think I was next."

Madi covered her mouth. "Is Maeve all right?"

"Does every noble know everyone else?" Orrin asked. "Maeve buried the person who came after her. Literally."

"We spent a lot of time together during state dinner functions and treaty negotiations. All the kids get sent off to mingle," Madi explained. "You're lucky you found us. We only came this way again because we'd received word that a large group was moving north from Veskar. This was supposed to be a recon mission only."

Orrin and Finley exchanged a look.

"You think—"

"That's probably—"

They both nodded at each other.

"What are you two talking about?" Madi's hands rested on her spear, back to its short form on her hip. "What is it?"

"Fin was going to be sent out on a patrol and killed by that group from Veskar, but I doubt they're actually from there. Anabella is trying to start a war with Veskar and blame them for the deaths of the other lords' kids to back her claim to rule Mistlight," Orrin explained.

Daniel watched Orrin. He slapped Gertrude, his giant sword, on his back. "You have a plan. Out with it."

Orrin smiled. "You're going to like this one. It's as crazy as you are. The Sanerris family wants a war. Let's bring them what they want."

Chapter 49

As Orrin hoped she would, Madi rolled her eyes and scoffed. "How do you expect to make war on the ruling family of Odrana? Don't forget that Lord Sanerris already forced us to flee during our last fight."

Orrin pointed at Finley.

Finley turned to make sure nothing was behind him. "What?"

"Finley has the backing of his dad. Maeve is bringing her dad to the Mistwater Lanterns. Iona—um, that's Rhys's bodyguard—is going to bring Lady Tonsa there as well. I think if we can convince them to stage a coup, we don't need an actual war. Lord Sanerris and his mommy have been fighting so much lately that they seem to have forgotten that there are other people with power."

"You are suggesting we instigate a civil war?" Madi asked, tucking one of her braids behind her ear. She'd changed her hair again. "Orrin, if I'm caught anywhere near that situation, all of Dey will be dragged into the fallout. No offense, Finley, but any surviving lords of Odrana would take umbrage with my help in a power struggle."

Finley chuckled. "He suggests overpowering and ousting two of the most powerful members of the most powerful family in Odrana and you automatically assume we'd survive."

Daniel cracked his knuckles. "Damn right we will. I've been working on something special for that slippery fuck."

"I'm more worried about Anabella," Orrin confessed. "She's powerful and scary . . . but I can take her if it's just one-on-one. I think we can weaken them both first if we get them to fight."

Madi's eyes narrowed. "Explain."

Orrin recounted the conversations he'd had with Anabella, telling the group about her comments regarding time-delayed attacks and their fraught history. "She's thought about ways to take out her son. They've known a Demon Lord was coming for years. He wants to attack the demons and wipe them out, but she played a longer game. If she thinks the demons have reached the Pass, she might feel rushed and make a mistake. Madi, I need you to help me convince the other leaders to push her into fighting her son. I don't know what they need to do, whether it's vote for a new chancellor or make them duel to the death. I've got half an idea but not enough information to make it work."

Madi tapped her finger to her lips for a minute. "Finley, how much do you know about the appointment of your chancellors?"

Orrin smiled as they started talking. Brandt asked him a few questions about his experience as a prisoner. Orrin could tell he was worried to have left him behind while being rescued, so he lied and denied any real torture had happened.

"Maybe playing Kala with Anabella," Orrin joked. "That was painful."

Tem, the [Mapmaker], coughed pointedly and Brandt excused himself, muttering about hired help. Orrin waved at the elf, Reyhana. She ignored him.

"You're really fine?" Daniel stood close to him. "We tried finding you, I swear."

"I know you did," Orrin said, putting his arm around Daniel's neck. "Are you all right? I heard you did some serious fighting out here."

Daniel remained quiet for too long.

"If you want to talk, I'm always here. I won't push," Orrin whispered just for his friend. "No more splitting the party."

"Come with me." Daniel's grip above Orrin's elbow didn't hurt, but he'd need to [Teleport] to get out of it. Orrin let himself be steered farther from the main group. Daniel's eyes glittered in the light streaming through the trees. "We can't bring Madi with us. Her father is angry that she's out here as it is. I promised him that I would keep her safe after we . . . almost lost you."

There's more to that story, but he's hanging on by a thread. Orrin simply nodded. "Whatever you think is best."

Daniel released Orrin's arm and let out a long breath. He scratched at his beard. "She'll be pissed off, but Brandt will keep her back. Silas took him to the Hospital himself. Good to know that missing fingers can be regrown, but Brandt said the pain is intense. Silas also had a talk with him, and Brandt doesn't leave her side now."

Orrin nodded toward Tem and Reyhana. "Are they worth bringing with us?"

"Tem should stay. He's no good in a fight. I'd love to bring Reyhana, but she won't go. Her orders are very clear." A hint of distaste entered his voice. "She doesn't leave the trees no matter who is getting killed."

Yeah, Daniel's not okay. Orrin let a [Calm Mind] seep out toward his friend. He frowned when the magic disappeared before it touched Daniel.

"It's rude to cast spells on people, you know?" Daniel punched Orrin lightly in the shoulder. "Did you try [Calm Mind]?"

Orrin nodded. "I thought it would help. You seem on edge. How'd you block it?"

"New skill from my class. I can . . . sort of eat . . . any magic that is thrown at me, to a degree."

"Explain," Orrin demanded. "If I can't buff or heal you, that isn't something that—"

"I can let things through if I want," Daniel interrupted him. "It's like a black hole that takes in all the magic that comes my way, but I can move it away. It won't block anything I subconsciously want to get to me, though. I don't need healing right now. I just want to live in this moment for a minute. You're alive. Bad shit is happening. The Demon Lord picked up speed and is going to arrive at the outskirts of the Pass in a week or two. It helps to feel alive."

"The good and the shit . . ." Orrin murmured.

Daniel laughed a small breath of air. "Yeah. I forgot to turn in some stupid assignment in English class last year and my dad told me off for not being on top of things. My mom waited for him to leave the room and said something similar. That I needed to learn from my mistakes just as much as I needed to enjoy the good things happening in life. I made a few mistakes while you were gone, O. I don't want you to numb my brain right now. I want to enjoy having this good thing back."

Daniel shook Orrin's shoulder.

Madi waved at them. "What are you two doing over there? Come back. We might have an idea."

The seven people moved together, with even Reyhana the elf pushing herself off a tree to join.

"Before we discuss this in detail," Daniel said first, holding up a hand. "Reyhana, I'm assuming you won't join us if we move into Odrana."

The elf shook her head once, keeping her silence.

"Once Madi explains the plan, I want you to tell Arandir everything. Tem, you'll take Madi and Brandt back to Dey to report to Lord Catanzano."

Immediate arguments came from Madi and Brandt.

Orrin was impressed with Daniel. He let Madi and Brandt vent for a minute before clapping once. They both quieted.

"You said it yourself, Madi. If you get caught in Odrana, it'll look bad for Dey. I'm not bringing Brandt back, either. For all we know, there's a warrant out for his arrest or something." Daniel stood taller, and Orrin noticed his friend actually was taller.

He used [Identify] and frowned. Daniel had reached level twenty-two, outpacing him again.

Brandt crossed his arms but accepted Daniel's orders. Madi was a different matter entirely.

"The plan needs me to be there, Daniel. If I can't convince Lady Tonsa, the entire thing falls apart."

"Tell us the plan. Maybe we can tweak it," Orrin offered.

"Not until you promise I can go," Madi said, digging in her heels. "I'm not letting you two go off to do something stupid."

"I can tell you," Finley cut in. He raised an eyebrow at Madi. "Don't give me that look. This is my country we're talking about."

Madi's hand closed around her spear haft, and Orrin sighed as he walked toward her. "Come with me for a second."

As he walked Madi away from the group, Finley yelled after them, "Can I have a secret conversation with you next? I'm feeling left out."

Orrin raised a middle finger over his shoulder.

Madi started trying to make her case before they stopped walking. "Orrin, you can't ask me to make a plan and then tell me I can't go into the fight. I'm not even doing anything dangerous, just talking with Lady Tonsa. She's the key."

How would I feel if they left me behind? Oh wait, they already did that a few times before we rescued Brandt. Orrin shook the thought out of his head. It wasn't helpful.

"I'm going to give you what you want," he said simply.

"Good. Let's go back and I'll explain everything. The way the Odranan chancellor council is set up, we can—"

"Not that. I'm going to give you what you want and then ask Tem to [Teleport] you and Brandt back to Dey. You'll be helpless for a while."

Madi tilted her head in confusion.

This is worth it. Daniel wants to keep her safe, and I only have an hour to get everyone back to the dungeon. It's the quickest way to keep her out of harm's way.

"I'll change your class to [Superior Prism Conjurer]," Orrin whispered. "But on the condition that you go back to Dey and prepare. You need to have your father power level you, because you're going to be level one."

Madi glared at him, her hands clenching and unclenching as she tried to breathe. "That's not fair. You can't ask . . ."

"Daniel is worried about you. I don't know what happened while I was gone, but he's my friend. He wants you safe, and I'll do what I have to. I'm offering this to soften the blow, Madi. We can't risk you going into Odrana."

Orrin kept her gaze until she broke and looked away. "I know. I don't have to like it, but I know, okay? If those idiots would just stop their fighting, we could all focus on the real threat. We can't let the Demon Lord through the Pass, O. It'll be the end of the world. You have to stay safe."

"I'll keep Daniel alive, don't worry."

Madi punched him in the shoulder, mimicking Daniel's earlier hit. "Not just him. We need both of you if we're going to survive."

She lowered her voice. "I need both of you."

The vulnerability hit Orrin like a Steel Boar. *How did I miss it? Madi's better at hiding her trauma, but I should have seen . . .*

"What happened to you guys?"

Madi flinched.

"This entire thing might be a bad idea if you and Daniel are this messed up. Madi, I want to help."

"There was a patrol," she whispered, staring down at her feet. She spoke with the monotonous voice of a soldier giving a report to her superior. "They stayed near the edge of the forest and wouldn't come close enough for the elves to attack. Brandt was in Dey, recovering still. Daniel and I offered to drive them away."

Orrin clucked his tongue. He could see Daniel getting impatient, but Madi usually kept him in line. She must have read his thoughts, because she let out a pained, sarcastic laugh.

"I should have talked him down, I know that. He's a great guy, but he's young and stupid sometimes, just like you. I was angry at what they'd done to Brandt and angry at my father and angry at everything. I agreed with him and we attacked. There were twenty soldiers around the edges. We counted after . . ."

Orrin no longer wanted to hear this story.

"They'd dressed up another twenty people in leather armor and some chain mail. None of them could have been above level ten. We didn't even realize until . . ."

Madi stifled a sob. "One of my [Lightbeams] went right through a girl who couldn't have been more than eighteen. Daniel used a [Gravity Well] and some of them lost their grips on swords . . . spears . . . In all the confusion, it took us a minute to realize the Odranan soldiers were attacking each other. They killed their own people. Arandir said later that they were probably under orders to bring the bodies back as proof that the elves were evil and killing commoners, but we didn't give the soldiers that chance."

Orrin wrapped his arms around his friend as she tried not to cry. "You aren't responsible for their deaths. They would have been killed regardless."

"We could have saved them if we'd taken our time and paid attention," Madi whispered into his chest. "One of the soldiers had a short-range teleportation skill. He kept running, but Daniel caught him. I've never seen him so angry. We tried to ask questions, but the soldier laughed and Daniel . . ."

Orrin hugged her tighter. "It's not your fault. It's not Daniel's fault."

Orrin used [Calm Mind] on Madi, waiting until she disengaged from the hug to let go.

"Arandir buried the bodies in the forest. He said they would find peace under the trees, but those people had families that will never know what happened to them," she said as she blinked hard, rubbing the tears away. "That's why I want to be part of this. I need to avenge those innocents."

Orrin thought for a long moment and picked his words with care. "Let me do it for you. Tell me your plan and I'll convince Lady Tonsa. Take the class upgrade and level yourself up. If we can end the war, you might even get a chunk of experience from the Quest. We need you preparing in Dey. Avenge those people by saving their families from the Demon Lord."

Madi wiped a leaf off his shirt. Some of the trees rustled in the wind, letting more fall to the ground. "When did you get so eloquent? A few weeks at the Sanerris School and you come back this confident . . ."

Orrin smirked. "I'm still the same idiot."

Madi smiled back. "Yes. You are." She sighed heavily and steeled her shoulders. "Do it. End this war and bring your idiot self and that other idiot friend of ours back alive. I'll go to Dey and get everyone ready."

Chapter 50

Orrin returned with Madi to the rest of the group. The small grove of trees was calming to him. The moon shed enough light that they could see each other while keeping the rest of the forest dark. He would have had to go to the edge of the trees to watch the Odranan border if not for his [Map] skill.

Madi gave Finley a thumbs-up, signaling for him to explain the plan as they approached.

"My father has given me proxy rights for his chancellor vote," Finley started, pulling a fine silver chain out from under his shirt. On the end of the chain hung a heavy gold ring. "It's not the first time that I've had to vote in his place. Veskarian raids happen even during prescheduled chancellor votes."

He smiled at his joke and rolled his eyes when nobody else appreciated it. He continued. "Currently, Lord Sanerris is chancellor of Mistlight. He holds the power to rule the city and its immediate surroundings, as well as control of direct trade between the rest of the territories. A quorum of three chancellors is needed to call a vote to replace another chancellor. If Maeve can bring her father and Lady Tonsa shows up, we'll be able to start the voting process with this."

Orrin studied the ring Finley held into the air. The top was flat, with an insignia of five small rubies arranged in a circle. Finley dropped the ring back under his shirt.

"The three of us won't be able to name a new chancellor for Mistlight behind his back. That requires an in-person vote of all the chancellors. When Lady Sanerris was removed from her position, she was forced to give her ring to her son. Lord Palmer objected, but Lady Sanerris accepted the transfer of power without violence."

"What's to stop Lord Stopwatch from ignoring you and staying in power?" Daniel asked, trying out a new nickname for Sanerris.

"Without a rightful claim, he has no power to vote or make demands of any other territory. I'll recall every Ronden soldier and suggest the Tonsa family and Wellans do the same. Lord Palmer has scouts and supplies but no standing forces. Mistlight supplies mages and trade goods, but without the gold from Goldenhall, the food from Ceraun, and the leadership from my family . . . the war with the elves will be over."

Orrin smiled at that, checking the Quest.

Stop the War in Odrana
Reward: 200,000 XP and Variable
Failure: Loss of 10 levels

They'd shared the Quest with a lot of people, including the elves. There was going to be a huge increase in levels coming their way, just in time for the demon invasion. Orrin salivated thinking of how close he was to level twenty. Doing the math in his head, he tallied up the increased experience threshold for each level.

If the pattern stays the same for each level . . . adding a thousand to the last experience goal . . . I should gain ten levels plus a little left over. That's insane! I'll skip the entirety of the twenties.

"This plan won't stop Lady Sanerris from trying to take over or Lord Sanerris from attacking you as soon as he finds out he's not in power," Madi continued. "This is where Orrin is going to have to be convincing. After the three chancellors officially vote him out, they have to vote her in."

Orrin didn't like the sound of that. "That's exactly what Anabella wants."

"Three votes cast will activate the rings. They're linked with magic, and the gems glow when a vote is cast. It's the way they signal each other that they need to meet for an important issue," Finley continued. "You'll need to convince Lady Tonsa to put Lady Sanerris back in charge."

"Lady Tonsa voted her out last time," Orrin said, not liking how everyone was ignoring him. "Anabella will want revenge, and she'll know that. How am I supposed to get her to do it?"

"Once the vote is cast to remove Lord Sanerris, the chancellors will meet to discuss his replacement. He gets a vote on his replacement." Finley reached out and put a hand on Orrin's shoulder. "Palmer will vote for Lady Sanerris and so will Arvin when he sees the way things are going. He'll want to keep the power in the family so he can try taking over again later. Once they've cast their votes, I'll bring up that Lady Sanerris tried to kill me and Maeve. Lord Wellan or Lady Tonsa will refuse to vote and demand Lady Sanerris be brought to answer for her crimes."

Madi was practically bouncing on her heels. "When she arrives, Daniel crashes in from his hiding place and announces that the Demon Lord has arrived in the Pass, requesting forces from Odrana despite Lord Sanerris's attempt to capture or kill him. In tow is his party member Orrin, who points out Lady Sanerris's plots as well. It should bring their squabbling to a head. If they don't fight outright, it should be enough for even Palmer to see how crazy they've both become."

Finley nodded along. "This is the part you have to get Rhys's mom to agree to. She needs to step in and demand satisfaction from the Sanerris family. They'll both be busy slinging accusations at each other, and if she times it right, she can force a four-member vote to replace the Sanerris family outright. Palmer is an opportunist at heart."

"That's the plan," Madi finished. "Any questions?"

"When this all goes to shit, do we kill Arvin and Anabella?" Daniel asked, cracking his knuckles.

"Killing the leader of our country should be the last resort," Finley said slowly. "I'd rather we imprison them and try them for their crimes through proper judicial avenues."

"They won't just . . . let their family's power go," Orrin pointed out.

Finley smiled. "If they attack the other chancellors or even the [Hero], they might find themselves outmatched. Lord Sanerris is strong, but he's not invincible. The same goes for his mother."

Daniel and Finley talked a bit more about the logistics of a possible fight, while Brandt and Madi whispered.

"Madi, when you get back, will you check something for me?" Orrin stepped in and interrupted her now that the main part of the plan had been explained. He pulled the ball of glass that he'd stolen from Wren's office from his storage and tossed it to Madi. "Have you seen these before?"

Madi caught the glass globe and held it gingerly. "A spell glass. I haven't seen one in years. People can store their spells inside for later use or to sell. My father keeps people on staff or retainer for spells we need regularly, so we rarely need them. What does this one do?"

Orrin smiled. His hunch had been correct. "It creates a sound barrier for private discussions. I'm pretty sure that Graem . . . a professor at the Sanerris School cast this for his sister. How much would it cost to make these, and are there any restrictions on the spells?"

Madi handed the ball back to Orrin, who swiftly made it disappear. "I'm not sure on either count. I can look into it when I return . . . if you still want me to go back. Lady Tonsa might argue against—"

Orrin waved his hand. "We agreed. You're going back home to Dey."

Orrin noticed Brandt smile and nod at him.

"Fine. I have nothing more to contribute, then. Finley knows the plan and will be best suited to figure out any small changes in the moment. Do you need to prepare or anything?"

"I'm ready now if you are."

Madi peered over her shoulder at Brandt.

"I trust in you," he whispered softly.

She stood straighter and took a deep breath. "I'm ready."

Orrin shook his head and brought up Assign Class, selecting Madi as the target.

Choose Class:

He scrolled until he found the superior version of Madi's current class. "This is your last chance. I can change your class back, but once you've switched, I can't give you back your lost levels."

"Don't back out on me now," Madi said through gritted teeth. "Do it."

Replace [Prism Conjurer] with [Superior Prism Conjurer]?
Yes or No?

"Good luck," Orrin said, accepting the cost of another Administrator Point. "It's done."

Madi stumbled and Orrin rushed to her, but Brandt was quicker. His knee hit the ground as he caught her and helped her to her feet.

"I feel weaker," Madi murmured as her eyes glazed over in the universal sign that she was reading her own blue screen. "All my stats are back to where they were when I first earned my class. Except . . . yes. I think I was able to keep those bonus points from the dungeon we destroyed and the Quests completed."

Orrin filed that knowledge away as he turned to Tem, standing off to the side of the main group. "Can you get them both to Silas's house?"

"Yes, sir. I have a location nearby on standby. I live in the city." The man spoke quickly, nearly tripping over his words. "Would you like me to return here and wait for you after I bring Lady Catanzano home?"

"Nah, rest up. I'm sure Madi will need your help soon enough," Orrin said, pausing at a thought. "How far into the Pass have you gone?"

"I've never been that far west. I'd only traveled in Dey and Odrana before I was hired for this job."

Orrin said a few words to Brandt, as Madi was still excitedly reading some class changes.

"It'll be dangerous for them. It's not a combat-heavy class usually," Brandt countered Orrin's idea.

"Tell Silas. Maybe he can arrange protection during transport."

"What are you talking about?" Daniel asked, coming back from talking with Finley.

"I asked Brandt to get as many people with [Teleport] to explore the Pass," Orrin answered. "If we survive this, it might help if we have a few people who can move a bunch of troops around quickly from Dey to the front and back again."

Tem paled a little. "You want me to go into the Pass?"

"You'll be fine. You're a higher level than we were when Daniel tried to fight some demons in the Pass. We survived," Orrin tried to convince the level-thirty-two [Mapmaker], who looked more and more like he was going to puke. "Only if they volunteer, Brandt. We don't want people who will run. It'll be a huge tactical advantage against the demons and might save lives."

Orrin watched as Madi and Brandt went through a round of goodbyes. Daniel gave a concerned look at Madi's weakened state, but she whispered what happened in his ear and he gave her a high five. With a final hug from Madi to Orrin, they circled up with Tem.

"Come back safe," Brandt commanded before the three of them disappeared.

The elf Reyhana placed a hand on Daniel's shoulder. She had snuck up behind him.

"If you're not going to come with us, can you tell Arandir the plan? He might be able to get the elves ready for the demons."

She nodded and turned to leave but paused. "Be safe," she whispered without looking at Daniel before leaving the forest at a run.

"That's the first time I've heard her speak," Daniel said with a smile.

Daniel Has Invited You to a Party
Yes or No?

"Finally, we're back together," Orrin said as he nudged Daniel with his hip. "Batman and Robin."

"You're Robin," Daniel answered with a smirk. He lowered his voice. "Should I invite Finley, too? Does he know about your buffs?"

"Invite him," Orrin said as he began casting [Ward] on the trio. "I trust him enough to let him see some spells."

Five minutes later, Finley stared into empty space with an open mouth. "You . . . you . . ."

"I'm awesome. I know. I could totally have kicked your ass in Battle Class, but I'm a benevolent person."

Daniel laughed. "No, you're not. You probably just had a plan to keep hidden and then act like you'd grown in strength or something."

Orrin turned red at how close to the truth Daniel's guess hit.

Finley turned. "How much longer do we have before we need to meet with Maeve?"

"Probably ten minutes or so, but I can [Teleport] us there directly," Orrin answered. "I think it might be best to land a little ways out and walk in, though. Just in case."

Finley's smile turned evil. "Want to fight before we go?"

Orrin slapped himself in the face. "No. We are literally trying to save the world. We do not have time for . . . Damn it, Daniel. I said no."

But he was too late. Finley and Daniel were moving quickly enough that Orrin could only catch glimpses of their bodies hitting each other before they bounced away.

Finley slid on his heels to a stop a few feet from Orrin with a large grin still etched on his face. "This [Hero] is great."

He had two daggers out and rushed Daniel again. Gertrude, Daniel's sword, pointed down at Fin's feet. Daniel swung with a speed that Orrin had yet to achieve with his own summoned swords, but Finley stepped on the flat of the blade, running along the length sideways before tackling Daniel.

The dust settled with Gertrude against Finley's neck but one of the daggers pressed against Daniel's belly.

"Are you two done? We might be heading into a huge fight with two of the strongest mages I've ever seen and you . . ." Orrin sighed and rubbed his eyes. "I swear, I might kill you two myself."

Chapter 51

Lord Galt Wellan, chancellor of Ceraun, was concerned.

His daughter, Maeve, the blooming flower of his life, had visited home unannounced less than an hour ago. Her story of political maneuvers and new friends worried him as much as it gave him hope for her future. Many pieces had fallen together, clearing up mysteries long worried over as she spoke. Now, he found himself waiting outside the Mistwater Lanterns dungeon.

It was for the best that he doted on Maeve. He didn't ask enough questions but came at her insistence. A trusting father following his heir's wishes. Galt might not have if he'd known who else would be here.

Another chancellor of Odrana and a conniving shrew of a woman stood across from him in the blocky building that housed the entrance to the dungeon. Lady Oyinlola Tonsa. One of the wealthiest persons in Odrana and the member of the council he struggled with the most.

Ceraun supplied the majority of food to the rest of the country and beyond to Dey. Some of their farms even sent vast convoys of food to trade with the more civilized city-states within Veskar. While the Sanerris family in Mistlight controlled the trade routes and shipping lanes, setting export taxes and stipulating prices, Goldenhall was the Odranan treasurer. Money that could be used to upgrade equipment and personnel, expand food production, and minimize casualties and injuries was instead spent on expansion efforts or wasted lining the pockets of the already wealthy. Galt was a simple man who would rather spend time helping his ranch hands calm a rampaging

Delkabeast than argue in a closed council session. Lady Tonsa rarely agreed to half his budgeting requests.

The Wellan family was one of the two remaining original families to carve the wild lands into the thriving country of Odrana. Families fell through the years due to sickness, marriage, or bad investments. The Ibarra family that had ruled in Goldenhall before the first Lady Tonsa rose to power had been invested in bringing up the standard of living for everyone in the country. Galt's father and mother spoke kindly of them even after their family's fall from grace. Lady Tonsa's use of indentured prisoners serving reduced sentences in her mines was a sore subject during their council meetings as well. The Wellan family had opposed slavery and banned it in their lands since the founding of Odrana. They had championed the dismantling of the orc slave camps with the Ibarra family. While that may have played a small part in their loss of ruling Goldenhall, few of the Ibarra family regretted what they'd done. As much as Tonsa stymied the flow of investment for his agricultural needs, Galt kept her attempts at reinstituting widespread slavery to a minimum. He couldn't stop the slave trade completely, with both Sanerris and Palmer invested in the market, but he could keep it illegal in his own lands. The Madvarr family in Ronden also held antislavery views. Goldenhall was surrounded on all sides by Ronden, Ceraun, and the sea. Slaves would have to travel through their lands to reach Goldenhall. Neither would let that happen. Unless Goldenhall started enslaving its own people, slavery was dead in the northeast.

Or so Galt had thought.

The current Lady Tonsa had instituted a policy of rehabilitation reform for prisoners. What at first had seemed like a small and altruistic venture had turned into a way for Goldenhall to supply its mines with free labor. Convicts would receive reduced sentences if they agreed to be moved to Goldenhall for hard labor. It wasn't until years passed that Galt learned of the punishments for minor infractions that increased the jail time of even a simple pickpocket to multiple years.

When he'd complained, Lady Tonsa pointed out that prisoners were released per the agreed-upon terms and moving prisoners through the land was not the same as transporting slaves. He'd been outvoted, even with Lord Madvarr not getting involved.

Galt cursed himself for the third time for not bringing along guards. Tonsa stood next to her son, each with a bodyguard standing close behind. Maeve's request for speed and secrecy had afforded him no time to summon his own trusted men. He smiled sadly at her innocence.

At least Professor Wren is here as well, or I might be dead, Galt thought with a shake of his head.

"Iona, Orrin said an hour, correct?" Maeve asked the Tonsa boy's bodyguard as she crossed the open expanse between the two parties, Wren standing between them. "They're late."

Galt studied Rhys's bodyguard, not realizing she was the same girl who had played with his daughter years ago.

Maeve and Tonsa's son, Rhys, had played together from time to time during meetings of the rulers of their country over the years. He was younger then, and his innocent demeanor at the time helped Maeve connect with him. Now, Galt could recall the other girl playing along with them. Maeve rarely connected well with others after her mother's death.

The pain stabbed Galt's heart, as it always did when he thought of his wife.

You'd be so proud of our daughter, my dear. She has your heart.

"Wellan, what information have you received from your daughter? Are our children truly in danger?" Lady Tonsa spoke for the first time. She'd simply nodded at him upon entering the dungeon's entrance facility and dismissing the guards stationed there. "If this is a ruse, I will be most displeased."

"Never mind, I hear them coming now," Maeve said, turning her back to the Tonsas and skipping back toward her father. She grabbed his hand. "Come meet Orrin. He's powerful but kind."

Two men and a boy who had to be younger than Rhys came through the doors. Finley Madvarr was easily recognizable. Galt smiled. The young man was coming into his own and filling in for his father on the council from time to time.

The other man's beard added age to his face, but once they were closer, Galt reassessed. He was young as well. The sword on his back was massive, but there was a draw to the warrior's aura that made the chancellor step in front of his daughter.

Dangerous. The word flew through his mind.

"Don't get in my way, Dad," Maeve said as she pushed him. "Orrin, is this your friend?"

Galt watched his daughter run up and stop a few feet from the young boy. She kept her hands behind her back. The boy's hair was light, and his smile at seeing Maeve brought up Galt's estimation immediately. He noticed the way his eyes traveled around the room as well, assessing.

Also dangerous, but not to Maeve.

The boy's next words made Galt's smile twitch and die on his face.

"Lord Sanerris wants to kill your children."

Orrin waited for a response. His read of the room when he entered boiled down to one word: tense.

"Who are you?" the dark-skinned woman standing next to Rhys asked. "I was told that the [Hero] of Dey would be here, or was I misinformed?"

Orrin didn't like the way that Rhys's mom looked at Iona as she said the last few words.

"I'm a member of his party but if I'm not good enough to talk to you, let me introduce . . . all the way from Dey . . . the one and only [Hero] . . . Daniel Kayson, Kayson, Kayson." Orrin repeated his friend's last name in a declining hush as he bowed and gestured at Daniel with both hands.

Daniel hit him in the back of the head.

"I'm sorry about him." Daniel stepped forward. "Thank you for coming. We have a lot to discuss."

Daniel spoke succinctly, telling Rhys's mom and Maeve's dad what had been going on, with a few key elements held back. Orrin watched their reactions, doing exactly as Madi had suggested. Lady Tonsa valued cunning and intelligence.

Be your normal idiot self at first, but then let her see it's an act. Madi's words played over in Orrin's head.

"I'm not an idiot," Orrin muttered.

"You're not," Maeve whispered, making him jump. She'd quietly moved near him.

Ignoring Maeve for now, Orrin kept his eyes on her father instead. The man was wearing normal clothing, with no weapons or armor showing. He wore shoes, unlike his daughter. Other than being in the same room as Lady Tonsa, Orrin would never have picked him out of a lineup as a leader of Odrana.

He looks like a suburban dad who would rather be mowing his lawn.

Lady Tonsa stood tall in a robe of rich umber. Red lines marked the wrists, waist, and bottom of the cloth, swaying centimeters above the ground. Her eyes left Daniel as he spoke and caught Orrin staring before he turned away.

Rhys was whispering something to Iona, both still paying attention to the information that Daniel was delivering. Professor Wren stood closer to the Tonsa family but had the nervous twitchy presentation of a rabbit about to take flight.

The last person in the room was an unknown guard standing behind Lady Tonsa. The man wore heavy plate armor on his chest and shoulders, with chain mail hanging down to his knees. Laced-up sandals covered his ankles and continued upward under the chain. It made for an odd look that Orrin hadn't seen before, but he ignored it as another class quirk.

". . . want to keep your families and your country safe, then I suggest you get rid of Lord Sanerris as the leader of Mistlight. I believe that Finley was given the right to vote by his father," Daniel finished, suggesting stage one of his plan.

"What proof do you have?" Lord Wellan asked. "Beyond your word. Maeve told me she was attacked, but there is no evidence that Arvin was behind it."

Lady Tonsa raised a hand to stop Daniel before he answered. "I can confirm large amounts of gold have moved from the Sanerris accounts recently, with no reason given. The timing suggests the assassination attempts on my son and your daughter were perpetrated by Lord Sanerris."

"To what end?" Maeve's father ran his fingers through his hair and stomped back and forth as he paced. "We helped put him in power. I've never gone against him directly on an issue he feels is important. Sure, I argued against further encroachment on elven lands, but his and Palmer's reports of their attacks were enough to change my mind."

"Those are lies, by the way." Finley stepped forward. "The elves don't leave their forest. The entire attack has been a land grab by Lord Palmer and some sort of personal vendetta for Lord Sanerris. I've spent the last week there, and every soldier I talked to said the same. Palmer wanted to kill me when I suggested we stand down."

"He wastes our money on an unneeded war?" Lady Tonsa hissed. "What about this Veskar assassin sent to kill my son? I could find no money in her accounts to account for her attack."

"I can answer that one." Orrin stepped up, explaining how Sloane had been alive when they left the dungeon. "They killed her for a convenient alibi. I think the other member of our party knew something was going to happen, but he was also killed."

Lady Tonsa stared at him long enough to make him uncomfortable. He kept his head high and didn't turn away.

"In my father's name, I move to strip Lord Sanerris of his power as chancellor of Mistlight," Finley stated with authority. "Does anyone second my motion?"

His ring took a dim glow as he held it toward the other two members of the Odranan council.

With a nod from his daughter, Lord Wellan raised a closed fist. His ring shone a dull green as he spoke. "I second."

Lady Tonsa stepped forward. "Who would we put in his place? Lady Sanerris? She would take revenge on us or Arvin would convince each of you to put him back in power within the year."

She turned from her fellow chancellors and asked Daniel directly. "What is your plan? Finley will have told you that four are required to name a new chancellor. Palmer won't agree to deposing the entire Sanerris family. What is your next step?"

Orrin's alarm bells went off. This was not what they'd thought would happen. He was supposed to convince her of this path alone. Finley and Madi had agreed that Maeve's dad was not a good actor, and they had to convince Lord Palmer to vote. They had to sow chaos.

Orrin's mind raced. Maeve reached out and touched his shoulder. The gentle reminder that he had allies here helped him.

"The next step is easy. We get all of you in a room and tell the entire story. Both Arvin and Anabella have been playing with your kids' lives and trying to start wars to keep themselves on top. Put them in a room together and let them fight. If they don't, we can come in and stir up a little more trouble. The Demon Lord is almost to the Pass."

Lord Wellan chuckled.

Lady Tonsa waved her hand in disregard. "Those are rumors—and unfounded. I've had no concrete proof that demons are attacking Dey in numbers beyond normal. Certainly nothing to suggest—"

She stopped talking and blanched. Her eyes stared at something straight ahead. Maeve's father's laughter turned into choking.

"Does that convince you?" Daniel growled. "I'm here for a reason, and it isn't to fuck around with politics."

"What is he talking about?" Maeve asked Orrin.

"I think he just shared a Quest with them."

"A Quest? I've never had a Quest before. What kind?"

"To stop the Demon Lord."

Chapter 52

Orrin worried that Daniel's ploy might have backfired. Lady Tonsa and Lord Wellan dragged Finley a distance from everyone and began to have an animated chat. The Tonsa guard nodded to a quick command from his boss and motioned for the rest of them to move back.

"Professor Wren, this is Daniel. Daniel, this is one of the teachers at the school I've been at. She helped arrange this." Orrin introduced the remnants of the meeting, ignoring the large man hovering menacingly a few dozen feet away. "That's Iona; we fought together in a dungeon. She's levelheaded and keeps Rhys in check."

"Hey, what is that supposed to mean?" Rhys said petulantly, turning away from his attempts to eavesdrop. He turned up his lip at the guard, getting a snide smirk back in response.

"That's Rhys. He's usually quicker with the banter, but he did just survive an assassination attempt." Orrin chuckled as Iona covered her mouth. "His mom is Lady Tonsa."

Orrin grabbed Maeve's arm and pulled her around front. "This is Maeve. She's smart and helped set this up with Iona over there. Wren helped, too, I guess."

The oldest person in the current group frowned at that. "I helped orchestrate the entire meeting. I created excuses for the guards to be—"

"Super helpful and not at all responsible for us almost getting assassinated."

Wren wisely stopped talking.

"Everyone, this is my friend, Daniel . . . the [Hero]."

Orrin stepped back and smiled as the group of more politically minded individuals swarmed Daniel.

"He's anxious," Maeve said from his side, watching as Rhys, Iona, and Wren asked rapid-fire questions.

"He's been dealing with a lot," Orrin whispered back. "Now he's in the middle of a different type of battle, but he'll be fine. He's stronger than he looks."

Maeve shook her head. "He's worried about you. He keeps his body turned to keep you in sight whenever you move. You being away must have scared him. You're important to him."

Orrin didn't say anything. He was learning that Maeve's perception of the world was different than his own. He shifted to the side a bit and felt a knot form in his stomach as Daniel sidestepped as well.

"He's always trying to protect me," Orrin muttered. Turning to Maeve, he asked, "Do you want to ask him questions, too?"

"No. He's your friend, not mine. After Lord Sanerris is taken down, you, Daniel, and Madeleine should come visit us in Ceraun. My dad might want to ask him questions. We have some books about [Heroes] of the past—not that they are any help to us."

The mention of books reminded Orrin that Maeve wanted access to the Sanerris School library to read up on a project. He'd blown her chance at getting a mentor for a thesis project with his small attempt to help during a class assignment that failed spectacularly.

"I'm sorry that I screwed up your chance to get access to the books you wanted. I can talk with Professor Graem if we all survive. He might let you break the rules a bit," Orrin said. Lady Tonsa was pointing at their group and gesturing at Finley. "What books did you want to read at school? Do you have a specific project in mind?"

"I want to create a self-sustaining crop field that self-harvests and reseeds itself. There are some berries and small fruit trees that have similar abilities, but only in singular circumstances. If I could get even a small field of wheat to self-propagate and spin itself into sheaves, it would reduce labor needs enough that our farmers could focus more time on increasing their own classes and spells."

Maeve's voice carried more passion than Orrin had ever heard her use before. "We could diversify more into other industries. More [Healers] and [Teachers]. If the price of food was reduced throughout Odrana, everyone would prosper. That kind of self-replicating magic is kept restricted—for good reason—but I'd hoped that I could prove myself to the professors."

Orrin hadn't thought about the way magic could impact something as mundane as farming, even with his [Tilth] spell. He only had the earth magic spell for the corresponding ward it gave him. *I should spend some time looking up earth magic spells related to farming for her later.*

"That's amazing, Maeve. I'm sure we can wrangle some concessions out of whoever takes over Mistlight. You'll be feeding the world in a few years."

Maeve beamed.

"If the [Hero] could join us for a moment." Lady Tonsa's voice rang through the stone room, stopping all other conversations. "We have logistics to discuss."

Orrin made to move when Rhys's mom held up her hand. "Just the [Hero], please."

"He goes where I go," Daniel answered for Orrin, waiting for him to move. "We're a package deal."

Orrin heard a light snort as Maeve suppressed a laugh behind him.

"Very well." Lady Tonsa didn't push the issue, although Orrin could see she wasn't pleased. "The rest of you may return to your homes. Rhys and Iona, please make sure Goldenhall is locked down. The next few days may be trying."

"Maeve, please see to it that our people pull back to the central regions. Build up fortification walls in the fields to the north and west. Leo will help with the logistics," Lord Wellan directed his daughter. Orrin noticed the man was no longer wearing regular clothing but heavy plate armor. He had no idea when he'd put it on.

Likely a spell of some sort, Orrin thought, glancing to see how Maeve took her dismissal.

"If that's what you think is best." Maeve nodded at her father. "Good luck, Dad. Be safe."

"What do you require of me?" Professor Wren asked, stepping forward and moving past Iona and Rhys, who were arguing among themselves. "I can be of great—"

"You've done enough, Professor," Lady Tonsa said with disdain. "Your services will not be needed tonight."

Wren flitted between a half dozen emotions that Orrin could see. Fear, anger, relief. She settled on the last and bowed once before leaving with Maeve.

Lady Tonsa narrowed her eyes. "Rhys? Why are you still here?"

The guard nearby clenched his fists, audible popping echoing through the room.

Rhys shook his head and forcefully moved Iona's hand off his arm before turning to face his mother. "Iona can initiate safety protocols on her own, Mother. I strongly urge you to reconsider and let me join you. I know Orrin from our time in the dungeon and can lend my voice as an additional witness to the council."

"That won't be needed." Lady Tonsa spoke with such disinterest that Orrin felt bad for Rhys. For a second. "You are dismissed."

"Your boy makes a fair point, Oyinlola," Lord Wellan said, resting his hands on axes resting on his hips. "These two aren't from Odrana. His standing as your son also gives greater credence to his testimony. It might help us convince—"

"I will not have my son put in danger again. He will return home and await my instruction."

Orrin raised a hand. "I can [Teleport] him away if there is any danger."

"You are here at the [Hero]'s request but will not accompany us, either." Lady Tonsa's eyes sparkled with rage at all those around her. "This is a meeting of the Odranan leadership, not a—"

"Shut up," Finley snapped, cutting her off.

The room darkened to Orrin's eyes as everyone held their breath. From the little interaction that Orrin had witnessed with the woman, Finley's interruption seemed a dangerous choice.

Rhys's mother turned slowly to Finley, who leaned against the wall, one knee bent with his foot planted against the stone.

Effortlessly cool, Orrin thought as he rolled his eyes. *I wonder how long he practiced standing like that in a mirror.*

Finley winked at Orrin.

"You may have your father's ring, young Madvarr," Lady Tonsa said in a whisper, her fingers tapping against her thighs, "but don't think for a moment that you have the right to speak to me that way."

"Orrin and the [Hero] are not obligated to listen to your demands as Lord Wellan and I are." Finley kicked off the wall and moved toward Lady Tonsa. "Your son can listen to the plan, at least."

He stopped within striking distance of Lady Tonsa and leaned closer. "Unless you believe he would betray Odrana."

Orrin's eyes stayed on her hands. The atmosphere in the room had changed drastically in the last minute, and he was ready to cast a few spells and flee. A single step brought him closer to Daniel, and his foot nudged his friend's shoe, ready to [Teleport] away.

Daniel cleared his throat. "If you all fight each other, I'm not sure my Quest gets completed."

Lady Tonsa stepped away from Finley. "Would you be willing to share the Demon Lord Quest? I would pay you well."

Orrin breathed a sigh of relief. Daniel hadn't shared the Quest, only throwing the blue box screen to the others. He'd known Daniel wasn't that much of an idiot . . . maybe.

"We can deal with this later," Finley said. "If you won't cast the third vote, this entire meeting was a waste of time."

Daniel moved quickly, stepping between Finley and Lady Tonsa. "We can figure things out now. I've learned rushing in without a plan isn't the best idea."

Looking back and forth between the two, Daniel sighed and put his hands down. "If you can't work together and take constructive criticism, we can leave. Now that Orrin is here, I can just kill the idiot family that is behind this mess."

Orrin winced at Daniel's comment.

"Orrin's strong, but a [Wind Mage] isn't going to stand a chance in a direct fight with either Sanerris," Finley said from behind Daniel's arm. "Lord Wellan, can you convince this control freak to calm down?"

Maeve's father chuckled. "Let the boy stay. It'll be a good learning experience for him."

"Fine," Lady Tonsa growled. "Rhys, you may stay, but you will leave the moment I say so. Am I understood?"

"Yes, Mother." Rhys smiled at having gotten his way.

"Iona, see to the defenses."

"Yes, ma'am."

Orrin noticed the guard was still standing off to the side. "What about him?"

"Mind your tongue, child. You may be a member of the [Hero]'s entourage, but you have no voice in these proceedings." Lady Tonsa unleashed her pent-up aggression at Orrin.

After being jerked around the last few weeks, Orrin's temper was already frayed. Watching Rhys's bully of a mom be rude to everyone around him, he felt himself calling his power. Just a few casts of [Decrease Dexterity] and she'd be on the ground begging for his forgiveness. He'd need to hit Rhys and the guard as well. Maybe Lord Wellan . . .

Orrin gritted his teeth and called up [Mind Bastion]. He cast [Calm Mind] for good measure, letting the coolness flow through his head. *She isn't the enemy. There is no threat here.*

Daniel punched Orrin in the shoulder. "I'm proud of you."

Finley and Rhys gave Daniel confused looks.

"You almost dropped everyone, didn't you?" his friend whispered. "I'm making plans and you're not overreacting. Are we maturing or what?"

"Dropped everyone?" Rhys mumbled to himself just loud enough for Orrin to overhear.

Orrin nudged Daniel to turn back around. Lady Tonsa wasn't pleased at having the [Hero] turn his back on her.

"We're all here," Daniel stated. "Orrin has a point. Is the big guy here part of the plan?"

Lord Wellan struggled to hold back a smile, and Lady Tonsa ground her teeth. "I don't travel without Niels. This is known."

"Well, if this is known," Daniel repeated her words, dripping with sarcasm, "I know you heard our plan, but you obviously know your laws better than we do. Any major changes we should be aware of?"

Lord Wellan put his hand on Lady Tonsa's shoulder and moved in front. "The plan remains similar to the one you brought us. The three of us can vote to remove Arvin. I'll have a message sent to Anabella immediately to meet us in the Sanerris castle. She'll know what that means."

Finley nodded. "The problem is that if she sees you, she'll leave. She's smart enough to know that if you are in Odrana, her plans failed."

"There is also a concern that Lord Palmer won't care about the invading Demon Lord. He will be easy to convince to remove Arvin, but he's always been loyal to Lady Sanerris. We need to time your arrival well in order to convince him that removing her, too, will be best for his own well-being," Lady Tonsa added.

"Who will you put in charge in his place?" Orrin asked, ignoring Lady Tonsa's glare. "That's a fair question. I'd like to start coordinating troops to help reinforce Dey right away."

"If we successfully remove the Sanerris family from power, the four remaining chancellors will have to discuss the replacement at length. We will need to secure both Lord and Lady Sanerris after we take over. It is likely they will resist," Lord Wellan answered.

Daniel cracked his knuckles. "Good. I hope they do."

Chapter 53

After a few more details were discussed, the odd group of temporary allies relocated from Mistlight's dungeon, traveling through the darkness to the city. Rhys tried his best to disappear from his mother's sight so she wouldn't send him home. She was focused on other matters, and nobody complained when Rhys moved out with them.

Lady Tonsa's whispered orders kept the guards at the gate from asking questions, and within thirty minutes, they were standing outside a government building.

"We will have them meet here. The enchantments on the building allow for a total lockdown and should prevent either Sanerris from escaping," Rhys's mom explained as they walked up the steps to the unassuming dark-blue brick building. The doors were locked, but a key magically appeared in her hand. Orrin allowed himself to be ushered inside.

"Are you sure being trapped in a building with Lord and Lady Sanerris is wise?" Lord Wellan asked nervously as they entered. "I think we should have a few more guards here in case things go badly."

"Nonsense." Lady Tonsa shook her head. "We have the numbers and the strength."

Ropes on poles created waiting lines in the front room. Booths with closed metal shutters lined the far wall, with a heavy metal door in the corner. The entire location reminded Orrin of a bank.

"What is this place?"

Maeve's dad pointed to the stone booths. "Petitioners can place grievances with clerks. Mistlight has an administrative force of adjudicators that investigate and attempt to bring justice, or at least fair results, to each person. Anything from property disputes to blood feuds can be brought here for official reckoning. It inspired my family to do the same on a smaller scale." He laughed, his heavy armor rolling about on his shoulders. "Our problems are usually who gets to keep the extra calf, though."

Lord Wellan, Finley, and Lady Tonsa led them through the entrance hall into a back room. Orrin took in the tables, chairs, and wooden lockers. *A break room for employees.* Rhys and Niels, the Tonsa bodyguard, sat to the left.

He slowed and elbowed Daniel gently.

"What?" Daniel murmured.

Orrin gestured with his head to the other side of the room and moved away from the rest of the group.

"When this goes to shit, we're running," he whispered as quietly as he could.

"They picked this building for its defenses. If we want to go, we should get out now." Daniel picked up a small glass bauble from a locker. "What do you think this is?"

Orrin grabbed the item and put it back. "I don't trust her. Rhys was halfway decent and I like Maeve, but I don't know her dad. I know this was partially my idea, but I'm getting a bad feeling."

Daniel put his hands on Orrin's shoulders. "We need all the help we can line up to fight the demons. Silas's scouts were able to get an estimate of their numbers. We're going to be facing at least six thousand of them. Dey can muster up a few hundred actual fighters, with maybe two or three thousand regular people who can shoot a bow or hold a spear. The elves sent a thousand to help, but we need more. The Pass isn't easily defendable. If we can get even a few hundred more high-level mages from Odrana, it could help save lives."

Orrin knew Daniel was right, but he didn't have to like it. "I'm just saying, be ready to run."

"If you want to leave, we go. I think it's worth the risk, but I trust you, O. You know these people better than I do."

Orrin considered it for a moment. Daniel would stick to his word and leave. *Lord Sanerris can only freeze one of us at a time. If Anabella knocks him out, the rest of us should be enough. Even if she doesn't, I think we can take him together.*

"We'll stay, but under my [Camouflage]. If shit goes sideways, I'll [Teleport] us out."

Daniel squeezed Orrin's shoulder.

"Rhys, I want you to go to our apartment here and wait. Do not leave," Lady Tonsa ordered.

Orrin spoke up immediately. "Not saying we don't trust you, but Rhys can stay here."

Her dark-brown eyes turned on him. Orrin stood straight. He'd faced down both Sanerris and his mother. He'd fought monsters from his wildest nightmares. This was just another human.

"I will not have my son in danger. He leaves or this alliance is at an end."

"He can join our party and stay undercover," Daniel suggested, stepping into the middle of the room. "There is no reason for him to come out from Orrin's [Camouflage] spell, and we can always [Teleport] out."

"This location is warded against [Teleport]," Lady Tonsa explained, waving a hand through the air. "There is no reason for him to be here."

"It helps us trust you a bit more," Orrin muttered.

He hadn't expected her to hear him. Orrin stumbled back at the rage in her eyes.

"Mother, please," Rhys said, rushing to his mom. He moved to block her view of Orrin, both hands touching hers. "I'll be no safer anywhere than by your side. Show them what our family can do. Show them who we are. I can take down the back wall if I need to. If there is a Demon Lord coming, the world will need the [Hero]. Let me play my part."

The Tonsas spoke more, but Orrin tuned them out, watching Finley's and Lord Wellan's responses. Neither seemed to care if Rhys stayed or left. *They must have a lot of faith that Anabella and Arvin will roll over.*

Orrin pumped up his and Daniel's stats with a [Utility Ward]. He'd top them both off before the party started for real.

Rhys left the three in charge behind and approached Orrin and Daniel as his mother called over Niels.

"Orrin, I want to apologize for how I acted in the dungeon," Rhys started, holding his hands behind his back. "Iona was right to trust you. You saved our lives and are here doing it again at great personal risk. I cannot undo the damage that my immature actions caused between us, but I will try to be better in the future."

Orrin squinted at Rhys. "Who are you and what did you do with the overly self-confident Rhys I know?"

Daniel rolled his eyes and stuck out his hand. "If he's making jokes, you'll be fine. Join the party?"

Orrin heard the ding of the system as Rhys joined, shaking Daniel's hand.

"Let's get situated over there." Rhys pointed to the far corner. "It's not likely that we'll need to escape, but the wards are weakest there."

"How can you tell?" Daniel asked as they moved to the farthest part of the room from the doors.

"I can sense metal," Rhys answered with a shrug. "There's less in that spot."

Niels left at Lady Tonsa's request to send a message to Anabella. He was gone for ten minutes. As soon as he returned, the two chancellors and Finley gathered to call for a vote of the Odrana council.

Finley repeated his earlier words, calling for Lord Sanerris's removal. His ring shone bright. Lord Wellan seconded the motion, his own green glow lighting the room more.

"Motion passed." Lady Tonsa spoke calmly but with fear in her eyes as her own ring gave off a blue hue.

"When your powers combine . . ." Orrin joked. Only Daniel heard him, but he got a small chuckle.

Daniel, Orrin, and Rhys bunched in tight, and Orrin cast [Camouflage] at level two on all three of them to be safe. He could have used his ward but felt the extra utility of being able to attack without breaking the spell would be worth it, just in case. Lady Tonsa let out an audible sigh of relief.

"That's not a bad spell. I might pay for information on that later."

Orrin ignored her and buffed himself and Daniel to the maximum stats. He threw a general [Ward] on himself and Daniel.

After another thought, he added [Ice Ward] on everyone in the room.

Everyone waited.

Lord Palmer was the first to arrive. Orrin thought the man had to be in his sixties, but even with the gray hair hiding in his deep brown mane, the man moved like a tiger. He entered the room, sweeping his eyes across every corner. Orrin held his breath, but his spell held up to the scrutiny of the ruler of Idrisid.

"What happened? I'm in the middle of a wa . . ." He trailed off and pointed at Finley. "What is that traitor doing here?"

Finley held up his father's ring. "Acting as a representative of my father. Don't push it, Palmer. We have a long night ahead of us still and a longer day tomorrow."

Lord Palmer exchanged looks with both the other chancellors. "The boy speaks for you two as well?"

"We've removed Arvin from his position of chancellor," Lady Tonsa tutted at the other two before stepping forward to speak on their behalf. "The war with the elves is a ruse for personal power. They have not attacked. You will want to investigate how Arvin suborned your lieutenants, who lied to you about elf attacks. Surely you did not know?" Her voice turned up at the end, giving Palmer a choice.

Clever. Orrin noticed Finley's hands were on his knives. *If he accepts her offer to side with them, he can feign ignorance of the fabricated reasons for the war. He can't admit to knowing Sanerris was already removed, crippling any alliance he might have.*

Lord Palmer glared at Lady Tonsa. He studied Finley and Lord Wellan as well before he burst out in laughter.

"Damn, it's a coup d'etat. I'll back your play, but I want to keep the lands I've captured."

Orrin almost choked on his disgust for the man.

"I'm sure Arvin is on his way and . . . let me guess? You want my vote to put Anabella back on top. Has she been informed, or was this her play all along?" Lord Palmer walked between Finley and Lord Wellan, grabbing a chair and dragging it loudly back between them. He set the chair between Wellan and Tonsa before settling himself down. "Well?"

Orrin smirked at the tightness in Lady Tonsa's jaw. *She doesn't like being compared to Anabella.*

"Arvin and his mother will be here soon."

But she's smart enough not to give away the play quite yet. Orrin didn't trust Rhys's mom, but he could respect her intelligence. She was doing all she could not to tip off Palmer.

"Should we vote now? There isn't a need for Arvin if we . . . Never mind. I can feel his magic. He's arrived."

Orrin doubled-checked all his wards, buffs, and camo spell.

Lord Arvin Sanerris, chancellor of Mistlight and ruler of Odrana, swept into the room. He ignored Niels, who stood by the door, and moved to Lady Tonsa first. His hair fell over his eyes as he bowed his head and kissed her outstretched hand.

"Oyinlola, how have you been? What is this emergency meeting?" His eyes moved from Wellan, to Finley, and settled on Palmer last. "I . . . see. This is a most unfortunate time. Will you let me explain or have you already voted?"

"Arvin Sanerris." Lord Wellan spoke with an authoritative voice that Orrin hadn't heard before. "You have been removed from your position as chancellor. The council will vote on your replacement. Your last act as chancellor will be to gracefully step down and cast your vote. Will you choose a peaceful transition or treason?"

Orrin's training with the flow of magic in the last few weeks paid off. While he wasn't yet a master in any way, a small part of his brain nudged his attention away from the scene in front of him. A familiar presence near the door where nobody stood.

What? Who?

Orrin stared at the open door beside Niels. The man's arms were crossed, but he stood close enough to close the door at a moment's notice. *No, the door . . .* Orrin tried again and felt his vision move back to the guard.

Shit. It's [Camouflage]. He tapped his foot against Daniel and whispered, "By the door."

"I will not fight and take power from our country," Arvin said with a sad tone in his voice. "Palmer, I am disappointed. Who do you have in mind? Not my mother, surely? You two hate each other, Oyinlola."

"I can work with those I dislike," Lady Tonsa snarled. "I cannot abide those who seek to harm my family and the lives of our people."

Orrin could feel Daniel's tension. They couldn't know for sure who was standing by the door. It wasn't yet time for them to make themselves known, since Anabella wasn't here, but every moment was a risk with an invisible potential threat in their midst.

"If it is all the same then, go ahead and vote her in. I need to get back to dealing with the true dangers facing our country," Arvin said, already back to his normal self. "I don't have time to wait for her to make the trip in. I'll give Palmer my proxy and be on my way."

Finley's fingers moved to the hilt of a dagger. Wellan's fingers stretched and cracked as he made fists. The air around Lady Tonsa began to almost crackle with energy.

"You will wait for her to arrive and cast your vote, as is your duty," Lord Wellan said. This time, his voice didn't hold the same authority. This was a hiccup in the plan. An unforeseen variable.

Orrin readied himself. *If he attacks, we'll have to move in. Anabella might go free, but at least . . .*

"That won't be necessary. I'm here." The figure at the door appeared. Lady Sanerris, Arvin's mother.

She can use [Camouflage]?

"Before you vote, I do have a concern to express," Anabella said as she strode into the room like a queen. "It seems in your haste to vote my son out, you failed to perform an adequate safety sweep. There are interlopers in this very room. I suggest we ask them to join us, don't you?"

Chapter 54

Daniel materialized, letting Orrin's [Camouflage] spell fade. With a cold smile plastered on his face, the [Hero] strode across the tile floor toward Anabella, undaunted in his approach.

"Hi everyone. If you don't know me, I'm Daniel, the [Hero]. I've been keeping your invading armies away from the elves for the past few weeks." Daniel's voice dripped with vitriol. "That blond dick has been lying to you and sending your people to die for no reason. The elves don't want a war . . . but I'm not here to talk about that."

Arvin took a more defensive position, furtively moving to where the other chancellors would block Daniel's path toward him. Orrin kept his own [Camouflage] on for now. It wasn't his turn yet.

Stick to the plan. Don't improvise.

"I'm here to force your hand. This is what passes for the leadership of Odrana, is it not?" Daniel stopped halfway between Lady Tonsa and Lady Sanerris. "You are the ones who call the shots with this piece of filth?"

Orrin ignored Lady Tonsa as she moved closer to Daniel, calling him out for invading the sanctity of their land and all the other planned bullshit in their attempt to confuse the Sanerris duo. His heartbeat picked up when he saw the smile on Anabella's face. He'd seen the same self-assured smirk each time she baited him into a trap playing Kala.

What are you up to?

". . . possible reason you could have for being here?" Lady Tonsa asked, finishing her masterful acting class. The woman's fury at

Daniel's supposed intrusion chilled Orrin, and he wasn't even the target.

Orrin moved slowly, positioning himself behind Anabella. From his interactions with the Sanerris family, Orrin believed her to be the more dangerous one. Her abilities were mostly unknown, while Daniel had promised he could take Arvin now. He trusted his friend but still planned on getting a few kicks in on his former torturer.

"The Demon Lord has reached the Pass and will breach Dey's walls in a few days. Against my recommendation and pleas, the lords of Dey sent me to ask for your aid." Daniel's acting juxtaposed with Lady Tonsa's was cringey. His friend was not good at this.

Arvin Sanerris finally spoke, pushing in front of Lord Wellan and pointing at Daniel. "What Demon Lord? You have no proof to back up your claims. Are you truly the [Hero] or a spy sent to—"

"Arvin, dear." Anabella's low voice cut through the room and stopped her son in his tracks. "Don't overplay your hand. You've known a Demon Lord was coming for months and told no one. This is the [Hero], and if you can't feel his power, I've failed you."

She turned to Daniel and bowed her head to show respect. "You are sure of the timing? The Horde has arrived?"

"You are Lady Sanerris, aren't you?" Daniel asked woodenly. "The person who has my friend Orrin? We missed you at your cottage."

Orrin groaned internally at Daniel's terrible acting. Thankfully, nobody else seemed to pick up on it.

"I believe you are talking about the young man that I rescued from assassins and helped educate in my school," Anabella said with a smile, spreading her hands in a supplicating manner. "He can be here within the hour. Your party members can relax; the daughter of Lord Catanzano is safe in Mistlight."

"Madi is . . ." Daniel paused. "I think we should keep this between us. You'd release my friend? Just like that?"

"He is of no further use to me," Anabella answered, moving closer to Daniel again. "I protected him from my son after you rescued your friend. I thought it best to keep him under my protection until

Arvin's rage had cooled. Know that there is still one Sanerris willing to work with the [Hero] to stop the demon threat to Asmea. How long until they attack Dey? Odrana will supply forces, but we need time to coordinate with Dey's armies and travel there."

"Lady Sanerris, I'm sorry, but you are not in a position to promise anything," Lady Tonsa said, drawing all eyes back to her. "Have you forgotten that you are no longer a member of the Odranan leadership?"

Orrin was quite enjoying watching from the shadows. He was tired of being the center of these shenanigans. *Let Daniel deal with the problems for once.*

"I have already prepared extensively for this," Arvin said as the group of lords and ladies began arguing. "It is no small part of the reason our forces are fighting the elves. They are in league with the demons and must be stopped. I vote that I retain my position as chancellor and we can begin moving our forces to Dey at once."

The disputes and bickering devolved. Arvin tried to convince the group that he had moved only in Odrana's interests, while Anabella simply pointed out that he'd already been removed, showing the council's lack of trust in him.

The air in the room stilled when Arvin gestured to Lord Palmer. "Palmer, you have worked with me and helped tremendously with the war effort. Tell the others how the fighting has helped our men get ready for the demons' arrival."

"The best thing to do now," Lady Tonsa shouted, raising her hands up to calm down all parties, "is to vote for Mistlight's chancellor. We have both members of the Sanerris family present. Does any chancellor have a statement or vote to bring forward?"

Finley sauntered into the middle with his arms crossed over his chest and both hands resting on his knives. His leather armor holding the braces of daggers glinted as he moved through the light. "I have something to say."

"Madvarr stays home and sends his pup," Arvin muttered loud enough for all to hear. "Too scared to do what is necessary himself. If he joined the fight with the elves, none of this would be needed."

Finley smiled at the former ruler of Mistlight. "Lord Sanerris drew Odrana into an unnecessary war with the elven nation without just cause. We have already voted for his removal. What this council may not know is that Lady Sanerris attempted to do the same with Veskar."

Lord Palmer went still.

Finley turned and pointed at Anabella. "Did you send a strike team to kill Rhys Tonsa and place the blame on a Veskar native?"

Orrin could feel Anabella's icy glare even positioned behind her. "I deny that accusation."

"Did you pay Veskar mercenaries to attack my planned convoy in an attempt to kill me?" Finley played with the strap holding his dagger in place.

"I deny that accusation."

"Did you attempt to have Lord Wellan's daughter killed?"

"No. Your information is poor if you believe I would harm Maeve. I believe my son may have insinuated that he would harm her before. Isn't that correct, Lord Wellan?"

Finley popped the button and held the dagger tight in his left hand, ignoring her comments. "Did you send a spy into the Sanerris School to keep tabs on me, Rhys, and Maeve?"

"No. I have no reason to spy on children of Odrana."

Finley smiled.

"I think you lost this one, Lady Sanerris," Orrin said, appearing behind Anabella. "She hired me to befriend all three of you in an attempt to take her position back from her son. I witnessed the attack on Rhys and questioned the woman they say was responsible. She was innocent and was killed for it. Veskar had nothing to do with the attack."

"Not the young Catanzano," Anabella sighed, her head turned over her shoulder at Orrin. "I missed something. How frustrating. Well played."

"You asked me to become friends with them and then tried to kill them," Orrin condemned her. "Was being in charge worth so much?"

Lord Wellan watched the exchanges, his head moving back and forth. Orrin almost missed when Lady Tonsa stepped on his foot.

"Lord Palmer, did you know of the plot to kill Finley? You are in charge of the western front, are you not?" Maeve's dad asked.

All their planning and plotting came down to this moment. They'd already voted Lord Sanerris out of power. Palmer had voiced his support for Anabella before the charges of attempted ruler-on-ruler homicide. Orrin knew his reputation was one of survival, but Lord Palmer's history with Anabella was a concern.

Sweat soaked his silver-streaked hair. The hunter was intelligent enough that he'd seen this coming. His eyes moved from Lady Tonsa to Lady Sanerris and back.

"I kne . . ." He wiped his forehead. "I know I was given orders to move the young Madvarr on reconnaissance missions far outside the normal patterns. Now that I hear this troubling news . . . I see that he would have been close to the Veskar border. If Finley was killed, it would be easy to place the blame on Veskar."

"Who could give you orders like that?" Lady Tonsa took charge again. "Madvarr's accusations are serious. Do you remember?"

"Why would Lord Palmer accept orders from me?" Lady Sanerris asked. "I am not my son. I have no power over Odranan forces fighting the elves."

"Everyone knows that your son comes to you for martial advice, Anabella," Lady Tonsa stated. "He may have personal power, but he is single-minded in his approach to problems."

"You bitch," Arvin snarled.

Lady Tonsa wagged her finger. "Making my point for me."

"The orders came from Lady Sanerris, as they do from time to time." Lord Palmer spoke softly, knowing he was defeated. His only chance at retaining his power was going with the trio's plan. His animalistic bearing had been reduced to that of a timid mouse trying not to be noticed between the large predators surrounding him. "Finley, I apologize for my words and actions when you returned against orders. Instead of court-martialing you, I should be giving you a medal for saving your men. To think that I was almost party to your murder."

Finley's smile was vicious. "I would have survived and come for answers, Lord Palmer. We can call this a win for everyone."

Lord Wellan didn't need a nudge to remember his lines this time. "I vote that the Sanerris house be stripped of the Mistlight chancellorship and a new family be instated for leadership."

Lady Tonsa kept her face devoid of joy, but her voice was lighter than normal as she seconded the motion.

Finley spat toward Anabella when he added his voice to the vote.

Lord Palmer kept his face down. "Yea."

"Motion passed. Arvin and Anabella Sanerris, you may leave. This is a closed meeting of the chancellors' council of Odrana." Lady Tonsa pointed to the door. "If you would be so kind?"

Orrin was waiting for it. They'd pushed both Anabella and Lord Sanerris to the brink. While the other leaders of Odrana said time and time again that they would accept the power change, Orrin watched. He caught the power building in Anabella.

"Arvin, you are an idiot. If you would have shared your findings when I told you to, none of this would have happened. We can't allow this." Anabella's voice was tired and sad as she raised her hand toward Lady Tonsa. "I apologize to all of you."

Orrin cast [Decrease Strength] and [Decrease Will] on Anabella just before she cast her spell. *That should drop her to the grou . . . What?*

Anabella stayed on her feet. The spell that she cast felt familiar to Orrin. A few weeks ago, he would have needed to see the results of the magic hitting, but his new education let him see the turns of power as it left her body. He knew what was going to happen before it hit Lady Tonsa.

Rhys's mom dropped to the ground.

Orrin used [Identify] as spells began to fly. Lady Tonsa's dexterity had been reduced to zero.

Chapter 55

Orrin made up his mind quickly and began casting his buff spells on the Odranan chancellors and Finley. His own will was topped out at one hundred after a few castings of [Increase Will] before a [Utility Ward] for him and Daniel. All his stats were at maximum.

At level three, an [Increase Strength] spell increased the target's strength by four points for twenty minutes. One cast from Orrin brought Lady Tonsa's strength up to forty. He could cast the spell five times on a single target but only needed three. Two and a half, really, but the mana cost the same. Orrin smiled as his mana pool barely dipped. His spells were cast at a tenth of their base cost with his current intelligence.

Buffing his allies was a calculated risk. The twenty-minute time limit for a third-level casting didn't increase, and Orrin had yet to find anyone besides himself and Daniel who didn't suffer severe withdrawal symptoms from the boosts after a certain point. If he didn't keep an eye on the time and recast the spells, the temporary gain could backfire, leaving everyone writhing on the ground in pain.

Lord Sanerris used the moment to attack as well. A handful of hazy orbs moved from his hands as he ran toward the door. Lord Palmer shot nine arrows in the span of Arvin taking two steps. Most clattered to the ground around Arvin's shield spell—the one that had frustrated them during their last fight. A few of the arrows hit the orbs and distorted as they traveled through the air bubbles. Dust blew away on the slight draft in the room.

Lady Tonsa's guard, Niels, moved in front of the chancellors. A six-foot-tall tower shield appeared in his hands. Slamming the sharpened bottom edge into the stone with a yell, Niels glowed with magic under Orrin's eyes. Five copies of the man stood in a line, blocking the softball-size globes.

For a moment, Orrin had hope. Palmer shot more arrows at the fleeing Arvin. Rhys's mom was slowly getting up from the floor, dizzy after her sudden lost-and-found strength experience. Lord Wellan placed his hands on the stone floor. Orrin felt a rumbling deep underground. The stone cracked and vines climbed out, slowly spreading across the ground. Orrin could tell the spell was strong, but it was slow . . . too slow.

The first bubble of time magic hit Niels. It moved through the shield without stopping. Two of the clones faded into dust. Three Nielses screamed in pain before the center figure fell away from the shield. The other copies faded from existence. Lady Tonsa grabbed the man's arm and pulled him from the slow-moving death balls. Niels held his hand against his body, rolling in pain.

Time bubbles? Orrin couldn't focus on Arvin, who was almost to the door. Daniel said he was ready. He would trust his friend.

He cast a healing spell at Niels, not waiting to see if it helped. There was enough health in his cure magic to keep him alive for now.

"How are you casting my spell?" Orrin demanded, turning toward Anabella and summoning his swords. A [Ice Sword] and a [Fire Sword] conjured in each hand, he stalked toward the regal woman. She stood tall and proud, a furrow in her brow the only clue that she was agitated. She tilted her head as she raised her hand, this time pointing toward Orrin.

"You are an annoying pawn. I should have let you die when I had the chance. You have ruined too many plans. A shame—your magic is fascinating."

Orrin saw the flow of magic gather. [Mind Bastion] knocked meekly at his thoughts, like a scolded child trying not to anger his father. He let the information flow in, reading the pattern with new eyes. *Her freeze spell.*

Orrin called a [Gust] through his [Fire Sword], bringing the blade in a skyward slash at the last moment. The sword disappeared in a burst of flames.

The magical matrices of Anabella's spell were beyond what Orrin could interpret. He'd understood that at a glance. All he could do was pray that Professor Hugh was right about different spell types and reactions. Fire magic had a slight edge on ice magic. He used the minimal amount of air magic from [Gust] to push the fire magic from his [Fire Sword] into the path of the incoming spell.

> **[Fire Sword]—Summon a sword of pure fire. Does minimal damage but will not be quenched in the bitterest of cold. Each sword lasts one hour. 1 MP per sword.**

The magic hit equidistant from each caster. The fireball that blossomed surprised everyone in the room, with both the intensity and cold heat that shot out in every direction. Orrin was launched backward in the air, tumbling head over heels before hitting a wall. A quick [Heal Small Wounds] brought him to his feet, and he searched frantically for the next attack.

The blast had knocked Lord Wellan against the far wall. He raised his hand toward the hole in the stone floor. Vines continued to climb from the earth, moving with purpose.

Anabella Sanerris leaned against the door, breathing heavily. It broke a moment later, the hinges melted from the heat of the back-draft. Burn marks covered her right arm up to her shoulder, and the dress she'd arrived in was covered in ash. For the first time since meeting her, Orrin saw fear in her eyes.

"That isn't possible. You spent less than a month in low-level classes at my school. How could you strike down my system-granted spell?" Lady Sanerris coughed as she tried to move. Her right foot gave out when she put too much weight on it, falling to her knees. "What are you?"

Daniel popped into existence next to Lady Sanerris and drove his fist down into her face. She dropped to the tile floor, limp.

Daniel rubbed his fist, Gertrude still strapped to his back. "He's Orrin. I'm Daniel. You fuckers should learn to stop messing with us already."

Arvin's scream of rage turned Daniel and Orrin's attention back to the pristinely dressed man. He clapped his palms together and . . . pulled the air. Orrin had no other way to describe it. A spell unlike anything Orrin had witnessed before began to form in front of the man.

Lady Tonsa danced around the room, using yellow balls of magic that splattered against the time-warp spells that still remained. Each target took multiple hits before fading. Finley abandoned his daggers and cast blasts of fire that exploded near Arvin's first spell missiles. Each landed nearly perfectly, turning the drifting balls of death away from the rest of the group.

A cry ripped from Lord Sanerris as he cast his spell. Orrin tried to read the magic again, grasping the barest elements of the mana before it struck Finley in the middle of throwing a blast of air. Finley froze in time. Lady Tonsa raised her eyebrows and abandoned the fight. She made it three steps toward the door, blown off its hinges by Orrin's rebounded magic before getting caught in the time spell. Niels threw Lord Wellan back, but it was too late for either of them. Lord Palmer reached the broken door, nearly tripping over Lady Sanerris's supine form. His hands reached for freedom before he too was enveloped and stopped moving. Like statues, the fighting force was frozen in time.

Daniel darted in front of Orrin, laughing. He pointed Gertrude at Arvin and shouted, "I've been waiting to try this on you."

A shadow of darkness surrounded Daniel in inky blackness before adjusting into a translucent sphere. Daniel glanced over his shoulder to make sure Orrin was inside. Orrin ignored everything else and tried to read the magic of Arvin's spell right up to the last moment. He had no counter to time magic, but if he could understand it, there might be a chance.

The wave reached them and nothing happened.

"Don't move a muscle," Daniel whispered. "On my signal."

Orrin kept still, trusting Daniel. He tried to see the spell that Daniel was using but could no more grasp it than Lord Sanerris's time magic. All he knew was Arvin's spell had not worked on them. Within the sphere, Orrin and Daniel were safe.

"I have been forced to use that spell twice since I unlocked it." Arvin huffed with exertion as he walked toward the still figures of Finley and Lady Tonsa. Tears of frustration filled Niels's eyes but wouldn't fall as the large man watched Arvin stand in front of his employer. "It is not pleasant to use."

Arvin knelt down and picked up one of Finley's daggers. "It's unfortunate that the [Hero] showed up during our council meeting and killed everyone in a rage."

The movements were quick. A few thrusts into Finley and a slash at Lady Tonsa's throat. A thin line of blood appeared along the wounds. He kicked the vines on the ground that had stopped moving as he approached Maeve's father. He left the dagger in the eye slot of the man's helmet.

Arvin tsked as he skipped back across the room. "Palmer, you rascal. I needed your men and your tracking abilities. I'll have to use someone inferior to find my target. Dey will be able to repel the Demon Lord. They are not the largest threat to us."

Orrin ground his teeth. *What are you waiting for, Daniel?*

Arvin kicked the lord of Idrisid in the head. His eyes found a nearby arrow that had missed him earlier. "Poetic."

Orrin took a half step forward as Arvin stabbed the arrow into Lord Palmer's heart.

Arvin looked up in confusion, his eyes widening. Daniel moved quickly, two steps bringing him within striking range.

Gertrude swung down in an overhand strike. Arvin's raised hand deflected the blade.

"How?"

Daniel attacked again, his giant sword moving through the air with a whistle. Each strike hit Arvin's shield, which seemed to cover him head to toe.

"You should be frozen in time," Arvin muttered, finally coming out from his daze. He pulled his sword and moved to strike.

Orrin hit the man with as many debuffs as he could. Arvin's shield flickered, and he stumbled.

Daniel's next strike glanced off Arvin's shoulder.

"His shield goes down if I hit him with enough spells," Orrin yelled, keeping Daniel between himself and the advancing time mage. "Try to time it with me."

"Now," Daniel shouted as he swung. Orrin recast his spells, using the moments in between to cast [Heal Small Wounds] on each person in the room. They might be dead, but if even one of them survived, the extra mana expenditure would be worth it.

The problem with announcing each attack became apparent as Arvin simply dodged the attacks now. Orrin had to give it to the man—with his best spells rendered useless, he still attacked with his sword. All of Daniel's training and system skills worked overtime as the blond man attacked with feints and thrusts that Daniel barely turned away. Arvin blocked one cut with his sword and almost lost hold of his weapon from the strength behind Daniel's attack. He didn't make the same mistake again.

Arvin skipped back and raised his hand, casting something. Orrin saw a bit more of the magical pattern before it fizzled against Daniel's sphere. Lord Sanerris cursed and glanced at the door.

"You aren't getting away, Sanerris," Daniel challenged him, using his foot to shove Arvin's mom away from the door. He planted his feet and raised his sword at the man, an avenging angel burning with anger. "You fucked with my friends. You made me fight in your pointless war. All to grow your own power. This ends today."

"If you kill me, all of Asmea will be overrun," Arvin said as he kept Daniel occupied with light attacks of his own. "The Demon Lord is just the beginning. They mean to end us all. The One Who Seeks won't stop. He hates humanity and will bring an end to our way of life. You should be working for me, not against me."

Orrin didn't know who the One Who Seeks was or if Arvin was making up some new distraction. He'd bet on the latter, as the man kept one hand behind his back. A small stream of mana was working its way into a new spell. The different aspects worked together in a similar way as Arvin's other spells. It almost seemed . . .

Orrin heard the ding of the system. No new notification popped up, but a quick check of the store showed a blinking cursor near his Spells selection.

> **[Time Ward]—Creates a ward around yourself and your party within 50 feet that protects against time magic. 20 MP. -1 AP**

Did I just break the system? Orrin assumed his study of Arvin's mana manipulation had given him enough understanding of the magic field to trigger a new ward type. He'd always needed to buy the spell before, but it made sense—the system gave him an inherently deeper knowledge about the magic type when he purchased a spell. *Could I just study different forms of magic to unlock more wards?*

Daniel tried attacking again, but Arvin's sword skills outmatched the [Hero]. He was slippery and damn near omniscient.

Orrin purchased the spell and cast it.

A bellow from behind them made all three turn.

Rhys had been in their party. Orrin had completely forgotten the young man was still in the room and covered by his initial [Camouflage Ward].

"You killed my mother," Rhys screamed. His glaive appeared in his hand, and bladed projectiles flew across the room. "You killed Niels. I'm going to murder you."

Arvin deflected the first two metal blades that were thrown and cast the spell he'd been preparing. The spell was similar to his earlier floating balls of death but condensed into one fast-moving ball of magic. It hit Rhys in the chest.

"The entire Tonsa family gone in one night," Arvin spat. "Such a waste of talent."

The next blade bounced away from Arvin's shield. He recovered quickly, but Orrin moved faster, hitting him with a round of debuff spells. Rhys landed three blades into center mass.

Arvin yanked the metal from his chest and narrowly dodged Daniel's next attack. His eyes widened as Rhys advanced, unharmed.

Daniel and Rhys positioned themselves on either side of Arvin, harrying the man back toward the corner of the room. Neither alone was Arvin's equal in combat, but together, and with Orrin knocking his shield down from time to time, blood flowed from multiple cuts. Arvin let Rhys hit him more, as Daniel's swings were backed by enough strength to break through his sword if he parried properly.

Orrin evened the field more by casting buffs on Rhys. His glaive overshot its target, and Rhys ducked to avoid a riposte from Arvin. His body literally hit the ground and bounced.

"Your stats are increased. You can move faster and hit harder," Orrin explained.

The fight took a turn for Arvin as the two men badgered him in turn. His spells fizzled against Orrin's constant upkeep of wards, and the long reach of both weapons outpaced his own shortsword.

"I surre—"

Gertrude struck Arvin's arm just as his shield went down. The sword clattered to the floor. The tip of Rhys's glaive pierced through his chest a moment later.

Arvin Sanerris, former chancellor of Mistlight and ruler of Odrana, was dead before his head hit the floor.

Chapter 56

Orrin ignored the cascade of dings that rang through his mind, focusing on the dying men and women around him. He sighed in relief as [Diagnose] and [Identify] confirmed everyone had been kept in a stasis of near-death, with his earlier castings of [Heal Small Wound] giving him a chance to save lives.

Arvin's spell had frozen everyone in time, and Orrin had hoped they wouldn't die until released. It was a risky bet, but he trusted Daniel. His friend had told him not to move. He valued Daniel's life and his own over anyone else in the room. With the enemy down and the spell broken, cries of pain and shouts for help rang out.

Orrin glanced at the nearest body. Lord Palmer's back rose as he inhaled ragged breaths, freed from Arvin's spell. [Diagnose] told Orrin about his specific injuries, including broken bones and a punctured lung. Nothing immediately life-threatening, as Arvin had missed the strike to the heart.

To the right, Niels held a ripped piece of Lady Tonsa's dress against her neck, trying to stanch the blood. The wound was deep, and the cloth was turning dark fast. Finley held his stomach in a grimace, but the multiple stab wounds didn't appear to require immediate attention. He was in pain but not dying yet.

Lord Wellan weakly reached a hand up to his face but missed as he struggled to grab the knife still embedded in his eye. Blood poured from under the man's helmet, coursing over his chest in a steady stream.

"Lord Wellan, don't touch the knife," Orrin ordered as he ran forward. The statuses from [Diagnose] worried him more than the others—[Perforated Optic Nerve] and [Prefrontal Cortex Laceration]. Orrin remembered enough anatomy to know Maeve's dad had a brain injury. He'd seen enough pop culture movies about lobotomies to worry about the man wiggling the knife. "Daniel, Rhys. Hold him down. I need to heal him and remove the knife as carefully as possible."

"Heal my mother, Orrin," Rhys demanded. "Lord Wellan can wait."

Orrin blasted nearly two hundred points of mana at Lady Tonsa as he ran, closing her sliced neck in a few seconds. "She'll survive. Niels, give her one of these." Orrin pulled a healing potion from his [Dimension Hole] and tossed it to the man. The bodyguard snatched it from the air and gently poured it into Lady Tonsa's mouth. Her coughing fits eased a bit.

Lord Wellan was strong, but Rhys and Daniel held his arms tight as Orrin dumped as many [Heal Small Wounds] as he could. He cast a few [Purify] spells for good measure. Orrin was glad the man wore a helmet. The grating screech of the knife against the eyehole as Orrin slowly removed it drowned out the squishing sounds behind the mask.

"You both stood back and watched this happen," Rhys accused. "If my mother or Lord Wellan die—"

"It'll be because you didn't shut up and help," Orrin snapped. "Daniel saved us. You got your revenge. Arvin is dead. Stop being a dick, Rhys, and hold him down."

Orrin focused his mana behind the eye, willing things to knit themselves back together. Lord Wellan's breathing evened out, and he stopped struggling after a minute. Orrin kept healing until the man spoke.

"Take care of the others, son. I'm through the worst."

Orrin nodded and checked on Lady Tonsa, making sure to heal the puckering red scar along her throat. Niels's hand was atrophied but moving, so Orrin moved to Finley.

"You never really tried in Battle Class, did you?" Finley choked out, coughing some blood on Orrin. "I demand another match."

Orrin rolled his eyes. "You're lucky that asshole sucks at killing people. He missed everything important." Orrin focused on letting the magic spread across the deep stab wounds, finding the mana move a little easier to the places he willed it. *All this healing is good practice, I guess.*

"I have to apologize again. It doesn't matter why you stood still. All that matters is you saved everyone," Rhys said gently.

Daniel was searching the room and was close enough to overhear. "Rhys, right? I told Orrin not to move. My spell takes a minute to spread out. We moved when we could and not a moment later."

"I'm going to want to hear all about this new spell later," Orrin sighed at his friend. Daniel dragged Arvin's body to the side of the room.

"Nothing to tell really. [Space Domain]. I can—"

"Later, D. Stop telling everyone your secrets."

A moan from the side of the room pulled Orrin's attention away. "I better heal him, too."

Lord Palmer reached a hand toward Orrin. His earlier search for what was wrong with the man had shown injuries, but nothing life-threatening. A yank on the buried wooden shaft just to the left of Palmer's spine brought the arrow out of his lung. Two [Heal Small Wounds] with Orrin's still-boosted will closed the bleeding hole, with his light concussion cured by [Purify].

"Thank you, young man." Lord Palmer slowly moved to his knees and stayed sitting on the ground. "I owe you a—"

"Daniel, what are you doing?" Orrin ignored Palmer.

"What does it look like? I'm tying up the prisoner," Daniel said, holding a rope he'd found over Lady Sanerris's unconscious form.

Orrin double-checked to make sure Anabella was alive and actually out cold. Daniel's punch had been backed by his fully buffed strength, but with her high level, Orrin was worried she might have recovered already. She wasn't faking, but ropes were not going to hold Anabella Sanerris. He considered for a moment before pulling something from his [Dimension Hole].

"Lady Tonsa, do you know how to use one of these?" Orrin held up his slave collar. He'd picked it up after Professor Wren deactivated it, thinking he would study it later to figure a way out. He was never going to let someone collar him again. However, this would be the best solution to control the woman for now. He had no idea how she would react when she woke to find out her son was dead.

"They are not hard to use," the woman replied in a soft voice. "I will accept responsibility for her imprisonment."

"That okay with you, D?" Orrin nudged his friend.

"Hmm? Yeah, sure."

"Daniel?"

"Shut up, I'm reading."

Orrin handed the collar to Lady Tonsa and opened his own notifications.

> **Quest Complete**
> **Stop the War in Odrana**
> **Reward: 200,000 XP and 3 stat points**

That is a stupid amount of experience, but we did almost die. Extra stat points are always nice. I don't remember that as the Quest reward. Orrin's eyes widened as the levels came in. *Holy shit, I did the math wrong.*

> **Experience Gained: 200,000 XP**
> **Level 20 obtained!**
> **+10 AP**
> **Level 21 obtained!**
> **+10 AP**
> **...**

Orrin scrolled to the bottom.

> **...**
> **Level 31 obtained!**
> **+10 AP**

Another blue box appeared immediately after he closed the last one. He continued reading.

Congratulations on obtaining Level 20!
10 stat points have been awarded.
Congratulations on obtaining Level 30!
10 stat points have been awarded.
Usable Stats for Utility Warder:
Strength
Constitution
Dexterity
Will
Intelligence

I miscalculated. I just earned twelve levels and a hundred and twenty ability points. I need to figure out some things and spend these points before we fight the demons. And another twenty-three stat points? I could put them all into my will and have a base of fifty-one. Maybe I should even my stats out a bit, though . . . or should I put everything into constitution? I can't buff that, and having a larger health base could let me get into the fight without too worrying as much. Orrin pushed the thoughts aside for now.

Quest Complete:
Obtain Level 20
Reward: [Hero Kit Level 3] Unavailable Reward

More? Oh, shit. Not this again . . .

Quest Reward Unavailable
Debug
Error
Administrator Access Override
Reward List Patch

Select your reward:
Upgrade one spell or skill
Increase Strength Stat +5
Increase Constitution Stat +5
Increase Dexterity Stat +5
Increase Will Stat +5
Increase Intelligence Stat +5
+10 Ability Points
Change Class

Orrin looked at his status and whistled. "Daniel, now I know why you've been quiet. This is crazy."

Reward List Patch is new. Maybe the system remembered what I did last time?

Orrin looked over his selection. With the ability points that he had before, he now had a hundred and thirty-eight total to spend in the store. The points that he had scrimped and saved so long for were now a drop in the bucket. He felt rich. *I would buy a bunch of spells for new wards, but after what happened with Sanerris . . . maybe I should save these for something better. I can get a sword skill!*

He also had twenty-three stat points to assign, or twenty-eight if he picked a stat-increase reward. The level-twenty Quest rewards were the same as they had been when Orrin hit level ten. He was already flush with ability points and saw no reason to add another ten on top. There was no way that Orrin was changing his class. Upgrading a spell or skill might be useful, but his build was unique already. He was never going to find someone who could tell him the possibilities that upgrading [Increase Will] or [Ward] would bring.

Picking where to assign the points wasn't easy. He looked at his status.

Orrin	**Utility Warder Level 31 (15,918/23,000)**	**Ability Points: 138 Administrator Points: 23**

HP: 140/140	MP: 954/1,100	
Strength: 9 (100)	Constitution: 14	Dexterity: 11 (100)
Will: 28 (100)	Intelligence: 11 (100)	

As much as he wanted to put one point into strength to round it out to a double-digit number, Orrin refrained. *Strength doesn't help me. I can boost it. It's going to be between will and constitution.*

Intelligence would reduce the cost of his first spells, but Orrin didn't care about a negligible amount of mana when he could max his intelligence out with buffs and wait a minute for [Meditation] to cap his MP again. Dexterity would let Orrin move quicker, but if he couldn't use his [Increase Dexterity] spell with the speed of his mind, the extra speed of his feet wasn't going to make a difference.

Will was the sexy stat to Orrin. It made his spells and buffs better. It gave him a bigger mana pool to draw from, which could come in handy if he needed to blood cycle. He hadn't needed to use the combination of healing and [Blood Mana] for a while, but every bit of help would be welcome when they fought a Demon Horde.

Orrin remembered the orc teacher, Professor Hugh, arguing the merits of a higher constitution. Enemy spell attacks would do less damage overall with a higher constitution score. Someone in the class had also mentioned keeping the spellcasting stats near the same number for greater synergy. Orrin wasn't sure about the reason behind that. Anabella had also mentioned to Orrin that a higher constitution would help a person acclimate quicker to his buffs. A higher constitution would mean he could use the full power of a level–one hundred strength or run faster than the wind with a maxed-out dexterity.

Orrin selected the plus-five constitution for the level-twenty Quest before he could talk himself out of it. He put two points into will to bring it to thirty and eleven into constitution. Part of him wanted to split the remaining ten between strength and intelligence for nice clean numbers, but he resisted.

Should I split them or go all in? The logical thing to do was go all in on constitution. It was the only stat that Orrin couldn't buff. Orrin went with his gut and put the last ten into will.

HP: 300/300	MP: 991/1,100	
Strength: 9 (100)	Constitution: 30	Dexterity: 11 (100)
Will: 40 (100)	Intelligence: 11 (100)	

"We need to complete more Quests," Orrin muttered. "That was insane."

Chapter 57

"Daniel, are you still leveling up?" Orrin watched as his friend's eyes darted through the air, reading his status. "That was an insane amount of experience."

Daniel held up a finger. "Too. Much. Math."

Orrin waited patiently, ignoring the whispers between the chancellors of Odrana. Finley hobbled over gingerly, holding his stomach.

"Thanks for the healing. I thought I was done for," Finley said as he came to a stop next to Orrin. "You two are acting like you leveled. You're not demons, right?"

Orrin shook his head. The rumor was that demons could kill other sentient beings for experience. That wasn't the case for anyone else. "We're human. We had a Quest. I'm surprised you know that much about demons, though. Not everyone knows as much. Are you still hurt? I can heal you more."

Orrin raised his hand, but Finley stopped him. "I'm fine. Full health, but I keep expecting to feel the pain again. My body is clenching in anticipation of pulling a wound open that isn't there anymore. It's a weird feeling, I'll tell you."

Lady Tonsa spoke sharp words to Rhys and gestured. The young man pulled his sleeves down as he left her side and moved toward Orrin and Finley.

"Be kind. I'm not sure the boy has killed before," Finley whispered quickly.

Rhys stopped and bowed a few feet from them.

"Thank you for saving our lives," Rhys said while looking at the ground. "For the second time, no less. I don't know what spells you cast, but you gave me the opportunity to defend my family and my country. My family and I owe you and the [Hero] a debt that we can never repay."

Orrin closed the gap and grabbed Rhys's shoulder. He gently tugged him upright, waiting for Rhys to meet his eyes. "You fought well. None of us would be here if you hadn't helped Daniel take that man down. There is no debt between friends."

Rhys smiled in disbelief. "My mother would like to speak with you and Daniel when you are ready. She plans to send Niels with Lord Palmer to the front lines immediately and end all aggression with the elven community. From what we've learned here, reparations may be necessary."

Orrin saw Lord Palmer standing nearby, eyes nervously scanning the broken door to freedom. He had his suspicions about what the man knew, but they'd completed the Quest. Getting more involved in the politics of Odrana was not on his to-do list. "We'll stay for a quick chat, but we need to get back to Dey. The Demon Lord is still coming."

Rhys went back to tell the remaining chancellors his words. Finley stretched his arms above his head and yawned.

"Tired?"

"I've been awake for almost two days, Orrin," Finley complained. "I'm going to get someone to magic me home as soon as this is over. My father can take this job back. A good fight is one thing, but all the political nonsense is boring."

Daniel signaled he was done and motioned to the hallway outside the broken door.

"I'll be back. Can you keep everyone from listening in on us?" Orrin asked. "I did save your life, too."

Finley rolled his eyes and pushed Orrin gently toward the exit. "No debt between friends, or was that bullshit? Go on, I'll keep them busy. Tell Daniel that I want a rematch before you kick off back to Dey. Would you also put in a good word with the lords of Dey for me? I want to join the fight with the demons."

"Sure, Fin."

Daniel was waiting when Orrin approached.

"Did you get the Quest?" his friend whispered as soon as they were close.

"What? What Quest?" Orrin frantically searched his system messages but saw nothing.

"Damn it," Daniel muttered. "Did you go up too many levels? Never mind, I used [Identify]. Good for you, man. I tried to share the level-thirty Quest with you, but I guess the experience from the war Quest hit too fast."

Orrin's eyes opened wide. "I missed out on an extra five points for stats?"

"You worked your Administrator mojo on the level-twenty Quest, didn't you?" Daniel smiled. "Here, I can share the level-forty Quest."

Daniel, Hero Level 33, is sharing a Quest.
Quest: Obtain Level 40
Reward: [Hero Kit Level 5] Unavailable Reward
Would you like to accept it?
Yes or No

"Did you get all your weapon skills up to level four?" Orrin asked, jealous of his friend's growth. "Level thirty-three is pretty good."

Daniel confirmed his new skills with a wide grin. "I also have over a hundred ability points again. I had used most of mine up."

"Me, too. I was trying not to buy anything new while I was a prisoner. I was worried that the collar might fuck with them somehow, or someone would learn I could buy more spells. What was that sphere thing you did?"

Daniel's hand clenched into a fist when Orrin mentioned the collar, but his eyes shone bright when he asked about his new ability.

"It's called [Black Hole]. It's only at level one and uses almost my entire mana pool, but it creates an impenetrable shield against magic attacks for me and any party member within range. Madi's never heard of it before, and I'm half convinced I got it as an option after level twenty because of you." Daniel spoke with increasing excitement. "I was getting jealous thinking about your [Ward] ability and then . . . poof . . . I have this new spell I can purchase. It kept Sanerris from hitting us. Any spell he cast gets sucked in and disappears. I was surprised that the Rhys kid was within range. I thought he was too far away."

Orrin thought back to the magic Arvin had cast at Rhys. It hadn't disappeared in the fizzled way the attacks against Daniel had. "I think my new ward protected him, not your new spell. He was behind me by a bit when you cast it."

Daniel cocked his head to the side. "Your new [Ward]?"

Orrin explained the best he could the appearance of [Time Ward] in the middle of the fight. "Maybe I was just lucky again. It felt like I could see the magic."

Daniel punched Orrin on the arm. "I told you to pay better attention in school. You're a genius. You've got to teach me to see mana, too."

Orrin let out a sigh of relief. Unconsciously, he had worried that Daniel might resent him taking his thunder. "Your spell saved the day. If Arvin had frozen us all in time . . ."

"Rule one is survive. We made it through." Daniel squinted playfully at Orrin. "Now, if someone would stop breaking rule two and stay by my side . . ."

Orrin huffed in feigned annoyance. "So what did you end up increasing? I'm betting more strength for the meathead jock."

Daniel shook his head. "Take a look. This meathead is learning."

Orrin used [Identify]

Daniel	Hero Level 33 6,305/27,000	Ability Points: 114
HP: 436/440	MP: 20/150	
Strength: 30	Constitution: 22	Dexterity: 20
Will: 15	Intelligence: 10	

He's evened out his stats a bit but still avoiding more intelligence. Orrin considered Daniel's build. It didn't make sense for him to use spells that often, focusing more on his stamina-based skills.

"I'm proud of you. It must have been hard to make the smart choice and not dump every point into strength."

Daniel beat his fists on his chest, making gorilla noises. "I'm dumb and strong. Only Orrin is smart."

Orrin held up his hands. "Yeah, yeah. I get it. You can make good choices on your own."

A flash of something went through Daniel's eyes, but he forced a fake smile. "Now that you're back in the party, I'll never increase anything but strength."

Orrin remembered too late Madi's story of the townsfolk outside the elven forest. An awkward silence settled between them.

"I can [Teleport] us back. Lady Tonsa wanted to speak with you before we go."

Daniel sighed. "This is why I keep Madi around. She keeps the fans at bay."

Orrin ignored Daniel's comment and led him back into the room.

Rhys's mom spent the next hour apologizing to Daniel and Orrin for the failures of their council to see through the deception of the Sanerris family. She made comments at times that sounded like an attempt to foster a closer relationship with Daniel—and Dey, in turn—but Orrin had decided to let Daniel do the talking.

Daniel did no talking.

Lord Wellan's chuckles became more pronounced as time went on until he interrupted Lady Tonsa. "Oyinlola, that's enough. He is smart enough to not commit to anything. Arvin destroyed our chances of a good relationship with the [Hero]. Perhaps, in time, we can prove ourselves."

Orrin nudged Daniel.

Daniel sighed. "I have little faith in your country, it's true. That doesn't mean that the people of Dey would turn away help. The Demon Lord is coming to attack. We have begun our planned response and have elven forces training anyone who can lift a spear or shoot a bow. Maybe you can reach out to Lord Catanzano and find a way to redeem yourselves."

Finley crossed his arms. "I'll fight with you, Daniel."

Rhys peeked out from behind his mom. "I'll see to it that Goldenhall sends fighters to Dey. Maybe I'll come, too."

"You will do no such thing," Rhys's mother said sternly. "You are in enough trouble as it is."

Orrin coughed to hide his laugh. Rhys might be about the same age as them, but his mom treated him like a child. Niels tightened his lips, not willing to call out the man who had saved his life and the lives of nearly everyone in the room.

"Your son is a decent fighter. Don't hide him away. If we fail at turning the demons back at the Pass, you might need him to defend Odrana when the armies turn their sights farther east," Daniel said calmly, ignoring Orrin.

Lord Palmer spoke next. "If you can keep my men separate from the elves, I can send scouts out and bolster your main fighting force as well."

Lord Wellan, not to be upstaged, stepped in front of Palmer. "We in Ceraun will send food and a few small herds to Dey, free in their time of need. Any volunteers to fight for Asmea from my lands will be given a stipend for their time away."

The two men began one-upping each other, offering more each turn. Daniel clapped once. A loud echo tore through the room.

"Discuss with Lord Catanzano what is needed. I appreciate the gestures. We need to be going, but what are your plans for . . . her?"

Orrin glanced at the still-unconscious form of Lady Sanerris. Anabella, his captor, looked smaller with the collar around her neck. He shivered, still not fully comfortable with using the evil thing. He reached up and rubbed his own neck.

"She will be tried for her actions and likely those of her son. Despite her power, she committed treason. Her sentence will be death," Lord Wellan said, sorrow in his voice. "It will be a loss. Anabella Sanerris pushed our magical education system to great heights."

"She also helped kidnap Orrin and enslaved him," Daniel seethed. "She killed more to cover her tracks."

Orrin remembered the men who'd tried to kill him and shivered.

"She will answer for all her crimes." Lady Tonsa answered Daniel's unspoken question. "But we cannot execute her twice."

Orrin briefly considered bringing up an argument against capital punishment but fought his urge to argue. This was a world of magic, intrigue, and new situations. He was learning his old way of thinking wasn't going to keep him alive. He cast [Purify] on everyone he had buffed as he shook hands with Lord Wellan and Niels.

Finley and Rhys exchanged goodbyes with Orrin before the friends left the building. As soon as they were free from the teleport wards in the room, Orrin used his spell. A few more casts of [Teleport] and Orrin stood in front of the Catanzanos' manor with Daniel. The dark sky would hold the night captive for another hour or two, but soon the sun would rise and the city of Dey would start a new day. Orrin hoped it had more than a few new days left.

"What are you thinking?" Daniel asked quietly, watching his friend closely. "How are you feeling?"

Orrin hadn't turned on [Mind Bastion] for a while. He liked the rush of emotions he felt as they walked the cobbled street. The joy and relief of freedom. The worry about the future. The solid friendship at his side. The despair at the death of such a powerful man who could have been a strong ally.

"I'm tired," Orrin answered truthfully.

Daniel stopped their walk by grabbing Orrin's arm. "If you need anything, I'm here. Madi and Brandt are as well."

Orrin scuffed his toe against a raised stone in the street. "There is something . . . but no, it can wait."

"What do you need, O?"

Orrin looked up at his friend, the concern evident. Orrin almost felt bad when he answered.

"Can we get some coffee?"

Chapter 58

Orrin sat at the dining room table inside the Catanzano house, letting the steam from his mug soak his face. He breathed in deep, ignoring Daniel as he butchered his cup of coffee with heaping scoops of sugar and milk.

"Tell me everything that's happened since you were taken," Daniel said, settling into a chair next to Orrin. "We've got two or three hours before people start waking up. I want to hear it all."

"We could get some sleep," Orrin offered up, taking a sip. "I'm sure Silas has a lot of things planned for you to do tomorrow."

"Fuck that. We can sleep in as late as we want. Talk to me." Daniel's face showed his concern.

So, Orrin talked, telling Daniel about his time with Arvin and then Anabella. He glossed over his fear and anxiety during his captivity and instead told Daniel about what he'd learned. He spoke of Graem, Wren, and his other professors. He told Daniel about the classes he'd taken and the friends he'd made. Daniel had met a few of them, but Orrin found himself laughing as he told Daniel about finding Ellis outside his room. The danger of the assassination attempt had been tempered with time and retelling his friend over a hot cup of coffee. By the time he finished explaining a few bits and pieces of magical theory, Orrin felt better than he had in weeks.

"Sorry I talked so much."

Daniel drank some of his abomination before speaking. "I'm glad you're alive. For a bit, I thought . . . It doesn't matter. You're here. Until we have to go fight again."

"What have you been up to?" Orrin asked, uncomfortable with Daniel's morose attitude. "You guys didn't spend the entire time fighting troops and looking for me, right?"

Daniel's eyes stared past Orrin.

"D?"

"I'm tired, too, Orrin. The kind of tired that can't be fixed with extra sleep. We've been here for months with nothing to show for it but more power and magic. What if we defeat the Demon Lord and nothing happens? Do we get more Quests and keep leveling up? Solving more problems in this world? Fighting stupid old people who don't care about anything but more power? I miss my family, man."

Daniel slumped in his chair. "I want to go home."

Orrin reached out to cast [Calm Mind] on Daniel but stopped before the magic coalesced. Magic was not the answer to this problem. He could push Daniel's feelings down like [Mind Bastion] did for him, but it wasn't healthy for either of them. "Other than your family, what's the thing you miss the most about home?"

"O, we might never find a—"

"Humor me," Orrin interrupted before he could finish the sentence. "We hop through a portal or cast some big spell. Poof! We're back in front of Cara's house, with no stupid trucks in sight. What do you do?"

Daniel sighed and shrugged his shoulders. "I don't know. Get a milkshake?"

"You'd walk off from your girlfriend's house and get food?" Orrin asked in surprise. "Seriously?"

"I mean, in this scenario, did she move on after we died? Or did we die? I think getting hit by a truck would kill us, right?"

Orrin had considered this a lot as he struggled to fall asleep at night. They'd been naked when they arrived, not covered in blood. "Maybe, but we're alive here. If . . . When we get back, we can figure out a story. Nobody is going to believe we've been living in a world of magic. If there were bodies, then Cara was lucky."

"What? Why?" A small light burst back in his friend's eyes. "She'd have seen us get crushed by a truck. That's traumatic as fuck."

Orrin downed the rest of his coffee before answering. "If we disappeared, she'd have told the police or our parents that a truck ran into us and then we were gone. That's how people end up in the mental ward of a hospital. Delusions or hallucinations—I'm not sure what the doctors would call it. Either way, I guess you wouldn't have a girlfriend."

"I'm on a different planet. I don't think I've had a girlfriend for a while."

"A shake, though?"

"I miss ice cream."

Orrin snorted a laugh.

"What would you do, then?"

Orrin didn't have to think long. "Go with you for a shake. You can't be trusted alone."

Daniel kicked his chair, missing Orrin's leg.

"I'm serious. You'd try to get a banana shake or something gross. How could I ever live with myself . . . Hey, don't throw coffee at me," Orrin said with a laugh as Daniel picked up his mug and feigned tossing it at Orrin.

Orrin was glad to see his friend smirk.

"You're stupid."

Orrin shrugged and considered another coffee, but he could feel the fatigue in his bones. *When was the last time I slept?*

"Want to get some sleep?" Daniel said, watching him closely. "You look like you're about to drop."

Orrin nodded and stood. The exhaustion hit, and only a few castings of [Heal Small Wounds] got him to their room. He listened to Daniel toss and turn but drifted off to sleep before he could do anything about it.

"Wake up, you two. It's a beautiful day and we've got training to do." Madi's voice chipped away at Orrin's grogginess. Her enthusiasm was too damn much for this early in the morning.

"We need more sleep," Daniel complained, throwing a pillow at her.

Madi caught the projectile and threw it right back at Daniel. "It's already noon. You've slept enough. The guards said you came in early this morning. I'd ask if the plan worked, but I woke up to a very nice surprise."

Orrin put his head under his pillow and pushed the edges in against his ears. "Too early."

Madi pouted a little and sat on Orrin's bed. "Don't you want to know?"

"Madi, we fought that asshole and his mother. I don't know how long Orrin went without sleep, but you said you know what time we got back. Whatever you want can wait," Daniel said, sitting up in bed. "One more hour."

"Fine." Madi reached over and ruffled Daniel's hair. "But only because I'm in such a good mood. You ended the war, after all."

Orrin bent his pillow and glared at Madi. "You got all the experience, didn't you?"

Madi smiled wickedly. "I'll be back in an hour."

Orrin groaned and sat up. His feet hurt. He'd forgotten to take off his shoes. He glanced at Madi and used [Identify].

Madeleine Catanzano	**Superior Prism Conjurer Level 29**	
HP: 130	**MP: 200**	
Strength: 10	**Constitution: 13**	**Dexterity: 12**
Will: 20	**Intelligence: 20**	

"Damn, we timed that right, didn't we?" Orrin whistled.

Madi gave Orrin a funny look. "You planned this? I didn't even think about the Quest. I was planning on going out with Brandt for low-level monster exterminations today. I went to bed at level one. It's a terrifying feeling being so weak again. The new class you gave me even earned more ability points per level and more stat points at levels ten and twenty. I'm stronger now than I was yesterday."

Orrin stretched and shook his head while yawning. "No, I didn't even think about the Quest until the system alerts at the end of our fight. Wait, didn't you have Daniel's level-twenty Quest as well?"

"Yes, but it has an unavailable reward. I was hoping if you had some time . . ." She trailed off.

"Sure, Madi. Let's grab some breakfast and you can pick your Quest reward." Orrin answered her unasked question as he looked around for a clean shirt.

Madi bounced from the room while Orrin left to take a shower and change into something that didn't smell like day-old blood and sweat. Daniel rolled over in the bed when he got back into their room.

"Get up. I need to get to the front of the Pass so I can [Teleport] back and forth. If this Demon Lord is coming, we can't sleep in again."

Daniel grumbled but left with soap and a towel. Orrin didn't wait for him and found Madi sitting next to her father in the dining room. Breakfast foods were piled high, with pastries, bacon, eggs, and a large carafe of coffee waiting by his seat.

Orrin frowned as he entered the room. "Isn't it noon? I hope this wasn't all for us."

Silas Catanzano, Madi's father and one of the rulers of Dey, put down the stack of papers he was reading through at hearing Orrin's voice. He wheeled himself from his spot at the head of the table and approached Orrin.

"I owe you a debt, Orrin." Silas's eyes pierced his own, holding his gaze. "You saved my knight. You prioritized my daughter's life and escaped at the expense of your own capture. You returned with Daniel after stopping a conflict well beyond my ability to interfere with. And somehow, I'm sure that I have you to thank for her . . . new power."

Orrin started to deny having any part of that, but Silas simply held up his hand.

"I've come to realize that my daughter will benefit from an open friendship with you more than any subterfuge or devices I could conceive. We've had our differences, and I admit my failings. If you will accept my apology, I promise to answer any questions you have in the future. You have but to ask and the full might of Dey will ride behind you and Daniel. If we survive the upcoming Horde, that is."

Orrin knew Silas had a half dozen reasons for his speech. Madi was already looking at her father in admiration. There was no downside to playing nice as he'd been doing all along. That didn't mean he'd trust Silas, but hopefully it meant no knives in his back in the meantime.

"Thanks, Lord Catanzano, but it was Madi who saved me. She and Daniel searched for me and I got lucky that a new friend recognized my description."

"Regardless, you have my ear should you need anything."

Orrin sat and ate, waiting for Daniel to join. Orrin enjoyed the fresh food and coffee while Daniel recounted the fight and outcome in Odrana. When he finished, Silas excused himself to report to the rest of the lords of Dey.

"If they are sending more troops, we may stand a chance. The last report I received said the Horde is within a week of the Pass. I'll be back as fast as I can be. Good luck." Silas left, gesturing for guards to follow.

"I guess it's time to go get some more sleep, right, Orrin?" Daniel asked, stretching his arms high in the air. "All that food made me tired again."

Orrin caught the wink. "I might go out and say hi to some friends. I haven't seen Tony or Amir and want to check—Ow!"

Madi picked up another cinnamon roll and held it menacingly. "I know you're both messing with me."

Orrin and Daniel laughed, with Madi joining in after a moment. Orrin found he'd missed her. She might be irritating at times, but underneath her upbringing and training was a kind woman who wanted to help others. She was just a bit misguided at times.

Orrin realized that could describe Daniel as well and sighed. *I surround myself with idiots.*

He had Madi open her Quest reward and received the same prompt as he had for Brandt in the Aqua Chambers all that time ago.

Unlocking Limited Reward Set for Nonadministrator_
Increase Will Stat +4
Increase Constitution Stat +4
Increase Intelligence Stat +4
+5 Ability Points

"I'd recommend bringing your constitution up," Orrin said, taking another look at her stat distribution. "I learned a few interesting things at the Sanerris School."

Madi raised an eyebrow. "What kind of things?"

Orrin smirked and summoned an [Ice Sword]. "Let's go out to the courtyard and I'll show you."

Chapter 59

Madi ducked as Orrin's combination of [Gust] and [Fire Sword] superheated the air above their heads.

"A new spell?" Daniel asked, leaning against one of the columns and peeling an orange. "That isn't a great argument for increasing constitution over strength."

Orrin considered using [Ice Sword] and [Gust] to freeze his friend in place, but Madi narrowed her eyes and moved between them.

"Stop with the childish antics, Orrin. What did you want to show us?" Madi held out her hand and Daniel tossed her a quarter of the orange.

"It's not a new spell. I'm combining two spells," Orrin protested. He remembered the first time he'd seen the flow of mana and slapped his forehead. "Have either of you tried to see your mana when casting a spell?"

Daniel raised an eyebrow. "What does that even mean?"

Orrin did his best to describe seeing the mana, using [Tilth] for his friends in an attempt to let them see what he could. He went over the lessons from both Wren and Anabella, leaving their names out from his explanation but cycling through different spell types. He had Daniel cast a few spells, but his friend couldn't see the magic.

"You don't see the way the mana comes out of your body in spirals?" Orrin pointed to the fading remnants of [White Dwarf].

Cracks in the tiles spidered out from under Daniel as he lifted a foot to inspect himself. "Nope. Nothing there."

Maybe an offensive spell would be easier for him to see? Orrin considered. [White Dwarf] increased Daniel's weight, making it harder to move him and increasing his own power output if he used his body as a weapon. *[Tilth] isn't an offensive spell, though, and I could see the mana while using it. If he can't . . .*

Orrin's thoughts trailed off as the spirals around Daniel began to form a pattern. It wasn't something he'd noticed at first. Just as Orrin felt he was about to figure it out, the mana disappeared.

"Daniel, cast that again." Orrin blinked his eyes, feeling a slight headache begin. He was so close to understanding the wibbly-wobbly spirals.

"Okay?" Daniel stretched out the word into an unasked question. He cast [White Dwarf] again.

A moment later, Orrin smiled at the sound of a ding in his mind.

> **[Space Ward]—Creates a ward around yourself and your party within 50 feet that protects against space magic. 20 MP. -1 AP**

"Yes. It wasn't a fluke!" Orrin cheered, to the confused glances from his friends, and purchased the new ward. He threw the new skill box to Daniel. "I can stop your attacks easier now."

"Did you buy a new space spell?" Daniel asked while reading.

"Nope. I figured out the mana of your spell. I told you that every magic type is unique. I might not have to buy spells anymore for new wards." Orrin used [Identify] on Daniel, searching his spell list. "I don't think you have any types of magic that I don't already know. I need to find a metal mage and maybe visit Tony. Maybe I can block his mind magic spells."

Madi took another bite of her orange slice. "Seeing the mana gives you that much of an understanding of the magic?"

Orrin shrugged. "Why don't you cast something and try to see the mana leaving your body?"

"[Sunbeam] might be overkill for a demonstration, and I haven't spent my ability points yet."

Orrin paused in his teaching attempt. "What? Why?"

Madi finished the last of her fruit and struck a pose of annoyance, her hand on her hip and her eyes boring into Orrin's. "You reset my class last night. I have plans but need to read a few books before spending points on anything."

"That's . . . a good idea. Did you not see anything from our spells?"

Madi shook her head.

"Orrin, if this is you pulling our leg . . ." Daniel trailed off as he threw the peel into a waste bin.

"I thought you two would be able to see it," Orrin muttered dejectedly. He knew that he'd skipped a class in school. Even Rhys was taking Sensing Magic before Mana Signatures. "Trust me. There's a way to see your magic spells. The mana is different as it forms for each type of magic. I guess I really am a prodigy at it for some reason. Once you can see the mana, there is a way to combine spells as you cast them. I take the air mana from my [Gust] spell and infuse the fire mana from [Fire Sword]. At first, I could only make a little hot air—"

"This sounds like hot air," Daniel whispered loudly to Madi.

"—but now I can heat my [Gust] to the point that it burns holes through people who interrupt me," Orrin finished.

"How does this help us, O?" Madi entreated. "We can't see the mana like you. We don't get new spell options like you from random spell purchases."

"You'll need to practice until you can see the mana. I'll contact Professor Wren and get her to help you two sense magic. It's the least they can do," Orrin said. He could [Teleport] the woman to Dey for personal lessons if needed. "I wanted you to see the magic in action, because it's easier to understand with the math."

Daniel glared at Orrin. "Now I know you're fucking with me."

Orrin shook his head. "There is some overlap in two of the classes I was taking. In one of them, we learned how every type of magic has a different signature. There's a core equation that each magic type relates to . . . but I'll explain that later. In the other class, we learned how different magic types interact with each other, like how fire magic is weak against water magic. There are mathematical equations that can balance that out if you force more mana into a spell or have higher stat points. It's all super interesting, but constitution plays an important role. Knowing your own spell and the structure of them helps in figuring out the best way to attack two different targets."

Orrin did his best to teach what he'd learned from Professor Hugh. Constitution gave more than health points—it increased your resilience to surviving attacks and let your body handle more powerful castings as well. Madi seemed interested in the formulas, at least.

He also explained the few bits and pieces that Anabella had taught him. The way that even a newly increased strength stat couldn't be fully utilized until a person acclimated. Constitution played a large part in the speed that Orrin's increase-stat spells or even a normally leveled-up stat could be used to the max.

"Madi should increase her constitution so she can survive attacks better and benefit more from your buffs?" Daniel asked.

Orrin reminded himself that his friend was not an idiot. He was smart when he wanted to be.

"That's like . . . the bare minimum of what I just explained. If you pay attention in a fight, you can use all this to figure out exactly how to win. Or know that you should run in an unwinnable scenario."

Daniel nodded and then grinned. "Or I could keep you by my side to do it for me. You tell me where to hit and I'll swing Gerty."

Orrin groaned as Madi covered a smile.

"I'm messing with you, O. This is super interesting, and I agree we should prioritize con a bit more. If I can use the entirety of a boosted one hundred strength, it'll be worth it. Oh, before I forget, I should share this," Daniel said as he waved his hand.

Obtain Level 40
Reward: [Hero Kit Level 5]

"Sorry, Madi. I can't share the level-thirty Quest."

She shrugged. "I'm grateful for what I have. I'm at a higher level than my father was at my age, and something tells me I'll keep growing if I keep you two around. Orrin, if you have a few minutes, I would love to write down some of those equations. It sounds a little like something Emily told me in the past, and I want to test a few things."

Orrin agreed. They spent time in the Catanzano library, with Daniel getting bored within the hour. He excused himself to train with one of the weapon masters that Silas kept finding for him. The morning passed quickly, and Madi also left.

"I'll be in my room until dinner," she confided in Orrin. "I've got spells and skills to buy."

Orrin sighed as he looked at his own ability and administrator points. He'd put it off for long enough. The fear that anything he bought would be sealed by the slave collar was fading, and he'd hoarded the points for long enough.

It's time to go shopping.

Orrin stayed in the library alone, his status screen open in front of him.

"I have one hundred and thirty-seven ability points. That's insane," he murmured as he checked over the skills and spells he had. "I should find a metal mage for a new ward. If it works, I might be able to get a ward for every magic type."

Orrin scratched some notes on a piece of paper. The store had thousands of spells, most of which were useless to him. He had no need for [Reheat], a spell used to increase the temperature of a liquid. [Protect Seed] would be immensely helpful to a farmer who needed to keep bugs away from his fields, but Orrin already had plant magic through [Tilth]. The crossover between plant and earth magic was something he hadn't studied at all, but if the one useless in combat spell wanted to count itself as both, Orrin was glad for a double ward.

Going through, he wrote down the fields of magic to investigate. To Daniel's dismay, he'd purchased the [Space Ward]. Metal and mind magic went on the list. After a few minutes of searching the store, Orrin found a few spells for lightning. While lightning could be a type of fire magic, he wrote it down anyway. He found glass, wood, shadow, and blood magic spells as well.

A thought scratched in the back of his mind, and he pulled up the Demon Lord Quest.

"Dark Essence as a reward. It might be another type of magic."

Orrin wrote it down on the list.

I can find some people down at the Guild who have the different types of magic I need. There's no reason to spend my points on anything useless if it works. I wonder why [Blood Mana] didn't give me a ward option.

Orrin cast a few buff spells, waiting for his mana to get low enough. He used [Blood Mana] slowly, trying to find the mana. He could feel something within himself changing but couldn't see the mana. He wrote "figure out blood?" on his list.

He looked at his spells and skills again. There were a few sub-skills of [Create Poison] that he could get, but there wasn't a particular need for that. [Alchemy] was still on his list of possible interesting things, but there were more important things to consider with the Demon Lord approaching.

Orrin could buy any spells or skills in the store. He thought about what to buy first. The way that he'd been fighting with wind magic and two swords had been born of necessity to hide himself at the Sanerris School, but he'd come to enjoy using the combination. He'd seen what even a few levels of knowledge in a weapon could bring watching Daniel.

> **[Sword Proficiency] Level 1—You are adept at using swords. -10 AP**
> **Would you like to purchase for 10 AP?**
> **Yes or No**

Orrin smiled as he selected yes and imagined Daniel's face during their next bout. He'd freeze him using the [Ice Sword] and [Gust] combination and tap him with the [Fire Sword].

"One hundred and twenty-seven left. This is going to take a while."

Chapter 60

The malicious grin on Orrin's face would have sent shivers down Daniel's spine if they'd still been in the same room. With his first big purchase out of the way, Orrin decided to let loose. He'd spent his captivity scared to make more purchases, worried that Anabella would find out he had points to spare and make him into a guinea pig for system knowledge. While he hadn't bought any spells or skills in Odrana, he had planned for the moment he escaped, biding his time.

This was his moment.

Orrin's offensive capabilities were finally coming along. Between his ability to combine [Gust] with his summoned swords and [Way of the Water], he'd taken down monsters in the Odrana dungeon by himself. He suspected that [Way of the Water] might have a surprise or two in store for him if only he spent the time to complete another few percentage points with Styx. He knew his powers were growing and felt that he could give Daniel a run for his money without using his debuff spells at this point.

Speaking of which, there were no more buffs or debuffs to buy. He'd upgraded [Decrease Dexterity] already. [Decrease Strength] was so close to level two that he could taste it.

I'd cast it on myself, but with my high will stat, there is a chance I knock myself out. Orrin shook his head at the thought of Daniel finding him choking on his own tongue.

His [Increase Strength] and [Increase Dexterity] skills were likewise close to the ten thousand experience mark, so he cast them both a few times as he looked through the rest of his status screen. He should be able to hit ten thousand in each within a few days.

[Heal Small Wounds] was available to upgrade. The elven healer Lyra had told him not to take [Heal Moderate Wounds] if he planned on taking other healing-type spells. The upgrade to his base healing spell would supposedly lock out other spells and healing paths. Anabella had told him that wasn't true, but Orrin trusted the person who hadn't set him up, enslaved him, and tried to murder him.

Orrin sorted the spells in the store by type. Healing magic gave a few options.

[Calm]—Calms the target. 5 MP. -2 AP
[Excise]—Remove corrupted area. 5 MP. -5 AP
[Numb]—Remove sensation from a localized area. 5 MP. -5 AP
[Heal Moderate Wounds]—Heal up to 100 HP. 40 MP. (Upgrade) -12 AP

"Is [Calm] a weaker version of [Calm Mind]?" Orrin asked the empty room. "I could spend my points on something better, but I want to see what else is available. I could help Amir figure out the best way to create different healing classes."

He imagined what Silas's face would do when he announced he was opening a free clinic. He purchased [Calm], [Excise], and [Numb]. *Another twelve points down.*

Orrin cracked his knuckles when he saw the low experience cost to upgrade each one of the new spells.

"I can do a hundred points of mana into each of you."

He cast [Calm] on himself. The experience tracker moved up, but he felt no change.

"Maybe I need to cast it on someone else?" He tried [Numb] next, pointing toward his arm.

Orrin immediately lost feeling from his wrist to his elbow. "That feels weird. Now to heal it."

Orrin cast [Heal Small Wounds] and frowned. "Shit."

His arm remained numb. He wasn't about to [Excise] himself, either, after that failure.

"I'll come back to healing later," Orrin muttered, looking at another spell blinking with an exclamation point. "I thought you didn't have an upgrade?"

> **[Remetabolize]—Change the toxicity and structure of a toxin. 50 MP (1,000/1,000)!**
> **Requirement met: [Create Poison] ability.**
> **Would you like to upgrade [Remetabolize] for 8 AP?**

Orrin read the box twice. "I guess I should have taken [Create Poison] first? What a joke. I'm not going to poison anyone."

Orrin's attempts at making acid had failed to get him out of the slave collar. He had no need for an enhanced version of [Remetabolize].

There were other spell modifiers that might help in battle. [Increase Durational Spell] might double the time of his buffs. If he went up and down the line of defenders, he could make an army of juggernauts for more than the twenty-minute timer he currently had available. [Far] would let him target enemies before they got close with debuffs.

Maybe I can split a debuff and hit an entire line of demons with [Decrease Strength] before they get near the Pass?

It took ten minutes for his arm to regain feeling. In that time, Orrin spent another eight ability points on the two spell modifiers.

> **[Increase Durational Spell]—(Spell Modifier) Modify a spell to increase duration. 5 MP. -4 AP**
> **[Far]—(Spell Modifier) Modify a spell to target double normal distance. 5 MP. -4 AP**

He smiled and reordered his status a bit to combine the new spells and skills. His eyes narrowed at two of his skills: [Analyze] and [Identify].

He used [Analyze] predominantly for inanimate objects. The more he knew about something, the more information he'd receive about it. He could spend time learning about the object with more use of the skill.

[Identify] was a system reward for saving Daniel's life. Since his early days on Asmea, he'd found there was an inferior version that most people had, whereas Orrin's [Identify] was upgraded to let him see a person's spells, skills, and general stats. It had come in handy on more than one occasion.

Orrin had tried to [Merge] the two once before, but no options came up. Instead, Orrin wanted to try something different. He'd once used [Mind Bastion] and [Analyze] to give himself data on his own injuries. It was essentially what [Diagnose] allowed him to do. If [Mind Bastion] enhanced one spell, then there was a chance it could do the same for the others.

Orrin turned [Mind Bastion] on, letting the cool relief flow. He felt more awake and remembered a half dozen things he'd forgotten to do. He quickly wrote down the list of people to visit and things to check up on before moving on to the main event.

I've never used [Merge] with [Mind Bastion]. I bet it would give me amazing skills. Logical analysis or the ability to control spells with my mind. Why have I never tried this before? Orrin felt the thoughts surface with a sense of déjà vu. He hadn't tried this before . . . had he?

Merge: [Analyze] and ______?

[Mind Bastion], Orrin thought, trying to select the skill. For the first time, [Merge] failed to accept the selection, and the window timed out. *What the hell?*

Orrin tried again, but [Mind Bastion] could not be used in [Merge]. *That's weird. I should write this down on my list of things to check up on.*

He left the skill running and tried using [Analyze]. A book on the shelf that he'd never picked up gave a quick and detailed reading. More than Orrin would have gotten on his own.

A shadow from the window stole his attention. He checked and saw a guard walk by on the terrace below. [Identify] gave the normal breakdown status of the woman's every skill, but something more tickled at the edge of his mind.

Yes. This is what I want. I know her spells. I know the math. Make a subskill that can calculate how much mana I need to spend to defend or attack against her spells. Orrin's glee snuck through [Mind Bastion] for a moment. *Come on, Orrin. You can do it!*

The guard finished her loop and moved out of sight. [Identify] dropped her stats.

"Damn," Orrin said with a smile. He knew it was possible. He could feel the subskill just out of reach. He dropped [Mind Bastion]. "I can do it on my own; I don't need to combine . . ."

Orrin trailed off and frowned. He grabbed his list and smacked his head. "I need to ask Madi about those spell glass things. I almost forgot about that."

He left the room to search for her. When Orrin had first seen Professor Wren use one of her glass orbs to cast a silencing spell around her office, he'd thought it was one of her abilities. The longer he spent with her, the more he realized the spell was outside of her spell set. He'd asked Madi to look into the spell-holding glass balls because he'd had an idea that might protect the people of Dey and give him something meaningful to do. It would also keep him safe and away from the front lines, which was the last place he or Daniel should be.

We have an army. Let's use it.

If the ability to store spells within the spell glass was something he could replicate, Orrin could cast buffs into the spells. The guards and volunteers of Dey, the elves, and anyone from Odrana or Veskar who showed up to fight could increase their will for a stronger first spell assault or their dexterity to run away in a last-ditch attempt at survival. All his planning in that direction hinged on being able to use the spell glass. If he had to, Orrin would be up front with Daniel fighting the demons.

"Someone needs to keep him from going crazy." Orrin kept talking to himself as he walked down the hall toward Madi's room. "Daniel went feral and chased the demons the last time they came within miles of Dey."

"Orrin? I thought I heard your voice."

Brandt was climbing the stairs and waved.

"Hey, Brandt." Orrin raised a hand in a quick, lazy wave back. "What are you up to? I'm going to ask Madi about something."

"Perfect timing." Brandt nodded at Orrin. He held an ornate wooden box in his hands. "I've just finished running an errand for her. You can go first. I can wait."

Orrin shook his head. "It's not urgent. I'll wait outside. What do you got there?"

Brandt tucked the box into one arm and opened the lid a few inches. "The errand. Madi wanted me to get spell glass. Nobody uses them within the city, but having a stored healing spell for accidents or a water spell for fires is a requirement in the smaller towns and settlements. I bought the few blanks that I could find."

Orrin lit up. "That's what I was going to ask her about. I'm the one who asked her to look into them. How many did you get?"

Brandt stood straight and smiled. "I found nine. I thought I wouldn't be able to find five in the city, but I have a friend in the Guild who deals with rare items. He brought me to a . . . less reputable shop I didn't know of. The store owner charged an extra silver each since they're rare around here."

Orrin's smile died.

"They weren't too expensive," Brandt hurried to say, interpreting Orrin's stoic look as disappointment in the price. "Madi said not to spend over five gold, and they only cost three to four silver each. If they're too expensive for you, I'm sure Lord Catanzano can requisition some gold. You more than deserve it."

Orrin put his hand on Brandt's shoulder. "I was hoping to find a lot for an idea I had. If we had a lot, we could let everyone boost their strength or will before the demons attack. Sorry you wasted your time. Unless we can find someone who can make more, it's a dead end."

Brandt was practically dancing as he shifted from side to side. "The store owner made them. She charged me more because she made them in front of me. Complained that it was a waste of mana."

Orrin felt his hope rekindle. "Lead the way!"

Orrin	Utility Warder Level 31 (15,918/23,000)	Ability Points: 107 Administrator Points: 23
HP: 300/300	MP: 500/500	
Strength: 9	Constitution: 30	Dexterity: 11
Will: 40	Intelligence: 11	
Abilities: [Analyze] [Blood Mana] [Create Poison] [Create Corrosive] [Diagnose] [Dimension Hole] [Identify] [Mana Pool] [Map]—[Party View]; [Monster View]; [Trap View]; [Zoom] [Meditate] [Merge] [Mind Bastion] [Obscure] [Side Steps] Level 3 (84/300) [Sword Proficiency]	Healing Spells: [Calm] (20/100) [Calm Mind] [Excise] (0/100) [Heal Small Wounds] Level 3 (10,000/10,000) [Numb] (5/100) [Purify] Spell Modifiers: [Boost]—(Spell Modifier) [Far]—(Spell Modifier) [Increase Durational Spell]—(Spell Modifier) [Split Spell]—(Spell Modifier)	[Increase Intelligence] Level 3 (10,000/10,000) [Decrease Strength] Level 1 (985/1,000) [Decrease Dexterity] Level 2 (400/5,000) [Decrease Will] Level 1 (740/1,000) [Decrease Intelligence] Level 1 (740/1,000)

Level 1 [Through the Ages] [Way of the Water]	Ward Spells: [Ward] [Utility Ward] [Camouflage Ward] [Earth Ward] [Fire Ward] [Ice Ward] [Light Ward] [Plant Ward] [Poison Ward] [Space Ward] [Time Ward] [Water Ward] [Wind Ward]	Other Spells: [Camouflage] Level 2 (7,980/10,000) [Fire Sword] [Gust] [Ice Sword] [Inverse] [Lightstrike] [Lightstrikes] [Remetabolize] (1,000/1,000) [Teleport] Level 2 (2,325/10,000) [Tilth] [Toxic Touch] [Water Reservoir]

Chapter 61

Brandt ran ahead to let Madi know where he was off to. She stuck her head out of her room to question Orrin, asking if he wanted her to tag along. She seemed conflicted between wanting to help and finishing up her spell selection. Orrin waved her back into her room.

"We won't be gone long."

Brandt questioned Orrin nonstop as they left the Catanzano residence and made their way into the city. He wanted to be filled in on their adventures before his rescue. Orrin could barely believe it had been only weeks before that Brandt had been a prisoner, tortured and broken. Silas had hired the best from the Hospital to care for his returned guard, and the man's body had recovered. He filled out his armor well and moved with the grace of a seasoned veteran, watching every side street and eyeing threats with a gaze that would drive all but the most desperate thieves away.

Under the facade, Orrin wondered how much the man still suffered. Orrin's ordeal hadn't lasted nearly as long, and he found himself reaching for his neck often.

"How are you doing, Brandt? Not physically but . . . you know," Orrin asked when the tall man took a breath. "If you ever need to talk to somebody, I'm probably the worst option, but I'll listen."

Brandt nodded directions for the next two streets, walking in silence. They approached a more run-down side of Dey near the northeastern gate. Refugees from villages near Odrana waited in bread lines. Small children wearing threadbare clothes kicked a half-inflated ball against the wall of a store. Orrin watched the storekeeper raise her broom threateningly at them as the kids scattered, the ball left behind.

"I appreciate the offer, Orrin. I don't think I'll ever be ready to talk about . . . everything . . . but hearing about how you and Daniel took care of Madi while I was gone is nice. It helps to keep busy, too. One good thing about the demons attacking us is there is no shortage of tasks that need doing." Brandt offered a dry chuckle. "If I remember correctly, the shop was down this street."

Orrin considered a hundred different things to say. He wasn't a psychologist. The extent of his trauma was being scared and being detained. Brandt had been tortured. *What could I possibly do to help?*

In the end, Orrin simply nudged his shoulder against Brandt's arm. "I'm glad you're back."

Brandt gave a tight-lipped smile and nodded.

The street in question was barely an alley. A few small doors near the end looked like no more than outdoor storage sheds for the local businesses. Halfway down and blocking most of the space between the two buildings that made the narrow back street, a man with greasy hair dug the tip of a long knife into the wooden crate he sat on. Dark circles framed the bloodshot eyes that stared at them as they approached. Two more men stood guard outside one of the doors on the left a few yards behind him.

The man spoke only when they were close enough to smell him. "Nothing down this way for fancy folk like you. Turn around and find another street to bother."

Brandt frowned and put his hand on the hilt of his sword in a not-a-threat-but-totally-a-threat sort of way. "I'm not sure we've met. I was here this morning visiting a shop and decided I needed some more items. We mean no harm."

The man leaned over and spat a wad of phlegm at their feet. "No shop here. Go away."

The sound of something shattering echoed from farther down the street.

"Brandt, is there a law against incapacitating but not harming a resident of Dey?" Orrin asked while he rubbed his neck.

"What?" the [Knight] asked in confusion without taking his eyes off the man in front of them.

"What's impacitating mean?" the filthy man asked, butchering the word. He raised his knife and pointed it at Brandt. "Is he making fun of me? There are more of us than you. Get going before I get angry."

Orrin dropped all three with [Decrease Strength]. He smiled at the flashing light in his blue box, not paying attention to Brandt drawing his sword.

"Yes, I will buy level two, thank you very much," Orrin said aloud while selecting the yes prompt. The two ability points were worth having the second level of the spell. "Don't worry, Brandt. They can't move for five minutes. Let's get going before Greasy here gets angry."

Orrin tossed a few copper pieces on the man's still form as he walked by. "Take a bath—you stink."

Brandt sheathed his blade. "It's been a while since I've seen you in action. I might take you out with me on patrol sometime. There are a few places that clear out too quickly for even a group of guards to capture everyone."

"I've got [Split Spell], so I can hit a bunch of people at once. I'm not sure how many targets I can hit, but I'm getting quicker at casting," Orrin said as he put his back to the wall next to the door. He nodded at Brandt.

"What are you doing?"

Orrin looked at the door and back at the brown-haired knight. Brandt's arms were crossed, no weapon drawn.

Orrin sighed in frustration. "Come on. These guys are obviously shaking this store down and we are saving her from a protection racket. Kick the door down and let's save your storekeeper friend."

Brandt laughed and pointed at the door opposite the two crumpled bodies. "Her store is right there. This is an outhouse."

Orrin blushed and stomped away. "You could have told me."

Nina was a tiny woman in her late fifties, with gray hair tied in a bun, glasses that tried to escape her nose every time she let go of the frames, and an attitude that Orrin could only describe as batshit crazy.

In contrast, her store was immaculately organized, with prices on small cards laid out next to the random assortment of potions, herbs, wands, and household cleaning supplies on pedestals or counters. A small bench separated a section of the room into an office, bedroom, and workshop. Nina was braiding long twigs together when they walked in.

She swatted Brandt with a bundle of tied-together sticks smelling of cinnamon three times as he entered the small room and introduced Orrin to her. She hit him another ten times when he knocked a candle off a stand on accident.

"If you break it—"

"You buy it," Orrin finished her sentence with a smirk. He knelt and picked up the candle as it rolled his way. "We're sorry. Brandt, maybe you should wait outside?"

Nina glared at him, which would have been scarier if her glasses hadn't tried to jump off her nose. "If you break it, it might kill you. Some of these items are magical beyond what you can understand. Mother Nina's Store of Curios and Magical Relics is dangerous for the uneducated and unwise."

Brandt patted Orrin's shoulder as he walked out. "Good luck."

Orrin offered the clump of wax with a string as a wick back to Nina.

"Two gold pieces and this can be yours." She tossed the cinnamon branches behind her. The sweet-smelling switches landed on her tiny bed. "A candle to light your way. Follow its flame and you'll never be lost."

Orrin held the thing he was hesitant to call a candle up a little higher. "How do you follow a flame? Wouldn't it stay on the wick?"

"Exactly!" Nina said and jumped, swiping it from Orrin and placing it back on the stand. "You can't get lost if you never leave."

Orrin closed his eyes and took a breath. "Brandt came in earlier and bought some spell glass orbs from you. I need more. Like, a lot more. I was hoping that—"

"I sold him all I can make today. If you come back tomorrow, we can make a deal. You look like a young man in need of love." Nina reached out and touched Orrin's chest gently. "I can help you. Here."

She darted behind her counter and dragged a box of clinking glass vials on the ground with a hideous screech. Nina peered close to one vial, then the next, as she lifted them out of the box. On the fifth vial, she giggled maniacally and placed the glass into her pocket. The sixth potion she offered to Orrin.

"Two drops of this on your inner elbows before you go to sleep. In four days, unless there is a full moon next week, then make it six days, your true love will confess to you," Nina said while holding Orrin's hand. Her glasses magnified her clear blue eyes. She winked.

"Thank you, but no," Orrin said with a shudder and handed the vial back. "If you can't make more spell glass, that's fine. Can you tell me what skill or ability I need to make it myself? It's important. It might save lives."

"Information is what you seek, then." Nina nodded so fast her glasses sprang up to catch on her hair. She blinked around in confusion. "Where did you go?"

Orrin helped her free the edge of her noseguard from her hair and settled her glasses back on her face. "How do I make spell glass? I'll pay you. I'm sure I can find it in a book, but we only have a few days before the demons attack."

"The demons already attacked, dearie. They came from the east and destroyed my town. Destroyed my shop." Nina's energy plummeted before she whispered, "Destroyed my family."

Orrin didn't move or make a sound. Since he'd entered the small shop, nothing had felt dangerous. The stillness of the older woman now scared him in a way he couldn't register. He listened to his instincts.

"Mother Nina moved to Dey. I'll rebuild my shop. I'm too old to start another town. Don't use that potion around me, I have no time to start another family with you. But no. You want information about my spell glass. You can buy that for . . . three silver?"

Orrin looked at the misshapen candle she'd tried to sell him for two gold. "I'll pay you a gold piece."

"No negotiations!" Nina screamed. "Take it or leave it or die!"

"All right, three silver," Orrin said, hurrying to pull the money out of his pocket. "I didn't mean to offend you."

Nina made the three coins disappear and curtsied. "You can unlock [Spell Orb] after you learn the spells [Storage] and [Mana Shield]. Just so you know, nobody needs [Spell Orb] anymore . . . Nobody needs you anymore."

"Nobody needs [Spell Orb]? I thought it was useful in small towns for—"

"Nobody needs you, Nina. Nobody needs Nina. Nina needs nobody," Nina muttered, repeating the same thing over and over. She turned woodenly, the erratic life sucked out of her, and walked away from Orrin. He watched her crawl into her too-small bed and pull a sheet over her body.

Orrin backed out of the store slowly, careful not to bump any of the stands as Nina sobbed and laughed. Brandt was talking to some guards outside. The three men that Orrin had attacked were gone.

"You get what you need?" Brandt asked after shaking hands with the guard captain. "Turns out you were partly right. These three were charging people to use the outhouse. Someone had already reported them. You made somebody's job easier today."

"She's not well," Orrin spoke softly, looking over his shoulder. "Something is wrong with Nina."

Brandt scratched the top of his head and looked away. "I thought so, too. I asked around after meeting her. Her village was burned to the ground by some thieves or the Odranan army, I don't know. She's a refugee, but nobody knows her. Just turned up in a local store owner's outbuilding and he didn't have the heart to kick her out. She's one of thousands of refugees that have flooded into Dey. My contact only knew her because she does get her hands on some interesting items, but there's nothing anyone can do for her."

Orrin shook his head. "No. I know someone who can do something."

Chapter 62

"You want me to heal someone's mind?" Amir asked incredulously. He raised a finger to a customer and continued grinding coffee beans. "You've been gone for weeks and nobody will tell me where you are. Then you show up, order five pounds of coffee, and want me to run off to heal something that the highest members of the Hospital rarely attempt. I want to make sure I'm hearing you right."

"Amir, you must take orders from paying customers before talking with friends, yes?" An older copy of Orrin's friend poked his head out from behind the steam-spitting knobs and copper pipes. Amir's father.

"Yes, Father," Amir answered, mouthing a *sorry* to Orrin. He quickly pushed two cups of fresh black coffee and the first pound of ground beans across the counter before turning away to help the waiting line.

Orrin and Brandt took their coffee and sat at one of the small tables outside the shop to wait.

"Do you think this is a good use of time?" Brandt stirred some sugar and milk into his coffee, ignoring Orrin's disapproving glare. A splash of milk he could tolerate, but the knight was essentially drinking sweet milk at this point.

"Compared to what? Daniel knows my suggestions for defending Dey and Madi can argue my points better than I could ever hope to do. I'm not going to spend the next few days trying to power level myself and I've missed my friends," Orrin replied, sipping his coffee. The blend was a bit darker than Amir usually gave him, so he added a drop of cream. "While we wait, can I ask a favor?"

"Anything," Brandt answered immediately. "You know how much we owe . . . how much I owe you."

Orrin sighed and pulled one of the spell glass orbs from his [Dimension Hole]. "I don't know how many times I need to say this before it sinks in, Brandt. You don't owe me or Daniel anything. I'm going to put a [Increase Strength] into this and I want you to break it."

Brandt frowned in thought and then opened his eyes wide. "You want to take [Spell Orb] and make them yourself. I'd argue against the mana expenditure, but you can already use more than anyone else I know. Give it here."

Orrin held the clear ball in his hand and cast the spell at its weakest level, targeting the glass. He trailed the mana through his fingers and watched it swirl about inside the globe in his palm. "I think I did it."

Brandt took the spell orb and crushed it in his fist. His eyes glazed over and he smiled.

"It worked?"

Brandt nodded. "How many can you make?"

"I have to buy the spells first, but I have a lot of points left after the Quest reward."

Orrin considered buying the spell while waiting but held off. It was a nice day and his coffee was delicious. He talked with Brandt and relaxed a little. The entire world might end in a few days, and there was little he could do about it right now. The sun peeked through the clouds and warmed the area around him. Orrin closed his eyes and smiled.

"If I knew that being part of the [Hero]'s party meant sitting around being lazy, I would have joined up years ago," Amir joked as he slumped into a chair next to Orrin. "He gave me ten minutes off. Tell me what the problem with the patient is."

Orrin recounted what had happened in Nina's shop, giving Amir a few theories. He might not have psychological training, but he'd watched enough medical procedural shows and listened to his mom on Earth. That gave him a better working knowledge of the human psyche than perhaps anyone on Asmea. As far as he knew, psychology wasn't a field of study here.

"If she has trauma to the soul, that is not a physical injury that I can heal." Amir sighed and rubbed his eyes. "I'm sorry, Orrin. I work here during the day and spend my nights trying to start my small clinic. I heal others but must work slowly. Lord Catanzano promised me protection, but I would rather not have to ask for it. Slow progress is my future, and I have yet to unlock more healing spells than when last we spoke."

Orrin nodded. He'd figured as much, but the extra few pounds of ground coffee sitting in a bag near Amir's feet was more than worth the stop. "It's fine, Amir. The elf I talked to told me about a class . . . [Mind Walker], I think. I hoped it would be something easier, but I can just pop over to the elven forest and ask for some pointers."

Amir raised an eyebrow and then laughed. Brandt chuckled as well.

"What? What's so funny?" Orrin pouted.

"You just suggested talking with elves about a probably hidden class by teleporting hundreds of miles to help a random lady you met this morning," Amir pointed out, holding his side. "If anyone else said something like that, I would bring them to the Hospital myself. With you, it's another day's work."

Orrin grumbled but stopped when Brandt put his hand on Orrin's shoulder. "You have a way of caring for others that society has forgotten. It helps me keep my perspective and reminds me why I became a guard in the first place, but you are becoming powerful. This isn't something you have to do."

Orrin knew in his mind that there were a dozen things he should be doing instead. The spell orbs idea worked, and if he were smart, he'd head back to the Catanzano estate right now. Every minute he spent filling those glass balls with buff spells was another person's life he could theoretically save. He suppressed a laugh, realizing for the first time exactly why his mom worked so much at the hospital.

"Mom, why do you work such long hours? You don't have to pick up every shift. I can get a job after school and help with the bills," Orrin had asked his mom one night shortly after entering high school.

He had seen her only once in three days, catching her between her second double shift. "Someone else can look after your patients. You aren't the only doctor working there."

Orrin's mom had had her wet hair tied back, having had enough time to shower but forgoing using the hair dryer to spend a few minutes asking about his first weeks in ninth grade. She poured a mountain of coffee into her extra-large mug that she carried everywhere. The dark circles around her eyes were a little less pronounced after her six-hour nap, but it would be ten hours before her next break and a day before she came home again.

"Orrin, honey, you don't need to worry about me. Focus on school. Helping people gives me purpose and is something I'm good at. You don't need me around as much, and if I can help one more person by going in, it's something I want to do."

Orrin stored the extra coffee, pushing the bags into his pocket, where they disappeared. "It's not something I have to do, Brandt. It's something I want to do. I can help her now. I'm not Daniel. I can't help with logistics. But I can help someone today."

Brandt put his cup down. "You should at least check with the elven reinforcements first. There might be some [Healers] here already."

Orrin noticed Amir glance back into the shop. "We can go in a few minutes. I'm being a shitty friend. Sit down, Amir. I'll tell you what I've been up to."

When Amir's father came looking for him fifteen minutes later, Orrin was recounting his and Daniel's fight against Lord Sanerris. The older man waited for Orrin to finish before pouring a fresh coffee into his mug.

"Was that a true story?" he asked quietly. "Telling lies of killing powerful men is a dangerous pastime."

Orrin nodded in thanks and slurped a little hot nectar before answering. "Lord Sanerris is dead and the council is replacing the leader in Mistlight. The war with the elves is over and, hopefully, reinforcements will arrive in time to help fight the demon Horde that is coming for Dey."

Amir took his father's hand and squeezed. "We'll be safe, Father. Orrin and Daniel will save us."

Orrin felt awkward after that and answered a few questions. The general information that a Horde was coming had been disseminated, but there was something different from hearing an official announcement and learning something from a trusted friend. Amir shook his head as his father returned to behind the counter.

"He didn't even yell at me to come back to work," he muttered. "Orrin, would we be safer if we left the city for a bit?"

Orrin didn't even consider lying. "If the Demon Lord gets through the Pass and attacks Dey, I'm not sure anywhere will be safe in the long run, but I'll bring you and your dad to Odrana if you want."

Amir considered while Brandt sat quietly between them.

"We'll stay. I believe what I told him—you'll find a way to save Dey."

Amir gave Orrin a hug .

"Once this is over, I'd like to visit your elf friend. I have questions about healing but no one to ask," Amir said with a smile. "Sorry that I can't help with your other problem."

Orrin rapped knuckles with Amir when they broke apart. "Keep a fresh pot ready for me when I get back. Keep up your training."

Amir waved from the door to his shop as Brandt guided Orrin to the elven encampment set up along the Wall.

The entire elven command was a picture of organization and order, a distinct difference from Orrin's time in their forest. The elves had set their camp away from the Wall but within running distance. The muted green and brown canvas tents sat in lines, with clearly marked paths and signposts designating directions to command, the mess, and latrines set farther away. Brandt spent time delivering messages between the captain and the lords of Dey and walked the paths with confidence.

"Brandt from House Catanzano for Captain Leanthun," Brandt announced as he knocked on the wooden post outside the captain's tent. "With a special guest."

An ancient elf with brittle white hair pulled back the tent door and beckoned them inside. "Welcome back, Knight Brandt. Your timing is fortuitous. We have reports for Lord Catanzano and Lady Timpe. What news from the west?"

The inside of the tent was spacious, with a wooden table taking up nearly half of the inside. Elves moved around a crudely drawn map of the Pass, with markers for different troops moving as various strategies were discussed.

Leanthun, the first elf that Orrin had met and the leader of the elven forces in Dey, stared gloomily at everything with his arms resting on the table. The gust of fresh air that traveled into the tent with them caught his attention, and he smiled warmly as his eyes fell on Orrin.

"You survived," he said simply. "Did they find you or did you escape?"

Orrin was worried that their allies were not being kept informed and shot a look at Brandt that promised a long talk later. To Leanthun, he rolled his eyes and cracked his knuckles over his head. "What do you think?"

Leanthun laughed and clapped twice, loudly. "Give us the tent for five minutes. Return to training and make sure we get those supplies set up for quick transport. I want us ready to move at the first sighting."

Everyone cleared out except the old elf who shuffled to the side and began cleaning up the mess left behind. Leanthun gave the man a long-suffering stare but was ignored completely. He leaned against the table, readjusted his khopesh so it didn't ding the wood, and crossed his arms. "I told my uncle not to worry when the [Hero] told us of your capture. You survive situations like a fated cat. No one knows how you land on your feet, and yet here you are again. What can I help you with?"

Chapter 63

Orrin got straight to the point. "I want to talk with a [Mind Walker]. I met someone who might need their help."

Leanthun tilted his head. "Who would need such healing before battle? A [Mind Walker] works for months after fighting to calm our minds. For anyone else, I would answer no, but I'll hear you out. Your actions made our people stronger, and all of Asmea may yet survive because of you and Daniel. Talk and I will listen."

Orrin recounted a quick and dirty version of his last few weeks, including his idea to use spell glass orbs to enhance the armies of Asmea. He told Leanthun about Nina and his desire to help her in some way.

"If they don't want to spend time or mana curing her, I'd settle for talking for a few minutes. I have a lot of healing spells and maybe I could do—"

"Listen carefully, Orrin. Do not attempt to pry into or heal anyone's mind. [Mind Walkers] are rare for a reason. Training takes decades, and no member of our Hospital would give you the tools that you seek. I will relay your request, but promise me that you won't try anything. You didn't do anything yet, did you?" Leanthun looked worried at the prospect.

"No. The most I could have done was [Calm Mind], but she needs more than a temporary fix."

Leanthun let out a sigh of relief. "That is a good spell for clearing your thoughts but has little effect on the horrors of the mind. I'm glad you didn't . . . It doesn't matter. Is there anything else that I can help you with?"

Orrin still wanted to talk with a [Mind Walker] but figured it could wait. He'd had interesting conversations with Anabella about healing the body and was convinced that something as simple as his high school anatomy class would have improved any regular healing by leaps and bounds. Maybe he could give a few pointers on psychology that could help cure Nina.

Leanthun wasn't going to change his mind, though, and Orrin had other things to do. Leanthun was also busy, and Orrin didn't want to take up any more of his time.

"I'm sorry if I wasted your time, Leanthun. I don't trust the human Hospital. If you do hear back, she owns a small shop near the . . ." He gave directions, which Leanthun wrote down in a small notepad.

"My door is always open for you, Orrin. I can't speak for a member of our Hospital, but rest assured our [Healers] are good people. I'm sure someone will look in on your friend." Leanthun assured Orrin, ignoring the old elf who kept poking him. "Yes, Draenadal. You can call everyone back in. I'm sorry, Orrin. There is much to organize. You humans are willing to learn our archery but slow to improve. I must go."

Orrin and Brandt said their goodbyes, with the knight taking an armful of letters to deliver to Silas. They made their way back to the Catanzano house, silence beating down on them like the sun above.

Brandt spoke first. "If you'd like, I can have Lord Catanzano arrange for someone from our Hospital to look in on Nina. It's kind of you to care for her, but she's gotten by for this long. She'll be fine until after we win this fight."

Orrin knew everyone in the Hospital wasn't rotten, but his only encounters with them had soured his view. He wasn't sure they'd forgotten about the invisible healing angel that stole half their work and saved a dozen lives. He hadn't forgotten the dejection on Amir's face for being demoted for doing his job.

"Thank you, Brandt. Maybe. I'll let you know. I'm going to go upstairs and start making spell orbs. What should I even call them? Strength spheres? Increase-stat orbs?"

"Buff balls?" Brandt offered with a straight face.

Orrin wiped tears from his eyes when he finally stopped laughing.

Orrin pulled out the remaining eight spell glass orbs.

"You better be worth it," he threatened.

Before committing to spending his ability points, Orrin experimented. He knew a low-level [Increase Strength] worked, but what about the other three stats?

"Please work."

Unfortunately, Orrin had to use the orbs to make sure the spells triggered. He used three of the costly glasses to confirm all his buff spells worked. When he used a level-three [Increase Will], the ball exploded in his hand.

Damn it. That's not the end of the world, though. Even a few extra points in a stat can make all the difference, Orrin rationalized. *Let's see how much this is going to cost me.*

Orrin couldn't find [Spell Orb] in his store, confirming his theory that some spells and abilities wouldn't show up unless he found the hidden combination that unlocked it. He did find [Storage] and [Mana Shield].

> **[Storage]—Create a magical barrier around a selected container that keeps items fresh. 2 MP. -4 AP**
> **[Mana Shield]—Create a shield of pure mana to reflect a physical attack. 2 MP. -5 AP**
> **Would you like to purchase for 9 AP?**
> **Yes or No?**

"That's a lot of points." Orrin considered his options.

He had over a hundred ability points. *One hundred and five.* He checked to make sure. *If these unlock [Spell Orb] and it costs a hundred points, I'm going to be pissed. It shouldn't cost that much. I should have checked Nina's level. That would have given me a clue.*

If he spent the points and decided [Spell Orb] was too expensive, it wasn't the end of the world. More spells would give him more options in [Merge], and Orrin had already thought of a few ways to use [Mana Shield]. Whether the wording of reflect in the spell's description meant simple protection from a physical strike or turning the damage back on the attacker, the spell was low-cost and high-reward either way. If he could use [Split Spell] with [Mana Shield], he could create another low-cost barrier like [Ward] to protect people. From the description, it would only work once, but Orrin had seen one strong attack take down powerful fighters and mages.

[Storage] was probably the kind of thing that people used to keep produce fresh during the journey to the markets. Amir might know how it was used from his coffee shop experience, but Orrin doubted there was a fighting application he could exploit.

"I hope I don't regret this," Orrin said as he clicked the yes and bought both spells. "If [Spell Orb] isn't available, I'm going to be pis— There it is."

A new option appeared in the store under his search.

> **[Spell Orb]—Create a storage device that can contain one spell with variable mana capacity. 1 MP cost minimum. Variable MP cost. -25 AP**

Twenty-five points was more than he'd wanted but less than he'd feared. The low and variable mana cost raised a few questions about the quality of the orbs he had remaining, but Orrin was in a unique situation. With [Meditation], he already recovered his mana naturally throughout the day. His [Mana Pool] ability gave him an extra hundred points of mana to spend, and if he buffed his stats before getting to work, Orrin's daily mana expenditure could rival a small town.

He told himself again this would save lives and spent the ability points. Holding his hand out, he activated the spell with the minimum mana cost. A fragile ball of light-blue glass formed in his palm.

Orrin carefully cast a level-one [Increase Will] into the glass with a building sense of excitement. *This is going to—*

The glass exploded.

"Fuck."

It took ten minutes of testing and resting before Orrin worked out the mechanics and kinks in his new ability. Spell orbs could be made with one mana point, but they couldn't hold any of his spells. *They could hold a single [Ice Sword], but what's the point in that.*

If Orrin wanted a level-one [Increase Will] spell orb, the initial casting needed to be five MP or the same cost of the buff. The mana cost wasn't actually five points, given his intelligence and the way the magic costs and stats interacted. Orrin let out a joyful cheer when he made a level-three [Increase Will]. He set the stat orbs into different piles.

If intelligence reduces the price of the initial item creation and I buff my will to maximum, I should be able to make . . . Orrin reached into his pocket and pulled out one of the notebooks from school. He scratched the math down.

If I have both intelligence and will at a hundred, I'll have eleven hundred points of mana. A single casting of a level-one buff costs five MP. That means five MP for the spell orb as well. With maxed stats, that should come out to ninety percent of the full cast or one MP to make the orb and one MP to fill it. I can make five hundred and fifty stat-increase balls. My will would be maxed as well, so the original plus one stat increase should increase to ten. A ten-point buff for two points of mana? That can't be right.

Orrin tested his theory. He raised his will and intelligence to one hundred. He created the spell orb. He cast the [Increase Strength] at level one.

"Daniel is going to freak out," Orrin said with a smile. He grabbed the orbs from his bed and rushed out of his room. "Guys, it worked!"

Brandt, Madi, Daniel, and Silas sat and stood around the table as Orrin explained his new ability. Silas held one of the spheres of glass in his hand.

"You can make hundreds of these?" the lord of Dey asked. When Orrin nodded, he crushed the one he held. "Remarkable. Brandt, bring me everyone—Leanthun, the other lords and Lady Timpe, anyone from the Hospital that can be spared, the merchants, the Guild. I want resources pulled from everyone."

Brandt smiled and left immediately.

"Resources for what? I'm not sure anyone else can make as many of these as I can or even unlock all the spells. I guess I could enchant more spell orbs, but I don't think it would be worth the mana cost to make them," Orrin asked, confusion apparent on his face.

Daniel walked over and threw his arm over Orrin's shoulder. "You know all those ideas you had about creating choke points throughout the Pass and building extra fortifications to retreat and regroup at? Madi, Silas, and I have spent a lot of time in meetings with . . . basically everyone trying to come up with mana-efficient ways to pull it off. Everyone said the same thing: it would take too long. We don't have enough people. We can't risk mana exhaustion before a Horde attacks. You beautiful idiot, you solved all their complaints."

Orrin chuckled nervously as Daniel and Silas began talking about various people to get involved. Madi sighed and dragged her chair closer to Orrin.

"Before the entire town descends on you, how do you feel about becoming a production line of these things for the next few weeks?" Madi asked quietly.

Orrin shrugged. "If it helps us prepare for the Horde and saves even one life, I'll do it."

Madi shook her head. "That's not what I meant. I know and Daniel knows that you'll put your head down and do what needs to be done. You should set limits, though. Don't tell anyone, even my father, that you can make more than five hundred a day."

"How do you know I can—"

"Stop," Madi interrupted Orrin, putting her hand on his arm. "You have an infuriating way of breaking down everything I thought I knew about magic. You also put everyone else above your own needs.

We both know you are going to be by Daniel's side when we fight the Demon Lord. Negotiate with leadership. Demand that you are allowed to visit the Pass and create teleport points for fast travel time. Make sure you don't get locked into a room making tools for others."

Orrin was touched that Madi felt the need to look out for him. She made good points. He hadn't thought about the possibility of being forced to sit there making the orbs day and night. He probably could do it, though. If he used a penidrop mana-regeneration potion, he could increase his mana output even more. A mana-regen potion would give him one MP back every second. That meant an extra three thousand, six hundred points of mana a day. *I could make eighteen hundred spell orbs in an hour.*

"You're doing the thing," Madi complained, knocking on his skull. "Are you in there? Tell me that you can hear me."

Orrin laughed and brushed her hand away. "You're right. Thanks, Madi. I'll make sure to set limits for myself. You are a good friend."

Madi rolled her eyes. "Obviously. Now, tell me what you want to get out of this and I'll make sure my father helps."

She pulled out a stack of paper and found a pen. "How many orbs do you want to make a day? Keep in mind this shouldn't be the maximum amount but something you can do in an hour or two."

Orrin glanced at Silas and Daniel still going over a map and talking animatedly. He leaned in close and whispered to Madi.

She froze and the pen fell from her fingers. "You told my father five hundred for a full mana pool. How? What did you do?"

Orrin smirked. "I broke the rules again."

Chapter 64

Orrin slumped down against the wall in the courtyard of the Catanzano house and covered his face with his hands. "That was a nightmare."

Daniel laughed at his side. "You did well. Madi had to save you once or twice, but I don't know where the timid Orrin who never raised his hand in class went. You told Guildmaster Pritus to fuck off."

"I told her she was being unreasonable. I did not tell her to fuck off."

"Tomato, tomato."

"You're supposed to enunciate tomato differently each time. Toe-may-toe. Toe-mah-toe. Get it?"

Daniel reached over and ruffled Orrin's hair. His friend had somehow found the time before the meeting to shave and cut his hair, but Orrin's own was getting long. His mom would have called him mangy.

"I'm messing with you, O. You did something incredible today," Daniel praised him. "That Hospital principal guy might be a dick, but he had a point about the side effects of your buffs. I hope they can find a solution."

Orrin grimaced at the mention of Principal Mangin. The creepy old man smiled with too many teeth and had shark eyes. His questions about how Orrin's spells worked without mana exhaustion were ignored, much to his annoyance, but the few arguments he'd made against overuse of the new weapon were sound enough.

"I have a few ideas but nothing concrete. I'm sure the Hospital could cure the status effects, but that asshole didn't seem like he wanted to help much," Orrin said as he began making [Increase Will] spell orbs at level one. They'd been the most requested by far, with the ability to give a mage extra mana to spend. "We could talk with an [Alchemist]. I'm sure they have something easy they could brew up. I could even make [Purify], orbs but I think Madi wouldn't approve. I'd need to make them in a one-to-one ratio, but as long as everyone uses them like we instructed, there shouldn't even be side effects."

Daniel snorted. "If you believe that people are not going to hoard those things and use them all at once, I have a seaside cottage in Dey that you should buy. I'm tempted to take a bunch of those things from you just to practice with increased strength. I think I'm improving in using more strength, but every bit will help when we fight the demons."

Orrin closed his eyes, letting the afternoon sun warm him. The lunch spread that Silas had put out for all the visitors was modest in fare but abundant in quantity. He'd tried a lot of new dishes. "Do you think you can control yourself around demons? Last time some came close to Dey, you went on the chase pretty quick."

Daniel rolled to his side and pushed up against the wall. He stretched his arms over his head before answering. "I think I'll be okay. Plus, I'll have you to keep me in check. Madi and Brandt, too, if Silas gives the approval. I don't know why he wouldn't."

"Everyone is going to have to fight," Orrin agreed in a whisper. "Silas asked if I wanted to scout the Pass with you tomorrow. The Guild and the unions are putting out quests for [Stone Mages] and other building classes. They want to get a small wall and fortifications up at the far side of the Pass within the next two days. Then we have to find as many narrow parts of the Pass as we can, make sure any climbable areas are reinforced or trapped, and keep any monsters in the area in check while doing it. It's going to be a busy week."

"Don't overdo it. We've got an army behind us this time. Have you seen the elves training with their bows? If we set them up on a wall, they can pin down the enemy from a mile away. With your buffs, our mages can put out more spells than any demon, and if the Demon Lord shows his face, we can kick his ass."

Orrin stood and motioned for Daniel to enter the sparring area with him. "We should practice some. I have all these new spells and combinations that I figured out in Odrana. Check this out."

Orrin summoned his [Ice Sword] and used [Gust] to cover a training dummy with ice when he hit it. "It isn't strong enough to freeze someone in place for more than a second, but if we time it right, it'll be like I'm setting you up for an easy dunk."

Orrin and Daniel talked, showing each other their new spells. Daniel had some interesting new attacks as well. His influx of new ability points had gone to upgrade a few of his key attacks, but he'd also branched out into a few spells. The floating balls of darkness around Daniel reminded Orrin too much of Lord Sanerris's attacks. They made Orrin's magic do weird things, like go off course or even circle back toward him.

He dodged another [Lightstrike] that Daniel's new spell rebounded just as Madi and Brandt entered, arguing about something.

"Hey, guys, you come to get some practice in?" Daniel let Gertrude rest on the ground. His spells fizzled out as well.

Madi shook her head and handed a letter to Orrin. "We got the final contracts drawn up and everybody we spoke to agreed to the important terms, but the Hospital sent this."

Orrin read the letter, his rage building the more he read. "Are they serious? Everyone could be dead in a week and they want to use this to . . . I don't know . . . make a healing monopoly in Dey?"

"What's going on?" Daniel asked, stabbing his sword into the dirt and joining the group.

"That asshole Mangin and his cronies will heal the troops only if we pay a daily rate. They also want full control over all healing magic in Dey and the surrounding areas in return for their 'help,'" Orrin answered. His hands were shaking and he handed the letter back to Madi before he ripped it into pieces. "Can they do that?"

"The Hospital is an independent faction," Brandt explained. Orrin noted his fists were clenched, too. "They don't have to answer our call for help, but there might not be enough [Healers] in Dey to cover their loss if we turn them down."

"I could make healing orbs," Orrin offered. "I can push myself a bit more than we negotiated in there. If we get a few [Healers] that we trust that aren't part of the Hospital, they could distribute them as needed."

Madi frowned. "We can't have you do that, Orrin. We can't ask that of you, and we can't put you at risk like that. If the Hospital catches word that you are healing all of Dey . . . again . . . they might come after you. A civil war within Dey would be devastating."

Orrin let out a scream of anger and threw his remaining [Ice Sword] at one of the archery targets. It stuck true. Not in the middle, but a few months ago, Orrin would have tripped and missed it completely. A small part of his rational brain congratulated himself on the growth.

"This is an initial bargaining point," Madi said after letting Orrin calm himself. "My father is going there in person to negotiate. He may pay more, but he won't give that much power to another group. It'll be fine."

Brandt and Daniel faced off and practiced sword forms together while Madi began testing her new spells. Orrin tried to focus, but the anger he felt at people playing games and making power moves while everyone was in danger overwhelmed his thoughts. He tried casting [Calm Mind] on himself, but within a few minutes, he knew it wasn't working.

"I'm going out. I need to get some more penidrop mushrooms for regen potions, and I might visit Tony. I'm too worked up to concentrate," Orrin announced, interrupting Madi's demonstration of her kaleidoscope-of-lights attack. "Sorry."

Madi let the spell die. "Do you want some company?"

Orrin shook his head. "I need to walk and think. I'll be back in an hour."

Brandt and Daniel waved before falling back into a ready stance. *Those two would beat on each other all day if they could.*

Orrin visited the same [Alchemist] he'd used in the past and purchased the full penidrop mothershroom along with a few regular clippings. He held the plant in his hands as he walked the street toward Tony's townhome, half-hoping someone would try and mug him.

"You survived Odrana. I was worried I might have to make a trip." Tony's voice hit Orrin's brain with a light chuckle. "I've been hearing lots of interesting things today. What did you do this time?"

Orrin smiled as he rounded the corner and saw Tony waiting in his doorway. "Sorry, I cut the vacation short. You could have come out for a visit, but the Sanerris family kept me under house arrest. Wouldn't have been much of a trip for you."

Tony raised a bushy eyebrow and waved Orrin to join him. Leaving the door open, he moved back into his sanctuary. "Come inside and talk. Or keep standing there with your thoughts all askew. I'm not the only person interested in you today, it seems."

Orrin heard a shout and heard feet slapping as someone ran away behind him.

"Thief?" Orrin asked as he closed the door and moved inside.

"Spy. Somebody wants to know what you are doing. Another will take his place, but we can talk in private here." Tony's voice carried a calmness that Orrin clung to. He was sure it was the Hospital. He felt the anger building again.

"I'm sorry if that makes trouble for you," Orrin said through clenched teeth. "I didn't think visiting you would—"

"Shut up, boy," Tony said, turning and giving Orrin a rough and clumsy hug. He grabbed his shoulders and looked down into his eyes. "You can visit whenever you need. Now, come have some tea and tell me what new adventures you've had. The Sanerris family, you say? Anabella or her sniveling son?"

Orrin smiled and waited for Tony to turn before wiping at his eyes. The dust from Tony's dirty walkway was totally the reason his eyes were watering. "Both, actually. We went to find Brandt and bring him home, but when we got to Mistlight . . ."

Orrin spun his tale as Tony made tea, which Orrin poked around with a spoon but refused to drink. *Dirty leaf water.* Tony's eyes danced when Orrin told him about beating Sanerris the first time, and he let out an actual physical laugh that was more strangled cat than chuckle when Orrin finished with the restructuring of Odrana's leadership.

"You could walk into a hurricane and find a way to calm the Seasnake that cast it," Tony said with wonder. "I would have found a way to leave, but I guess you gained some new spells and knowledge."

"And knowing is half the battle," Orrin joked.

"Knowledge comes with a price. Sometimes it's worth the cost." Tony spoke darkly. "What did you teach the leadership of Dey that has them running around searching for old villagers?"

Orrin sighed. He shouldn't have been surprised that the other lords were trying to edge into this new market, but there it was. "I figured out a way to store my increase-stat spells in spell glass. I got [Spell Orb] and can make a bunch for those that fight the demon Horde that's coming toward Dey. Actually, now that I'm here . . . I met this woman near the eastern gate, Nina. She's had some trauma and is a little . . . *crazy* isn't the nicest word, but yeah. Do you know any way to help her?"

Tony rested his hands together over his cup and stared into his cooling tea. "I hope you didn't try to heal her in any way. There are few that would attempt such a thing, but you rush into situations without thought sometimes."

Orrin held his hand over his chest in mock outrage. "Who? Me? No!"

Tony pulled his lips into a straight line.

"I didn't. I asked a friend who is a [Healer] and even asked the elves if I could talk with a [Mind Walker], but dead ends all around so far. You didn't answer my question, though."

"I can talk with her, but there is little help that I know of for loss other than time."

Orrin felt the shadow of Tony's past falling over the room. He hadn't come to depress his friend. "I bought a plant today. Do people in this world name their plants? It's a mushroom, and I'm supposed to keep it in a dark place. What do you think?"

Tony rolled his eyes at Orrin. "I'm glad that you've found a way to release your frustration. I don't name my plants, but I talk with them in my own way."

"I was thinking of naming it Tony," Orrin announced, putting the penidrop mothershroom on the table.

"I regret ever meeting you."

Chapter 65

Orrin stared out at the plains filled with tall, yellowing grass. The land beyond the Pass was beautiful in an undiscovered and unconquered kind of way. The trees within the Pass stopped a few yards beyond the mountains to either side . . . or they had a few days ago. An army of workers had corralled the tree line back, creating an open space for the daring project. It was a beautiful view that Orrin ignored as he read his status for the tenth time that day.

The overlook that Orrin stood on was one of several that spanned the length of the Pass's opening mouth. At Silas's request, a [Locationist] had teleported Orrin to the far side of the Pass, negating the long trek needed for his own [Teleport] ability. Orrin's near-limitless mana let him bring parties of workers out and back to Dey without fear of getting stuck. Fortifications, towers, and more went up in hours, with reinforcements and additional supports built up daily.

Orrin's schedule filled his days to the minute. He spent an hour in the morning creating [Increase Will] and [Increase Intelligence] spell orbs for the people building the initial strongholds and wall. He'd heard the people calling it the Outer Wall already, describing something that had taken hours to build as if it had stood defending Dey for centuries. At first, Orrin had wanted to be in charge of handing out the glass spheres. He needed to explain how dangerous they could be if overused. A few [Alchemists] had worked with him to create potion versions of [Purify] but the ten-minute time limit was hard to enforce. Orrin tried using [Increase Durational Spell] in combination with his buffs and could create an orb that lasted a total of nineteen minutes, but the extra point of mana cut into how many he could create. In the short term, quantity over quality was needed.

Luckily, Madi and Silas came to his rescue with schedules, time sheets, and threats of docking pay if anyone fell ill due to their own negligence. After watching one man vomit from will overuse and a [Nausea] debuff, the workers passed the word around to not slack off.

"It's quiet out there," Daniel said from his side. The [Hero] and his best friend had slept out behind the original Wall of Dey the last three nights. While Orrin prided himself on being a gamer, knowing the nerdy ins and outs of stats and min-maxing, Daniel wasn't a complete neophyte. He knew tower defense strategies, but more than that, Daniel worked hard to keep the workers motivated. Everyone still remembered him from his victory tour throughout the city of Dey, and having the [Hero] bring refreshments helped make the tired and mana-drained workers keep going.

"Leanthun's scouts returned this morning," Orrin said between bites of the sandwich that Daniel brought him. "The demons should be visible in the morning. They're moving north along the mountain range. They have to enter the Pass to get through. The dwarves all swear the mountain range is impenetrable."

Orrin didn't bring up his fears about that. He knew some of the dwarves traded with demons. If the demons could get a small group behind the mountains and attack Dey from the rear, it would be a disaster.

Daniel grunted and waved with a large fake smile at some people below carrying a large tree. "Did Madi tell you about the alchemist guild?"

Orrin frowned. "No. I didn't see her this morning."

"She came in for an hour to check in on our progress and drop this off," Daniel explained and pulled out a familiar book. "Odrana arrived in force. I guess Lady Sanerris 'donated' this with instructions to give it to you."

Orrin reached out and took the Twin Book of Sending from Daniel. He reached into his pocket and used [Dimension Hole] to yank the other one out. The two books looked identical as he held them in either hand.

"She's still alive?"

Daniel rolled his eyes. "I asked the same thing. Madi said 'politics' and left it at that. She also told me about the alchemy problem. They're saying the price for the purifying potion ingredients is going through the roof and they won't be able to keep up production."

Orrin closed his eyes and counted to five . . . something he'd been doing more of lately. "I'll drop one of these off with Madi and teach her how to use it. We can save a few [Teleports] for communication if we use them. Does she think the Hospital is behind this? Did they get to the [Alchemists] we know or are they buying up ingredients? How much of a margin do we have for error here?"

Daniel threw the last bite of his bread out into the air and ruffled Orrin's hair. "I have no idea. I'm just a pretty face who hits stuff with his sword."

Orrin ducked and pushed the hand off his head. "I could take [Alchemy] and make a bunch of potions. I've been thinking about doing it anyway."

"What about your orbs?" Daniel asked.

"I've got a stockpile. I made a handful of these, too. Meant to give them to you earlier but forgot," Orrin said and pulled a box out of his magical storage.

"Where'd you get the box? This looks custom," Daniel commented as he took the item from Orrin and opened it. He whistled. "Covered in cloth and shaped to hold the orbs. This is new."

"Silas ordered them. There are crates of these back in Dey now. Each is marked with what stat they increase. These are different," Orrin explained and pointed to the four rows in turn. "[Decrease Strength], [Decrease Dexterity], [Decrease Will], and [Decrease Intelligence]. I'm not making a lot of these and giving out none to anyone but you and maybe Madi if she wants some. They're all level three."

"Nice," Daniel said, elongating the word into a hiss. "These will be fun to use."

"Just keep them safe. It'll be bad if they get— Where did the box go?" Orrin blinked in confusion.

Daniel looked over his shoulder and tried to hold a straight face. "What do you mean?"

"D . . ." Orrin started threateningly.

Daniel broke and laughed. "I copied you. Got myself [Dimension Hole]. A few things opened up for me after hitting level thirty. The ball breakers are safe."

"The . . . what?" Orrin asked stupidly.

"Your orbs that decrease people's stats and break them. Ball breakers. I came up with it just now. What do you think?"

Orrin walked to the edge of the wall and looked down. "That has to be . . . thirty . . . forty feet?"

Daniel joined him and raised an eyebrow before looking over the edge. "I think more like fifty. Why?"

"If I throw the [Hero] over the wall, do you think anybody will care?" Orrin asked with a wink.

Daniel laughed but backed away with his hands raised. "I'd care. I can't fly. Yet."

Orrin discussed some issues he'd seen in the next fallback point with Daniel before he jumped back to Dey. He needed to explain the relic book to Madi. As much as it pained him to admit it, Anabella's choice to hand it over would help a lot of people.

"If you tap the stylus three times like that, it clears the messages," Orrin explained to a dumbfounded Madi twenty minutes later. "There's no notification or alert, but it doesn't cost mana. It can move around with a designated commander, and we don't have to worry about a [Locationist] teleporting into an area overrun with demons."

"Orrin, this is a relic," Madi repeated for the third time. "You can't just give this away and—"

"Take them. The only thing they mean to me is bad memories. I trust you to figure out the best way to use them," Orrin said, putting the two black notebooks into her hands. "Daniel mentioned an alchemy guild. Tell me about that."

One good thing about Madi was that she could compartmentalize with the best of them. Orrin knew Madi or her father would try to pay him for the books, but honestly, he barely used the gold he had. There would be time after they survived to talk about the relics, but that could only happen if they didn't die.

"The [Alchemists] delivered a quarter of what was promised and need more time to complete the order," Madi said, still holding the two books tight to her chest. "We put pressure on them, but nobody is breaking their story. The ingredients needed for the potions are in low supply and high demand right now. We've sent messages to Odrana and Veskar and expect answers by tomorrow."

"I can [Teleport] to Mistlight and ask Maeve if her people can help. They grow things."

Madi shook her head. "Who do you think I asked, Orrin? You won't find her in Mistlight anyway. She's returned to Ceraun with her father. I think they're our best bet. If they can help, I might send you there on a supply run. With [Teleport] and [Dimension Hole], you can bring back most of what we need within an hour."

Orrin agreed immediately. The orbs were supposed to save lives, and the tainted side effects were a known factor. If Orrin was going to ask people to risk their lives using his buffs, he would need to find a way to supply the antidote as well.

Madi had two meetings to attend and promised to stop by before dinner. Orrin made his way to his room and locked the door.

He pulled up his status again. After spending his first two days making nothing but will- and intelligence-boosting spell orbs, he'd made a batch of the physical-stat orbs this morning. It was the boost Orrin needed to hit a threshold that he'd worked on for ages.

> **[Increase Dexterity] Level 3 (10,000/10,000)**
> **(3/4 Completed)**
> **[Increase Strength] Level 3 (10,000/10,000)**
> **(4/4 Completed)**
> **Would you like to upgrade for 50 AP?**

No prompt saying level four like it should. Orrin scrutinized the text for some hidden clue. When [Increase Will] hit the needed ten thousand mana points, Orrin wasn't worried about the one-out-of-four completed notification. He assumed a level-four set of spells would appear after he completed leveling all four stats. *Not this hidden bullshit.*

The number of ability points wouldn't be a problem. He could purchase the upgrade right now. The only reason he didn't was his uncertainty and fear. A fear that the spells would be lost. He couldn't . . . no, the entire city of Dey couldn't afford that right now. He didn't tell Madi or Daniel what was going on. They worried he was taking on too much. He worried that he could do more.

I might not be the [Hero], but I'll do everything in my power to help my friends survive . . . to help us all survive.

Acknowledgments

Buckle up, here we go!

Shout-outs are most deserved by those who helped keep me sane while writing and editing book three. Why should people who defecate on me, make me cry in frustration, and drive me insane on a daily basis get acknowledged? Because they're my kids. They also snuggle, read with me, and listen to my rambling bedtime stories. To my sons, may you never be kidnapped in a magic land, but know that if you are, I'll rescue you.

To my team at Podium, which has grown into my writing family. Julie, Brian, Kyle, Leah, and Sara. You keep me honest-*ish* with deadlines and motivated with praise. The amount of work you do for this series and for the other authors with Podium is not unseen. Thank you a hundred times.

To Nick Podehl, for giving these characters a voice outside of my head. You do impeccable work and I'm blessed to have you along on this crazy adventure.

To my family at large, who might accept that I'm not just a lawyer now that I have three books published. Mom and Dad, thank you for buying me Every. Single. Book. that I wanted growing up and always encouraging me to read, even when I was staying up too late on school nights. To my brothers, for the encouragement with each new book and threatening me over the book two cliff (I'm sorry).

To my long-suffering D&D group. NO. I will not put your character names in my book. I know you picked stupid names on purpose.

Thank you for reading my books, listening to my anxious rambling, and keeping my monk alive when he rushes into trouble.

To my readers. The ones from the beginning on Royal Road. The ones we picked up along the way. And the ones on Patreon, who copyedit my initial chicken scratch and keep me flush in sweet, glorious coffee. Thank you for giving me the chance to live my dreams.

To Sarah . . . again. Because however smart/cool/funny you might think I am, she exceeds me in every way. I love you.

About the Author

SourpatchHero is the author of the LitRPG series I'm Not the Hero. When he's not writing new stories, you'll find him spending time with his two sons and his wife, reading, or playing video games.